THE

J.A.P.

CHRONICLES

a novel

ISABEL ROSE

BROADWAY BOOKS

new york

First Broadway Books trade paperback edition published 2006

Book design by Nicola Ferguson

The Library of Congress Cataloging-in-Publication Data has cataloged the hardcover as:
Rose, Isabel, 1968–
The J.A.P. chronicles : a novel / Isabel Rose.— 1st ed.
p. cm.
1. Reminiscing in old age—Fiction. 2. Female friendship—Fiction.
3. Jewish women—Fiction. 4. Aged women—Fiction.
5 Reunions—Fiction. I. Title.
PS3618.O784J15 2005
813'.6—dc22   2004045550

ISBN-13: 978-0-7679-1837-4
ISBN-10: 0-7679-1837-1

1 3 5 7 9 10 8 6 4 2

*For my parents,
who have made everything possible*

Acknowledgments

Deepest gratitude goes first and foremost to my editor, Deb Futter, for her belief in me and for the distance she helped me travel with this project. And thank you to everyone at Doubleday who enabled this book to see the light of day. Scott Waxman, you are my hero for getting me my amazing agent, Sally Wofford-Girand. There are not enough thanks in the world for either of you. Sloane Miller, this book would not have existed had you not hatched the title and met me every day for a year so we could work on our books side by side, and thanks to Pain Quotidien and to 71 Irving for letting us write through countless cups of decaf and a bagel. Amy Brownstein, special thanks for your tremendous support and for getting me to the fantastic Meg Mortimer and to my wonderful crew at UTA—Jay Gassner, Marissa Devins, Liz Ziemska, and everyone else who has helped me there. Enormous thanks also to Robbie McDonald, Scott Klein, and Keith Sherman. You are the best publicists around! Thanks also to Judy Hieblum and Victoria Rowan for editorial expertise and advice. Gary Yantsos, thanks for saving my computer's life and therefore mine. Dianne Choie, thanks for fielding my endless inquiries with grace and kindness. Elinor Lipman, Abigail Thomas, Alice Mattison, and Susan Dodd, thank you for being the first to encourage my writing, and great thanks to everyone at the Bennington Writing Seminars who helped fan the flames of my desire to learn. David Alvarez, Albert Sax, Cary Zateslo, Ben Feldman, Cyn Rossi, Randy Slifka, and Aimee Schoof, you each helped me in special ways to grow this book, to dig deeper into the material, and to believe in myself.

To my extraordinary family—Susan and Elihu Rose, Amy and Jeff Silverman, Abigail Rose and Michael Blum—you are my home team, my ultimate support. I love you and thank you for a lifetime of nurturing. Lily, my precious daughter, you are my raison d'être. And to my extended family of Roses and Wechslers; to Suzanne Ronson; to Anita Sarto-Trillanes; to my great and life-sustaining network of friends: you have each helped me more than you know. I thank you with all my heart.

THE

J.A.P.

CHRONICLES

Back to Willow Lake

✳

"Is this about religion?" Renny asked.

Ali looked up from the *New York Times* and said, "It has nothing to do with religion, and you know that."

"Because I'll convert if it's that damn important to you," Renny persisted.

His large frame filled the door to the kitchen, cutting off Ali's escape route. She thought the conversation had concluded when they came in from their early-morning walk through Chinatown.

"When have I ever gone to temple since you've known me?" she asked. Some crumbs from her apple Danish rested on the table next to the newspaper. She wiped them into her hand and popped them in her mouth.

"You can take the Jew out of temple, but you can't take the Jew out of the girl," Renny replied. He didn't sound sarcastic.

"Oh, and Catholicism just disappears once you move to the Lower East Side?"

The scar that ran through Renny's left eyebrow crinkled in irritation. "This is no time to act all cutesy or belligerent, or even

1

cutesy belligerent. Catholicism plays no role in my life whatsoever. I haven't stepped foot in a church since I can't even *remember* when."

"It was last summer, when we went to your friend's wedding in Yonkers and the mass lasted an hour and a half and it was unair-conditioned and that woman in the hat fainted."

"Well, don't blame *me*," Renny said. "It wasn't a reflection of *my* religious affiliation. And please don't tell me you've suddenly started making judgments about the variety of my friends, because then I actually *wouldn't* want to marry you. I wouldn't even want to know you."

Ali went to the refrigerator and took out a carton of milk. It was always a careful balance with Renny. So gentle and good-natured on the surface, he'd retreat into a quiet, unreachable anger if she pushed too hard. She decided to keep it light. "I think it's very generous of you to consider converting"—she paused to take a swig of milk—"but if you did, we'd never have any more children, because we'd never have sex again, because I've never once in my life been attracted to a nice Jewish boy." She took another swig and put the carton back.

Renny wasn't amused by any of it.

"Come on," she cajoled, "if you converted, our relationship would stop shocking my sisters, and shocking them is one of the great pleasures of my life. You wouldn't want to deprive me of one of my greatest pleasures, would you?"

Renny stared at her, the expression in his dark eyes flat. Then he said, "At the end of the day, you're exactly like them."

"Sticks and stones," Ali quipped, hoping he'd drop it. "Sticks and stones," she said again, wriggling past him into the narrow hallway where her suitcase sat.

"I just don't understand what you're waiting for," he said, following her to the front door of the ground-floor apartment on Norfolk Street they had shared for the last two years. "I'm ready. You're ready. *We're* ready."

"You know what I'm ready for?" Ali did an abrupt 180. "I'm ready for one more apple Danish!" She gave Renny a peck on the cheek and returned to the kitchen. She didn't really want the Danish, but they'd been through the same conversation over and over and Ali couldn't stand to go through it yet again, especially when she was already running so late. The pastry wrapped in a napkin, she headed for the door.

"At least let me help you with your bag," Renny said, picking up her small valise. "Not bad for a J.A.P." He winked as she passed.

"Not bad for a mick." She winked right back.

They walked together down to Delancey and found a taxi quickly. After putting Ali's bag in the trunk, Renny pulled her in for a tight hug. "Call me when you get to Maine." He kissed the top of her head, her forehead, her cheek, her neck. He smelled like sweat and Tide. He smelled like comfort.

"Call me when you get to the market." She forced herself to pull away. "I feel like I might want you to pick something crazy up for me, but I can't tell what it is yet."

"Do you really have to go?" Renny looked so sincerely pained, it melted the all-business igloo Ali had put herself in. "I don't like the idea of your traveling right now. Didn't you say you felt some cramping last night?"

"Nothing's going to happen to me," Ali reassured him, even though no one had had faith in reassurance since September 11, when every New Yorker realized there simply was no such thing.

"I'm only doing a two-day shoot. Let's just be glad it's paying so well."

Renny looked away. Ali knew she had touched a nerve, and she tried hard to soothe it. "Don't you want to start filming our Bosnian refugee project?" She caressed the side of his face. He hadn't shaved this morning, and the stubble tickled her fingers. "This'll fund it *and* another one. I'm not trying to be a downer, but things are about to get a lot more expensive. It's not like I'll be able to breast-feed forever. And then there's sitters and clothes and play groups—"

"And a wedding."

"And a new *apartment*. Did you hear those guys last night outside our window? It was insane how loud they were, which I wouldn't have minded as much if I'd understood them, but my teachers definitely never taught us *those* words in my high school Spanish classes."

"Maybe the baby will inherit my sleep genes," Renny said.

After fifteen years on film sets, Renny could sleep through anything and at any hour. The morning Renny and Ali got together, they were on their way home from a shoot that had started at 6:00 P.M. and ended at 4:00 A.M. Renny had been called in to sub for Ali's usual cinematographer, who had had to leave unexpectedly due to a death in his family, and the two had struck up a conversation on the drive back into the city from Newark, where they had been filming teenage prostitutes.

When Renny had arrived that night for work, Ali had seen only a tall, willowy guy with straight black hair cascading over slightly slumped shoulders that looked like they couldn't possibly handle the weight of a camera. It wasn't until much later that she noticed his hands, large and white, with bitten nails and ragged

4

cuticles but with long fingers that fluttered gracefully in the air when he was trying to make a point or explain a camera angle he thought would work. He was wearing army fatigues and combat boots and from afar looked almost menacing, but up close it was obvious that his large brown eyes were gentle and perceptive and his pockets contained nothing more harmful than soy nuts, which he liked to snack on instead of "the toxic crap on the craft services table." Ali found this out in the car ride home when she mentioned that she was starving.

"Open your mouth," he had said. Then he placed the nuts, one by one, onto her tongue.

"Yummy," she said after she had swallowed, her eyes never once leaving his.

"How'd you get the scar?" she had asked.

"Chasing after Marlene Fitzpatrick after Sunday school when we were both eight. Always have had a weakness for smart, attractive brunettes."

Neither of them had slept that morning. First they ate pancakes and eggs at an all-night diner on Delancey. Then they went back to his place because it was closer than her apartment in the East Village. They made love until noon, his white hands moving over her with slow, exhilarating skill, then they slept until four, ate again, and went back to work, a schedule they kept up until the shoot ended ten days later, by which time they were inseparable. They had decided to move in after two months, less as an expression of their mutual devotion than a necessity if they were ever going to see each other. Renny was on another shoot by then and Ali had her days free.

And so it went, with one or the other always working, sometimes on the same projects, more often not. It was an odd life, but somehow they made it work, especially because they both understood the demands of each other's schedules; and then there was the incontrovertible fact that they truly hungered for each other, not just physically but emotionally and intellectually, as well.

Good thing, that insatiable chemistry. They'd need it through the hard times to come. How could they have predicted that no one would shoot in Manhattan after September 11? How could they have imagined the independent-film world would come to such a halt? Of course it was only temporary, but it was a tough temporary, and Renny was working more parties these days as a bartender than he was working on films. Lately, he'd been looking for television and video work, which was lucrative but always made him feel like a sellout. He was even contemplating doing weddings and Bar Mitzvahs.

"I've got to get to the plane," Ali said, taking a step toward the taxi.

"Please," Renny begged, his hand catching her arm. "Think about it. You're hurting both of us right now. It doesn't have to be any big deal. We can hop down to City Hall one morning, or go to Vegas."

"Sounds classy," Ali said.

"Or we can do something big." Renny took his hand away in irritation, but his tone remained gentle—hopeful even. "Whatever you want, hon. I'm sure your mother would love to throw one last extravaganza. You don't have to be afraid. Being my wife"—his tone suddenly shifted—"well, I don't want to *convince* you to do it." He started to walk away, muttering, "This is sick."

"Come on," Ali said, grabbing his arm and pulling him back. "I don't want to get on a plane with any tension between us." She gave him a kiss on the mouth, which he returned. "But right now I gotta go. I'm already late, and you know how my sisters get." She blew Renny one last kiss, tumbled into the cab, and told the driver to hustle.

"So glad you decided to join us," Robin said when Ali arrived at Teterboro Airport forty-five minutes later. Robin was her oldest sister and usually launched the attack.

"You could have called," Andrea, next in line, added.

"You had to put purple in your hair for the occasion?" Mara said. "It's not even one of the team colors."

Karen got the last word, saying, "Lose the nose ring, Ali. We're not going to India."

"Nice to see you all, too," Ali said, laughing to herself at the uniformity of her sisters' appearance. It wasn't just their outfits, which were all similar versions of a floral miniskirt and pastel-colored tank top. They could have all been dressed head to toe in different national costumes and they still would have looked the same, since they each shared their mother's frizzy brown hair, their father's brown almond-shaped eyes, and each had had her nose done by the same doctor (a sweet sixteen "gift" from their parents, which Ali, to her sisters' disbelief, had resolutely turned down). Sure, Robin had the biggest breasts and Mara had recently added Japanese hair straightening to her list of hair manipulations. Sure, Andrea's nails were as long as an eagle's talons and Karen had a mole above her lip that made people liken her to Cindy Crawford. Beyond that, they were more or less interchangeable.

"What's wrong with my nose ring?" Ali said to Karen. "You're just jealous because my diamond's bigger than yours."

Of course it wasn't. No nose could possibly support the weight of a rock that was bigger than Karen's. Still, Ali chuckled to herself as she followed her sisters up the stairs and into the Learjet 35.

"You redecorated!" Mara shouted. "*Uch,* it's awesome. I love the chenille."

"This must have cost a mint," Andrea said, running her hands along the holly inlay in the mahogany walls.

"It wasn't prohibitive." Robin winked. "I just felt like the gray was too sterile."

"The pink is *much* better," Karen agreed.

"Please. We call it *salmon,*" Robin warned. "Otherwise, David gets upset. Let's not forget—technically, this is his corporate jet."

Ali took the plush pink seat closest to the bathroom, just in case she got sick, and pulled out her notebook. She hadn't prepared at all for the shoot she had been hired to do, and she wanted to write out a few ideas about how to structure the documentary. She wasn't worried. It wasn't much of a challenge, this job; nothing like her usual trek through urban jungles and juvenile detention centers. All she really needed to make was a commercial—an hour-long promo attesting to the wonders of Willow Lake. That was all Faye and Ron Stein, the current camp owners, wanted. They just liked the word *documentary* because they thought it sounded important. But they didn't really want a documentary. Otherwise, they would have asked her to incorporate footage and do research, express a point of view even, which, given Ali's history, could only have been mixed at best, scathing if she was feeling vengeful.

"Something to help us commemorate Willow Lake's centennial" was all they had specified. It was ironic that they'd come to her. She and her sisters had all gone to the camp when it was run by June Simon, an elegant grandmotherly type who always wore pristine white pants, pristine white Tretorns, pastel-colored button-down shirts, and a matching neckerchief. She took her job as Role Model seriously and spent her days wandering around campus in a golf cart, reminding the girls to "Always be a lady."

It was "Aunt" June, as the girls called her, who had first likened the Cohen sisters to the Kennedys; Aunt June who had said she had never known a family of such outstanding young ladies; Aunt June who had bestowed the Spirit of Willow Lake award on each one of the Cohen sisters, one after the other.

Of course, Ali had never won the award, but Faye and Ron Stein, the new owners, didn't seem to know that. As usual, she had been lumped in with her sisters, who now had their own children attending Willow Lake and were once again the talk of camp as their legacy continued. The mere thought of Willow Lake usually made Ali wince, but with a baby on the way and Renny unemployed, really this trip back to camp was just a job. That's all it was. She'd film the reunion guests as they went about their activities, give a little history about Willow Lake, conduct a few interviews, shoot the lake in the morning as the sun came up, and again in the evening with the moon shining down on the waves, put it all together, and send it off.

As she scribbled down the idea about the lake, Karen asked what she was doing.

"Just making some notes for the film," Ali replied without looking up.

"Nobody bother Ali," Karen shouted. "She's *working*."

Her sisters giggled, and Ali saw Mara roll her eyes. Still, they did leave her alone for most of the flight. Ali was glad. The snippets of conversation that floated back to her were like a foul odor she instinctively tried to avoid.

"The Four Seasons Nevis is the only place I like to go at Christmas, but it's so crowded you can't even get a massage, so why bother going?" Ali heard Andrea say to Robin. Later, Robin told Mara, "I know the name of a great tutor if you want one for Nikki. I heard she was having trouble with mazes during play group last week, and that's one of the things they test you on for pre-pre-K." There was also some talk about a dermatologist who did amazing things with a chemical from France that hadn't yet been approved by the FDA, and a plan was hatched for the girls to meet at Karen's apartment to take private yoga classes from an instructor she had met at Canyon Ranch who was making women look ten years younger with an innovative routine taken from Native American dances.

The only time Ali's sisters addressed her directly was when Andrea asked Ali if she had ever heard from a guy named Josh Dubin. Ali said she hadn't, and Mara squealed, "Isn't he married?"

"Oh *please*," Andrea said. "Didn't you hear? His wife had an affair with her tennis instructor in East Hampton in June. They're so over, it's frightening. Apparently, they had it out at Nick and Tony's in front of *everyone*."

"I think you should go out with David's friend Arthur," Robin said. "He's losing his hair, but he was number one in his class at Wharton and he's making billions, not that that matters, but it doesn't hurt. I heard he bought twelve pairs of Manolos for

Rebecca Marsh. And Sara Greenblatt got like eight Marc Jacob purses from him *and* a trip to Parrot Cay."

"I've heard he rents the most insanely beautiful house in St. Bart's at Christmas," Karen added. "Shoshana Epstein stayed there once. But she said he's hung like a Tootsie Roll, so maybe he isn't all that great. The gift giving seems like major compensation to me. It sounds like he can't even get it up!"

"I'm extremely happy with Renny," Ali said, irritated enough to look up from her notebook.

"Oh *please!*" her sisters said, sounding like a Greek chorus.

Then Andrea said, "I just want to know if Renny's available to bartend a party I'm throwing next month for the parents of the Ninety-second Street Y. Amy Rubinstein said he did a great job for her." Andrea turned to Mara and whispered loudly, "When Ali told me he worked for Glorious Foods, I assumed she meant as a manager or something. I didn't realize he actually poured the drinks!"

Mara cackled, and Ali lowered her eyes to her notebook. It amazed her that her own flesh and blood could be so obtuse and narrow-minded. Well, if they had any real problems with Renny, they'd better get over them soon. Then again, she really hadn't been fair. If they knew she was carrying his child, they wouldn't say anything more that was inappropriate. They wouldn't say anything more about Renny at all other than "When is he going to convert?" and "When are you getting married?"—and what a ball of barbed wire that would unravel!

Soon she would start showing. Soon she would have to provide a reason for her choice. It exhausted her just thinking about how she would ever explain herself to them. They were as provincial in certain ways as the women she had interviewed once for a documentary about life in Appalachia. At least the mountain women could blame poor education and lack of exposure for their ignorance. She couldn't come up with a single suitable excuse for her sisters' views.

"I don't believe in marriage," she'd tell them, and they'd say, "You just haven't met the right man." But she *didn't* believe in marriage. How could she?

It had been a terrible shock when Ali's father, the pillar of their family and the person they had all relied on for sound judgment and advice, had admitted—the morning after the party the girls threw for their parents at the St. Regis to celebrate their thirtieth wedding anniversary—that he had been having a decade-long affair with one of the secretaries at his law firm. Those kinds of things only happened in sordid TV movies and romance novels. They weren't supposed to happen to a man who'd spent his entire married life perfecting his home on the Cohens' three-acre property in Scarsdale; to a father of five grown children and eleven grandchildren; to a man who was on the board of Con Edison and had once been the president of the Westchester chapter of UJA; to a man who had just purchased a two-million-dollar condo on Fisher Island so his wife could play tennis in the winter and keep up her beloved tan. It wasn't supposed to have happened, period.

Ali sighed, and Karen asked what was wrong.

"Just tired," Ali said, and she closed her eyes for the remainder of the flight.

When the plane landed, the girls got into a rented white van and drove forty minutes northeast. They sped along an unremarkable highway for most of the way, but when they got off at exit 7N, they immediately saw a familiar wooden sign in the shape of an arrow, with WILLOW LAKE CAMP, 3 MILES painted on it in a color Ali always thought of as "Willow Lake green," a green halfway between kelly and evergreen, the color of all the bunks and other buildings at Willow Lake.

"Look!" Robin pointed excitedly. "Three Brothers!"

All eyes went to a small pizza restaurant and the girls burst into a song Ali hadn't heard in seventeen years:

When your school lets out in June
Summer's heat brings up this tune.
Pack up your shorts! Pack up your shirts!
Leave your Mary Janes behind and come to Maine.
Come to Willow Lake, where you'll water-ski.
Come to Willow Lake, where you'll climb a tree.
Say hi to counselors and friends from last year.
Put your hands together and give a big cheer!
Here's to the best camp [clap]: Willow Lake!

Ali made the same hand gestures as her sisters and cheered at the end with feigned enthusiasm: the memory the song unleashed was not a pleasant one. Whenever that song had begun, it meant that in a matter of minutes the bus would stop at the head of campus and a counselor would board. It meant that in a matter of minutes Ali would hear the same names read off that she heard on the first day of camp every year, because her bunk mates stayed more or less the same for the entirety of her eight summers as a Willow Laker.

Laura Berman. Jessica Bloom. Arden Finkelstein. Wendy Levin. Beth Rosenblatt. Dafna Shapiro. Her own name came between Jessica's and Arden's. "Jessica Bloom," the counselor would read, and Ali would feel her stomach churn, knowing her name was coming next. Of course, she wouldn't have had it any other way. Ali's bunk mates were the most popular girls in their age group. "You're lucky we let you be with us," Wendy had said to her at the beginning of their third summer together. "If it weren't for your sisters, you'd be stuck in 10B." (10B was the bunk with girls like Pam Fink, who picked her nose and ate it, and Jocelyn Ehrenefsky, who was fat and sullen and walked around with an inhaler for her asthma.)

Only three summers had passed and already Wendy had established herself as the best at every sport. Only three summers, and already Dafna and Arden were considered the prettiest girls in their age group and Laura Berman was regarded as the funniest. Beth was attached to Dafna at the hip, which made her popular by association, and Jessica was their age group's star thespian. But what was Ali? The smartest? The most insightful? Those qualities didn't hold any currency at camp.

What was wrong with her, the other girls wondered. Why didn't Ali want to go waterskiing, or knot a macramé bracelet, or make an ashtray in enameling or a fake stack of pancakes in pottery like everyone else? Why didn't she yearn to shoot a bow and arrow like Pocahontas, or do a handstand on the balance beam like Nadia Comaneci, or play tennis like Chris Evert, or ride bareback like Lady Godiva?

They were correct in their suspicions. Ali *hadn't* wanted to do any of those things. She had wanted to stay in her bunk all day, reading books from the neglected camp library, books like *Emma, One Hundred Years of Solitude, Animal Farm,* and *Catcher in the Rye*—books the other girls made fun of her for reading because they weren't *Deenie, The Cat Ate My Gymsuit, Blubber,* or *Are You There God? It's Me, Margaret,* all perfectly good books, but ones Ali had read years earlier.

Every activity she went to was a torture. She hated the freezing lake. She cowered when the softball came toward her. Tennis was terrifying, especially when she was forced to work on her lob and the ball would speed toward her from on high like a deadly comet. Pioneering was boring and involved exposure to mosquitoes and spiders and, once, a snake. And her bunk mates—

Ali grimaced, even now, when she thought of them. Not all of them. Some were just spoiled, others simply irritating. But Wendy and Arden—*Wendy*, really . . . mean was too mild a word to describe her behavior. Ali wondered sometimes if she could still press charges. Had her self-esteem been higher back then, she would have turned Wendy in. Had her self-esteem been higher back then, she could have gotten immediate revenge, rather than having her need for it fossilize into something cold and sharp, like a stalactite waiting to drop.

But her self-esteem hadn't been high then at all. She had even returned for her final two summers. Turn someone in? Go crying to the head of camp? Request not to be sent back? It was unthinkable. Going to Willow Lake was what a Cohen sister did in the summer. There was no way Ali was going to be the one Cohen sister who couldn't cut it.

There she was every February, writing the names of her desired bunk mates on the Willow Lake form just like her sisters did, or had done, with *their* friends on *their* forms. There she was every May, sitting at the mustard-colored table in the cramped kitchen in Scarsdale (it was well before the big kitchen renovation), helping her mother sew the ALI COHEN name tape in her sisters' hand-me-downs. There she was every June, arriving at Willow Lake with a furrowed brow and a dash of hope. And there she was every August, back at the mustard-colored table in the kitchen in Scarsdale, relieved, exhausted, battered, and more determined than ever to prove herself in other arenas.

And prove she did: honors student, head of the debate team, editor of the yearbook, early acceptance at Brown where she won an award at graduation for the documentary she made about the university going coed. She had used her Fulbright to study film in Paris and her NEA grant to make her breakthrough documentary, *Out of the Dark,* which followed a fifteen-year-old girl as she went to high school daily from a homeless shelter where she lived with her mother in a tiny room with a single hot pot and one lightbulb dangling down from the ceiling.

The more she accomplished, the further her adolescent failure at Willow Lake receded in her emotional memory. Ali never saw a single one of her bunk mates ever again and only occasionally ran into a former Willow Laker, usually when she was uptown visiting one of her sisters, and once when she was shopping for shoes at Barneys.

She could still remember the hysteria that had accompanied those final good-byes for the other girls in her age group when the school bus pulled away from camp in 1985 to take them to the Portland Airport for the very last time.

There were no tears streaming down Ali's cheeks. *Good-bye,* she had said to herself, looking only at the road ahead as the bus bumped and jiggled its way out of camp. *Good-bye,* she had said to herself gleefully as the others ran to the back of the bus to relish a final view of their beloved Willow Lake as it melted into the horizon of pine trees.

And now, seventeen years later, the pine trees soared once more. The white van was hurtling down the road that led straight into camp. Maybe she should start the documentary with a school bus pulling up to camp! She scribbled down the idea as the van came to a stop in the small camp lot. Above their heads loomed a green banner that said in white block letters WILLOW LAKE CAMP, 1902–2002.

"We're here!" Karen screamed.

"Oh my *God!*" Andrea yelled.

Mara and Robin started singing and clapping:

> *We love you Willow Lake, oh yes we do.*
> *We don't love anything as much as you.*
> *When we're not with you, we're blue.*
> *Oh Willow Lake, we love you!*

Ali reminded herself that she was back at Willow Lake for a job, not the joy of reunion. She reminded herself it no longer mattered that she was the one Cohen sister who couldn't swing a bat, balance on a water ski, cradle a lacrosse stick, dribble a basketball, carry a tune, or even draw a straight line. She reminded herself that she was a documentary filmmaker with many awards to her name and one Academy Award nomination. She reminded herself that she was a professor at NYU, with students who were older than she was. She reminded herself that she was the one Cohen sister who had been entirely self-supporting since she left college. She reminded herself that the money Faye and

Ron had given her up front had already been deposited in the bank. Still, she looked around warily as she followed her sisters down the short hill that led to the main house.

"The Cohen sisters are here!" someone shrieked. And then Robin and Andrea were screaming and hugging two girls Ali didn't recognize, and Mara and Karen were asking about some mutual friends of the two unknown girls, and everyone was jumping and hugging and chanting an old camp cheer: "Chickee wee! Chickee woo! [Clap, clap.] Willow Lake!"

Ali reached for her video camera and filmed the spectacle, glad to have a real reason to stand outside of things.

"Water Ski Jack is still here!" one of the girls said.

"And Miss Carol—remember Miss Carol from lacrosse?"

Miss Carol had also been Ali's bunk counselor one summer early on.

"She's head counselor now. Can you *believe* it?"

Ali clung to her camera as if it were her baby blanket. Everything about Willow Lake was the same: the smell of pine and French toast that permeated the air; the muted green of the endless rolling lawns, mixed with the deeper green of the Willow Lake buildings, mixed with the occasional spots of dirt where too many feet had trod over the years; the quiet that enabled you to hear the leaves as they rustled in the breeze; the willows—the willows that served as the team meeting spot, the willows that defined the camp as much as anything else did—

Ali's heart was racing and she actually closed her eyes and took several deep breaths in an attempt to steady herself.

Better. She felt better. It was just a job. That was it.

She followed her sisters more steadily as they mounted the steps leading up to the terrace of the main house. The roofed-over terrace that encircled the house had always been the nexus of camp activity: the place where milk and cookies were served at eleven o'clock every day between morning activities; the place where friends met during free swim or after dinner; the place where everyone went to find out who had gotten what part in their age-group play, or who had been promoted in swimming, or what trip each age group would be taking on trip day.

This weekend, in honor of Willow Lake's big anniversary, a picnic table was set up in the center of the porch. Behind it sat two women Ali recognized immediately: Miss Carol, who still looked as firm and youthful as she had when she had attempted, unsuccessfully, to teach Ali to play lacrosse so many years ago, and, beside her, Miss Ruthie, who, conversely, looked like a withered apple. She had been ancient when Ali had been a camper. It was hard to fathom that she was still working. Did she really still ring chimes? Her eyes were barely distinguishable behind the many folds of flesh around them. Could she even still see?

"The Kennedys of Willow Lake have arrived!" Miss Carol shouted. She got up from the table and hugged each of Ali's sisters. She was wearing the same style of kilt and high socks she had worn when Ali had been a camper, and her blond hair was pulled off her face in a French braid as if no other styles had been invented since the early 1980s.

"Where's Ali?" she asked, her glance passing over Ali without recognition.

Ali smiled and stepped forward.

Miss Carol gasped.

"Yup," Ali said, "it's really me."

"Goodness!" Miss Carol laughed, giving her a hug. "You're all grown up!"

Ali was relieved to know she was unrecognizable. Whoever was looking for the pale, flabby girl with dark braids falling from a middle part down either side of her body to her waist would find instead a woman who, even in her third month of pregnancy, was taut and muscular, sporting a shock of short jet black hair highlighted on the tip of each spike with purple. Her makeup, too, was strong, especially around her eyes, which she lined in black, and on her lips she wore a color called "Kill 'Em Crimson."

"Is there anything we can help you with in terms of the documentary?" Miss Carol asked. "And may I add that we're all extremely honored to have someone of your caliber making this for us."

"Well, a paycheck does help," Ali said.

Everyone laughed, and Ali asked if it would be okay for her to interview some of the guests and have them sign consent forms. Miss Carol assured her it would be fine and then invited Ali to sign the contact sheet.

Ali scanned the list of names already on it. She recognized several of them but didn't see any of her former bunk mates on it, thank God. Not that it would really matter, but she had been hoping none of them would deem it necessary to return. Relieved to see they hadn't, she added her own name to the list.

It wasn't the photo albums or the old camp movies on display in the main house or the view from the terrace of the magnificent property or even her first look down the hill at the glistening lake. It was the particular smell inside the dining hall that did it, that took her back in the most visceral way to the summers of her youth. One breath and there she was, eating peanut butter and jelly on Wonder bread, shoveling fried clam strips drenched in ketchup into her mouth, breaking dried, crunchy amber-colored noodles over a plate full of chicken chow mein, slurping down a spoonful of vanilla ice cream and butterscotch sauce.

One breath and she could remember the feel of a wet bathing suit under dry shorts as she sat on a hard green bench waiting for food to arrive. One breath and she could remember the ache of her swollen feet as they marinated in sweaty tube socks encased in Adidas with frayed laces, and the way the ice-cold glass of Hi-C in her hand would soothe them. One breath and she could remember the salty odor of lunch meats arriving on aluminum trays at breakfast so each camper could fix an ultimately soggy, smushed sandwich for trip day.

"I have to get out of here," she mumbled to her sisters.

"You okay?" she heard Karen call after her, but there was no time to answer. The bile was already rising in her throat. She rushed through the screen door and galloped down the steep steps leading to campus. What a relief the fresh air was! Unfortunately, not relief enough: Ali just made it to the giant oak tree that stood at the head of campus when the vomit came up, landing in a relatively neat yellow puddle in front of her feet.

She looked around, panicked. A few women were wandering around campus, but no one seemed to have noticed. It was strange, this feeling of inferiority. She hadn't felt it in so many years!

Ali wiped her mouth on her arm and reached into her knapsack for a mint. Then she kicked some dirt over the vomit and sat down at the base of the tree. Before her spread the campus, as magnificent as ever, its circle of white canvas-covered tents and green bunks like a tidy necklace around the velvety expanse of grass. In the center was a flagpole, from which waved that ever-present American flag.

Ali wondered if everyone still stood outside of their bunk-houses each morning to say the Pledge of Allegiance while they watched two lucky campers help one of the counselors raise the flag. She herself had never been chosen for the honor. Who had decided which campers were chosen? Did they *still* do that? Did they even still raise the flag? Did Miss Ruthie still play the scratchy recording of "Taps" at night and the scratchier recording of "Reveille" in the morning? Ali felt disconcertingly out of touch with the rituals of contemporary campers. Could it really have been seventeen years since she had been one?

She looked from bunk to bunk and from tent to tent, trying to recall the ones she had inhabited, but her eyes returned to the flagpole and she was swept with a fresh wave of humiliation, even after all these years, as she remembered the morning she had stood outside some bunk or other and watched as her "little bloomies" underwear was raised along with the flag while the rest of Willow Lake stood by laughing.

Bunk 10A: She remembered that one. She found a dead frog on her pillow one afternoon after free swim in 10A.

Tent 7. Ah, yes. The Pringles and squirt cheese her parents had hidden in a care package beneath some shirts had disappeared from her cubby in that tent. No one had claimed responsibility, but Ali knew it had been Wendy.

Bunk 4B. Ali stared and allowed the memories to crowd in. Arden and Wendy had held her head in the toilet and flushed it over and over again in that bunk. They had stolen her favorite purple sweater and flung it up into the rafters, short-sheeted her bed, lopped off her hair in her sleep, and tore down her poster of Shawn Cassidy in that bunk. That was the bunk she had returned to after the atrocity in the woods. She had cried herself to sleep night after night in that bunk. She had sworn revenge in that bunk. She had *promised* herself revenge.

Tent 2, and the tide began to turn. Wendy didn't come back to be in Tent 2. Ali caught Arden smoking behind Tent 2 and told the head counselor, and Arden had been sent home the very next day, so there was an empty bed for the rest of the summer between Ali and the rest of the girls in that tent.

Bunk 1AB, at last. At last, for her final summer at camp, no Arden, no Wendy, no mandatory activities: peace. She got her period for the first time in 1AB. She shaved her legs for the first time in 1AB using baby lotion and a pink Daisy razor. She knew she'd never have to come back to Willow Lake after the summer she spent in 1AB and it was a relief.

Ali rose, stretched, turned away from campus, and made her way down the sloping hill, around the outside of the dining hall, past the canteen where campers got their Snickers or Three Musketeers or Charleston Chews after dinner, past the Newcomb court, past the steps leading up to the main house, around the four team willows, then continued on to the plateau in the hill where a row of Adirondack chairs were set up, offering the most spectacular views down toward the lake.

Ali sat in one of the large "Willow Lake green"–painted chairs and took in the scenery. After so many memories, it was nice to do nothing but sit and look. It was the same view she had admired every Friday evening of every summer for eight years as she had nestled among the other campers listening to the

Sabbath prayers float in the pure Maine air. It would make the perfect opening for the documentary, this view, and she gazed outward now with a surge of unexpected tenderness.

Ali cupped her hand around her eye so she could see the landscape as her camera lens would capture it. She could start with a broad shot—she widened her hand to increase the amount of scenery she could take in—and then she saw them. There was no mistake: Dafna Shapiro, Beth Rosenblatt, and Wendy Levin were greeting one another beside Aunt June's garden to the left of the infirmary.

Ali dropped her hand and slunk lower in her chair. Dafna and Beth were dressed like twins, wearing outfits similar to the ones her sisters had been sporting. (What was it with that outfit? Was it something that came with your apartment when you moved to the Upper East Side, like a welcome basket in a hotel room filled with fruit and champagne? *Welcome to the Upper East Side! Enjoy your Marc Jacobs skirt and top and these adorable Manolo Blahnik sandals!*) Dafna looked the best in it, elegant as ever, with a figure that had only improved with time. Beth was thinner than Ali remembered and her blond hair wasn't quite as wild, but she was still a dead ringer for Miss Piggy. And Wendy Levin—well, she still looked formidable with her statuesque build and broad shoulders, but her khaki shorts and Todd moccasins combined with her ashy blond hair to give her a preppier look than the others, if JAPPY could ever be aligned in such a way with preppy, which of course it could ever since Ralph Lipshitz changed his name to Ralph Lauren, his unspoken motto: Think Yiddish, Dress British.

Ali considered her own attire for a moment: low-slung black jeans that allowed her swollen belly freedom, a purple-and-black

T-shirt with the arms torn off, black slides on her feet—okay, they were from Prada, but there was no logo, so you couldn't tell. When she had chosen the outfit that morning, she hadn't thought much about what it would say to people. She had chosen it for its comfort and because it was more or less what she always wore. But here she could see the outfit screamed *Iconoclast*.

I could show these people some real iconoclasts, Ali thought. She tried to make herself invisible, but the girls were advancing directly toward her, closer, closer, until Ali really had no choice: she sat up and waved.

Wendy looked behind herself, and Dafna and Beth exchanged glances. Ali could tell they had no idea who she was. She waved more vigorously and reached into her bag for her video camera.

"I should start filming right now," she said as the trio approached. "The reunion of bunk 16B for the first time in twenty-four years. This is classic."

And suddenly they were right there, close enough to touch.

"Hey, Wendy," Ali said, grateful for the social skills that had been ingrained since childhood. "Dafna, Beth, how was your trip up? Did you come together?" Ali enjoyed their confusion for another moment, then said, "I gather you aren't sure who I am." She introduced herself. "Remember me?"

Wendy stared openly, but the other two did the same thing Miss Carol had done.

"Oh my God!" Dafna screamed, throwing her arms around Ali's neck. "Ali Cohen! Look at you! Where are your braids?"

"You're all punk!" Beth squealed.

"Very Kings Road 1984," they both agreed. "Very Moschino."

Ali looked at them in their practically matching outfits, then at the gargantuan diamond ring on Beth's finger, and thought, Very Upper East Side, but she didn't say it. Instead, she said, "Do you guys mind if I get you on film? I was hired to make a documentary about Willow Lake, and I'd love to do a little interviewing."

"A *movie*," Dafna said. "How glamorous." She squeezed Beth's arm in excitement.

"Can I just put on a little more lip gloss?" Beth asked.

"We heard from your sisters about your Oscar," Dafna said.

Ali explained it was just a nomination.

"Still," Dafna said.

"It's *incredible*," Beth agreed.

"Anyone know if Laura's coming?" Ali asked. "Or Jessica? Or Arden Finkelstein?"

"Laura's coming tonight," Dafna volunteered. "She sent me a text message from the Hamptons or something. Who knows. She's a super-duper power agent with lots of bigwig friends. I swear I think she was taking Spielberg's private plane up here."

Ali wasn't surprised. Laura had always been all business. She was the bunk mate who knew, by the second day of camp, when visiting day was and when the counselors' play, which day was pajama breakfast and which the inter-camp tennis tournament. She understood how the summer was organized on a macro and micro level and advised her bunk mates when to sign up for more waterskiing or fewer tennis practices, telling them, once they got older and anxious about weight, when it was okay to eat a lot of ice cream and when it was better to hold off on dessert due to an upcoming smorgasbord. And her cubby! Never a sweater or T-shirt out of place, and everything organized by color, shape, and size.

"How about Arden?" Ali asked. "I'm dying to know what ever happened to Arden Finkelstein."

"You haven't heard about Arden?" Dafna asked in a hushed tone.

"Why would she have heard?" Beth countered.

"I just thought it must have made the Willow Lake rounds," Dafna said.

"I'm not really in the loop," Ali confessed. "What's the big news?"

Dafna looked at Wendy and asked, "Do you want to share the saga?"

"You go ahead," Wendy replied. "You're a much better story-teller than I am."

Wendy's voice was different than Ali remembered it: softer, gentler, with a hint of uncertainty.

"Do you guys mind signing consent forms?" she asked. She explained what they were and all three agreed it was fine.

"So," she said after the forms had been returned. "What's the big news?"

"Arden was Wendy's nanny!" Dafna announced. "Is that insane?"

"It is," Ali agreed, enjoying how little Dafna had changed since camp. She asked how the bizarre situation had come to pass.

"Well," Dafna said, her perfectly groomed eyebrows rising as she geared up for a good one. "You're sure you want me to tell it, Wendy? It is your story."

"Go ahead," Wendy said.

Ali was struck immediately by Wendy's deference. It wasn't an attitude Ali associated with Wendy Levin.

"So, Wendy was in the city looking for a nanny since her nanny had just quit. Isn't that right?"

Wendy nodded.

"And she ran into Arden in front of Ralph Lauren—"

"In SoHo," Beth added.

"In SoHo. That's right. And—"

"My nanny had just quit on me the day before," Wendy explained, looking directly into Ali's eyes for the first time. Ali looked away quickly. Even with the intervening years, it was too hard to pretend their history together hadn't happened.

"She'd just returned from studying child psychology at Oxford," Dafna continued, "and her parents had just *died.*"

"This part is so tragic," Beth said. "They had some kind of freak kayaking accident on the Long Island Sound. Can you believe? And her boyfriend—"

"She was dating some kind of Eurotrash millionaire—"

"*Italian,*" Beth corrected. "He was Italian."

"Whatever. He kicked her out of their apartment and she was literally, like, homeless."

"I don't know if she was *homeless,*" Wendy said. She looked at the lens of Ali's camera, which Ali thought a clever solution. "But there you go. She was my nanny."

"Until you caught her screwing the snow-blower!" Dafna shrieked. "In the master bedroom! *Can you imagine?!*"

"And then what happened?" Ali prompted.

"Well, what do you *think* happened?" Dafna's eyes were wide with the obviousness of it all.

"I told her to get out, and she did," Wendy said. "I hadn't seen her since camp and she seemed very capable, but it just didn't work out."

"I'll say!" Dafna kibitzed.

"Did you check your jewelry?" Beth asked. "Do you think she stole anything?"

"She didn't steal anything." Wendy stood. "I honestly think

she was just lonely. I'm going to walk down to the lake. Anyone want to join?"

"What about Jessica and Laura?" Ali asked, ignoring Wendy as an idea began to take form. "Anyone know what happened to *them*?"

"Well, of course," Beth said. "Dafna knows what happened to everyone."

"No one wants to join me?" Wendy asked again.

Wendy's discomfort gave Ali pleasure.

"I'm dying to see the lake." Wendy looked positively pained.

Dafna and Beth stood, but Ali told them she had work to do and would remain on the hill.

"See you later!" Dafna chirped.

"*Ciao ciao,*" Beth echoed. As she waved, her enormous diamond engagement ring caught the sun, sending a splash of rainbow-hued circles across Ali's face.

Faye and Ron Stein decided to officially welcome everyone to the one hundredth reunion weekend at the traditional Shabbas service they normally held during the camp season on Friday nights at sundown. Ali's sisters were sitting together toward the middle of the pack, their miniskirts and tank tops replaced, like everyone else's, by jeans and cashmere sweater sets to warm them in the chilly August twilight. Dafna and Beth were huddled together farther down the hill with Laura Berman, who had walked into the bunk after dinner looking amazingly skinny and chic, dressed head to toe in black, her red hair styled in a pageboy cut that was very Anna Wintour, only on her it simply looked very Laura Berman.

Jessica Bloom was sitting with them, too. She had shown up

in all her blond perkiness during the pizza cookout, virtually froth-
ing at the mouth with the news of her impending turn as Sarah
Brown in a yearlong national tour of *Guys and Dolls*. She had
played the same leading role as a camper to great acclaim and had
even reprised one of the songs right there on the baseball diamond so anyone who might have had a murky memory of the
event or wasn't around at camp at the time could have a taste of
her artistry. The job was the reason she said she was going to eat
only watermelon, no pizza. "Don't need to show up bloated on the
first day of rehearsal," she had explained. Ali couldn't imagine that
a slice of pizza could do significant damage but she nodded with
the other girls and commented on Jessica's amazing discipline.

Where is Wendy? Ali wondered, scanning the guests. Wendy
was missing. Ali had a good view, since she was sitting above
them all, filming; filming and thinking; filming and strategizing;
filming and contemplating if what she wanted to do was possible,
interesting, entertaining, ethical.

Oh, she'd make Faye and Ron their little documentary. No
challenge to that. But why not make a second documentary?
Something about her former bunk mates. Really, why not? The
premise: seven girls, all Jewish, all from wealthy origins, spend
eight summers of their lives together in a bunk. Does the experience shape them in a particular way? Does being a Willow Laker
actually mean something specific? Do they all have things in
common now? And what about their evolution? Are they now
hardworking career women? Benevolent caretakers? Teachers?
Artists? Or have those Jewish American Princesses of yesteryear
simply become the Jewish American Queens of today, arranging
catered birthday parties for their three-year-olds and ordering
their personal shoppers to get them in first at Prada and Gucci?

"Baruch atah adonai," Faye began as she lit the Shabbas candles.

Ali joined Faye silently, adding "Amen" under her breath when they reached the end of the prayer.

The bonfire crackled, sending orange flames into the cold night. While waiting for Wendy to appear, Ali had been filming the reunion guests as they conjured up the forgotten folk songs of their childhoods. How they could still remember harmony was a source of wonder. She had hated those stupid folk songs as a camper and had never understood why girls like Jessica Bloom would cry and hug themselves when they sang songs like "Leaving on a Jet Plane," "Cat's in the Cradle," and "Circle Game." But now, as an adult, she had to admit the melodies and lyrics were beautiful in their simplicity. And how could you beat singing on the beach under a sky full of stars in August in Maine? Too bad she hadn't been able to enjoy this kind of thing as a camper.

Too bad she hadn't been able to enjoy a lot of things as a camper. Now she would have loved to take a canoe out on the lake, or a kayak, or a Sunfish. Now she would have loved to take a moonlit skinny-dip. But how she had despised those canoe meets as a kid! Why had the others thought it so much fun to purposely tip over in a canoe, fill it with water, then paddle back to shore? And what could possibly have been worse than diving into that freezing lake and accidentally touching the slimy wall? Ali turned away from the water, and there was Wendy.

Dressed in a bright blue fleece with a Hermès scarf around her neck, Wendy was walking toward the bonfire, holding a marshmallow on the end of a stick.

Ali put her camera away and followed. "Your first s'more of the night?" she asked when she reached Wendy's side.

Wendy nodded, then added, "I was just off checking on the kids."

Ali asked how they were and Wendy said they were all fine but that her husband was definitely overwhelmed.

"Must be tough," Ali said. "How many do you have?"

"Four," Wendy answered, the inherent exhaustion of the situation evident in her tone.

"Goodness!" Ali exclaimed. It was truly incomprehensible to her. "You must have started young."

"Not that young," Wendy said, and Ali had to acknowledge that in some circles, thirty-two was not too young to have four kids. Of course, she thought those circles were mostly in the South and Midwest, not as close as Short Hills, where Wendy now lived. In Ali's circle, children, period, were pretty much unheard of. Most of Ali's friends were filmmakers and writers, performers and activists. They were either too career-oriented or broke even to think of having children. One or two were married, but that was about it. She was certainly the first to get pregnant. It would be a big deal in her world when news got out.

"So, Dafna, Beth, Jessica, and Laura are over by the boathouse," Ali began, aware that she needed to lure Wendy in immediately, before the others wandered off, "and I wondered if you'd join us for a minute, after you've had a s'more, of course, so I can run a quick idea by you."

The marshmallow Wendy was roasting caught fire and she blew on it, but the charred outside fell off the stick and landed unceremoniously in the sand. "I'll make another one later," Wendy said, turning dutifully toward Ali. "Let's go."

It was great, the way they all acquiesced, Ali thought as she led Wendy over to the sandy knoll where the three other women were talking. What a difference! What a thrill!

Ali didn't want to waste a minute. "So I had this idea," she began. It was too dark to see the expressions in their eyes, but she spoke with as much enthusiasm and certainty as she could convey. "You know how I'm doing this documentary?"

The girls nodded.

"Well, I just thought it would be amazing if I could interview you each about what you've been up to since camp. Learn what you consider to be the real defining moment, or moments, of your lives."

Dafna and Beth turned toward each other in excitement and Laura asked Ali if she already had funding and which producers were attached since she had an excellent relationship with HBO.

"I'm not concerned about that end yet," Ali said. "I'm more interested in the general shape of the project. I just think it would be fascinating to get an idea of the directions we've all gone in." She paused because it felt like a good dramatic moment. "Are you game?"

"What do you mean by a 'defining moment'?" Wendy asked cautiously.

"I'm talking about the moments in your lives when you did something, or made some kind of choice, that somehow made it clear to you who you really are. Does that make sense?"

"I thought the documentary was just supposed to be about camp," Dafna said.

"Yeah," Beth echoed. "Memories and stuff. I brought my scrapbook down." She reached into her purse and produced a small square book. Ali shone her flashlight on it and found Miss Kitty smiling up at her in pink glitter.

"No pressure," Ali said. "If you don't want to do it, that's totally cool. I just thought it would be fun and interesting. If you'd prefer, I could contact you once you're home. I'd be happy to go to your apartments or houses, or wherever you'd like."

"I won't be home for twelve months," Jessica said, "but you're welcome to join me on the road. I'm hitting some pretty exciting locales—Wichita, Livonia, Tampa."

"Yikes," Dafna said.

"Although I can tell you right now," Jessica continued, "that my defining moment happened when I was in second grade at Brearley and got cast as Rumplestiltskin. Never wanted to do anything else my whole life."

"Than play Rumplestiltskin?" Laura deadpanned.

Dafna and Beth laughed.

Jessica asked if she'd qualify for her SAG card if she did the film, and Ali promised to look into it.

"My defining moment was the night you lost your virginity," Dafna said, pointing to Beth. "That was when I realized my life's calling was to mop up your messes."

Both girls squealed at the memory and Jessica said, "Do tell!"

"No, *don't,*" Beth said, but it was clear she wanted Dafna to talk.

"We were on a Putney teen tour—"

"This is *such* a virginity story," Laura said dryly. Her boredom was potent, but not a deterrent to Dafna, who barreled right on.

"Naturally, I lost my virginity first," Dafna said, "to Taylor. Dee. The Third."

She and Beth both swooned.

"*So* not Jewish," Laura said.

"Oh my God, he went to Hotchkiss or something!" Dafna shouted in glee.

"Deerfield," Beth said, "and then Syracuse. He wasn't very smart."

"Who cares?" Dafna shrieked. "The brain we needed worked fine. So there we were on a night train to Venice—what a cock. He was as big as a horse."

Jessica clapped her hands and shouted, "How fun!"

"No, *so* not fun. So *ouch* for the first time. Trust me," Dafna said, "it was *not* pleasant. Believe me, we broke up about five minutes later. If I recall correctly, he didn't buy me one of those glass candies when we went to Murano, and I was totally pissed. Anyway, to make a long story short, before I know it we're in Florence at the Hotel California—"

"Can you imagine?" Beth said. "The Hotel California, when we could have been at the Villa San Michele? I don't know what our parents were thinking, sending us on something so squalid—"

"—and Beth is shaking me in the middle of the night, sobbing and telling me she can't stop bleeding, should she go to the hospital, blah, blah, blah."

"He was as big as an elephant," Beth lamented. "You could have warned me."

"I didn't realize you were planning on using my discarded merchandise."

There was a moment of clear, unadulterated hatred that passed between them, but it only lasted for a millisecond. Then Dafna said, "Of course, quick thinker that I am, I tore the sheet off the bed and poured a bucket of ice in it and we sat together in the shower stall and laughed about it all and vowed to become virgins again by not having any sex until we got to college."

"You actually *were* awesome," Beth agreed. "I thought you'd be furious with me, but you were so cool and levelheaded. I really could have bled to death."

"Oh, don't be so dramatic," Laura said. She was simultaneously checking something in her Palm Pilot. "No one's ever died losing their virginity."

"So what was *your* defining moment?" Dafna asked Laura, a hint of competition in her voice.

"Haven't had it yet," Laura replied.

"You probably just need some time to think about it," Ali suggested.

"My defining moment was this morning when I left," Wendy said. "Seth was like, 'What does Sam eat for lunch? Do the kids have a special bedtime?' I handed him a printout with each activity of the day highlighted in a different color. I'm hoping he can at least handle getting the boys to their play dates and putting Sam on a swing, but you never know."

The four of them laughed and Ali joined them. Make friends with the animals, she thought. Offer them treats. "I'd be happy to tell you my own defining moment," she offered. For a second, she caught Wendy's eye and Wendy looked away. In fear, Ali thought, a smile spreading in her heart. *In fear.*

Five P.M. was the hour of deep fatigue, the hour when being pregnant seemed like a terrible idea. Ali dragged herself out of the Adirondack chair anyway and made her way down the hill, heading toward the stables, where she had seen them disappear into the woods.

At least she was moving. She had been waiting for fifteen minutes in the hard chair for Wendy to show up for her interview. She'd been about to give up, when, scanning the horizon, she spotted Wendy and Miss Carol.

It was right here, she decided, studying the unmarked trail to the left of the riding rink. She turned into the woods. It was much cooler beneath the vast pine trees and it smelled like early autumn. The flies, however, reminded her it was still summer. "Shoo," she whispered, swatting them away. She didn't want to make too much noise. Something told her to tread with care.

After a few minutes, she came to a small clearing where a shack stood. A wooden sign above it read PIONEER PETER'S PAD. Around Peter's pad, several small green tents had been erected. Ali's legs started to tremble almost immediately and she thought for a moment that she actually might fall down. The sight of the tents was too much. It was all rushing back without any preparation: the horror of being gagged, the terror when Wendy forced down her pajamas, the pain when the mascara wand went into her anus. Ali broke into a sweat, her eyes riveted on the tents. The trembling in her legs increased and she went over to the shack and sat.

It took her several long moments to calm herself. It was during that time, when her own breathing felt so labored, that she became aware of other labored breathing. She caught her own breath and listened. She heard moans, soft moans, the moans of lovemaking, the moans of lust. She raised her head, her attention rapt. The sounds were coming from one of the tents. She rose and placed her finger on the recording button of her video camera like a cop in the movies cocking a weapon.

There were six tents in a ragged circle. She tried to pinpoint the origin of the moans but it was hard. She put her ear to the first tent: nothing. On the side of the tent was a small mesh window. She peaked inside: empty. The moaning continued and she went to the next tent: nothing. She made her way to the third tent and the moans got louder. Someone was in there. Dare she intrude?

She went to the mesh window, raised her camera, pressed record, then put her eye to the viewer. Miss Carol, in a pair of white underpants and a bra, was going down on Wendy, who was naked. Ali stifled her own gasp and averted her eyes. Without thinking, she tiptoed out of the campground and retraced her steps back to the main campus. Her heart was beating hard, as if she herself had been caught in flagrante. She returned to the Adirondack chairs in a state of amused shock. She almost couldn't believe what she had seen, but when Wendy and Miss Carol returned from the woods some ten minutes later, there was no denying it. They were holding hands, which they quickly dropped once they hit the wide open field in front of the stables, an area that was clearly visible from where Ali was sitting.

Ali rewound her camera and checked the replay. It looked like a cheap porn video. She closed the camera quickly and looked around. Her sisters were over by the Newcomb court. Uncertain as to how she would use the footage, but certain that something momentous had just occurred, she got up to join them.

✳

As Ali made her way into the dining room for supper, Wendy came running up.

"I'm so sorry about the interview!" she lamented. "I fell into such a sleep! I think I was exhausted from all the activities. I don't know what happened."

"Don't worry about it," Ali said. "We'll do it another time."

"Perfect," Wendy said.

"Perfect," Ali echoed. "Wouldn't want to put a damper on anyone's good time."

"You'd think I'd be used to all this activity, but I feel like I could sleep for a week!"

"I imagine you must be pretty spent," Ali said. For a moment, she considered mentioning the pioneering tents as a nice place to nap.

"Well, don't *you* look radiant!" Dafna said, sauntering up to the twosome and staring at Wendy. "You look like you just got laid. What's your secret? And don't say *lacrosse toss*, because I just don't buy it."

"Talked with the kids," Wendy said. "It was just good to hear their voices."

"I'll bet," Ali said as they all sat down.

"So what do we think?" Dafna asked, sliding over to make room for Laura and Beth. "Do we wish we could all go back to camp?"

"Of course," Beth said.

"Over my dead body," Laura declared.

"I'd love to come back," Ali said, aware that she needed to

participate if she wanted the others to, "but only if I was the person I am now."

"What about you, Wendy?" asked Dafna, persisting with her questions. She was obviously in one of her "Let's all share" moods. It seemed clear to Ali that Dafna wanted to say something herself but was waiting until everyone else had spoken so she wouldn't seem like a conversation hog.

"I'd do anything to reexperience the pleasure of this place," Wendy said, a flush creeping into her cheeks.

Ali smiled as she filmed, loving the subtext that only she understood.

Jessica, who had already packed her bags and was leaving after dinner, said she wished she could have the freedom of a whole summer off again. She began to cry, and Ali saw Laura smirk ever so slightly.

"Well I, for one, feel like writing my parents a thank-you note," Dafna declared, satisfied now that everyone else had said their bit. "I feel like, what could have been more magical and perfect than those summers we spent here? And I feel like it really helped to shape us into nice young ladies, just like Aunt June wanted. I mean, we always laughed when Aunt June said that, but look how well we all turned out!"

"Missy Marx got so fat, I didn't recognize her," Mara said.

The plane was taking off and Andrea asked her to repeat herself. Once Mara repeated the comment, she decided it was inadequate. "Fat doesn't do her justice. Goodyear blimp is more like it. I don't know how her husband stands it."

"If that ever happens to me," Karen said, "please just do an intervention."

"There's really no good excuse for being overweight," Mara said. "The No Carb thing works like a charm. And if you really can't stick to something, just do what the stars do and spend a week at a spa."

"Spas don't work," Robin said. "I *gained* weight at Canyon Ranch. Of course, it was mostly just bloat. The food was so full of bran, I did nothing but fart."

"It's not the bran," Karen said. "It's those jicama sticks. They're lethal. You may as well be gorging on raisins. And the raw broccoli? Forget it."

"You don't need a spa to stay in shape," Mara said. "Just go to Lotte Berk. Or get a trainer at Reebok or Equinox to help you out. Or hire one of those people who follow you around and make you stay on your diet—you know, *a life coach.* Chloe Bernstein became a size two that way."

"Oh, *please,*" Andrea said. "Chloe had lipo."

"Yoga's the answer," Karen said. "This woman we're going to work with, I'm *telling* you—"

It was at this point in the conversation that Ali checked out. Her mind was reeling with the potential of her idea. Her bunk mates were just as she had expected: grown-up versions of their JAPPY childhood selves. If she could just get them on film, she'd capture a whole culture and indict it along the way. How perfect! And the footage of Wendy and Miss Carol . . . Ali was almost overcome with how easy her vengeance would be.

"Romy Plotnik looked amazing, didn't you think?" Mara was saying too loudly to ignore.

"She uses Dr. Orentreich," Andrea said. "He's a fucking genius with a needle—the father, not the son. But I think she's already had her eyes done, too."

"Like *done* done?" Karen asked.

"Like the same thing I did," Andrea said. "I mean, I was wearing dark glasses, but I'm still pretty sure it was her I saw in Dr. Aston's waiting room."

There was a hush in the cabin as the girls acknowledged the bravery required in having "the real stuff" done before turning forty.

Ali was tempted to film her own sisters, but she didn't dare. It was one thing to indict her bunk mates, another to alienate family. She decided to take notes, though, on their conversation. She realized suddenly that they were her way in—just the guides she'd need if she was going to completely win her bunk mates' confidence over the course of each interview.

"What's wrong with Orentreich's son?" Ali asked.

There was a slight pause as Ali's sisters processed her interest in the conversation. Mara actually raised a brow. Then Andrea said, "There's nothing wrong at all with the son. I just prefer the father, although there's apparently some Indian guy down in TriBeCa who's the best of the lot."

"Do you know his name?" Ali asked, her pen poised.

Renny was waiting with two bouquets: one for her, one for the baby-to-be.

Ali melted the moment she saw him with the bundles of dahlias, her favorite flower. It was good to be home, good to be

away from the chatter and frenetic energy of three hundred as-
sembled Jewesses.

"Did you get some good footage?" Renny asked after they
had kissed and hugged and held each other.

"You have no *idea*," Ali said.

"So it was a good time?"

Ali loved the way Renny looked when he was enthused
about something, as if he'd just found out Ali was going to serve
him a Baskin-Robbins mint ice-cream cone with rainbow sprinkles, his favorite.

"I think I hit the jackpot," Ali said, pulling out her camera. "I
have something you need to see. I think I have a second film
here."

"Do a little J.A.P. chronicling?" Renny asked.

Ali pressed play and told Renny to get ready.

The nausea was overwhelming the next morning. Even so, Ali got
out of bed and went to her computer.

August 26, 2002

Dear Dafna, Beth, Wendy, Laura, Jessica, and Arden,

As some of you know, I was inspired by the camp reunion to make a documentary about you, my former
bunk mates. I'm interested in hearing what you consider
to be the defining moments of your lives, which is to say
those moments when you made choices or had experi-
ences that helped you clarify who you are or hope to be.

It would be my great pleasure to come see you at your choice of location. I have a preference for conducting interviews in your homes but would be happy to accommodate you elsewhere. I think this could be an exciting project and hope you will participate with enthusiasm. Please get back to me at your earliest convenience to schedule interviews.

Best regards,

Ali Cohen

Ali Cohen

She had to stop typing twice to throw up, but eventually she managed to print out six copies and get them all into addressed envelopes, and made it to the mailbox on the corner of Norfolk Street before the 10:00 A.M. pickup.

The Last Sick Day

Even in the dismal light of a gray Valentine's Day dawn, Dafna Shapiro could make out the unkempt line of her eyebrows in the sterling silver hand mirror she held up to her face. They looked like two furry caterpillars resting on the pale slope of her forehead. There was no way she could go to the Valentine's Day benefit for the Israeli Philharmonic at Lincoln Center tonight. Not unless she got them waxed.

Dafna tried to think calmly as she sat up in bed. If she called the office now, no one would be in. She could leave a message on her boss's voice mail. Food poisoning. Not oysters, though. That would be too obvious. Sea urchin maybe. Or eel.

She pushed the duvet aside and hoisted herself up, only to realize by the time her feet hit the carpet that she had already used food poisoning, and only a few weeks ago, the day she left at 2:00 P.M. to get her nails done in preparation for a date she was having that night with Andy Silverman. It was the last time she had seen Andy (Dafna's brows knit together at the fact) and she needed to see him tonight if she was going to remain in contention.

Would she hurt her chances if she showed up with her brows in this condition? Definitely, Dafna decided as she trudged across her bedroom toward the bathroom. How perfect life would be if only she could take another sick day! Alas, another sick day was not an option. She didn't have any more sick days to take. She had already used up all ten and had even used up her vacation week, and she had only been employed at G.L.M. Advertising for seven months. Not that Dafna was particularly prone to sickness; on the contrary, she was quite splendid, physically speaking. But there were those days when matters other than arranging for her boss's business lunches and dinners required her attention, and those matters just happened to take place out of the office. So what if the matter was a shopping spree at Bergdorf's or a thermal plankton/alpha-hydroxy treatment combo with an essential oils rejuvenating massage at Elizabeth Arden. Matters were matters, and this morning she had one.

Dafna despaired as she brushed her teeth, the usual refrain running through her brain like a mantra. *If only, if only, if only—*

If only she hadn't made so many mistakes!

Back in the days when she still worked for her father at Piró, the family-owned-and-run cosmetics company, no one had made her justify her whereabouts if she needed to step out of the office for an hour or two. But those halcyon days were over. Her father had fired her fourteen months earlier, after she wiped out the entire company database and then blamed the incident on her father's secretary, Miriam, who had been with the company for thirty years.

Dafna wasn't a bad or vindictive person. She knew she had done a terrible thing. Blaming Miriam hadn't been her first idea.

It had happened only because the mahogany doors to her father's office had flown open and out he had come in a rage, his whole head crimson, his Hermès tie askew.

"What's happened to the system?" he yelled. "I was in the middle of a huge transaction with Paris!"

Dafna could have kept her mouth shut. She could have looked up at him and shrugged her shoulders. Instead, she'd felt she should at least take some sort of responsibility for her action. After all, it hadn't been a pretty moment for her, either, when she realized that whatever combination of buttons she had been fiddling with while she was busy booking a facial had deleted everything in the system file!

Dafna looked toward Miriam's office across the hallway. Miriam usually knew what to do at times like this. But Miriam's office was empty.

The seconds ticked by, and Dafna's father awaited an explanation.

"Am I going to stand here like an ignoramus," he said, "or is someone going to tell me what's going on?"

"I think Miriam may have pushed a wrong button, Daddy," Dafna whispered, the fiction arriving without thought to consequence. "I saw her shake her head at her computer and run out of here pretty upset, and that's not like her. Maybe we should call the tech guy up so it can get fixed before Miriam gets back."

Dafna had assumed there would be some dork on call who would fix the problem in ten minutes. How could have known that no such dork existed on staff?

And then Miriam returned to her desk and Dafna's father began to rant.

Miriam's eyes opened wide at the injustice of the accusation.

"Are you telling me my daughter lied? She saw you press something on the computer, she saw the look on your face when you realized what you'd done, and then she saw you leave here upset. If it was an accident, which I'm sure it was, it's not a tragedy. But I don't like liars in my employ."

Miriam swore on her mother's grave she was telling the truth.

"Did *you* lie to me?" he asked, turning toward Dafna.

Dafna shook her head, a five-year-old unwilling to be caught with her hand in the cookie jar. And then a computer dork *was* called in from some agency, and after an hour of tinkering, he timed the trouble as having occurred at 12:04. Out came Miriam's lunch receipt from Wendy's—11:59, it read. She hadn't even been in the office when the event had transpired.

Dafna shrugged and shook her head, her eyes wide in indication of her innocence. But then the guilt overwhelmed her and she admitted that perhaps she hadn't been paying close enough attention to the keys she had been pressing, and perhaps the accident had happened as a result of *her own* silly mistake. She had thought it sounded charming, her little confession, but her father wasn't amused: she was fired and cut off until further notice.

"Don't you think Dad's being a bit extreme?" she had said to her mother a week later, when he still hadn't relented and given her the job back.

"He was very disappointed in you," she said, looking at her daughter with as much sadness as she could convey, given her recent round of Botox. She sipped her cappuccino without taking her eyes off Dafna, the attempted expression of sorrow returning to its induced state of surprise. "He feels like you really betrayed him, sweetie. You asked him for the job and he gave it to you, even though you had no background in marketing or business. I mean, you have to admit that since graduating from college, you've never even held a real job. Not that *I* had any problem with it. We were both proud of the benefit work you were doing. But Daddy wasn't thrilled with the way you handled things with Evan, either, so I think the combination . . ."

It was true. She certainly had made a mess of things with Evan Stone, the son of her father's most important buyer. Three months into their engagement, Evan had returned home one night to the apartment they were sharing to find Dafna in bed with Kali (né Josh Blumberg), her private yoga instructor. Evan was supposed to have been on his way to Switzerland for a color-trend conference! How was she supposed to know the flight had been canceled?

Dafna had actually gotten on her hands and knees to beg forgiveness. "Come on," she had said, getting up and kissing Evan's neck, just behind his ear, where he liked it. It was a terrible lapse in judgment; it would never happen again, she swore. Kali had seduced her and brainwashed her while she was in *shavasana,* otherwise known as "corpse pose." She had not been responsible for her actions. She'd been a corpse, for heaven's sake! She swore she was sorry, *extremely* sorry; she felt like a life-form lower than a rat!

She even hauled out the scrapbooks she had made him on each of their two anniversaries. "Look how happy we are," she said, pointing to photos they had taken in Cap Juluca and on safari in Kenya. She reminded him that they were both rich enough to enjoy the good life without anyone feeling uncomfortable. She thanked him again for the beautiful diamond earrings he had given her for her thirtieth birthday, and reminded him of the professional-series Viking grill she had gotten him for his house in the Hamptons, and of the burl humidor that sat on his desk at work. She reminded him how well matched they were: they both skied (so the Stones' house in Aspen was a plus), they both played tennis (they had met, in fact, at Tennisport, which Dafna had joined in hopes of meeting a husband), they both rooted for the Knicks (her father's courtside seats didn't hurt), and they were both Reform Jews who agreed on celebrating High Holidays plus Shabbat once they had kids (she had recently been turned on to a caterer who did the most charming things with brisket and had some kind of nouvelle noodle kugel dish, so the thought of producing a sit-down dinner once a week was no longer intimidating). He was the perfect man for her!

What she didn't mention in her monologue was that most of her peers were already engaged or married. One or two even had children. Even Beth was engaged. It was unthinkable. The girl who had played second fiddle to Dafna since they were eight years old was going to walk down the aisle first?! How could it be? She, Dafna Mina Shapiro, who had never been short of boyfriends, wasn't about to end up an old maid!

No matter how hard she tried to convince Evan of the error of her ways, he remained resolute: their engagement was off. Not long afterward, Evan's father followed suit and called off his engagement with Piró. All in all, it was not Dafna's finest season.

Trying to pick up the pieces quickly, she had prevailed upon mutual friends to set her up with David Hershon, the real estate heir, but he never got in touch; nor did a number of other possible boyfriends. Whether they thought she was damaged goods or past her peak was something about which Dafna tried not to speculate.

And if all this hadn't been bad enough, to intensify matters there had been the hullabaloo over her sister Jennifer's career at Piró. Jennifer had never taken a sick day. Jennifer was the model employee. So when she was promoted to creative executive of Styles and Trends, Piró decided it would be a good idea for her to get her own PR person. Jennifer could become a role model for young women all around the world who used Piró products, the "real" face of Piró: young, successful, and pretty in an accessible way that the supermodel who did most of the Piró ads never would be.

It happened in a flurry. Suddenly, there Jennifer was, on the cover of *Gotham,* featured in *Vogue,* mentioned in blurbs in *Marie Claire, Mademoiselle, Elle,* and *Harper's Bazaar.*

Jennifer Shapiro Goodman, shown here in cream suede pants by Marc Jacobs and a white sweater by Malo, is the very essence of today's modern woman. She balances her busy career and thriving social and philanthropic life with a strong devotion to her husband and one-year-old daughter. And she still finds time to do a combination of yoga, Pilates, gyrotonics, and spinning at least four days a week because, as she put it so eloquently herself, "You can't ask other people to respect you if you don't respect yourself."

Dafna had called her sister to congratulate her on each feature and displayed the magazines prominently on her own coffee table, but really it was too much. Everyone knew *she* was the family beauty!

For a few painful weeks, Dafna languished at home. Then she got her idea: she'd go to work! It would be the perfect move. Not that she had needed something to take up her time. She had been terribly busy with a plethora of boards and charities. And if her philanthropic commitments didn't take up all her free time, then certainly the remainder of it was eliminated by sessions with her personal trainer, personal shopper, nutritionist, therapist, chiropractor, manicurist, hairdresser, reflexologist, acupuncturist, astrologer, and masseuse.

But a job—a *real* job—that was something else entirely. People respected women who worked.

"Please," she had begged her father, "I feel so horrible about what happened with the Stone account. Let me work here and make it up to you."

So much for that! Where had it gotten her? To her bathroom on Valentine's Day morning, plucking stray hairs from her brows!

Frustrated, Dafna dropped the tweezers onto the sink top with a clatter and ended the activity. It was like bushwhacking through the jungle and would most likely result in something as bad as a snakebite: uneven brows.

Panic began to mount. Something had to be done. Something had to be done about her brows. Something had to be done so Andy Silverman would sit up and take notice. Sit up, take notice, lean in, get a hard-on and ask her to marry him.

Andy Silverman was the answer. Andy had been listed in the January issue of *Avenue* magazine as one of New York's most eligible bachelors. Did it matter that his tan looked store-bought and his chin merged in a faintly reptilian way with his neck? Not a bit. There were a dozen women, most of whom would be at the benefit tonight, who would swear on their *mezuzahs* that he was a looker. And why not? Thirty-four years old and already he was taking his father's hedge-fund empire to new heights.

If her father continued to refuse her access to her trust fund, well (Dafna had recently begun to fantasize as her bank statements showed an increasing deficit), she could always *marry wisely,* as her friend Shari liked to put it. Shari's parents hadn't had a cent to give her after college (they lost everything after her father went to jail for insider trading in the late eighties), so Shari caught herself a big-deal developer, got pregnant on the honeymoon, and the rest took care of itself: nanny, housekeeper, cook, floor-through on Park Avenue, beachfront property with pool and tennis court in Southampton. And Shari had made that match without half the social connections available to someone of Dafna's family's stature.

Dafna ran to her dresser and looked at the invitation once more. There was his name, in curly script at the top of the invite: Andy Silverman, chairman of the benefit committee. She *needed* a sick day! What could she say? A urinary-tract infection? Up all night with hives?

Rumors had been swirling about Andy for as long as Dafna had known him. She remembered hearing back in the seventh grade that he'd gotten a blow job from Kim Bamberger in the men's room of Midtown Temple during Kol Nidre services. And there was some sort of scandal that involved either cheating or the purchase of a term paper, she couldn't remember which. He was two years older than she, and they had run in slightly different crowds both at Dalton and the U of P (he liked Eurotrash, while Dafna preferred the pseudo-Jewish jocks in Sigma Nu), but they had always said hello when they bumped into each other at benefits and in front of the Golden Pear in East Hampton. Andy's reputation as a womanizer was so well honed by the time Dafna was in her twenties, she always scoffed when people mentioned his name as a possible date. But when he had called and asked her out a few weeks ago, she'd been pleased.

For their first date, he had chosen an acceptably chic restaurant and been surprisingly good company. He knew how to order a bottle of wine, and his repartee had been witty and flattering. She had even found him attractive, which she had sworn to all her friends she never could. But there really was something magnetic about him. Whether it was all the rumors that added to his sheen or the fact that he had thought nothing of ordering a seventy-five-dollar glass of Sauternes, she couldn't tell, but when he kissed her good night on the mouth, she had kissed him back. The next morning, he had sent her a bouquet of flowers, and by five o'clock that afternoon they were set for a date the following week at the opera.

That date had led to drinks at Café Luxembourg and a night spent at his place, but now ten days had elapsed since she'd heard from him, and she was beginning to feel anxious. Of course, she was sure Andy's inattention was due to his involvement chairing the benefit. Still, he hadn't even called to see if she would be attending; to ask her to be his date; to make sure she was sitting at a good table, preferably his!

Forlorn, Dafna began the routine that, as the daughter of a beauty magnate, had served to reinforce her celebrated face since early adolescence: wash, tone, wait, wipe, and moisturize (even if her father *had* fired her, she still felt Piró products were the best). Then she turned on her special examining light and inspected herself in the supermagnifying mirror she had recently had installed so as not to miss any extra-fine wrinkles as they began to creep in around her lips and eyes.

Dafna gazed at herself. Aside from her eyebrows, she really was quite—

And then she saw it. A shiver of horror rippled through her and her neck muscles tensed. There was hair—there was!—on her chin and upper lip, and, now that she was looking closely, her eyelashes were in desperate need of a tint.

Appendicitis? Swollen lymph glands? A sprained ankle? Gout?

Dafna checked the time. It was getting late. A decision had to be made.

She tried to create a plan as she dressed. She could go to La Belle Complète during lunch. Surely Rosa would make time to do the waxing. But what about the lash crisis? There was no way she'd be able to get uptown to Lucia on Eighty-sixth and Park and back to G.L.M. in midtown by 1:30. Not with all the slush. Even if she dared to take a subway!

Menstrual cramps. She hadn't used that one in a while and there was nothing her boss could say about it, either. Richard was a jerk, but he wasn't that big of a jerk, unless he hadn't gotten enough sleep.

A miraculous thought suddenly occurred to her: she didn't have to go to the benefit at all. An evening at home of mindless TV and some herbal tea might be nice. Then she'd have a reason to call Andy. She'd apologize for not making it to his benefit and then ask him when he wanted to get together again. The idea made her smile, and for a moment, she felt calm and resolute. Then the phone rang. It was Jennifer, calling to make a meeting plan for that evening, since she, too, was going to the benefit.

"I haven't decided whether or not to go," Dafna confessed. She related the details of her predicament.

Jennifer told her not to be ridiculous. "Besides," she added, "I wouldn't let this opportunity pass."

"Opportunity for what?"

"To support a worthy cause," Jennifer said after a quick pause.

"You can tell the truth," Dafna said. "I'm almost thirty-two. I can take it. You wouldn't let this opportunity pass to meet a *husband*. To meet a nice rich Ivy League Jewish boy who will love me, and cherish me, and buy me an apartment on Fifth and a summer house in the Hamptons!"

"Why don't you just convert to Catholicism?" Jennifer said. "Then you can sit up at the Cloisters all day and meditate on the theme of responsibility."

"Look, Jen," Dafna said, careful to remove the whining tone from her voice, "you *know* how hard I'm trying. FYI, I hate my job *and* I'm working my tail off. And I don't think it would kill you to mention that to Dad."

"Show up tonight or don't," Jennifer said. "I'll be with Valerie Steinman. Dean's out of town tonight on business. We're meeting at the fountain at six-fifteen."

"Why so early?" Dafna asked, thinking she might be able to squeeze in the procedures after work but before the benefit.

"It's not so early. Cocktails start at five-forty-five."

"Who can make it *anywhere* by five-forty-five?"

"Apparently, quite a few people."

"Like I'm really looking forward to seeing everyone we ever went to Willow Lake with. If I wait awhile, I'll see them at the reunion."

"If you're that stressed about it, don't go," Jennifer snapped. "I'm only going because it's good for business. Let's get things into perspective. We're not talking heart surgery here."

"You wouldn't know of any places in midtown that dye lashes?" Dafna asked.

"*Please,*" Jennifer said. Then in a lowered voice, she added, "Try Sigrid of Sweden. Ask for Viveka. Tell her you're my sister."

"You're the best!" Dafna said, slamming down the phone.

There was no time to waste. She ran to her closet and pulled a new black cocktail dress off the hanger. Next she contemplated stockings: old-fashioned black ones with a seam up the back, or fishnets? For a moment she wavered, but intuition led her to a fresh package of Calvin Klein French-cut black sheers with a control top, and she always tried to go with intuition. Next came shoes: black spike sling-backs, or the lower black silk mules? She grabbed both pairs, plus a third (just in case), and was in the process of throwing everything into a suitcase when the phone rang again. This time, it was her mother, calling from Boca.

"I can't talk now," Dafna said.

"Yes you can," her mother insisted. "Wait until you hear this! Guess who I ran into at the Boca Beach Club yesterday?"

"I'm in a rush, Ma!"

"Barbara Silverman, Andy's mother. Can you believe what a small world it is? Their cabana is literally next to ours!" Ronnie paused to give her daughter a moment to appreciate the wonders of the universe and then forged on with her story. "I never really knew her before, but she's adorable. So peppy. She was running off to yoga and then to golf, which you should certainly learn. I see all sorts of young people out there. It would be an excellent way to meet someone, and Babs *did* mention that she keeps Andy's clubs in their condo so he can play whenever he feels like hopping down."

"Is there a point to this?" Dafna reminded her mother that she had to get to work.

"Patience," her mother urged. "She didn't just mention Andy's golf clubs. She also happened to include the interesting fact that Andy is chairman of the event at Lincoln Center tonight."

"So?" Dafna said.

"So I assume you're going."

"I might."

"Don't be a fool! Obviously, Andy has talked about you to his mother! And his father is a real *macher*. Nice, too. On the Beth Israel board with me. A big-deal giver to the UJA—"

"I'm not dating his father," Dafna said, thrilled to know her name had been bandied about the Silverman household.

She wished her mother love, asked her to put in a good word to her father, and hung up. It was already after 9:00 A.M. If she wasn't in by 9:30, Richard would have a fit.

She was halfway to her suitcase when something caught her attention outside: the clouds, dark and heavy, spiraling downward upon the city, obscuring the skyline almost entirely from view.

Life could be so oppressive sometimes!

Dafna retreated to her room and reached for the orange container of pills on her night table. One pill at night to help subdue anxiety wasn't doing much. How could another one hurt? One tiny blue dot—down the hatch!—and she bundled up in her Calvin Klein camel hair coat, picked up her suitcase, put the pills in her pocket, and left.

＊

It was 9:45 when Dafna—having been safely transported to midtown in a taxi whose driver had been disappointed to find out that his fare wasn't an airport run, "what with the luggage and all"—pressed the intercom on her desk to let her boss know she had arrived.

"Get in here!" Richard roared.

Three of the secretaries at surrounding stations looked up. It always irked Dafna that these women considered her to be of the same rank. Dafna was an Account Operations assistant, according to the contract she had signed at the beginning of August, after looking unsuccessfully for a more glamorous job. Her cubicle, however, was out in the hall with the other secretaries and, despite the title, there was really no difference between their respective functions. Only Dafna's wardrobe suggested a slight superiority; she still received roses from Richard on Secretaries Day.

"When I say *now*, I mean now!" Richard yelled through the intercom.

Dafna raised her coffee cup in a mock toast to the other secretaries, took a quick sip, smoothed her lustrous shoulder-length brown hair, and went in to face the company pit bull.

Richard Thompson was the kind of guy who would have made a great prizefighter had he not had such good grades in school. He was naturally pugnacious and always chose a spat over a peaceful disagreement. He was tall and imposing-looking, with an angular face pockmarked from an acne-riddled adolescence. He had hands that looked like they could crush a champagne bottle with a simple squeeze around the middle and feet the size of bread loaves. His suits always looked slightly abused, as if he writhed in them, rather than simply took the subway to work, sat behind his desk for most of the day, walked to the gym, and caught a cab to the dinner Dafna had most likely booked for him.

Rumor had it he did coke. Rumor had it he had spent time in rehab. Rumor had it he had once been married to a model who left him for his best friend a year into their marriage. As tough as that was, it still didn't excuse his behavior, in Dafna's opinion. She felt his rudeness to her was a result of his attraction to her, which would explain why he could barely look her in the eye.

"The Triple Stuff Cookie Crunch account is ready to go." He was pacing the room and tearing at one of his cuticles with his teeth. "The marketing exec over there is waiting for the final contract. He's a guy named Phil Fisher. I'm not done yet with all of the changes, but I'll want you to type up the edits when I finish, print it out, and run it over to the Nabisco Building yourself. I told Phil you'd be there by noon."

Dafna raised one of the self-offending brows and queried, "Why not use a messenger service?"

"I want the personal touch, if you know what I mean." Richard winked. "Not that I expect anything untoward, but Phil's an important client. And if you ever want to advance in this business you're going to have to start meeting some of the clients face-to-face, right?"

"Sure," Dafna said, hopeful for the first time in months that a promotion might be on the horizon. She stood and excused herself. She was almost out the door when Richard added, "Not that it matters, but I happen to also know that Phil was recently divorced, so if he asks you to lunch . . ."

"Richard!" Dafna exclaimed, pretending to be shocked.

"Seriously," Richard continued, "if he asks you to lunch, go." He smiled beneficently, which made him look handsome, and Dafna wondered why he had never asked her out himself. "Read the contract while you're typing up the changes so you can talk to him about something. Just make sure you get your lovely self back here by two. Flannery's coming down this afternoon for a briefing, and if I don't have that contract signed and in his hands, I'm gonna need surgery to remove his shoe from my ass."

"No problem," Dafna replied, nodding and puffing out her lower lip slightly, trying her best to look capable and sultry at the same time. "I'll be back with it by two. You can count on me."

Richard winked at her, and Dafna gave him a sexy exit. She didn't need to look back to see if he had appreciated it. She knew the power she had over men and enjoyed it. The second Dafna returned to her desk, however, the momentary high she felt knowing she had been appreciated collapsed as the reality of her predicament returned. What if this Fisher person asked her to lunch? She'd have to go. *Have* to. No lunch break, no waxing. How could she go to the benefit without waxing? No lunch break, no waxing, no benefit, NO HUSBAND. She would die— impoverished—*alone*.

Overwhelmed, Dafna ran to the bathroom, locked herself in a stall, removed a small Mason-Pearson hairbrush from her purse, and rubbed the flat back of the brush against her crotch. Anxiety always made her horny, or maybe it was a side effect from the little blue pills. Either way, she needed some relief from the conflict that was distorting her day. Just as she was nearing orgasm, a toilet flushed in the next stall. Dafna stopped immediately, readjusted her blue wool skirt and jacket trimmed in blue velvet, composed herself, flushed the toilet, and left the stall.

Gwynne, the receptionist, who was only a few years younger than Dafna, was drying her hands at the blower next to the full-length mirror.

"How's it going?" Dafna asked, her heart still waging war inside her chest.

Gwynne rolled her enormous blue eyes. "You'd think the switchboard would explode, so many people have called this morning." Gwynne talked with a deep Long Island accent, which Dafna abhorred. Still, she needed one friend at the office, and Gwynne was it, mostly because, in addition to being chatty and sweet, she had an enviable figure and a cute sense of style. Today she was wearing a red angora sweater tucked into a white wool skirt, an outfit, Dafna noted, that would have made anyone except Gwynne look like a moose. She resembled one of those models on a bottle of suntan oil: tiny, shapely, perfectly proportioned, and perpetually tan. Dafna wasn't jealous. Her own taste and figure were superior. Still, she felt a small pang of envy: Gwynne's brows were sublime arcs of tweezed perfection.

"Cawffee at eleven?" Gwynne asked.

"Why should this Wednesday be different from all other Wednesdays?" Dafna replied, smiling at her only friend at G.L.M.

✳

It was 10:35 when Dafna returned to her desk. Almost another whole hour to get through before her break with Gwynne! Dafna separated the small paper clips from the large ones and put them into separate containers inside the top desk drawer. Then she tested all the pens she kept in a mug to see if any needed to be thrown out. Only after she completed these tasks did she dare to call La Belle Complète to find out if Rosa had an opening around noon.

While Dafna was put on hold by the receptionist, Richard came out of his office and dropped a thick packet of papers onto her desk. "Get to it," he said. "And I reconfirmed with Fisher. He's expecting you at noon."

"I'm your girl," Dafna said brightly.

Thank God Richard had returned to his office by the time the receptionist came back on the line. Tragic news: Rosa was booked solid until 7:00 P.M. What now? Dafna flipped through the packet. It was no small document, there were a million changes, and her typing skills were far from lightning-fast. Nevertheless, she did not begin the job immediately. First she picked up her purse and retrieved the vial of pills she had put there when she arrived at the office. Another small blue pill down the hatch—and she put in a call to Sigrid of Sweden.

It couldn't have been easier. Viveka would squeeze Dafna in whenever she stopped by. Silently blessing her sister, Dafna picked up Richard's packet and set cheerfully about the revisions. Just wait until Andy Silverman saw her tonight. He'd be *begging* her for another date!

"So what was with the suitcase this mawning?" Gwynne asked, emptying packets of sugar into her mug. "Going somewair?"

"Benefit."

"Is it in New Yawk?"

Dafna nodded.

Gwynne finished stirring her coffee and went to sit on the black leather sofa in the corner of the small conference room. Dafna poured her own cup and turned toward the sofa, but as she crossed the room, the heel of her pump caught a snag in the tattered nylon carpet, which sent her careening forward. She managed to regain her balance without spilling too much of her coffee; her purse, however, and most of its contents went flying.

"Don't tell me you take Prozac?" Gwynne exclaimed as Dafna scrambled to pick up the vial of pills that had rolled out into the middle of the room.

"Traxim," Dafna said, snatching them up.

Gwynne's face lit up. "I tried Traxim! I *loved* Traxim." She almost spilled her coffee in the zeal of her recollection. "Traxim was great. Traxim was my first." Gwynne sighed. "But it made me see double." She sipped her coffee and tossed back her crispy overprocessed hair. "Traxim! God, that was a lifetime ago! I've tried everything since then—Klonopin, Mersak, Xanax. You name it. One of my friends from high school works at a pharmacy. He swipes me samples of everything. But they're awful. All of them. Except Paxil. Paxil's great. You can even booze on it."

"Lucky you," Dafna said, wiping her hands and composing herself on the sofa. "You're not supposed to drink at all on Traxim. Of course I do anyway, but—did any of them ever really help you?"

"Sort of," Gwynne said. She thought for a moment, then added, "You gotta be careful with pills, you know? This one time"—Gwynne made a face of horror—"well, let's just say you should follow the directions on the label."

"Sure," Dafna said, averting her gaze. After a moment, though, she looked back up into her friend's face. "Gwynne," she whispered, reaching for her friend's arm. "Look at me. *Tell me.* What do you see when you look at me?"

"Duh! I see *you.*" Gwynne giggled.

"I'm serious," Dafna said. "Look at my face. What do you see?"

Gwynne sat up straighter and studied Dafna's face. She shrugged. "I see a beautiful girl."

"Look *harder.* Look as if we were at a party together and you thought I was trying to steal your boyfriend."

"But I don't—"

"Gwynne!" Dafna cried. "This is an emergency!"

"What's going on here?" Gwynne looked miserable. "Is this some kind of game? I'm sorry, but I'm not sure what it is you want me to see."

"My hair," Dafna prompted.

"Your *hair?*"

Dafna nodded.

"What about it? It's gorgeous. I don't know a single person who wouldn't kill—"

"Not my *hair* hair," Dafna whispered, her vision blurring as tears filled her eyes. "My *eyebrows.*" She caught her breath. "My *upper lip.*" She stifled a sob. "My *chin.*"

"What about them?" Gwynne asked cautiously.

"Tell me the truth!" Dafna begged. "Do you think I need to wax?"

For several long seconds, Gwynne studied Dafna's face. Only the *drip-drip* of the coffee falling into the pot could be heard in the room. Outside, the Xerox machine hummed and the occasional high-pitched secretaries' "G.L.M. Can I help you?" rang through the air. "Maybe," Gwynne finally stammered, "maybe just a little, in, you know, in the arches."

Dafna's grip relaxed on her friend's arm.

"But listen," Gwynne went on, "I read an excellent article in last month's *Elle* that said if you have any style at all, you don't need to have a hairless face. I mean, it didn't actually specify *facial* hair. It was talking more about any feature you consider flawed, like a fat ass or no tits or what have you. The bottom line is this: no one will notice your brows if you carry yourself with confidence."

"Thanks," Dafna said. "You're absolutely right." She smiled at Gwynne and the two enjoyed the rest of their coffee break, but in her heart, Dafna knew what she had to do.

Shortly after noon, Dafna was riding the elevator up to the forty-ninth floor of the Nabisco Building with the revised contract safe in a bright yellow G.L.M. envelope snuggled tightly under her arm.

Come in, Phil mouthed, waving her in with the hand that wasn't holding the telephone to his ear.

Phil was a handsomish man somewhere in his early forties, with salt-and-pepper hair and a classy shirt-tie combination. It might be fun to have lunch with him after all, Dafna decided. Maybe she *was* being ridiculous about this whole waxing thing.

Phil mouthed for her to take off her coat and sit, rolling his eyes and making a talking gesture with his hand. Dafna smiled and shrugged to let him know it was okay, then slid off her coat and hung it on the rack next to the door. Seating herself, she crossed and uncrossed her long, shapely legs several times while pretending to take in what she imagined must be a fabulous view on a day without snow. Finally, after the amount of time it would have taken to have both brows and a lip waxed, Phil slammed down the phone.

"*Christ,*" he said. "You'd think that *schmuck* never learned the word *good-bye.* So. Sorry. You're the girl from G.L.M.?"

"That's me," Dafna said, holding up the contract.

"Fine fine fine." Phil reached for the envelope, ripped it open, flipped through it, reached for a pen, and signed. "Like working for Richard?" He thrust the contract back.

"Um-hmmm," Dafna purred, as if he had asked her if she liked having her toes sucked. She took the contract from him and smiled coyly.

"Good. Great. Dick's a great guy. I used to play racquetball with him over at Reebok." He paused and looked at her for half a second. Then he ran a hand through his hair and began to rummage around his desk as he said, "Sorry to be so abrupt, but I have to run to a lunch meeting." He looked up at her for another split second. "You give Dick my regards, will ya?"

"My pleasure," Dafna said, smiling.

In the elevator down, Dafna could feel the eyes of the other businessmen on her appreciatively, but not Phil's. He probably wouldn't even be able to tell his lunch partner the color of her suit!

As she made her way through the lobby and out into the street, a horrid thought occurred to her: had Phil Fisher noticed her brows? Had he noticed her chin hair? Had he spotted the hair over her lip? Dafna checked her watch. It was only 12:30. If

Richard thought she was having lunch with Phil, she could stay away at least until two o'clock.

There was plenty of time!

✳

Dafna sauntered up to the check-in desk of Sigrid of Sweden and waited while the receptionist finished up with a middle-aged, big-haired bleached blonde with a southern accent.

"—and I need a full hour for the blow and set, in *addition* to my standing noon appointment," the lady said, pointing a bejeweled and manicured finger at the receptionist's book. "I like the lunchtime slot. Always."

"No problem," the receptionist replied dutifully, but as soon as the woman was out of earshot, the receptionist looked up at Dafna, an expression of disgust on her face. "Some people," she said.

"Really," Dafna agreed.

"You'd think her whole entire life depended on a blow-dry."

The receptionist looked at Dafna for confirmation of the absurdity of it, and Dafna rolled her eyes, but inside she felt sympathy for the blonde, fully aware of how stressful it could be when you just wanted a little service. It really was just a question of tone. If the woman had asked nicely—

"So, who are we here to see?"

Dafna gave the information, smiling sweetly throughout.

"You're not in the book today. Viveka must be squeezing you in. Why don't you sit down and I'll let her know you're here."

Dafna sat on one of the white-and-cream-striped chenille banquettes, closed her eyes, and inhaled the happy, familiar fumes of nail polish, shampoo, and peroxide.

"Dafna?" she heard someone say in a sharp-pitched foreign voice.

A tiny middle-aged woman with bright red glasses, powdery white skin, and canary yellow hair came scuffling toward her. Dafna rose, an expectant smile on her face. She followed Viveka down a long, dimly lit hallway and into a small, even more dimly lit room.

"So," Viveka said, "ve begin vith de vax. Let me look."

As Dafna lay down on the table, a sheet of paper crinkled unsettlingly beneath the weight of her body. Once she was settled, Viveka pulled over a magnifying glass, covered Dafna's eyes with a cold cloth, turned on a bright light, and grabbed Dafna's chin. She turned Dafna's face to the left and to the right and tilted it all the way back. Then she announced her verdict: "Uh-oh."

"What is it?" Dafna ventured.

"You haf some very stronk hairs. And a few ingrown under the chin. You are using exfoliant?"

"Every week."

"But that is too much. No vonder."

"No wonder what?"

But Viveka didn't answer. She was already busy with the wax. When the burning emollient made contact with Dafna's skin, she couldn't help shrieking slightly.

"What kind of wax do you use?" Dafna gasped.

"Bee's," Viveka said, spreading more of the burning emollient across Dafna's entire chin and underneath it as far as her throat. "Something is the matter?"

"It's a little hot," Dafna managed.

"It's supposed to be hot," Viveka chirped back. "It's vax."

Viveka pressed a thin strip of cloth across a section of Dafna's jaw, then tore it away with a violent yank.

"Thank you," Dafna said, though the pain was piercing. "Get it all. Just get it all."

The procedure took an excruciating ten minutes. Each time Viveka tore the wax strips from Dafna's face, it felt like a layer of skin had gone with it.

"All done," Viveka announced after some final tweezing. "Now ve do de lashes. Look up."

And then, while Dafna's eyes were still open, Viveka began to apply dye to Dafna's lower lashes. Lucia never did it this way! Dafna jerked her head away.

"Hold still," Viveka ordered, "or I get dye on de skin."

Dafna forced herself to be still, but her heart was racing. The dye felt wet and runny, not dry and clumpy like the dye Lucia applied.

"And close," Viveka said.

Dafna had a vision of herself crossing the street with a Seeing Eye dog.

"I think this is a mistake," she murmured, trying to get up from the table. "Thank you so much for—" But she couldn't continue. The skin under her eyes felt as if it were on fire.

"Help!" Dafna cried. "Wipe it off! Please!"

It wasn't just the skin under her eyes that stung; now it was also her chin, lip, and brows. Her entire face was alive with stinging. "Ohhhhh," she moaned. "Wipe it off. Just wipe it off!"

Viveka applied some damp cotton compresses, which helped.

"I need to get back to work," Dafna said, removing the compresses after a few moments and getting up. She hurried toward the door, though her face still tingled and throbbed. "I apologize for taking up your time. I'll pay for everything."

"I am the one who is sorry. I've been doing—"

But Dafna didn't stay to hear the rest. In a flash, she was halfway down the hall, on her way to the bathroom. In the sanctuary of this haven, she splashed handful after handful of cold water against her pulsing face. Little white blisters, like whiteheads, were sprouting up all over her chin. She could even make out the distinct mark of strips in a few places.

There was only one person who could fix her now, and Dafna wasn't going to wait to find out if she could be squeezed in or not. This was an emergency! She paid, leaving a generous tip, since Viveka had, after all, squeezed her in as a favor to Jennifer, whose face was clearly made of tougher stuff than Dafna's.

La Belle Complète was only a few blocks away, and Dafna was there faster than you could say "Is anyone free for a lash tint?" The receptionist there said she didn't see Dafna's name in the book.

But I'm Dafna Shapiro, she yearned to say, *daughter of Howard Shapiro, CEO of Piró, in case the name alone doesn't ring a bell*. But she didn't. She took a deep breath and said evenly, "I'm not in the book, but whomever I spoke with this morning told me to just show up. She said Rosa would squeeze me in."

"The *whomever* you spoke with was *me*," the receptionist said irritably. "I told you Rosa *might* be able to take you at the end of the day."

"Oh," Dafna said. "Really? Are you sure that's what you said? I could have sworn—"

And then, a miracle: enter Rosa, whose mouth broke into its wide toothy grin as soon as she saw Dafna, but just as quickly the smile faded when she spotted the situation on Dafna's face.

"Who did this to you?" Rosa demanded. "Who? Tell me. I must know."

"Can you help me?" Dafna begged.

Rosa, whose soft, warm, lavender-smelling hands had so often administered a soothing touch, enveloped Dafna in her bosomy embrace. "I could try a soothing mask and some calendula. At the very least, I could reduce the swelling. Are you my next?"

"She's not your next," the receptionist interjected. "Your next is coming down from Pedicures right now." She shot Dafna a scornful glance, then checked the appointment book. "Beth Rosenblatt."

"Beth Rosenblatt?" Dafna said, relief sending her voice into the stratosphere. "But I *know* Beth Rosenblatt. She's my best friend! I'm sure she wouldn't mind if I switched appointments with her."

"You don't *have* an appointment to switch," the receptionist said. "If Beth wants to *give* you her appointment—"

The elevator door opened and Beth got off wrapped in a pink terry-cloth robe. She was sporting open-toed paper slippers and scarlet toenail polish, the strip of cotton separating her toes still firmly in place. "Hiiiiii!" she said in her sometimes too-perky voice (now being one of the times it struck Dafna as way too perky). "How funny! What are you doing here? I thought you were stuck at work."

Beth didn't work. She had worked until her engagement a few months ago to one of Dafna's rejects. Now her job was planning her wedding, the details of which she never seemed to tire of disclosing and dissecting with Dafna, much to Dafna's chagrin.

"I'm on my lunch break," Dafna explained, trying not to pounce too quickly.

"I assume you'll be at Lincoln Center tonight," Beth said.

"I was planning on it," Dafna concurred, taking a step closer and lowering her voice, "but I just got the worst waxing job of my life. Look."

She jutted her face forward and Beth said, "Holy shit."

"I can't possibly be seen now unless Rosa gives me a quick calendula treatment. The only thing is"—Dafna's shoulders tensed as she checked the time—"I have to get back to work in less than an hour."

"Bummer," Beth said, her expression wilting. "I thought we might be able to grab a Caesar salad together. My mother's making me nuts over the choice of a florist. She wants me to use Thom LeBaux. Can you imagine? He's so pretentious, and the flowers he did for Amy Miller's wedding were a joke. He had purple roses in these black rectangular vases that looked like roach motels. *Vile.*"

"Sounds it," replied Dafna hastily, knowing the seconds were ticking on the clock. "I'd love to hear more, but I was actually wondering, could you possibly give me your appointment with Rosa right now and then we could talk about the florists at the benefit?"

A look of anguish crossed Beth's face. "I'm so sorry," she said. "I'm on a tight schedule today myself. I have to get to Cristoff Cuvier by three for my hair and—"

"No, of course," Dafna said. "No need to explain. It was rude of me even to ask. I just thought it was worth a try."

"But I'm totally devastated you had a bad reaction to the

wax," Beth offered. "Remember the time I broke out in that rash from the collagen injection in my lip? Uch. It was awful. I didn't go to work for a week. I'll never forget how hard you laughed when you saw me. I found a great guy for lips, by the way. Carpolon. Dr. Phil Carpolon. On Eighty-sixth and Park. How convenient is that? He's amazing with a needle. I never feel a thing."

"Great," Dafna managed to say. It was disgusting how self-absorbed Beth had become since her engagement. "I better get going."

"And I better get to Rosa." Beth tilted her head to the side with an apologetic sigh. "Ciao for now?"

"Ciao for now," Dafna said with a little wave.

Back on the street, Dafna felt dizzy and exhausted. Snow flew around her in blinding swirls and her feet, clad in snow-soaked suede pumps, were as frozen as the ice beneath her, which threatened to take her down with each slippery step. She made her way over to a wall and collapsed against it. After a moment, she peeked out of her coat and tried to get her bearings. She was leaning against the wall of a synagogue—*her* synagogue—which was located so conveniently close to most of New York's major midtown retail and beauty emporiums. (What other lucky congregants could slip off to Bergdorf's after the morning service on Yom Kippur and return in the afternoon with a whole new look?)

A few quick steps up a short flight of stairs, a small detour around a homeless person wrapped in a blanket, and all at once everything was quiet—quiet and calm and warm. Never had Dafna been more relieved to be inside the magnificent sanctuary.

Near the pulpit, a maintenance worker was vacuuming. Otherwise, the house was empty.

For High Holiday services, which was the only time she attended, Dafna sat with her family in their assigned seats in the fifth row, a prime location—given only to the highest donors of the temple. Although she normally enoyed being the center of attention, today she tiptoed down a side aisle and sat down in one of the pews far in the back. These pews faced the pulpit on a diagonal. It felt nice to be on the side, in the back. For the first time in her life, she felt alone in the presence of God.

Dafna didn't usually think much about God when she was in temple. She was always too busy hiding her ring finger (she knew everyone was looking!) or trying to turn around strategically to check out the status of her fellow congregants. Marcy Landau, who had been in the same Hebrew School class with Dafna all the way through their tenth-grade confirmation, always sat in the balcony just above Dafna's family's seats. Over the years, they had refined their gestures to a subtle science and, with a few finger twirls and neck rolls, were able to indicate to each other who was looking fat as opposed to pregnant, who had gotten engaged or separated, and who looked like he might have gotten hair plugs.

Today there were no distractions. Dafna had never been good at praying, unsure if you were supposed to do something formal, like put your hands together, or clear your throat and say, "Are you there, God? It's me, Dafna." She opted today for something simpler: she closed her eyes. After a few quiet minutes, she came to a decision. She would not go to the benefit tonight. Instead, she would stay home and read. And not a magazine, either; a book, one of the ones from freshman English that she'd never gotten around to. That would be better than going to some stupid party just to get the attention of an overtanned, pompous renegade she hoped to use as a bankroll.

Dafna returned to the street inspired with newfound determination. As she marched back to work, she decided she was being exactly the kind of girl her father had wanted her to be: a girl with good values. Dafna was delighting in this thought while she waited for a streetlight to change, when her cell phone rang.

"Where are you?" It was Gwynne. "Richard wants the contract."

"I'm on my way," Dafna said, ending the call as she sailed across the street. But just as her feet hit the pavement, she had one of those sixth-sense premonitions that something was missing. She took a quick inventory and realized, to her horror, that she was no longer in possession of the contract.

She didn't even wait for the lights to change. Zigzagging through the traffic, she retraced her steps to the temple. No envelope there. It was 1:50. Her heart beat wildly. She plunged into the crowded, slushy street and proceeded to Sigrid of Sweden. First she checked the ladies' room, then the banquette and the coffee table piled high with magazines. Nothing. She ran down the hall and knocked on Viveka's closed door. After an interminable moment, Viveka poked her yellow head out.

"Did I leave something in your room?" Dafna asked breathlessly.

"Nothink," Viveka said, and the door closed in Dafna's face.

One more blue pill and it was back out to the street.

The receptionist at La Belle Complète was shaking her head even before Dafna spoke.

"Listen," Dafna said with the intensity of someone dangling over a cliff, hanging on to safety by a single thinning thread, "I just need to know if I left a yellow envelope here with the initials G.L.M. on it."

"No one turned anything in," the receptionist said with a smirk, "but feel free to look around."

With half a glance, Dafna took in the entire waiting area: stylists rushed by the long corridor, wielding color-carts and curlers; maids in pink uniforms covered with white lace aprons carried trays of Oriental chicken salad and cappuccino to women waiting in plush chintz chairs for their toes to dry. The envelope wasn't there. *It wasn't there.*

A message from Dafna's brain told her body to leave, although for what, she didn't know. She couldn't return to work. Not now. Probably not ever.

She was almost at the elevators when she heard someone call her name, and there was Rosa, careening across the plush carpet. "I gave the package to Beth," she said breathlessly. "She said she'd be seeing you tonight."

"God bless you!" Dafna gushed, throwing herself into Rosa's arms for a brief embrace before pulling out her cell phone.

Gwynne answered on the first ring. "Dafna! Where are you? Get your delinquent ass back here. Richard's raving."

"Tell Richard that Phil kept me late at lunch."

"Richard already called Phil's office. He knows you left over an hour ago. He *knows*. Just get back here, Dafna. *Pronto.*"

"I'll be there in ten minutes. Hold him off for ten minutes. Can you do that for me? *Please?*"

It was 2:15 when Dafna arrived, pale and panting, at the check-in desk of the famed Cristoff Cuvier hair salon. It was not until

2:20, however, that one of the harried but perfectly coiffed army of receptionists dressed from head to toe in black paid her any attention.

"I'm looking for Beth Rosenblatt," Dafna said for what was, by now, at least the sixth time.

The receptionist scanned the book and announced, "She's with Yuki."

"Where would I find—" But the receptionist had already disappeared. Daunted but determined, Dafna puffed up her chest, threw back her shoulders, raised her slightly swollen but hairless chin, and walked straight back into the stylists' section. She found Beth in color, chatting away with a tall, emaciated-looking Asian man in a black jumpsuit covered with a white apron. He was wrapping Beth's wet purple-painted hair, section by section, in tinfoil.

"Daaaf!" Beth called out, waving. "Do you have an appointment here, too, or did you bite the bullet and call in sick?"

Dafna winced. She did indeed feel frighteningly sick. The room was spinning like it did when she came in from a particularly debauched night and her mouth was dry as a corn nut.

"Don't worry," Beth said. "I won't tell anyone. Oh! I have your envelope!"

"Head still," Yuki ordered.

Beth held still and ran her fingers across her lips to show that she was zipping her mouth shut.

"Can I have it?" Dafna said.

"Of course," Beth whispered. "Sorry, Yuki, it'll just take a sec." She reached into her enormous brown leather Louis Vuitton purse and pulled out the envelope. "I was a very good girl. I didn't even peek."

Dafna snatched the envelope and pressed it to her chest, closing her eyes in profound relief. The ordeal was over. Now she could get back to the office. She checked the time. It was 2:30. She was only half an hour late. Dafna thanked Beth and excused herself, eager to touch base with Gwynne.

In a quiet nook near the ladies' room, Dafna pulled out her cell phone and dialed. Gwynne answered immediately.

"You are in big trouble," Gwynne announced, her voice snippy and low. "I'm sorry to have to tell you this, but Richard just fired you."

"I can fix everything," Dafna said. "I have the contract."

"Flannery *left,* Dafna. He's gone. *Adiós. Ciao.* It's too late. Richard went—well, *insane* is putting it mildly."

"I have the contract," Dafna repeated. "I can be there in fifteen minutes. Ten if I run."

"It's too late," Gwynne said. "If I were you, I wouldn't come back. Not today anyway. Wait until tomorrow. Let Richard simmer down."

"But I can—"

"I gotta scram. Take my advice. Stay away. I'll take your suitcase home with me and you can get it some other time. Here comes Richard. Gotta go." And that was that.

Dafna stood statue-still for some time. Nothing seemed real. She pinched her own arm and felt nothing. She slapped herself across the face. There. She felt that. A woman wearing a white towel turban-style around her head asked Dafna if she was okay. Dafna nodded, put away her phone, walked over to the waiting area, and sat down.

So. She couldn't go back to the office. She had gotten her sick day after all. Tears sprang to Dafna's eyes and her throat constricted. In a vision, she saw her future of ski vacations at Vail and her summers in East Hampton glide away like a train pulling out of a station. *Good-bye*, she waved. *Good-bye* forty-five-dollar Fogal stockings! *Good-bye* benefits! *Good-bye* doorman apartment on the Upper East Side! *Good-bye* children in swank Carnegie Hill private schools! *Good-bye* ballet and piano lessons! *Good-bye* Willow Lake! *Good-bye! Good-bye!*

And yet, even as she sat there envisioning all these things pulling out of the wreckage of what had once been the sumptuous, impregnable station of her upbringing, a part of her mind was fast at work, trying to figure out how to reassemble the rubble.

The answer seemed simple enough: back to plan A. And a short time later, she was lying in a reclining chair, her head in a sink, while a Caribbean woman massaged Château Lafite finishing rinse through Dafna's brown locks.

When the stylist was through, Dafna paid with her MasterCard, using the last of her cash to tip everyone generously. Beth was paying at the same time.

"Is your dress tonight long or short?" Beth asked.

"Uh, short," Dafna said, realizing that she'd have to buy a whole new ensemble since she had left her suitcase at the office.

"I was going to go long to practice for the wedding," Beth said, "but I don't want to overdress. Do you think some people will be going long?"

"Without a doubt," Dafna replied, already preparing what she'd do.

"So, what do you think?" Beth asked, flipping her hair. She'd had it straightened and lightened, but she still looked like Miss Piggy. There was nothing Beth could do short of plastic surgery.

She had a round face and a pug nose and large blue eyes. *C'est la vie.*

"It looks great," Dafna said, knowing all Beth needed was some reassurance.

"Do you think I should do it like this for the wedding? I've been trying to decide between up or down. And if I do it down, what do you think about straight versus curly? Because I like straight, but I'm not sure it really looks like *me*. And what do you do with the veil? I could also do half up, half down."

"Why don't we strategize tonight during cocktails?" Dafna said. "I need to race back to work right now."

"Oh! Of course!" Beth said with exaggerated compassion. "My God. Of course."

"See you soon," Dafna said, blowing a kiss as she dashed into the elevator just as the door was closing. She couldn't listen to one more word; hoped, in fact, that Beth would fall down the elevator shaft.

She raced over to nearby Bergdorf's and went directly up to the fifth floor, where she was greeted by a familiar salesgirl.

"Nice to see you again, Dafna," the salesgirl said. "Anything special I can help you find?"

"Just browsing today," Dafna said, not in the mood to chat like she usually did.

With the speed of an expert, she surveyed the floor. Nothing caught her eye. She took the escalator down to three, the designer floor. As a rule, Dafna did not shop in this department since the prices were exorbitant, even for her, but this was a special situation. She found a red strapless satin sheath that stopped just above the knee and had beads sewn in along the top and hem, as well as a matching silk bolero jacket that had beading down the sleeves. It fit perfectly. She asked the salesgirl to bring a pair of shoes, *et voilà!* Dafna was gazing at herself in the mirror, thrilled. This was no damsel in distress, but a stunning princess with the world at her Yves Saint Laurent–shod feet!

Still in the mood of surreal happiness that came over her while in Shopping Mode, Dafna handed over her MasterCard to the salesgirl, who swiped it through. Shortly thereafter, her forehead furrowed. She tried again. "Do you have another card?" she asked. "This one was denied."

"There must be some confusion," Dafna said, the protective carapace of her Shopping Mode shell cracking a bit as she fumbled through her wallet. She was out of cash and she didn't have any other credit cards. She asked if there was a bank nearby.

"Just around the corner," the salesgirl informed her. "I'd be more than happy to hold the dress for you."

Dafna glanced at the price tag. The sum was hefty, but this was not a time to be depriving herself. "Back in a flash," she said with a smile, and, once more, out Dafna dashed. Only one thing went through her mind as she made her way to the bank: that dress would solve everything. She would have to dip into her savings. Her grandfather had set aside $500,000 for each of his grandchildren. Since her disinheritance, she had used up $120,000 on rent, clothes, a rental in Sagaponack, and a trip over Christmas to St. Bart's. But there was still plenty left.

She opened her wallet and reached for her bank card. For a moment, she hesitated. The money in this account was really all she possessed. She might have to live on it for a while if her father persisted in the ridiculous folly of holding her back from her rightful millions. But this thought flitted through her mind like the brief gust of cold air that sweeps through the front door of a restaurant on a winter day and chills your neck but disappears by the time you've reached behind your chair for your coat. She withdrew the money and ran back to the store.

When Dafna arrived at Lincoln Center, the party was already well under way. She checked the Bergdorf's bag containing her work clothes and the contract and was handed in return a seating card that read "Dafna Shapiro, Table 103."

Clutching the card like a passport to paradise, Dafna took the escalator up and surveyed the scene. The entire first tier was packed wall-to-wall with tables, the guests were already seated, and an old man was making a speech at a podium in the center of the room, only the sound was muffled and no one even attempted to quiet their conversation, so it was impossible to comprehend what he was saying.

The room was a sea of red: red tablecloths, red chairs, red glasses, and red hearts hanging from the ceiling. The table numbers, which were white, were stuck into gigantic towering red flower arrangements in the center of each table. Like her ancestors before the Red Sea, Dafna forged her way through the tables, searching for table 103.

Table 24 . . . Table 16 . . . Table 21 . . . Table 8 . . . There didn't seem to be any logic to the number assignments, and forward progress was challenging. Waiters and waitresses rushed from table to table, picking up small plates, putting down larger ones. Table 45 . . . Table 59 . . . There was Dan Rosen, still looking as cute as he had when they went to Hebrew School together twenty years earlier, only now he had a lot less hair. Dafna waved and Dan waved back. They had had a fun night at the Four

Seasons a few months back, after the ICP benefit. Why hadn't they gotten together again? Oh yes. The holidays had come and she went to St. Bart's and Dan went to Vail and they had lost the thread somehow. Or maybe there were rumors of a girl he had met on the chairlift? Dafna couldn't remember.

Table 35 . . . Table 91 . . . Where was Andy? Dafna scanned the crowd. She wanted him to see her. Table 63 . . . Table 99 . . . She thought she saw someone waving at her from the farthest end of the room, all the way over by the window. She squinted. Someone *was* waving. It was her sister Jennifer.

Dafna waved back, forcing a smile on her face. What kind of seating was this? She couldn't be farther from the action if they'd placed the table in Yonkers! She slipped through the chairs and inched herself toward table 103. She passed Zoë and Michael Kramer with Steve Berman. *That* looked like a fun table. Why wasn't she at *that* table?

She was almost at 103. . . .

No, Dafna thought, taking in the situation with abhorrence. *It can't be. It can't be!* But as she got closer she saw that it was: *no eligible men.* There were no eligible men at the table! And on top of that, there was Beth, her boring fiancé, Michael, on one side, an empty seat on the other! If Dafna had to hear one more thing about the wedding, she'd go at Beth with a steak knife!

"I saved your first course for you," Beth said as Dafna arrived at the table. "I thought you'd like it. Beggar's purse. The caviar's actually pretty tasty."

"Thanks," Dafna said, taking the seat between her sister and Beth. On Jennifer's right, Valerie Steinman waved. Jennifer and Valerie had been in the same bunk at Willow Lake for their eight summers. Back then they had both been fairly popular but Dafna had always found Valerie insufferably boring. She talked slowly and in a monotone and her hair and skin color were beige, which pretty much summed up her entire personality. Everyone said the only reason Jennifer hung out with Valerie was to make herself look better. It did.

"I need to stretch my legs," Dafna announced, standing up to get a better look at the room. Andy had to be there somewhere.

Their eyes met almost on cue and Dafna's jaw dropped. There was Andy, his too-tanned head perched on top of a double-breasted tuxedo, his arm around a girl Dafna had never seen before. Not just any girl. A tall girl with a short blond bob and a straight boyish figure highlighted by the white and silver-sequined drop-waist flapper dress she wore. A WASP! A shiksa!! Andy looked away quickly.

"So tell me," Beth said as Dafna lowered her shocked self back into her seat. "What do you think of my makeup? Honestly. I had it done after you left."

"I'm sorry," Dafna said, turning on Beth with a ferocity she felt unable to contain, "but I can't focus on your makeup right now. I'm sorry. I can't. I mean, it looks great. You look great. I just—is it incredibly loud in here, or is it just me?"

"It's definitely on the loud side," Beth said, clearly wounded.

Dafna seized her wineglass and drew it swiftly to her lips. "Listen," she said after her first gulp, "I'm sorry. I just had an incredibly stressful time at work. Your makeup really does look great. But let's talk about how you want to do your hair. Honestly. Tell me all the options."

For the next twenty minutes, Beth yapped away about the pros and cons of up versus down versus half up–half down, straight versus curly versus wavy versus straight with occasional

85

tendrils, while Dafna nodded and uh-huhed and polished off her red wine and the glass in front of Beth's place setting, which Beth wasn't touching since she was off alcohol, dairy, sugar, and carbs.

Where did I go wrong? Dafna pondered, replaying each moment of each one of her two dates with Andy. She never should have spent the night at his place. That was it. He probably thought she was a slut—not potential mother-of-his-children material.

Dafna was deep in the analysis when she realized someone was talking to her other than Beth. "All through?" Dafna heard in a register decidedly male, and up she looked into the expectant face of a devastatingly handsome waiter.

Dafna looked down at her untouched dinner plate and back up at the waiter.

"Not a fan of quail, huh?"

She shook her head no. He had ice blue eyes, sharp Nordic features, and thick sandy hair slicked back with gel.

"I guess I'm just not in the mood for food," Dafna said, ducking her chin and looking up at him through her thick Lancôme-enhanced lashes.

He picked up her plate, lingering for a moment before he left the table. "Want a refill on the wine?"

"You know what I want?" Dafna said, running a hand through her hair. "I want a Stoli martini, twist of lemon."

"Sure about that?"

Dafna gave him her amused-yet-bored look.

"I only meant are you sure you want Stoli? Personally, I think Ketel One is a better brand, and it doesn't give you as bad of a hangover in the morning."

"Stoli," Dafna said, fixing her gaze on him with a challenge.

He gave her a half smile, took her plate, winked, and left.

"Don't make that face," Dafna said, noticing Jennifer's raised eyebrows, which, no surprise, were perfect. "You're drinking a Cosmopolitan. Valerie's got a—what is that? A Madras?"

Valerie nodded.

"So stop judging me," Dafna said, "and let's make this a party. God knows, it ain't gonna be unless we help ourselves out here. I don't know about any of you, but I think it bites shit that there aren't any eligible men at this table."

"Do you have to announce it to the whole room?" Jennifer asked. "Keep it down."

"Why?" Dafna said in a louder voice. "I think it's *abysmal. Abominable.* I think it *absolutely* sucks *ass cheese!*"

Their table had fallen silent, as had the table next to theirs. Beth giggled and Michael, who had spent most of the meal fiddling with his Palm Pilot, looked up. Across the table, Valerie picked at her dinner roll and Jennifer muttered "Oiy" with a look of stern consternation on her face. Then the silence that seemed to freeze the room in a moment of miserable judgment passed. Conversation resumed around them and the whirl and swirl of a benefit party mid-action continued.

Dessert arrived: crème brûlée and a chocolate-covered strawberry. Dafna wasn't interested in dessert; she was interested in the waiter. She looked around for him, but her eye caught Andy Silverman's instead as he crossed the room, alone. His nostrils flared and he looked away quickly; then he turned back with an embarrassed smile on his face, as if he'd been caught with his fly unzipped. Dafna motioned for him to come over to her table, but he shook his head and pointed toward the theater.

Dafna mouthed *Later* and waved, but her heart sank.

People were starting to head into the theater. The rest of Dafna's table had departed while she was lost in her moment with Andy, and she found herself, quite suddenly, alone. She searched the area nearby for Jennifer. It was at times like this that she felt comforted by Jennifer's self-assured presence. Jennifer, however, was nowhere to be found.

Dafna was at a loss. Panic set in. She felt perilously close to tears. Then: a tap on her shoulder.

"Sorry for the delay," the cute waiter said, handing over her drink.

"Thanks," Dafna said, downing the vodka in a few long gulps and handing the empty glass back. "See you at intermission."

Dafna's seat was twelfth row center, the best in the house, reserved for patrons like the Shapiro family, who were million dollar–plus givers to Lincoln Center. Even so, Dafna hated where they were. It was hell if you wanted to get up in the middle of a concert to pee or leave.

"We were beginning to wonder whether or not you'd make it in," Jennifer chided as Dafna slid into the seat next to her sister.

The conductor came out onto the stage and the hall erupted in applause.

"I'm glad you didn't let something as trivial as what you told me on the phone this morning spoil your day," Jennifer whispered, squeezing Dafna's hand as the orchestra began to warm up. Jennifer's hands were soft, her nails elegantly manicured, the perfect backdrop for her three-carat square-cut diamond flanked by baguettes, joined above and below by thin diamond and sapphire bands, which seemed to mock Dafna as they sparkled up at her.

Dafna waited for the exhilarating chords of a symphony to subdue her troubled mind and increasingly queasy stomach, but the orchestra continued on with their warm-up for an uncomfortably long time. After about five minutes, Dafna realized that it wasn't a warm-up at all, but the actual music. This is what everyone had paid five hundred dollars or a thousand, or even ten thousand in some cases, to hear: this *noise.*

Dafna checked her program. The first piece was by a contemporary composer whose name she didn't recognize, but Beethoven was up next, and after intermission she would have Brahms and Schubert, thank God.

"Yuck," Jennifer whispered as the racket reached a fever pitch. "Let's just hope it's short."

It wasn't. At least not short enough to end before Dafna's stomach revolted.

"Excuse me," she murmured as the first of the heaves began. *"Excuse me,"* she begged, pushing herself over people's knees and purses, briefcases and coats, until she finally reached the aisle. Up and up the endless passage she raced, the room spinning and the vodka wreaking havoc with the blue pills in her mostly empty stomach. Out into the lobby she ran, her three-inch heels click-click-clicking against the marble floor, the sound resounding in the vast marble emptiness. She fled to a door that opened onto one of the terraces, stumbled out into the cold New York night, and leaned over the rail, pleading with the tidal wave of nausea that had washed over her to retreat.

"Ready for another martini?"

Dafna jerked herself up and around.

"Oh shit," her waiter said. "You okay?"

Dafna bobbed her head up and down in her best approximation of a nod. "Fine." She hiccupped. "Can you excuse me?" She belched.

"Oh *man*," the waiter said as Dafna released the contents of her agitated stomach.

"Fucking shit!" Dafna cried between sets of vomit. "Jesus Christ!"

When the siege was over, Dafna sank down onto the icy concrete and buried her face in her hands. The waiter came over to her and draped his black blazer over her bare shoulders.

"Come on," he said, helping her to her feet. "Let's get you inside." He pulled her up and helped her toward the door. "You should have eaten more of the quail. It's not good to drink on an empty stomach. Don't they teach you private school girls anything?"

"My stomach wasn't empty," Dafna said, thinking of the warning on the label of her blue pills that said DO NOT MIX WITH ALCOHOL.

"I'm Lars," he said as they made their way down a long, dark hallway. He had a sweet accent.

"Swedish?" Dafna asked.

"Norwegian," he answered, "but close enough."

Lars led her toward a room divider. Behind it, Dafna discovered a world of silverware and champagne flutes; a world of Saran-wrapped platters filled with biscotti, truffles, pastries, and fruit; a world of rush and chaos as scores of waiters prepared for the postconcert dessert and dancing portion of the benefit.

"Twelve minutes till first intermission!" someone called out.

"I don't suppose you feel like sharing *your* name," Lars said.

"Sorry. I'm Dafna," she said, wiping away a strand of hair that was plastered to her cheek with vomit.

"Well, Dafna, I'm supposed to go work the bar now. Why don't you wait here? I don't think anyone will mind."

Dafna nodded, grateful for a place to hide. Her dress was splattered with puke and water stains from the snow, her makeup was all over her face, she had a poisonous taste in her mouth, and her hair was matted with sweat and everything else.

"I'll try to get you some ginger ale and a roll or something. There's a bathroom at the end of the hall if you want to fix yourself up. It's just for the staff, so you don't have to worry about running into someone you know."

"Why are you doing this for me?" Dafna asked, genuinely baffled.

"Because," he said, eyeing her with an expression she couldn't quite decipher. "Because you're the most beautiful and saddest and sexiest girl I've ever seen."

"Oh yeah," Dafna said. "I'm the very portrait of beauty now."

"I wasn't talking about your looks so much. It's just . . . I work so many of these jobs, and every now and then I see someone who seems different from everyone else." He laughed a little, shook his head. "Or I see someone who just seems horribly trapped—maybe *that's* it—and I usually can't talk to those people because guests are kind of off-limits and everything, but you talked to *me*, right? You're the one who talked to *me*."

"Well . . ." Dafna said, her eyes on the carpet.

"I'll need my jacket back," Lars said. "Sorry. It looks nice on you. It goes well with your red dress."

"Shit," Dafna murmured. "I had a jacket. A bolero."

"Don't worry. I'll find it for you. I know one of the ushers."

"I was sitting down front—twelfth row center," she called out to him.

"Don't you worry!" he yelled back. "Don't you worry about a *thing!*"

91

✳

The party was over, and although Dafna had a dull, throbbing headache, she had freshened up and was waiting on a bench by the coat check for Lars to meet her. She had agreed to one quick drink, even though she'd told Lars she was only up for tea. Lars told her he knew the perfect place and promised to have her home before her coach turned into a pumpkin.

While Dafna waited for him, she watched the other benefit guests as they retrieved their things and said their good nights. There was no sign of her sister. She couldn't even find Beth or Valerie. She did, however, see Andy help the blonde into a lovely white ankle-length fur.

They walked right by her bench and Dafna stood up. "Congratulations," she called after Andy. "You must have raised a fortune."

Andy stopped, wheeled around, then took a few steps toward her. "Dafna Shapiro," he said with a magnanimous air, as if they had been dear friends during childhood and hadn't seen each other since.

"I assume that's why you didn't call me," Dafna continued, refusing to play along. "I knew how busy you were with—"

"I've had an incredibly busy few weeks," Andy confirmed.

"I mean, I think it's incredibly rude that you didn't manage to pick up the phone and call. I think it's just incredibly rude, especially since I sucked your *cock* the last time we were together."

"What's going on here?" the blonde asked cheerfully, as if Dafna and Andy were just joking.

"You have nothing to say to me except *I'm sorry*," Dafna said to Andy. "That's the only thing you have to say to me. And you know what? I'm sorry, too. We could have given our parents a lot of *naches* getting together." Dafna looked straight at the blonde and added, "You can look that up in your Yiddish dictionary when you get home."

"I know what it means," the blonde said. "It's *me*, Dafna. Lynn Rosenthal. We were in the same Hebrew School class. Mrs. Zemesky. Remember? Second grade?"

Dafna searched the crowd for Lars. "Nice to see you again, Debbie," she offered.

"Lynn," the blonde chirped. "It's Lynn."

Dafna apologized, muttering something about how much Lynn reminded her of a girl named Debbie who had been in their class.

"That was Debbie Weinman," Lynn said. "I'm still friends with her. We should all have coffee sometime."

"That would be nice," Dafna agreed, with venom enough to take down a woolly mammoth.

Lars put a glass of water in front of Dafna and slid into the booth across the table. He had taken her to a dive in the no-man's-land of the West Thirties. It wasn't her usual upscale watering hole or even a chic downtown *boîte*, but it felt oddly right after the bizarre day she had had. *Nothing* was familiar anymore. She was beginning to get used to it. Even Lars had metamorphosed after the benefit. Gone was the dashing tuxedo, replaced by a pair of worn jeans, black work boots, and a nondescript gray sweatshirt. He looked alarmingly young, and Dafna felt a frisson of impatience with herself for having agreed to this outing when she knew she should be in bed, devising a strategy for retaining her job. Still, he had helped her in a horrible moment and she wanted him to know she was grateful.

"To rare circumstances," Lars toasted.

"To rare circumstances," Dafna echoed, smiling as if she were enjoying herself and sipping her water as if it were a glass of champagne. "So tell me about yourself," she said, putting her good breeding to practice.

Lars wasn't shy. Off he went, chattering away about the trials of being a cater waiter and describing his dream of making his living as a photographer. The more he talked, the more relaxed she became. There was something accepting, too, in the depths of his mesmerizing eyes that invited intimacy, and before long she was recounting her own tale, admitting all the choices she had made that had ultimately led her to the terrace at Lincoln Center that night. She told the story truthfully, sparing no detail, not even that she had lied to her father about destroying the database, or the fact that she had prioritized her looks over her job and would potentially now grow old alone and penniless.

"So what are you going to do?" Lars asked when she reached the denouement.

Dafna shook her head and shrugged.

"You see!" Lars exclaimed. "That's exactly why I haven't spoken to a single member of my family in four years."

He offered her a proud smile, but Dafna didn't smile back. She didn't believe him and told him so.

"That's your prerogative," he said, "but it happens to be true."

"But how can that be?" Dafna asked. "Don't you miss them?"

"Sometimes," Lars answered. "I mean, I *think* about them.

I'm not a heartless bastard. But my life is a lot less complicated now. A *lot* less. The only person I have to take full responsibility for is myself. If I screw up, the screwup is mine and I admit it and try to make up for it. But at least I know I'm living my own life, and there's a lot to be said for that."

"Sure," Dafna said, nodding, but a moment later she added, "Still, I don't see why you can't live your own life and also be in contact with your family. What if one of them got sick?"

Lars shrugged.

"Like *really* sick," Dafna said. "Like cancer or . . . or . . . a stroke. Wouldn't you want to know?"

Lars asked why he should want to know.

"Don't be silly," Dafna said. "You could just be there for them. Support them."

"Does your father support *you*?"

Dafna said she was sure, deep in his heart, he did.

"And if he got cancer or had a stroke, what would you do?" Lars asked.

"I'd go to his bedside and tell him I love him and that he has to forgive me right away."

"And if he wouldn't?"

"But he would!"

"But what if he wouldn't? And what if he didn't leave you anything in his will, either?"

"That's just ridiculous," Dafna said. "That just couldn't happen."

"He cut you off *when*?"

Dafna counted. To her dismay, fourteen months had elapsed since he had made his decree.

"And have you spoken to him during that time?"

Dafna shook her head. "But I've seen him!" she blurted out. "At Seder and Rosh Hashanah and . . . and Yom Kippur."

"Yom Kippur." Lars nodded slowly several times. "I'm not an expert on Jewish holidays or anything, but isn't that the one about forgiveness?"

"Let me explain something," Dafna said, on the verge of losing her patience. "My father is going to forgive me."

Lars asked why.

"Because I'm his *daughter*." Dafna's tone no longer sounded friendly, even to her own ears.

Lars seemed to get the message and stopped talking. They were the only people in the bar, and it was suddenly unnervingly quiet. Lars lit a cigarette and smoked it while Dafna chewed the final ice cubes in her glass. She found the silence almost as upsetting as Lars's line of questioning.

"Look, you don't know what my father's like," she said in a final attempt at explanation. "He's tough. He fought hard to get the company to the place it is today. His own father practically ran it into the ground, but he built it back up through the seventies and eighties, even when so many cosmetics companies were folding. And I messed up big-time. I lied. And that's one of those things my father doesn't condone. We were raised not to lie. It's, like, in the Talmud, or one of the Ten Commandments or something. It's against our religion! And I'm from a religious family. We celebrated Shabbas every Friday night while we were growing up, and my father is very involved with our synagogue and—"

Dafna paused. While it was true that her family had indeed celebrated Shabbas and observed all the major holidays, and while it was true that she had gone to a Jewish summer camp, and been Bat Mitzvahed and continued to go to Hebrew School once a week until she was sixteen, and that her family gave an enormous amount of money to the temple each year and that both of her parents had been invited to sit up on the bima on more than one occasion, still, it wasn't like they had been raised in some kind of ultrareligious house. They were "*very* Reformed," as she had heard her own mother say. They ate shrimp and bacon and snacked on Yom Kippur; they had never debated the Torah or any other Jewish literature. Mostly, Shabbas dinners had been a nice excuse to wear something pretty to the dinner table, and holidays were seen by Dafna as reasons to update her wardrobe.

"It's my own fault," she said to Lars. "I've made some very stupid decisions. But I'm not a monster, and neither is my dad. He's just stubborn. But I'm sure he'll come to his senses soon."

"I hope so," Lars said.

Dafna could no longer find a reason to stay. She stood up and grabbed her coat.

"Oh, don't run away," Lars said. "We're just beginning to get somewhere here."

"I don't think so," Dafna said, donning her hat and gloves.

Lars watched. Finally, he said, "You should try to enjoy your privileged life a little more."

"And you should try not to judge people just because they're rich," Dafna retaliated.

"Let me at least walk you out," Lars said. "If you want, we could go back to my place. It's only a few blocks from here. We don't need to have sex or anything. We could just hold each other. At the very least, let me photograph you."

"I don't think so," Dafna said, struggling to make her way through the tables with her large Bergdorf's bag in hand.

"I didn't mean to offend you," Lars said. He had followed her to the door and tried to help her with the bag. "Honestly. I was only trying to show you that there are other ways to live."

A taxi pulled up outside the bar, letting a couple out.

"Thanks," Dafna said, her dismay clear. Then she softened, remembering how kind he had been. "Listen," she added, "thanks for helping me tonight."

Lars stared down at her with a sad expression in his azure eyes, and for a moment she thought about inviting him to go home with her. Instead, she grabbed his threadbare coat collar and pulled his handsome face down toward her own. "I won't ever forget how kind you were to me," she whispered. Then she kissed his chiseled cheek, scrambled into the cab, slammed the door, and gave the driver her address without looking back.

By the time the taxi had passed Barneys, Dafna had finished composing the speech she would make first thing in the morning to Richard. She wouldn't ask for her position back. She'd simply give him the contract and then tell him "the truth": that she suffered from a rare blood disease which required lengthy medical treatments that often took her away from work at awkward hours. She would also come clean about the fact that her funds were running low, which was why she needed the job so badly, not for the salary as much as for the health insurance. At this point, she would stop her speech, tell him she felt a little weak and needed to sit. Hopefully her cheeks would flush a nice color of pink and that would be that: his heart would swell with compassion and he'd ask her if she needed a cool cloth for her forehead. She'd decline, she'd sigh, then offer to work for free as his assistant until she made up for the firm the amount of money they would have gotten had they won the Nabisco deal. Or maybe Nabisco would accept the contract one day late and they could all just get on with things.

Either way, she was sure she'd be able to get her job back. And that was what she felt she needed to have when she approached her father for forgiveness. As long as she had her job, she'd be able to appeal to his sense of justice and ethics. She had paid enough for her transgression. It was time for him to forgive her. It was also time for him to reinherit her, so she could continue getting her monthly deposits of twenty thousand dollars plus her rent automatically paid.

Should she ask for her position back at Piró? That was a tough question. She had enjoyed working there, and had especially enjoyed the way people responded when she told them she worked there. And of course it would be fun to have her own PR person, like Jennifer, and an ad campaign with her photo in it. But if she had to return to her former life of lunching and exercising and shopping and planning benefits, it wouldn't be that terrible. She was good at all that. And there was nothing wrong with doing what you're naturally good at. Wasn't that another one of the Ten Commandments? "To thine own self be true," or something like that.

The taxi pulled up in front of her building. She handed the driver the last ten in her wallet and went inside. The March issue of *W* magazine had arrived. She took it from the night doorman, collected the rest of her mail from her mailbox, and got into the elevator. Dafna studied the magazine. She hated what the cover model was wearing. The "poverty" look conveyed by the torn T-shirt repulsed her. Dafna noticed that the T-shirt logo was Versace. "Stop slumming it, Donatella," she said aloud to the shirt's designer. "Be who you are and stick to sequins."

Once inside her apartment, she dropped the Bergdorf's bag, the magazine, the mail, her coat; everything, actually, went straight onto the floor. She had the nagging feeling she had neglected to finish something, but she was too exhausted to figure out what that was. She had to sleep! It was an emergency! She rushed to her bathroom, brushed and flossed her teeth took off her makeup, put on her night cream, applied vanishing cream to a zit that looked like it might be forming beneath her left nostril, plucked a few hairs that had been missed under her chin, inserted her teeth-whitening trays and dove into bed.

Yes, *her father*, she remembered just as sleep began to claim her. She would talk to him in the morning.

And then she fell asleep before she managed to set the alarm.

She was awakened by a loud ringing anyway. It was the telephone on her night table. She reached for it out of habit even before her eyes were open.

"Hello?" she croaked.

"Dafna?"

It was a male voice. "Lars?" she said, trying to remember when she had given him her number.

"Uh, this isn't Lars," the caller responded. "But I could pretend to be, if it would make you happy."

Dafna struggled awake. The voice on the line was familiar, but it wasn't the waiter's. "I'm sorry. Who's this?"

"Dan Rosen. I didn't wake you, did I?"

"No, not at all," replied Dafna, removing the teeth-whitening trays so as not to sound like an idiot. She checked the time. It was after 10:00.

"Sorry we didn't get a chance to talk last night," Dan said. "I figured I'd catch up with you after the concert but you disappeared."

"I had another party," Dafna apologized, trying to sound girlish even though she felt as if her throat were lined with Kitty Litter.

"So I was thinking," Dan continued, "we had so much fun that night at the Four Seasons—"

"Didn't we?" Dafna said.

"And I was totally bummed that we kind of dropped the ball."

Dafna agreed it was a shame they had lost touch.

"So this is going to sound crazy, and I don't want you to take it the wrong way, but I happen to have an extra ticket to Vail, leaving this afternoon—"

"This afternoon?" Dafna was completely awake now and already beginning to go through a mental inventory of her ski wardrobe.

"It's a long story, but basically there's seven of us going—me, Zoë and Michael Kramer, Andy Berman, Pam Levis, Jill and Ben Singer."

"That's a fun group!"

"And Lisette Weiner just dropped out because she had some kind of freak accident in her spinning class yesterday—she fell off the bike and broke her arm—but the spot is paid for already. We're staying at the Sonnenalp."

"Oh, that's niiice," Dafna purred, flexing and pointing her toes in anticipation.

"And you'd have your own bed—I mean, we might need to

share a room, but I'm fine on the floor in a sleeping bag, or on the couch."

"Sounds amaaazing!" Dafna said, thrilled she had purchased the tight-fitting one-piece white Polo Sport ski suit in December on spec.

"I know it's last minute, and I forget what your work commitments are—"

Dafna, too, couldn't quite remember. Then she did. She remembered everything, including a dream she had had in which she flew down to Florida and told her father what an idiot she had been up to this point and how she was now absolutely reformed and ready to return to the family with a newfound respect for money and responsibility. In the dream, her father had smiled warmly and taken her into his arms and said he wasn't going to disinherit her any longer since he loved her so much. Then Jennifer showed up with her mother and they had a family celebration that concluded with a cake from Greenberg's, the chocolate kind with the little circus animals and chocolate squares that her mother used to serve at Dafna's birthday parties when she still wore a tutu and crown.

"So what do you say?" Dan asked.

Peering through her open bedroom door, Dafna could see the Bergdorf's bag on the floor of the living room, the yellow envelope containing the contract peaking out. It wasn't too late to go into the office. Richard would be in a better mood than he usually was first thing in the morning. His coffee would have kicked in and he would have yelled at other people by now, instead of just at her.

"You still there?" Dan said.

Outside, the gray sky deposited large wet flakes onto the city.

"How's the snow out there?" Dafna asked, stalling for time while she searched her soul. She simultaneously searched her closet. Her white snow boots with the fur around the tops would look great with the ski suit. She had had no plans whatsoever to ski this winter, but the boots and the ski suit had both been so irresistibly cute, and the trip would certainly justify the purchases.

"Supposed to be great snow," Dan said. "Fresh dump yesterday."

Dan Rosen was appealing if you didn't mind premature baldness, and according to reliable sources, he was the salt of the earth. Of course it was a little worrisome that he was thirty-five and still single. But then again, who was perfect?

"When does the plane depart?" Dafna asked.

"Eleven," Dan answered. "Sorry for the short timing. Do you think you can get ready in time?"

Dafna took a quick peek at herself in the hand mirror she kept beside her bed. Her brows this morning were glorious: two perfect dark arcs.

"I was born ready," Dafna said, a smile blossoming across her face.

Ali Uptown

✳

"That was so fun!" Dafna said, standing up and stretching after the two-hour interview. "I love disclosure. There's something so cleansing about it, like a mental colonic."

"Glad you enjoyed it," Ali said, careful not to let any sense of judgment creep into her voice. "Mind if I film the apartment?"

"Go ahead," Dafna said, "although it's about to become obsolete. I've already started looking."

Ali asked when the move would be taking place.

"Oh, not for another eight months, at least. By the time we find something, pass approval by a co-op board, renovate—and believe me, everything always needs renovating, even if someone's just fixed a place up."

Dafna's look conveyed a vast and dismal acquaintance with *sub par* decor. "Dan doesn't even know I've started looking. We aren't even engaged yet! But that's going to happen any minute. I'm sure he's just waiting on the ring. I told him exactly what I want and gave him my ring size about a week before the reunion, so it should be any day. He knows I'd like to have something to show off for the holidays, and Rosh Hashanah is in three weeks, I think. It's late this year, isn't it? Which I like so much better, since you can wear *real* fall clothes to temple instead of something that's obviously meant for summer. I hate when you have to wear a fall suit and end up broiling, or else you try to pass a spring suit off for fall. Everyone always *knows*." Dafna shook her head at the horror. "Honestly, I wish they'd always have Rosh Hashanah in October. Don't you?"

"Mmm," Ali said. She hadn't been to services on Rosh Hashanah or Yom Kippur in the last ten years and didn't own any suits, fall, summer, or spring, for that matter. "Well," she finally said, "congratulations in advance."

"Thank you," Dafna said, smiling radiantly. She'd had her hair and makeup done for the interview and truly did look stunning. "You're welcome to come with me as I start looking," she added, leaning forward and picking up a stack of floor plans that were resting on the coffee table. "You can't stay downtown forever if you plan to have children. Fun as I'm sure it is on the Lower East Side, there aren't any decent schools that go past fifth grade, and then you'll have to move your kid, and there are so few spots left by that time at the good schools—it's a chance you probably don't want to take."

"Have you ever heard of Friends?" Ali asked, wondering if Dafna suspected her pregnancy. "That goes all the way through senior year. And Saint Ann's in Brooklyn is excellent."

Dafna looked at Ali as if she had just suggested sending her child to a Nazi youth program. "In an age of terrorism, I'm sure you don't want your child going to school in a different *borough.*

Up here, you have a million to choose from, or you can send your kid to one of the campus schools in Riverdale and it's no big deal, whereas I'm sure you wouldn't want your kid making that schlepp from downtown."

Ali conceded that Dafna had a point. She was not unfamiliar with the debate. She had heard her sisters chatter about the same issues time and again. Still, she refused to give in to it. She wasn't going to let a school determine where she wanted to live. The Upper East Side had no soul, no flavor. There were no cool bars or restaurants, no funky stores, no sense of history. And the people! Ugh! All the girls had their hair blown to meet their friends for coffee and all the men wore Gucci loafers with their jeans. She could never be happy up here. And she could never afford it, so there was no point in even thinking about it. The only way she could live here would be to use the money her father had put aside for her, and that wasn't something she wanted to do. Her self-sufficiency had been one of her crowning sources of pride. Her sisters called it "stupid," but her father understood, since he was a self-made man himself.

Not that she wasn't concerned about where her child would go to school. But she and Renny had decided to look for places on the Lower East Side, where Renny had always lived, and in Brooklyn, where many of their friends lived. Fort Greene was a possibility, or Williamsburg, if they could find something they could afford. Ali loved Smith Street and Montague Street, and proximity to Prospect Park was enticing.

"I can't believe it's already noon!" Dafna said. "Would you like to grab a bite? It's so pretty, let's sit outside at La Goulue— although the whole world will be there today, so it might be hard to get the right table."

Dafna had a way of making everything she said sound simultaneously sincere and tongue-in-cheek, and Ali decided to extend their time together, since she found Dafna so amusing. As a rule of thumb, the more she ingrained herself into the lives of her subjects, the better the documentary would be. People always ended up saying more than they should when you had them in your confidence. It wasn't a technique Ali loved to use, but it was effective, and she was nothing but effective when it came to filmmaking.

Dafna was effective, too, at least when it came to her appearance. She had disappeared into her all-white bedroom to retouch her makeup, leaving Ali in the living room to continue her observations. "Be right there!" Dafna shouted.

"Take your time," Ali shouted back, her camera already capturing the contents of the cabinets in Dafna's kitchen. She hardly had a thing in her cupboards. Ali might have guessed the secret to Dafna's fabulous figure was starvation, but a Zagat guide next to the phone suggested a propensity toward dining out. Ali moved from the kitchen back toward the living room, opening every drawer and door along the way. The closet beside the front door was stuffed with so many coats that it looked like a designer warehouse. Dafna had one of everything: a shiny white Ralph Lauren ski parka, a black cashmere Prada three-quarter-length day coat, a camel hair Calvin Klein, a long fur, a short fur, a leather jacket, a fuchsia suede jacket, a Burberry raincoat, and on it went. Ali just had enough time to capture it on-camera before she heard Dafna shout from the bedroom, "Here I come!" and a moment later she swept into the living room in a cloud of perfume and at least eight layers of lip gloss.

They left the apartment and began the walk east. It was

outside of Starbucks on Lexington Avenue between Seventy-seventh and Seventy-eighth that they bumped into Beth Rosenblatt, her eye makeup smeared, her cheeks damp. She was clutching a white book to her chest and tightened her grip on it reflexively when Dafna squealed hello.

"My God!" Dafna exclaimed. "What is it? Did your mom change the fabric of the dress again?"

"Nothing. It's nothing," Beth managed. "I gotta run, though. I'm late."

"I just did the interview!" Dafna said. "It was so much fun! When are you doing yours?"

Beth looked around helplessly. "Soon. Soon. Now's just not a great time."

Now seemed like a great time, though, to Ali. She loved the thought of capturing one of the girls in the middle of a meltdown.

"I'll call soon," Beth managed, running off.

"Poor girl," Dafna said. "She's really losing her mind over this wedding. I have to make sure I don't let that happen to me."

"Does she live around here?" Ali asked.

"Across the street!" Dafna pointed to a salmon-colored building with a white awning. "You should interview her today—give her a chance to vent. God knows, she needs it, and I hate to sound like a bad friend, but I really can't hear any more of it."

Ali decided to pay Beth a visit after lunch with Dafna, an experience that turned out to be surprisingly fun. As Dafna nibbled on her Caesar salad and Ali made her way through a steak-frites, Dafna deluged Ali with questions about her work and her boyfriend, her sisters and her life on the Lower East Side. Dafna was surprisingly self-deprecating, referring to herself more than once as "just a J.A.P. from the right side of the tracks."

"Is that what you really are?" Ali asked at one point. "A J.A.P.?"

Dafna had shrugged and smiled, saying, "I *am* a J.A.P. if that means being Jewish and rich! But I *like* who I am, and I *like* my life, and I *like* shopping, and getting manicures and pedicures and facials and massages, and you know what? If someone has a problem with it, they're just jealous. You have to play the cards you're dealt in life, and I was dealt rich ones. I mean, *really*. What should I do? Sleep in Central Park and wear rags? Anyway, the last time I checked, *JAPPY* rhymes with *happy*."

Ali had to laugh at that, and said, "I guess you lead a JAPPY-go-lucky life!"

"Let's just hope I get to live JAPPILY ever after!"

"Don't worry, be JAPPY!" and they dissolved in laughter and a sense of mutual understanding. In fact, by the time their cappuccinos were drained, Ali had to admit she liked the woman across the table.

"Well, I guess we better get the check," Dafna said. "It's time for me to shop." She checked her watch. "Oh my goodness! It's almost three. I barely have time. I do have a standing mani-pedi every Tuesday at four-thirty."

Ali didn't know whether Dafna was serious, but she smiled, and so did Dafna, and the two parted with a hug.

It was a beautiful afternoon and Ali wandered in and out of a few stores on her way to Beth's apartment. Unlike the clothes in the boutiques in her neighborhood, the clothes up here were not so stylish that you couldn't wear them. She picked up two shirts and a pair of comfortable but chic flip-flops. Then she went to Beth's.

"May I help you?" the doorman asked.

Ali gave Beth's name.

The doorman rang Beth's apartment and, to Ali's relief, told her to go up to 6G.

Ali checked herself out in the mirror in the lobby en route to the elevator and decided that you still couldn't tell she was pregnant. Her sisters might know if they saw her, and her mother. She'd been avoiding them all for the last month, and it was becoming stressful. She would tell them soon, she decided as the elevator took her up to the sixth floor.

The front door was open. Ali rang the bell anyway and a weary voice called out, "Come i-iiiin."

Ali expected to find Beth wrapped in a blanket, lying on her sofa with her hands steeped in a bag of taro chips, but instead she discovered her on a stepladder in the kitchen, removing china from a high shelf.

"I'll just be a sec," Beth said. "Would you mind setting this down for me?"

Ali took a few steps into the small kitchen, where she took a large white china serving platter with a gold rim from Beth's hands.

"Just put it with the rest of the set on the floor in the corner of the living room. There"—she pointed toward the windows— "below the heater."

Ali turned the corner and found herself amid a crazy clutter of crystal, silver, appliances, china, picture frames, linens, pots, pans, and vases.

"Okeydokes," Beth said, joining Ali in the mess. Even though she was dressed in an oversized T-shirt and sweats, Ali could see she was close to emaciated. "I think that's everything. Can I offer you some water or a Diet Coke? I think I have a can of Fresca, too."

"I'm fine," Ali said, still in awe. Then she remembered what she was there for and asked Beth if she could start filming right away.

"I'd prefer if you didn't," Beth said. "I wasn't prepared for you to be here today."

"Okay," Ali said, trying not to display her disappointment. "Would you like to talk off-camera? Would that make you more comfortable?"

Beth's expression went from wary to wounded and worked its way to exhausted. "Forgive me," she said. "I don't mean to be rude. I just wasn't— Would you like to sit for a moment?"

She indicated the cream-colored sofa against one wall of the small apartment. Ali knew she should be polite and suggest a return visit some other time, but her curiosity was piqued so she took a seat. The decor was reminiscent of Dafna's apartment, only everything was a little smaller and a littler cheaper-looking. A large framed poster of Marilyn Monroe hung above the sofa, which faced a wall unit containing some books and a TV set. Other wall space and surfaces were taken up with photographs of Beth and her friends, images of her and Dafna dominating.

"I can come back another time," Ali said halfheartedly.

"It's okay," Beth said, sliding onto the sofa. "I just—I'm just a little spent. I've been through a lot."

"Maybe a defining moment?" Ali said hopefully.

"You could say." Beth sighed. She almost seemed to laugh for a second, but her eyes filled with tears, which soon began streaming down her cheeks. "I'm so frightened," she whispered.

"It's just such a risk." She bowed her head and brought her knees up to her chest.

"I'll come back," Ali said, standing. "This was a mistake. I'm sorry. I just got excited to see you, and I'm not in this neighborhood that often. Forget it." She was already at the door. "Give me a ring when or if you're interested. Really. Sorry to have barged in."

"Wait!" Beth shouted. She grabbed the white diary from its resting place on the coffee table and said, "Take this. It's all in here. Just take it."

"You sure?" Ali said, snatching the book greedily.

Beth nodded solemnly. "Get home safely," she managed before virtually slamming the door in Ali's face.

Ali didn't care; she could barely contain her curiosity. She opened the white book while still in the elevator and read it cover to cover on the subway ride downtown.

This book belongs to

BETH LEAH·ROSENBLATT

ENGAGED: Wednesday, January 14, 2002

CONGRATULATIONS ON YOUR ENGAGEMENT! *You are about to embark on the most important journey of your life: planning your wedding. Every detail should be perfect, every dream fulfilled, every moment a cherished memory. This book will tell you exactly what to do so you end up with a real showstopper without going too far out of your mind. We know there are literally hundreds of guides out there, each one promising the same results. But this guide is for you, the Jewish American Princess. Why waste time flipping through pages of sample budgets when we all know your parents are footing the bill? Why read about morning coats and what fabrics wrinkle least when you kneel? You are most likely getting married on a Saturday night after sundown and the wedding certainly won't be in a church, unless you're trying to give your parents heart failure.*

What else makes this guide specially designed for you? We know how much every Princess likes to share the minutest details of her life with all her friends and family. To avoid burnout from those people you most need in your life, this book has come up with a solution. It asks you, the glorious bride-to-be, to write down everything you're going through right here in the spaces provided. Think of this book as your new best friend. You will tell it everything, instead of burdening your mother, your sister, your brothers, your girlfriends, your manicurist, your hairdresser, the dry cleaner, and never—oi vay—your fiancé. Take it from us: no one wants to hear it.

If you heed nothing else in this guide, heed this: as you go through the arduous yet exciting planning process, try to remember that although you are producing an event aimed at impressing your friends, pleasing your parents, and possibly earning you a feature article in the New York Times "Vows" section, a wedding is ultimately a **simple ceremony** celebrating the commitment you and your fiancé have decided to make together—a commitment based on love, mutual respect, and a desire to share the rest of your lives together. So take a deep breath, turn the page, and enjoy the journey to your Ultimate Wedding!

How This All Began

SO YOU'RE ENGAGED. *Mazel tov! You finally reeled him in! Now, before you start freaking out about your dress or who your bridesmaids should be, take a minute to record the reason all of this happened.*

FIANCÉ: Michael Joel Solomon

HOW YOU MET: I was at the MoMA Winter Wonderland benefit with Nina Katz and Dafna Shapiro, and they introduced me to Michael, who knew Nina and Dafna from a summer share in Amagansett they all did two years ago. Dafna actually dated Michael briefly, but she said they didn't have chemistry and were now just friends. She claimed he'd be perfect for me, and I thought he was kind of cute, even though he does have a uni-brow and the mole above his cheek with hair growing out of it, so after the benefit when we all went to the Four Seasons and Michael asked me for my number, I gave it to him.

HOW LONG DID YOU DATE BEFORE HE SHOWED UP WITH HARDWARE/YOU GAVE HIM AN ULTIMATUM? We dated for a little over a year, and I never had to give him an ultimatum—thank you, God—even though my mother told me all last summer and fall that if Michael wasn't going to ask me, I should move on, since I'm not getting any younger. I was planning on bringing it up with Michael around Valentine's Day, but luckily he saved me from *that* vile conversation!

HOW HE PROPOSED: He took me to Jean Georges because I'd never been there and he knew I'd always wanted to and it was the anniversary of the night we met at the MoMA party, so I wasn't really expecting a proposal, just sort of a romantic night (but thank goodness I got that manicure!). For dessert, the waiter set a plate down in front of me with three scoops of raspberry sorbet and a larger scoop of lemon in the center, with this outrageous diamond ring resting on the top of it on a mint leaf! Around the edge of the plate the chef had written *Will you marry me?* in raspberry sauce, and I said, "Sure."

HOW YOU FELT: *Thrilled!!* Okay, I'm not going to lie. I knew the minute Michael insisted on ordering dessert what was coming. We don't normally order dessert, or else we just split something, but Michael was totally pushing dessert, saying we were at this great restaurant so we should just get something. Also, Michael was sweating, which he normally doesn't do, so I wasn't exactly shocked when the waiter put the plate down in front of me. Jake Gerstein proposed to Melissa the same way last year, and so did Lisa Newman's husband, whose name I can never remember. I'll admit I was hoping for something a little more original. I know that sounds stupid. I know that at thirty-two I should just have been grateful someone was asking, but the minute Michael insisted on dessert, instead of my saying, "Oh wow. You're proposing! This is so exciting!" I had to pretend not to know what was coming and then pretend to be really moved and happy, when really I was a little disappointed by his choice of how to break the news. Also, I told him one day when we were walking past Tiffany's that if I ever got engaged, I'd like a ring with two sapphires flanking a diamond set in platinum, so I was a little miffed when I saw the solitaire set in gold. Not that it isn't beautiful, but it's a little gaudier than I would have liked and it gets stuck in everything. It even ruined my favorite Agnès B. sweater yesterday!

It's funny. You see all these movies about men proposing and women being so happy that they cry, and I behaved that way, but I don't think I really felt *anything*. Okay. Wait. Not true. I felt relieved. Can't lie about that. Mom has been telling me for years that if I don't get married soon, I'll be too old to give her grandchildren. I told her Madonna had her children in her forties, and Mom told me that I'm not Madonna and that nice Jewish girls don't get impregnated by their trainers, either. Then I told her that Madonna's married now to a famous filmmaker, and Mom told me nice Jewish girls don't marry men who make movies called *Snatch*. (I guess she still gets her subscription to *People*.)

The bottom line is that I've seen what planning a wedding can do to people. I can say right now that it is my goal to maintain a healthy perspective during the next few months and to always remember what my father said to me the other day: "It's not the wedding that's important, but the marriage."

Where and When

NOW COMES THE FUN PART: *choosing the location for the wedding. Do you want to get married on the lawn of your parents' mansion in the Hamptons, like Aerin Lauder, or at the Plaza, like Joan Rivers's daughter, Melissa? Do you want your friends to schlepp down to Jamaica, or can they just hail a cab over to the Pierre?*

What?! You haven't had your dream wedding in mind since you were a tiny tot in a tutu? Don't worry! We'll get your imagination on the right track. Close your eyes, take a few deep breaths, and try to see the perfect location. Don't worry yet about the number of guests unless that's an important factor for you. Most Jewish American Princesses have somewhere between two and three hun-

dred guests, and more if their parents are on a lot of boards. But if intimacy is important to you, now's the time to make that clear. So think. *Put this guide down, close your eyes, and relax. Then open your eyes, pick up your pen . . . and start writing.*

WHEN YOU THINK OF THE PERFECT WEDDING LOCATION, YOU SEE: I don't see anything. Dafna always says that when she gets married, she's going to do it at the Breakers in Palm Beach. How does she know she wants to get married there? She claims her family went there for spring break when she was in seventh grade, before they started going to Half Moon Bay in Jamaica. Where did *we* go on vacations? Oh God, I'm *not* going to get married on a cruise ship! And I'm not going to get married in a ski lodge in Vermont. I hate skiing and I hate the cold, and besides, I don't want to wear a long-sleeved wedding dress. I like the idea of getting married somewhere warm, like Florida, but if I choose the Breakers, everyone will think I'm copying Dafna. I would be.

I guess I want something simple. Something on the small side. Maybe something in a garden. I love flowers. Maybe I should look into the Brooklyn Botanic Garden. Marcy and Ned Klein got married there. I didn't go to the wedding, even though I was invited. I never really liked Marcy (what a J.A.P.!!) and the thought of getting on a bus to go to a wedding in Brooklyn was very unappealing. Okay. Forget that. What about Mom and Dad's house in Bedford? The garden is gorgeous in June, when all the peonies are in bloom. We could definitely fit a hundred or so people in the yard. Mom likes to do everything BIG, but she already did the giant New York wedding thing for

Shelly at the Pierre, so maybe she'll consider scaling back for me. Of course, she's still upset that she didn't get to plan Brad's and Rob's weddings, so she may have a *lot* of plans for me, the last little bird to leave her nest, *finally*, and thanks, Mom, for never letting me forget that.

SO YOU RAN THE IDEA OF YOUR DREAM WEDDING BY YOUR PARENTS. HOW DID THEY REACT? Surprise, surprise, Mom said she'd be happy to do a garden "theme," but she's already reserved the Temple of Dendur at the Metropolitan Museum for two different weekends next January and one in February and is just waiting to hear back from the rabbi about availability. When I told her I want to get married in the backyard, she said Dad would have heart failure worrying about the weather but that if I don't mind having a recently widowed mother accompanying me down the aisle, they'd be happy to indulge my every whim.

Dress Time

NOT TO ADD TO YOUR STRESS LEVEL, *but let's face it: this is the single most important article of clothing you will ever purchase in your entire life. You want it to be both beautiful and functional, unique yet classic. This guide assumes you've already pored over every wedding magazine and book on the market and that you have a folder full of tear-outs of your favorites. Great start. Now pick up the phone with your date book in hand and make*

*yourself some appointments. You'll want to spend at least half a day
at each one of these stores, so if you have a job and haven't quit yet,
now's the time to give notice.*

*What? You want to keep working? Don't be silly. After the wedding, you'll be writing thank-you notes for weeks. Then you'll move
to a new apartment and have to start decorating, then you'll get
pregnant, and then you'll be a mom busy with mom things like installing video cameras to spy on your nanny and going to yoga and
spinning classes (and/or a plastic surgeon) in order to achieve your
former perfected pre-baby body! Be honest with yourself: work is not
for you. Say bye-bye!*

Notes:

Vera Wang—Tried on twenty-two different dresses, loved
three. Shelly and Mom were with me and they both like one in
particular (strapless, tight bodice, poufy skirt, lace on the edge
of the skirt), but I like a different one better. They both hate it
because it's *organza,* not satin. Mom said for a Saturday night in
January at the Temple of Dendur, I'll want satin, not organza,
because organza is definitely a summer fabric and wrinkles like
crazy. She said organza is really only right for a garden wedding,
so I reminded her that I want to get married in a garden, and
she shot Shelly a look, so I know she and Dad are waiting for
me to get over *that* one! But I discussed it with Dafna, and she
said, "Fight for it, Beth." I made a few calls. There's a nice
garden available in Riverdale and another one in Tarrytown, but

all of them involve a bus, and I know Mom and Dad will never go for that. Not sure I'm going for it, either.

Kleinfeld's—Tried on fifty dresses but was unimpressed with the selection. There was one, in particular, that I did like (Empire waist, A-line, silk, a detachable train). It was very Audrey Hepburn, but Shelly told me that I looked like I was in a nightie and to take it right off. Mom liked the Audrey Hepburn dress, too, but thinks the ones at Vera Wang are better and not all the way out in Brooklyn so it'll be easier ultimately for fittings if I can find something there.

Saks—Tried on nine dresses. Hated them all. Hate my nose. And my thighs. And my hair. Why did I cut it? I told Kevin to keep it at my shoulders, and now it's just below my chin. My face has never looked more round. If someone drilled three holes in the top of my head, you could bowl with it. I feel like suing Kevin. I hate him. I'm *not* going to have him do my hair for the wedding.

Bergdorf's—Tried on everything they have, which wasn't much. They wanted me to stay for some trunk show, but I left. Who wants to buy a dress out of a trunk? I'm starting to get confused and tired. I just want to get the organza one at Vera Wang.

Yumi Katsura—Nothing fit! You have to be a midget and size two to fit into any of the samples. Mom said the dresses aren't for Jewish girls and not to take it personally. It's awful, though, looking at myself in the mirror so much. I want to get a nose job and liposuction. I'm going to look into it this week. For now, I'm on a really strict diet (no sugar, no carbs, no alcohol, no dairy) and am going to begin working with a personal trainer. I'm also looking into Pilates and yoga and have decided to start training for the New York marathon.

Mathilde—Found a dress I love, and Mom and Shelly agree! It's strapless satin with a kind of netting over the whole dress that makes it look really ethereal. Mom thinks it's perfect for the Temple of Dendur and I think it's perfect for a garden, so we're all happy. Mom put down a deposit and I'm scheduled to have a fitting with the designer of the dress himself next week since he happens to be coming to town. I'm so thrilled! On a completely separate note, I want to report that I gave notice. I'm leaving Avon in two weeks. I'm upset. I actually enjoyed working there. The PR department was fun and I got a lot of great perks. But Dafna told me not to be silly. Then again, Dafna has enough money to live on forever. It's not like I don't have money from Mom and Dad, but it's not like it's a bottomless pit, either. Not that we've ever discussed it. We've never discussed money in our family. I just get a check for twenty thousand dollars every year on my birthday and that's that. Whatever else I want to spend, I need to earn.

Time to Make Some Decisions

THERE'S REALLY NO POINT IN GOING *on with your wedding plans until you've solidified the date and location.*

WHAT'S IT LOOKING LIKE? It's looking more and more like the Temple of Dendur. Mom is insistent and I just don't care enough to fight her on it. Dafna said the idea of getting married at the Metropolitan Museum of Art is very exciting. Her favorite benefit every year is the one thrown there by the Costume Institute. She said it's thrilling to pull up to those beautiful steps with the fountains all lit up and surging toward the heavens. The way she put it makes me feel excited. Still, it's a tomb. I'm getting married in a tomb. I know they call it a temple, but it's where they buried some pharaoh, isn't it? It's also alarming to me that as a Jew, I'm getting married in front of a pyramid. Didn't we do everything in our power as Jews to escape pyramids? I suppose I could view it as a statement of mastery. *(Look, you dead Egyptians. I'm so much more powerful than you now, I'm throwing a party at your grave!)* I don't know. It doesn't seem right to me. But who am I to argue with my mother? When I told her my concern, she said, "We built the pyramids. May as well use them!"

Choosing the Florist

WHEN INTERVIEWING FLORISTS, *here are some important considerations: Do you like this person, or does he or she make you feel like a tasteless idiot? What other weddings has this person done? You want to have heard of some of the weddings, be they celebrity ones or simply the weddings of friends. Ask around. Have your mother ask around. Chances are, she already has a list of names she's been hoarding for years. When you go to a benefit, if you like the flowers and other decor, find out who did it. Your florist can make or break your special day, so this guide suggests you research this as carefully as you did your college. Okay. Bad example. Some of you went to whichever school had your family's name on a building. So research this with the same care you give to who colors your hair.*

Notes:

Benoît d'Arte—Went to his apartment on CPW. Lots of gold and Louis the Whoever–looking stuff. Also a framed photo of his guru on top of a shrine. I was turned off right away. Showed us some slides. Kept droning on about how much the socialite Alice Sturgeon likes hedges and how he built a box hedge for her around the Palm Court at the Plaza, and about how Ellen Tress once had him make a maze at the St. Regis. For some newscaster I've never heard of, he did everything pink: pink plates, pink tablecloths, pink-edged crystal, towering pink cherry blossoms, pink lanterns. Very pink. Too pink. Made me think of Pepto-Bismol.

Martin Volel—One of Mom's recommendations, suggested to her by Brenda Rosenthal (apparently, her daughter Amy's wedding was one of the most beautiful affairs anyone's ever seen in history). Went to his office on Lexington Avenue above an Indian restaurant. Strong smell of curry made me hungry. Love curry and skipped breakfast. Have lost four pounds already by skipping breakfast and eating only salad with chickpeas for lunch and dinner. Martin is over six feet tall with skin so white you can see his veins. He's completely bald and his eyes bulge out of his head in a very unsettling manner. Martin is way over the top. I told him I want something "simple but original" for the ceremony, but I can see *simple* is not part of Martin's vocabulary. He instantly suggested an Egyptian theme, where I'm transported to the *chuppah* in a barge. Then he suggested floral arrangements made of papyrus in the shape of ankhs in the centers of all the tables. Thought Mom would *plotz*.

Troy Daniels—Recommended by tons of people, including Dafna, who said she doesn't do *anything* without him. Was supposed to meet us at Mom and Dad's at 11:00 A.M. Someone from his office called at 11:30 to tell us he was running late. By noon, Mom and I were both starving and Mom made some lunch. At 12:30, someone else called and said Troy would be there shortly. He finally showed up at 1:45 in a flurry of apologies and Prada and carrying a chihuahua in his bag. Mom offered Troy water and he said that *he* was fine but that

Angelica would love some, thank you so much, and did Mom have anything in the kitchen Angelica could have for lunch? Mom served Angelica some chicken, and when the little mutt was done, Troy asked if Mom had any cookies for Angelica's dessert. Mom asked if Milanos were okay and Troy replied that, honestly, biscotti would be better. Troy has an English accent, but when we mentioned the wedding is going to be at the Temple of Dendur, he said he spent some time in Cairo in his youth. Later, though, when he tried to sell us on marigolds and rose petals, he mentioned a childhood spent in Bombay, so I'm a little confused.

Harris Montgomery—Did the decor for the benefit at the Museum of Natural History I went to with Vicki and Marc Gold. Vicki was on the benefit committee and said Harris is amazing. I loved him right away. His office down in the flower district is a mess, with cats milling about and vases mixed up with flowers mixed up with everything from streamers to Viking helmets, but he listened to Mom and me for a long time while we each told him what sorts of ideas we have. He was very supportive of my lantern idea, too, even though I saw Mom roll her eyes. He was even amenable when I mentioned grapes. I've been having visions of grapes, for some reason, and really want them incorporated into the overall decor. I'm not that big into visions—it's really the first one I've ever had (I got the lantern idea from Dafna)—so I feel pretty strongly about it. He showed me a number of photos of centerpieces he's done with fruit, and they were all gorgeous. He admitted he's never worked with grapes before, but he has done quite a bit with lemons and oranges and seemed sincerely excited about the idea of working with a new fruit. I want to hire him, but Mom wants me to meet with a few more people. So far, he's my first choice.

Thom LeBaux—Mom's first choice but not mine. He made me feel like a tasteless idiot, and this guide recommends against that. He suggested stuff I've seen at a lot of other weddings (bowls of *just* papyrus or *just* calla lilies, or *only* candles) and he was not amenable to my ideas at all. He said grapes spoil and lanterns are passé. He seemed irritated that the wedding was going to be in the Temple of Dendur and kept answering his cell phone during our meeting. Mom wants to hire him because he re-created the Taj Mahal in Greenwich for Nina and Rick Horowitz's thirty-fifth wedding anniversary. She was also impressed by the scented candle he gave us as a gift from his own collection of candles. The candle, which is in the shape of a dress pump, says "Cinderella's Slipper" on the front, but I think it smells more like Sweaty Inner Soul.

Dillon Barnaby—He wants the waiters to dress in tunics and wear black wigs with bangs and blunt shoulder cuts. Need I say more?

And the winner is: *Harris!*

First Fitting

SO . . . HOW'D IT GO? What a horror! I've canceled the whole dress, but not without losing several nights of sleep and practically ending my engagement. Plus, I was unable to get my money back, so now Mom has to get her mother-of-the-bride dress at Mathilde unless she wants to lose eight thousand dollars!!!!!

In a nutshell, I went for my fitting with the designer of the dress himself and he was a big mean faggot who made me cry. Yes, cry. And I am not exaggerating. I put the sample on and the first thing he did was smirk. He literally smirked. To be even more specific, he smirked, then he frowned, and then he shook his head and mumbled something to Mathilde. I'm pretty sure he said, "She has the wrong body type." He said it in French, but I took enough French at Brearley and Penn to understand. Then he said loudly, "Looks good!" (The big phony!) He asked me to step into a fitting room and then he circled around me—well, *prowled* would be a better way to describe it—prodding me and pulling at the dress. At one point, he put his hand on my lower back and said to Mathilde, as if I were a mannequin, "She has a very *flat* back, no arch *at all*." I tried to stick my ass out more, but he told me to stand tall and keep my head still. Then he suggested *sleeves*. I said, "Why sleeves? I want strapless," and he said, "Well, you *will* have arm cleavage, but if you don't care, I guess I don't either, although this gown was definitely not designed to point out a bride's physical disadvantages." So I agreed to sleeves, and then, as if I hadn't endured enough, he suggested removing the netting (my favorite part), since he felt it made me look heavier than I am.

Okay. I had had enough. But *he* hadn't. He proceeded to inform me that the dress absolutely could not have a train (which, when I purchased it, Mathilde told me wouldn't be a problem), and when I insisted, he said if I really had to have one, he would attach one to the weird flat part of my back, at which point the tears just started pouring out and I took the dress off and got back into my jeans and just ran. I called Mathilde later and canceled the dress. Mom said she'd go back with me and we could try the fitting again, but I'll never step foot in that store again. Dafna agreed with me. She thinks I should sue for defamation of self-esteem.

Your Wedding Party

NOW YOU CAN BEGIN TO WORK *on the second tier of details. Let's start with the wedding party. Most of you brides-to-be will deal with a few tearful phone calls from friends who think they should be walking down the aisle ahead of you. Make a list of those people you want up there with you and say NO to everyone else. Your number doesn't have to correspond perfectly with your husband's, but it would look a little nicer if you did have an even count.*

I PLAN TO ASK THE FOLLOWING GIRLS TO BE IN MY WEDDING PARTY:

My sister, Shelly Silverstein

My sister-in-law Ronnie Rosenblatt

My sister-in-law Tammy Rosenblatt

My best friend from high school, Trish Katzman

My best friend from camp, Dafna Shapiro

ANY STRESSFUL MOMENTS TO REPORT? Rebecca Dickstein asked me out to dinner and then burst into tears over the chicken paillard. She said she couldn't take the stress anymore and that she simply had to know if I was going to ask her to be in the wedding party since it was so "meaningful" that I was in hers! I knew it was going to happen and I told Michael before he left for work that when it did, I was going to tell Rebecca that I have decided to have only family members, but then, when I was sitting with her face-to-face, I just couldn't do anything but say, *"Of course* I want you in my wedding party!" Now I have to have her, and I know she'll look awful in the bridesmaid dresses I've chosen, because they're spaghetti-strap sheaths and she's turned into a balloon in the last sixth months.

Unrelated, but I'm just bursting with the good news: I went to see two different surgeons regarding my thighs and my nose. I've decided that I don't want to tell Michael what I'm going to do, so I'm *not* going to do my nose, but I *am* going to go ahead with the lipo. I'm going to tell Michael that I'm visiting Laura Berman, an old camp friend, in L.A., but really I'm going to go up to Bedford to recover at Mom and Dad's place.

Michael and I haven't had sex in a month. Is that normal

for two people who are engaged? I've tried to talk to him about it, but he says he's getting his ass kicked at work right now and that we shouldn't worry about it. He says he loves me but that we never discuss anything other than the wedding anymore and it's getting on his nerves. I will start to read the *Wall Street Journal* every day so I have something to talk about with him when we have dinner. I read this morning that there's a nursing shortage in Ghana. Maybe we should talk about that. Or we could talk about politics. That's always an icebreaker. I'm going to read *Sports Illustrated*, too. Michael would probably be thrilled if I discussed football and ice hockey with him.

How is it that I once thought we had so much to say to each other? Was he always this distant and boring? Did I want to get married so badly that I chose a sullen snore? While we were talking about the groomsmen's gifts last night, I noticed he has some very long, coarse black hairs growing out of his ears. If he's getting hair in his ears at thirty-five, what's going to happen at sixty? Yuck.

Time to Register

NOW THE REAL FUN BEGINS: *it's time to register. This is an arduous process, so allow the right amount of time for the task. It will take a few weeks to go to all the places to assess your options. Then you will have to go back to each place and narrow down your choices. Before you've finalized things, you'll want to get your fiancé's approval. Many stores stay open late one night a week and all are open on weekends, when your fiancé may have more free time.*

You'll want to keep the following in mind while you register: what will your future apartment look like—the one you will move to in about two or three years? You know, the ten-room—full-floor—apartment on the East Side between Sixty-fourth and Ninety-sixth anywhere between Fifth and Lex. Because you'll want to choose things that will look good in this future apartment, not the little cookie-cutter you live in now.

Think about it. If you end up decorating this future apartment in a minimalist style, ornate Victorian vases might look incongruous, whereas large glass cubes may be perfect. Contemplate color, too. If you decorate your future apartment in beige and white, will a traditional Haviland china plate with royal blue and gold around the rim look right? Or might you do better with a Japanese-style plate with a contemporary crackle glaze in taupe or azure? Give thought to geography, too. Is there any chance your husband will get transferred somewhere like Miami? Would bright pink and turquoise be a better choice for your daily china than white Ralph Lauren Nantucket basket weave? Is Dubai in your future? Or Tokyo? Or Milan? Think. Imagine. And apply these questions to each piece you choose.

Notes:

I'm completely overwhelmed. I went with Mom to Michael C. Fina, Bergdorf's, Takashimaya, Scully & Scully, James Robinson, Nelson & Nelson, Bloomingdale's, Barneys, Crate & Barrel, Macy's, Bernadaud, Bardith, Baccarat, Villeroy & Boch, Georg Jensen, Tiffany, and Williams-Sonoma. Thank God I quit my job. How on earth do women do this while they're still working? This is my career now. Shelly said she felt the same way when planning her wedding, so I'm not feeling as freakish as I think I'm acting. I mean, how am I supposed to choose some of these things? How do I know what my future apartment will look like? Mom keeps pointing out objects I've never even heard of, telling me she couldn't get by without them. What on earth is a Dutch oven? What's a cruet? Why do I need oyster forks?

Thank God for older sisters. Shelly told me to get All-Clad pots and pans and Henckels knives and to make sure to get forks with four prongs instead of three, since she registered for ones with three and finds them disappointing.

I've limited my selection of china to four patterns and will go with Michael this weekend.

Michael hated all four and pointed enthusiastically to the only pattern I despise. We parted ways on Fifty-seventh and Park without speaking and didn't see each other again until seven o'clock, when he came home from the gym and went straight to the shower. Later we met Dafna for drinks, and I noticed Michael had twice as much scotch as usual and that he drank almost an entire bottle of wine by himself during dinner. I asked Dafna if she noticed, and she said I should come with her for a half day of beauty soon at Elizabeth Arden and that that will help more than I know.

We've registered at:

Bergdorf's: for formal china (Mozart Symphonia Limoges), crystal (Lalique water glasses, Baccarat wineglasses, William Yeoward champagne flutes), and formal silver (Christofle); we also registered for place mats, formal salt and pepper shakers, candlesticks, vases, decanters, linen cocktail napkins with small embroidered flowers on them (Mom insisted), some picture frames, a special caviar thing that keeps the caviar cold and has room for bread and onions and stuff, and one Lalique fish knife.

Tiffany: more vases, more picture frames, more decanters, some tumblers and beer mugs for Michael, and a small crystal ring holder for me.

Michael C. Fina: Seder plate, daily china (Hermès jungle pattern), several platters, Henckels knife set, daily silver (Gorham shell pattern), a Cuisinart and a Kiddush cup.

Crate & Barrel: All-Clad pots and pans, coffee grinder, daily salt and pepper shakers, colander, steamer, and various other odds and ends that Mom deemed necessary.

Nelson & Nelson: tureens, huge silver serving platters, cruets, silver sugar tongs, a champagne bucket, and a challah knife.

Notes:

In the end, I decided not to register for the oyster forks. Mom thinks I'll regret it in the event that I serve coquilles St. Jacques at a dinner party, but considering I usually just send out for sushi, I don't think it'll be a problem.

I know this section is about registering, but I also have a wedding dress update. I went back to Vera Wang *alone* and purchased the dress I loved to begin with—in ORGANZA. It's so beautiful!!! And I feel THIN in it and it's light, so I feel like I can really move and dance in it. I want to make it strapless and add a few extra little details like buttons down the back, and no one made me feel fat or mentioned "arm cleavage." The saleswoman said my arms are great. (I've been working out with a trainer three days a week and running every day, so I'm glad someone has noticed!) It cost $7,500 (gulp!). I put it on my AmEx. So who cares? I'll worry about it later. Wait until Mom finds out!!!!!!!!!!! Oh yeah. I forgot. I'm not telling her.

On a separate front, my liposuction date has been confirmed. I'll have it done two days after Michael and I come back from St. Bart's. I wish I could have it done sooner, but I'll have to wear some kind of huge girdle for three weeks following the surgery and will be terribly bruised, so I won't want to be running around in a bathing suit (which I hate running around in even when I haven't just had lipo!). The doctor also said I won't see any results until a few months after the surgery. At least I'll look good at the Willow Lake reunion in August. I'm still agonizing about my nose and wish I could do it. I've always hated it. But Michael asked me to marry him with *this* nose, so it can't be that bad.

Invitations

YOUR INVITATIONS WILL SET THE TONE *for the entire wedding: creamy thick card stock adorned with a gold crest tells your guests that this will be a black-tie affair; pink velum with confetti inside the envelope tells your guests the wedding will be more fun than formal, and women will show up in knee length or shorter. Do you want a satin bow on the top of the invitation? Do you want the invitation in the shape of a tree? You can design anything you want, so try not to limit your imagination. The invitation could arrive in a tube or a box, or even inside a small cake. One bride we know had her invitations printed on silk scarves!*

Notes:

Went with Mom to Kate's Paperie, Tiffany's, Barneys, Crane's, and our local stationery store. I saw several things I liked, but Mom and I disagreed on everything. She likes super-formal and I keep veering toward simplicity. She says the ceremony will be at one of New York's most prestigious institutions on a Saturday night, black-tie, and that the invitation should reflect that. Mom keeps saying she wants me to be happy, but then she goes ahead and tells me why certain things HAVE to be certain ways. I don't want to seem ungrateful for all the time she's giving this, or for the expense, which I imagine will be astronomical. Still, I'm beginning to feel like I'm the only person involved in this whose decisions don't matter.

I finally did concede on the invitation front and we chose something that, at least, shows a little creativity. We're going to send something in the shape of a triangle. (Get it? A pyramid?) Formal script, thick card stock, tissue paper and all that. But I think the shape is fun. And on a happier note, I chose my own personal stationery for thank-you notes, with my new name at the top: *Beth Solomon*. It's nice. It's the same number of syllables as Rosenblatt but looks a lot shorter, for some reason. It makes me feel thinner, too. Rosenblatt rhymes with *aren't you fat*. There's no rhyme for Solomon. It's sleek. I like that. A new, sleek me.

Michael and I haven't had sex in over two months now, almost three. At first, we couldn't have sex because of the lipo and my breast reduction (decided to do that, too, at the last minute and got a discount). I lied and told Michael I had a nasty yeast infection and that he shouldn't touch me until I gave him the go-ahead. But I've told him the infection is gone and that we can get on with it and he still won't come near me. It's disconcerting, but in a way it's a relief, too. I don't know. I'm just not feeling sexy these days, even with my new breasts and thinner thighs.

The other night while we were in bed, I asked Michael if he loves me. He told me he didn't find my constant insecurity particularly attractive, but he said, "Of course I love you. What a dumb question." Here's the thing: he didn't ask me if I still love *him*, and I'm glad he didn't, because I don't like to lie, and I'm honestly no longer sure. I even thought of breaking the engagement, but Michael's aunt and uncle sent all of our Christofle silver, and I just don't know how we'd handle that. Could it be returned? I'm not even going to go there. I know I'm just having normal bride-to-be jitters.

I think I'm also upset because I've developed tendinitis in my left ankle from running so much. I've joined another gym, one with a pool, so I can swim while my tendinitis goes away. So far, I've lost twelve pounds, but Michael doesn't seem to notice. Gary, my trainer, has promised me the perfect body for the wedding and says every woman in the room will want my back. I can't see it, so I hope he isn't lying when he says it's looking awesome.

Photographer

CHOOSING THE RIGHT PHOTOGRAPHER *is almost as important as choosing the right groom. This is the person who will capture your essence, capture your emotion, capture every aspect of the most important day of your entire life. Your photographer will be right there with you every step of the way, so you'll want a high amount of comfort level with him or her. Your photographer can make you late if he or she isn't organized, and can erase bad moments and replace them with good ones, depending on what he or she is able to capture or crop.*

Notes:

Met with three photographers and hired the third on the spot. His name is François Menton (French!) and he's so sexy I almost can't breathe around him. He has black hair past his shoulders and a five o'clock shadow, and his work is to-die-for gorgeous. He's one of the most in-demand wedding photographers in the city right now, so I know he'll be expensive, but he's the one for me.

Michael and I finally had sex last night. I imagined the whole time that it was François making love to me. Michael isn't that inspired a lover, so I pretended François was telling me I was beautiful and thin and that he tries really hard not to sleep with the brides he's photographing but that in my case he just couldn't hold himself back.

Sometimes I worry that Michael is so boring, I'll snap and jump out a window one day. When he tells me about his day, I *want* to be interested, but I'm just NOT. Then I tell him about *my* day, how the wedding plans are progressing, and his eyes go glassy. I'm trying to remember if it was always like this and I just didn't notice, or whether this is a new development that will go away as soon as we have the wedding. It's not just the conversation, either. He isn't helping on any level. For instance, I tried a new makeup person and a new hairstylist for the benefit last night at Lincoln Center for the Israeli Philharmonic. I hated my hair, which I had straightened, but I thought my makeup was pretty good. I asked Michael for his opinion and he said, "You look great," but he didn't even raise his eyes from his Palm Pilot! What the hell? He's the man I'm going to spend the rest of my life with and yet he couldn't bother looking up!

I also asked Dafna, and she was an unbelievable cunt. Her jealousy is so infuriating and obvious. I can't believe she's so self-obsessed that she can't be happy for me for once in her overprivileged life. She keeps *kvetching* to me about how her father has disinherited her. What a joke!! Oh, poor Dafna. She actually has to have a *job*. Welcome to the world the rest of us live in, Daf. And next time I ask you if you like my goddamn hair and makeup, *tell* me, you piece of shit spoiled bitch.

FYI: I decided that the mascara application was too heavy and am going to continue my search for the right makeup artist. Maybe I'll call François. He must have some names.

Videographer

THIS IS OPTIONAL, BUT *almost everyone gets one in the end, so you may as well start looking. A video will capture the wedding in sound and motion, whereas a photograph can capture only a single moment. Think about how much fun it will be reliving your wedding start to finish over and over and over. Think of the years of delight you'll derive from showing your children and friends your wedding video on holidays and rainy Sundays. Many brides worry that the videographer will be too intrusive a presence at the wedding, but there are many talented people out there who work with minimal lights and small, unobtrusive cameras. One piece of advice: watch a sample wedding video before hiring anyone. This guide suggests drinking a strong cup of coffee first, since these can really send you into REM state, but it'll be worth it.*

Candidates:

Larry McDougal—Really like his stuff and booked him immediately. François suggested him, naturally. I still feel nuts whenever I talk to François. Larry is also cute, but he's got a bit of a paunch and a boroughy accent, so I'm able to look him in the eye without blushing. He does a sort of documentary-style video that mixes black and white with color and makes the wedding seem both important and funny at the same time. He made *me* feel that way, too. We talked for a long time, actually, and he loved all my ideas for the wedding, including the lanterns and the grapes. He also told me I have a great smile, so I guess the bleaching trays worked. (Thank you, Daf!)

I asked Larry about François and he said François is a great guy. Then he asked me if I'd ever met François's stunning wife, Elizabeth. Here's the skinny: F. (I'll call François that from now on) met Elizabeth at a wedding he and Larry worked on together six years ago. Larry thinks F. is thirty-eight, so that would have made him thirty-two back then, my age exactly. Apparently, Elizabeth is quite a bit older than he is, so they got married very quickly and tried to have kids, but they don't have any, so obviously something went wrong there. Larry said Elizabeth is an angel but that he never sees her anymore because she's very into yoga now and spends all her time teaching. She does some kind of very special yoga and has a lot of celebrity disciples like Christy Turlington, Gwyneth Paltrow, and Sting. Larry says he took one of her classes once and almost had to be hospitalized afterward. He said Elizabeth can stand on her head for, like, twenty minutes. She sounds thin.

She sounds intimidating. She sounds like she exists, which is a little bit more sound than I want to hear.

Second Fitting

HOW'S THE DRESS COMING ALONG? I'm beside myself. I told Shelly about the dress and she told Mom, and then Mom—without telling me—called Vera Wang and told them to charge her credit card and to make the fabric *satin* instead of *organza*! I went for the first fitting, and the dress now weighs eight billion pounds! Plus, the satin doesn't hug my body the way the organza did, so I look pudgy again, even *with* my 34B's and thinner thighs. (Since the tendinitis, I haven't been able to do a thing and I've gained three-tenths of a pound. But I'm allowed to get back to Pilates at the end of the week and I can do ab and pec work, thank God.)

Have I mentioned that the dress, which now costs *ten* thousand dollars with the satin, is UGLY???? I'm totally devastated, but it's way too late to make changes, so I'm just going to have to deal.

Sometimes I really hate my mother. I also feel like I can't talk to Michael anymore. I can't even talk to Dafna. Her relationship with Dan is going so well, she's just full of joy and enthusiasm, and it's fucking irritating. The only person I feel like I can talk to right now is F. We went out for drinks two nights ago and he told me about his wife and about how all she cares about now is yoga. Apparently, she's off on some yoga retreat in Costa Rica until the end of the month. He said they got married too quickly, and then he asked me if I'm absolutely positive Michael is the man for me. I'm obviously having some very serious doubts about Michael since I made out with F. for about an hour after we had drinks. He tastes like tobacco, and I was so wet that I thought I'd die without having him inside me. He told me he thought it would be a big mistake to rush into anything. When I got home, I went straight over to the sofa and seduced Michael, who was sound asleep on it and grateful for the wake-up blow job, but I pretended it was F. the whole time. I wonder if Michael can tell? Does it matter?

Choosing the Menu

NOW'S THE TIME TO MEET *with the caterer and decide what everyone will eat. Do you want food stations during hors d'oeuvres or do you want passed food? Do you want a caviar bar or a chef preparing sushi? Do you want filet mignon or do you want to give each guest a choice of fish or fowl? How big a statement do you want to make with your wine selection?*

Notes:

I have good news and bad news. I'll start with the bad news, since I've sort of made that a precedent. The bad news is that we almost lost Daddy at the museum. I mean we literally almost lost him. What a nightmare. I don't know if we will ever be a family again. How did it even happen? We were all so drunk, it's hard to make sense of it.

Basically, we began tasting hors d'oeuvres—some sushi rolls, spanakopita, little truffle thingies, foie gras on toast—and out came the first three glasses of wine. I mean three glasses for each of us, not three glasses total. The caterer warned us to pace ourselves, but Mom always rushes the first glass no matter what anyone says and then she starts getting loopy. You would have thought that after planning Shelly's wedding she would have known to take it easy, that there were going to be twelve or more wines to taste. But there you go. She went and rushed the first three—not just the first one—and she was already sloppy by the time we'd moved on to the consommé. (By the way, what is it about consommé that's so great? It's like knocking back a little salty water. I don't want it, but Mom and Dad and the caterer agreed it can't be beat.)

Anyway, on and on it went and we all just got drunker and drunker, only Mom was superdrunk, which I've never even seen before, and we were all laughing hysterically because Daddy burped and then Mom said, "My first husband's father burped like that during his toast at the wedding." Well, *that* was a buzz kill. We were all like, "What did you just say?" Mom just giggled and said, "Oh, don't listen to me. I'm too drunk to make sense." But Dad got sober in about a second flat and insisted Mom explain herself. And then I was seriously curious, so I was also pressing her to explain. And then Mom says super matter-of-factly, "I was married briefly before I met you, Jerry. It was irrelevant, so I never mentioned it."

Dad's eyes got really wide and then he just keeled right over like a tree falling in the woods. He almost crushed me! Thank God the paramedics came quickly. Turns out Dad had a heart attack. Just like that. Just from the news. Or maybe he would have had one anyway, but that's the way it went, so it felt very $a + b = c$.

The good news is that Dad's all right. He had triple-bypass surgery but is recovering well. The bad news is that he's not talking to Mom right now and Mom has started smoking. I had no idea she ever smoked, but apparently she was a chain-smoker until 1972. Virginia Slims, can you believe it? How totally tacky is that?

The other good news is that we did decide on a menu.

FIRST COURSE: seared scallops with champagne
SECOND COURSE: salad with blue cheese, walnuts, endive, and truffles
PALATE CLEANSER: raspberry sorbet (Corton-Charlemagne)
MAIN COURSE: lamb with a selection of winter vegetables (St. Emilion)
BEFORE DESSERT: a selection of cheeses served with port (Fonseca)
DESSERT: individual chocolate soufflés, wedding cake, assorted chocolates and cookies on each table (Château d'Yquem)

Tomorrow I go for a colonic and then I begin a supervised fast with the same nutritionist who did last year's *Sports Illustrated* cover model.

Music for the Ceremony

YOU MAY WANT TO DEFER *to your mother on musical selections, since she probably knows the classical canon better than you. Feel free to choose nonclassical music, but don't expect anyone to think it's classy. "Here Comes the Bride" is always a fine choice.*

Notes:

I went over to F.'s apartment last night and we listened to a bunch of classical records. He helped me choose the piece I want to walk down the aisle to: Fauré's Pavane. He said the last bride he photographed walked down the aisle to it and it was magnificent. Then he told me *I'm* magnificent and we made love. I'm not going to lie. We made love on the black-and-white carpet in his living room and it was incredible. F.'s lips are so soft and mushy and he has this way of sucking my tongue so it feels like it's going to come out of my mouth. It actually hurts a little, but it's so different, it really turns me on. I wish I could actually feel what he does to my breasts. It looks like it would feel amazing, but I can't feel anything in that vicinity since the surgery. He licks my scars and calls me his "wounded bird." Have I mentioned he's not circumcised? I'd never seen an uncircumcised penis before and admit I was terrified and wishing it came with an instruction manual, but after some basic experimentation I have to admit it works pretty much the same as a circumcised one.

Should I call off the engagement? I've never felt so frightened and exhilarated in my entire life.

Choosing the Right Band

THE RIGHT BAND *is absolutely critical. You want everyone up and dancing, and the right band can achieve that, while the wrong band can cast a pall over your wedding like nothing else short of the groom not showing up. Consider every single song they'll play. Make sure you like each one. Do you or your fiancé have any particular favorites? Ask the bandleader if he'd be willing to learn them. Do your parents know any famous singers or musicians? Ask them to perform. It's always impressive. Do your parents have ties with any of the major cultural institutions in the city? Perhaps Plácido Domingo could be persuaded to do a short aria between courses.*

Notes:

If things weren't tense enough between me and Mom, now they've totally disintegrated. I flew to Rio (I used miles) to hear the Big Bang (Dafna heard them at some rain forest benefit) and have asked them to put January 21 on hold. I also reserved a DJ to come in at 11:00 P.M. so we can really rock. But Mom has shocked me, yet again, by declaring the fact that she's had the Tripp Pane band on hold since the day after I got engaged.

She's already made the down payment to reserve them and won't get her money back if she cancels!

I hate the Tripp Pane band. They're for old fogies. I don't know why Mom is so insistent on ruining my wedding. I've tried appealing to Dad, but he says he's sure everything will be beautiful, and then he usually walks away.

On a separate note, F. went with me to Rio and we had a ball. I can't believe someone with an eye as sophisticated as his actually finds me beautiful, but he does. He thinks I'm a knockout. He tells me all the time that I look like Brigitte Bardot. What am I supposed to do now? F. has told me straight out that he doesn't have plans to divorce his wife at the moment and certainly doesn't know where our relationship is headed. And Michael and I come from such similar backgrounds and have so many friends in common—not to mention the fact that my mother will most likely disown me if I cancel the wedding. I haven't told anyone about F., not even Dafna. He's my special gift to myself; the first thing I've ever done that Dafna didn't do first. She even had Michael first. F. is mine-all-mine-all-mine. Well, not really. He's his wife's, but for now I'm willing to pretend.

The Big Name Change

OH, PLEASE. DON'T BE TIRESOME ABOUT THIS: *keeping your own name is so passé. Just remember to change all your identity cards, such as your passport, driver's license, credit cards,*

frequent-flier cards, gym membership card, and anything else that
states to the world who you have become.

Notes:

It's over. I called it off. While we were at the Willow Lake
reunion, Ali Cohen asked if she could interview us and find out
what we consider to be the most important moments of our
lives. Dafna kept saying how mine was so easy, I could just say
getting engaged to Michael, but the more I thought about it,
the more terrifying that sounded. I don't want that to be the
most important moment of my life. I've been nothing but
unhappy since I agreed to his proposal, and I feel better now,
although I'm very disoriented and sad: sad because I wasted the
last year of my life; sad because I wasn't courageous enough to
do this sooner; sad because of all the energy Mom's put into
this wedding; sad because it's depressing to break up with
someone you thought you were going to spend the rest of your
life with, even if you're not happy with him. Thank goodness for
Prozac. I called Dr. Sayers and he's upping my dose.

It was pretty painless in the end. I met Michael at the
Starbucks closest to his office around 10:30 this morning and
told him I thought we should call off the wedding. He looked at
me as if I had just told him we should call off our plans to go
for a walk, then just nodded his head and said, "Agreed."

I didn't tell Michael about F., but I will sleep at F.'s tonight.
Hopefully, Michael will have packed enough stuff that he can

stay at a hotel until the weekend. Then I can go up to my parents' house and Michael can move out. We've agreed that he'll find a new place, since I worked harder than he did on the decor in our current apartment. He told me he's always hated the Upper East Side anyway and welcomes the chance to move to TriBeCa (ick), so that's that.

I feel like I just lost twenty pounds. Wait—I *did* just lose twenty pounds. Well then, I feel like I'm walking on new feet. I feel giddy, in a strange way. I feel brave. I feel free. I have no job, no fiancé. I have F. for tonight, but Elizabeth gets back from some yoga retreat she's been on in Mexico, and then who knows what will happen? I don't care. I didn't call off the wedding for F. I called it off because I'm not in love with Michael. I'm not even in *like* with Michael. He's just someone who's appropriate for me to marry because he fits all the right specs. Well, fuck it. So I'll turn thirty-three without a ring on my finger. *All right.* So I might not have children. *Yes I will!* I just know I will. I refuse to accept the fact that love has passed me by. So I won't have a wedding at the Temple of Dendur next time around. Good. I don't care if I get married in the back of a pickup truck. I just know that next time I'll do it my own way.

I'm now at Starbucks on Seventy-sixth and Third (I'll confess, I'm latte'd out). My parents just left. They said they were sad for me but not shocked. Neither of them tried to talk me out of the decision. They both agreed that if I feel it isn't right, it probably isn't. I thought for sure Mom was going to rant and rave and cry and threaten me, but she was hugely supportive. She hugged me and told me how brave she thinks I am. The one little problem is that I can't seem to stop crying now. Better head home. Gotta figure out what to do with all the loot. Should I give it to Goodwill, or will the stores take it back? I'm not the first bride who's called off a wedding. I'm sure there's a protocol for all this. I just need to learn it.

Hell, I did it! I called off my engagement. I am now a person who's called off an engagement, like Nikki Bernstein and Pam Miller. Like Julia Roberts and Jennifer Lopez. But you know what? All those girls got married in the end, didn't they?

And here's another thing: at least it's something Dafna didn't do first.

Ali Downtown

Ali felt like cheering by the time she finished reading Beth's diary. Thank goodness Beth had stood up for herself, but at what price? Ali shuddered. Beth would never be able to get her breasts back, or her thighs, but at least if she wanted to reenter the workforce, she could. Ali went to the phone in the kitchen. "I think you're very brave," she said when Beth picked up.

"I shouldn't have given you the whole book," Beth said. She sounded a little brighter. "I just couldn't imagine recounting it all this afternoon. I'm just wiped out. I'm sure you understand."

"Of course," Ali said. She shared the exhaustion. The baby was growing and she was ready for bed most evenings by 7:00 P.M. Ali offered to messenger the book back to Beth, then asked if she wanted to do an on-camera interview. Beth declined and Ali told her it was all right, then added that if Beth had a change of heart, she should give a call.

Ali hung up and went to the fridge. She was starving, but there wasn't anything appealing in it. She opened the pantry and removed a box of chocolate Pop-Tarts and a jar of peanut butter.

There had to be a way to get Beth to talk on-camera. There had to be a way to get *all* of them to talk. So far, she'd heard back from everyone but Wendy and Arden. Even Laura Berman had responded—via her secretary—that she'd be in touch soon. It was irritating that Wendy couldn't give her the courtesy of a reply. Ali was sure Wendy had received her letter. She'd taken the address straight off the updated Willow Lake contact sheet.

Arden was the real mystery. Ali had sent the letter to an address she had found on an ancient Willow Lake list from 1979. Whether or not the Finkelsteins still lived in Great Neck, though, was anyone's guess.

"Hello!" Renny shouted, bursting into the apartment. He'd been out for a run and came into the kitchen dripping with sweat. "How'd it go with today's J.A.P. chronicle?"

"Great," she said, watching as Renny drained a bottle of Gatorade.

Ali marveled at his muscles while he gulped. He'd gotten in great shape since he'd had so much free time this year. It was the only thing keeping him sane. There was still no business in the city. He had shot a few films out of town, but with Ali pregnant, he didn't want to go farther than a few hours' drive.

In a way, Ali wished he would. She needed some time away from him to think about why she was refusing to get married. He had said they could run down to City Hall; that they didn't have to go through the hell Beth had gone through.

Maybe she *wanted* that hell. . . .

Renny plunged his head under the faucet and let out a whoop of pleasure.

No! It *wasn't* what she wanted at all. She *didn't* want to choose a long white gown; *didn't* want the hassle of the gifts and the thank-you notes; *didn't* want to worry about where to throw the party; *didn't* want to hire a band and worry about bridesmaids and think about wedding vows and what her family would think of her marrying an Irish Catholic boy from Yonkers.

It was all about the dollar anyway. As long as women felt they had to get married in wedding dresses, people in that business would continue to overcharge for the dresses and women would continue stressing over finding the perfect gown and achieving a perfect body to look perfect in the perfect gown. It was all a giant scam by the capitalists. Make women feel insecure enough and they'll spend on anything.

"My parents are coming into the city," Renny said, drying off with a kitchen towel. "They want to know if we're up for dinner. Whaddya say?"

"Tonight?" Ali asked, unable to mask her annoyance. It wasn't that she didn't like to be with his parents. She far preferred Pete and Fiona McCann to her own parental options. But she was exhausted after such a big day uptown and also decidedly nauseous suddenly. She pushed the Pop-Tart away and said, "Please don't wipe your sweat on the kitchen towel, honey. That's what the towels in the bathroom are for." She sounded like her mother. It was scary.

"I can go out with them by myself," Renny said, ignoring her request. "Or else they can come here and we can break the news. I think it's time, don't you? My mom's gonna go ballistic. *Come on.* Her first grandkid? She's gonna go nuts!" Renny hung the towel neatly on the hook above the sink and turned to her, awaiting a response.

It wouldn't be that bad, telling Pete and Fiona. They were much more accepting people in certain ways than Ali's parents.

They were different. They had different expectations, not only for themselves but also for their kids. Renny's younger sister, Deirdre, never went to college and was currently working as a hairdresser in White Plains. Fiona and Pete were happy she liked her job and were pleased that she was dating the bartender at the Best Western near her salon. "As long as she's happy," they always said, and when they said it, it seemed sincere. They didn't undercut it by rolling their eyes or smirking, like someone in Ali's family might. Whenever Ali's mother said, "As long as you're happy," she always sighed and seemed resigned, as if being happy was a concession.

"As long as you're happy" was the McCanns' mantra. Their lives had been defined by concessions, and they seemed happier for it. Fiona and Pete were happy people—not that happy was synonymous with dullness or complacency. They were both very intelligent, but they seemed somehow less complex than Ali's parents, or perhaps they were both more satisfied with themselves. Renny's father, or "Pop," as Renny called him, was a retired electrician who played golf on the public course near his house in Yonkers when the weather allowed, and worked on his carpentry on cold days or when his back was hurting. Fiona had spent thirty-nine years as a public school librarian and had one more year to serve before she would retire and get her pension. Fiona planned to train her rosebushes to climb over the front fence once she had more time to herself and to travel a little, since neither she nor Pete had ever been out of the country. She wanted to go to Ireland to see where their ancestors were from, and to Paris and London to see the Eiffel Tower and Buckingham Palace. Pete wanted to go to Rome to see the Vatican and to Vietnam to see where his youngest brother had died.

Pete and Fiona were staunch Catholics, the kind who went to mass every Sunday and volunteered to teach Sunday school. According to Renny, Pete and Fiona didn't pass judgment against you if you didn't follow their faith. They didn't think you needed to be Catholic to be a good person. They weren't opposed to Renny's relationship with Ali because they saw that it made him happy, and that's what they cared about above all. Still, Ali knew they'd be crushed if he didn't have a Catholic wedding; even more crushed if the baby wasn't baptized.

And that's where the deep internal conflict over religion blinked awake deep inside Ali's mind, where it usually slept, and growled. It growled and bared its teeth and once or twice had swiped a claw, because she was a Jew. There was no way to deny it, and she didn't want to deny it, either. She was a Jew, even if she didn't do anything particularly Jewish. There was no way she could get married in a church; no way her child was going to be baptized. In fact, if it was a boy, she'd have to have a *bris*.

She was a Jew. If the Nazis ever came back to power, she'd be hauled off to the camps with the rest of them and she wouldn't try to pass herself off as something else. True, there wasn't a devout bone in her body. True, she didn't believe in God. True, she felt religion was something man had constructed to organize people and give their lives structure—as much a political tool as a psychological and spiritual one, which in and of itself didn't make it a bad thing, but she didn't believe in burning bushes any more than she believed in virgin mothers, saints, prophets, or messiahs. True, she and Renny had a Christmas tree. True, her sisters were offended she hadn't once joined them on a Friday when they took their kids to Tot Shabbat at Midtown Temple.

But she was a Jew nevertheless, as surely as she was a five-foot-six-inch pregnant white female.

Yes, she was a Jew—a Jew who loved the son of two devout Irish Catholics. If she told them tonight that she was both carrying their son's child and refusing to get married, it would certainly break their hearts, even with their great desire that their son do whatever made him happy. Of course, Ali wasn't making him happy right now at all. Things were tense where they used to be easy; Renny was apathetic, when he used to be so charged with enthusiasm about everything he did. He wanted to get married and was clearly taking her refusal as a personal rejection rather than as a reflection of her ideology. He didn't want to have a bastard, he had told her. She could keep her name; they could have a ceremony at City Hall; nothing had to change; he would even *convert*. Still, the thought of getting married made her feel overwhelmingly tired and sad.

"So what should we do?" Renny said. "They're waiting to hear back."

"Let's go out," Ali said, too tired to fight Renny anymore. "And you're right. It's time to tell. My tits are like two beach balls. If we don't start telling people soon, they're going to think I had a boob job."

Katz's Deli was not a fancy place. It was a cafeteria with long communal tables, fluorescent lights overhead, jars of pickles on the counters, and cylinders of salami hanging from the ceiling. As one of the oldest Jewish delis in New York, it was a standard tourist destination. Ali hated it, since it reeked of raw fish and onions, smells she hated even when not pregnant, but it was one of Pete's favorites—he claimed they made the best pastrami sandwich in the tristate area—he made a point to get one whenever he came down to the Lower East Side to visit them. It was not the sort of place Ali had imagined sharing the biggest news of her life, especially not with two other families and a young couple clearly on a date sitting beside her.

Nothing was going as Ali had imagined, either.

"No, it's not that I'm not thrilled," Fiona was saying for the umpteenth time, the tears falling faster than she was able to wipe them away with the back of her hand.

"Get ahold of yourself," Pete said, clearly mortified that his wife was crying in public.

Renny, who was holding his mother's hand, suggested a walk.

Fiona declined, then said maybe it was a good idea. Pete stood up, pulled out her chair, and the two left the deli, promising to return shortly.

Once they were gone, Ali and Renny eyed each other miserably from across the table.

"I had no idea she'd be so upset," Renny said apologetically. "I thought she'd be ecstatic."

"She is," Ali said. "You heard her. She's just upset because we aren't married and we aren't *getting* married."

Renny looked at her with the same look she had just seen in his father's eyes. It was a look of tolerance but not friendliness.

"And if we told her we were getting married under a *chuppah*? What do you think she'd do then? Cry more or cry less?" Ali asked. There was a twinge of hostility in her tone, and she wished she had been able to better control it.

The family in the seats directly next to theirs was doing their best to ignore the situation, but Ali saw the father give Renny a sympathetic look. Ali excused herself to go to the bathroom, where she washed her hands and looked at herself in the mirror, since she didn't have to pee. What had gone wrong? Pete and Fiona were supposed to have hugged her and Renny and clinked cream sodas and told her that if she and Renny were happy, they were happy, too. They weren't supposed to have received the news without emotion, then look at each other in fear. They weren't supposed to have asked, "What do you *mean*?" Fiona wasn't supposed to have cried for twenty minutes. Pete wasn't supposed to have pushed his plate away, his beloved pastrami sandwich half-eaten.

When Pete and Fiona returned to the table, they were all smiles and Ali and Renny weren't talking.

"Fiona and I are extremely happy for both of you," Pete began, his eyes only on his son. "We're certainly very excited at the prospect of becoming grandparents."

"We just don't understand why you don't want to become husband and wife," Fiona broke in, her mild tone no mask for the urgency of the question.

"Mother," Renny said, "I'm not sure it's really your business—"

"It's *me*," Ali said, unable to bear it for another second. "I'm sorry. I don't believe in marriage. It's just not for me."

Fiona allowed the words to sink in before she said, "But why on earth not? There's nothing more sacred—"

"Let's go," Renny said, standing up. "Ali, come on."

"We didn't mean to upset you," Fiona said, following Renny and Ali as they rose and moved toward the door of the deli.

"Let them go," Ali heard Pete say. "Just let them go, dear. Let them go."

✳

As soon as they got home, Ali went straight to the phone in the kitchen and called her mother. If she had to bear the crashing of the heavens as a result of her announcement, let her bear it all at once.

"What is it?" her mother asked, breathless and afraid. "Is everything okay?"

"Everything is fine, Mom. Great. Better than great. I'm calling to share some exciting news." Ali put down the phone and asked Renny to pick up the phone in the living room, which he did.

"Hey there, Sharon," Renny said. He sounded like he'd just run a marathon.

"So what is it?" Sharon asked.

"We're expecting, Mom. I'm due March first."

"Mazel tov!" Sharon shouted. "What wonderful news! Do your sisters know yet?"

Ali told her she was the very first person they'd called.

"This is just fantastic! You know how much I adore you, Renny, and I can tell you I'm going to spoil this grandchild as much as I spoil the rest of them. Can I call your parents, Renny?"

"It's too late," Ali said carefully. "Give us half an hour. Then you can call whoever you want. We're going to hang up now and call Robin."

"Well, this is just wonderful news," Sharon said again. "I'm sure everyone will be thrilled. What about a wedding? Are you going to get married or just elope?"

"Neither," Ali said.

"Well, we'll see about that," Sharon said. "I saw a fantastic spot for a wedding the other day, a new country club in Harrison."

"We have more calls to make," Ali said.

"Well, mazel mazel *mazel* tov!"

And that was the end of the conversation.

Her father came next.

"Isn't that good news!" he said. "Mazel tov. When are you due?"

She told him.

"I trust there'll be a wedding soon?"

"Nope."

A pause.

"Well, anything goes these days. Mazel tov. I'm thrilled."

Next she called her sisters.

"Mazel tov!" Robin said. "When are you due?"

"Mazel tov!" Andrea said. "How exciting! Does Mom know yet?"

"Mazel tov!" Karen said. "Who else have you told?"

"Mazel tov!" Mara said. "Are you and Renny getting married?"

"Not now," Ali said.

"That's so *rock star!*" Mara said. "Can I tell the world?"

"You can tell whoever you want," Ali said.

And then there was no one else to call.

The apartment felt emptier after she hung up the phone. It felt very quiet, but not in a bad way. It was peaceful. Then Renny came into the kitchen and got on his knees in front of her chair.

"You're so beautiful," he said, unbuttoning her shirt, which was really one of his: an old, soft, blue button-down he was wearing the warm spring night they walked across the Brooklyn Bridge and had dinner alfresco under a cherry blossom tree in full bloom. Renny put his cheek against her swollen belly, then kissed it. "That wasn't so bad now, was it?"

Ali shook her head as Renny reached up to cup one of her breasts. It was swollen and sensitive now, but he caressed her gently and she allowed herself to relax and enjoy his touch. Soon his lips were on her collarbone, her neck, her shoulder. Renny had soft lips and a kind of ripe pomegranate-nectarine sensuality that never failed to arouse her.

His mouth was working its way down past her navel when the phone began to ring.

"Fuck it," Renny said. "Let it go." He lifted her off the chair and sat her up on the table so her legs were dangling over the edge. In one quick movement, he removed her underpants and jeans and spread her legs. He pulled his own jeans and boxers down and took her right away.

"Baby," she murmured, trying her best to ignore the insistent ring of the phone. Finally, the machine picked up.

"Um, Ali?" The voice was instantly recognizable, even through the haze of Ali's mounting orgasm. "This is Arden Finkelstein? You sent me a letter?"

Confessions of a Dirty Jew

✳

Arden woke up disoriented, hot, and terribly thirsty. Next to her in the vast bed, Jude slept peacefully while Sushi snored in her dainty Pomeranian way on the pink silk pillow in the corner of the bedroom. Outside the apartment, trucks groaned up and down Hudson Street as they hauled away debris from Ground Zero. The air in the bedroom was stifling, but Arden didn't dare open the window lest she poison herself by breathing in all the toxins she was certain were out there. She pressed herself into Jude but was too hot to get comfortable, so she got out of bed and went to the kitchen for a glass of water and a cigarette.

While she smoked, she studied the "Save the Date" card to Willow Lake Camp's one hundredth reunion, which would be held the following August. It was still on the counter, where she had dropped it after opening it earlier that evening. How they had ever managed to track her down was a mystery; *why* was another.

Arden picked it up, went over to the sink, and set it on fire. She watched it burn with a strange mixture of sadness and elation until the flames danced too close to her fingertips. Then she dropped the charred remains into the sink and turned on the water. The paper disintegrated immediately and flew down the drain on its way to nowhere, a destination Arden almost envied, given her current predicament.

Would she ever come up with another idea?

She slipped back into bed. Three-fifteen turned to 3:30, and still sleep wouldn't come. She thought about masturbating but was too lazy in the end, so she watched a rerun of *I Love Lucy* with the volume on mute until sleep thankfully reclaimed her at some point during the episode.

She woke up at 11:00 A.M., exhausted and alone. Wrapped in a pink silk robe, she dragged herself into the kitchen, got a Diet Coke from the refrigerator, and wandered over to the divan in the living room, where she deposited herself with a grace and hopelessness someone, she felt, should have witnessed.

As tired as Arden felt, it was hard to stay calm. She reached under the divan and retrieved a cigarette from a pack she had stuck between some loose springs. It had been a month since the World Trade Center had gone down five blocks away, but between the terrorist threats and the vile, smelly air in her neighborhood, she was sure every breath she drew was bringing her closer to an early death. She doubted she would reach thirty-two. She would die at thirty-one, a terrible number: odd.

Arden hated odd numbers. That's why she and Jude had bought their current hateful apartment. Their old hateful apartment had been on the ninth floor of a West Side prewar building, and although the space had been charming and a bona fide movie star had lived on the floor above them, Arden felt, after consulting both a numerologist and a feng shui specialist, that the vibe was entirely too negative on an odd-numbered floor. She would never be able to create her follow-up one-woman show if she stayed there. At least that's what the numerologist and feng shui specialist had concurred. "Who could create anything on the ninth floor?" asked the feng shui specialist, who suggested they move to four, six, eight, or ten.

Arden smoked the cigarette listlessly. When she was through, she dropped the butt into the almost-empty can of Diet Coke and wallowed in her unhappiness as the cigarette fizzled out. A thin wisp of smoke wove its way out of the opening and she watched, disconsolate, as it did a bewitching dance into the air and disappeared.

Smoke! She sat bolt upright. That's what she would do! Smoke as a metaphor! She hurried into her office and grabbed her yellow legal pad. "Smoke," she wrote in minuscule script that leaned backward, as if the words were fighting against a stiff wind, "a story about"—she had to pause. She had no idea what it was a story about.

Arden reached into her desk drawer and got another cigarette, returned to the kitchen for another can of Diet Coke, and shuffled back to the bedroom, where she propped herself up in bed and stared at the tangerine walls she now hated despite having decided on the color with mad excitement only a few months earlier.

Nothing mattered anymore. Everything was an exhausting blur. Only one thing was certain: she didn't have any new ideas.

She closed her eyes and tried to think in an orderly, calm manner about the events that had led to this terrible moment of malaise. One year and three months ago, she had been basking in glory after her first solo performance piece had closed. It had been a downtown sensation, complete with her photograph in *TimeOut New York,* and positive reviews in the *Voice* and *Paper.*

Things had happened quickly after that. She broke up with the show's producer, her then-fiancé, Bennét Blitz, the famous party promoter, and hooked up with Jude Rosenthal, the tall, rakish son of a millionaire. Jude had dark hair that fell to the middle of his back, just like hers, and was making his name as a manager/promoter/general wheeler and dealer of up-and-comers like herself. Together they spent a sex-saturated, shopping spree–punctuated, nightclub-restaurant-lounge-resort-chain-smoking gluttonous month. Then Jude told her it was time to kick her career into high gear since her name was still on everyone's lips.

He arranged a trip for her to L.A. She spent a few weeks trying to put together a West Coast run of her show, but it never came together. She was bored with L.A. by then and ready to get to work on her next show. The only problem was, she didn't have any fresh ideas. Jude was paying her hotel expenses, so she stayed on in L.A. for another few weeks, hoping for inspiration but instead ending up only with a good tan.

Jude thought she might need a real vacation in order to release her creative spirit. He sent her a ticket and met her in Bora Bora. On their first night he presented her with a magnificent aquamarine engagement ring. They decided to get married in a beach ceremony officiated by a half-naked monk of some sort and returned to New York together with high hopes for the future.

On their first morning back, Jude got up at 7:00 A.M. and worked out before going to the office at 9:00. Arden joined him and was fully exercised, showered, caffeinated, and nicotined when she sat down at her desk at 10:00 A.M., pen poised over her yellow legal pad, ready to compose her award-winning follow-up show. The only problem was, she still didn't have any ideas.

She decided the 7:00 A.M. gym routine was a detriment to her natural creative cycle, and so on subsequent mornings she slept in until she felt like getting up. Still, she had no new ideas. She cut her glossy dark hair from midback-length to shoulder-length and dyed it chestnut, dyed it blond, dyed it black: nothing. She tried massage. She tried acupuncture. She consulted an astrologer. She consulted a psychic. Jude suggested tantric sex, but sex had never really been something Arden enjoyed, so she didn't bother trying. Jude suggested a week at the beach, but Arden found it boring after three days and asked if they could leave. They bought a new car, an adorable light blue convertible with a tan interior, but there was nowhere to go in it and parking was expensive and three long blocks away from their apartment, so it didn't help, either. At one point, she even cut bangs. Still, she had no fresh ideas.

Arden's first show had been about her coming-of-age: about how she had gone into the city on Saturday nights when she was fifteen with some older friends of hers from Great Neck South and about how she had hooked up one night at the Palladium with a once-famous punk rocker who was attracted to her wispy figure and advanced sexual know-how. She then described her instant rise to trivial fame when the then-famous punk rocker's song "My One and Only Arden" hit the top of the charts.

The show went on to chronicle her decision to drop out of high school and follow her famous rocker on the road. She was totally candid about how she had quickly gotten addicted to coke and booze; and about how, in a rare lucid moment in a suite at the Detroit Marriott Marquis, she had found her punk rocker in bed with two other women; and about how, in a not quite as lucid moment, she had opened the bathroom door of the tour bus to discover her rocker getting his cock sucked by the band's drummer, Hal. She enacted perfectly the Sunday morning she had finally summoned the courage to call her parents and admit that she had radically, supersonically fucked up (on stage, she made the phone call in a spotlight and often managed to cry night after night, which was what all the favorable reviews mentioned).

She then told how her parents had come to get her, Doris and Alan Finkelstein of Great Neck, Long Island, she a housewife and temple volunteer, he an accountant and runner-up for his golf club championship, fifty-plus. She told about how they had sent their Arden to a rehab facility in upstate New York to clean up (at this point in the show, she always yawned and rolled her eyes and said, "Rehab was such a *bore*," and for some reason people always laughed, even though nothing she said was funny). So she got clean ("what*ever*"—more laughter) and her mother got her a job (she always used her hands to make quotation marks around the word *job*, which also got laughs) teaching theater games to toddlers at a temple in Roslyn ("Oh, thank you, Mother, whose single act of creativity was naming her only child Arden, instead of Amy, Jill, Lisa, Sarah, Debbie, Michelle, or Beth"), but Arden hated the little screaming brats, so she quit and moved to the city and roomed with the incredibly famous model Tatushka, whom she had met in rehab. Tatushka was modeling again full-time and got Arden a job as a fashion stylist, something Arden felt was her true calling, until the coke and booze became a problem again and she had to quit and return to Great Neck for a little more R and R.

When she was ready once again for the city, she got a job through another friend from rehab, this time in a gallery showing conceptual art. Within a few short months she become the belle of New York's night scene, now that she was *in, in, in* with a group of Very Fabulous art-world people, most of whose names she could hardly pronounce let alone now recall. All the guys were gay—or should have been—and the women were all competitive and chic, with pointy noses and odd accents, which were explained, when inquired into, by a semester or two spent in Paris, London, Barcelona, or Rome.

It was on one evening, similar to so many (an art opening in Chelsea, a group dinner in one of the trendy restaurants nearby, drinks at a lounge, followed by drinks at a bar, followed by drinks at a nightclub, followed by the offer to do any number of drugs in a VIP room somewhere) that fate put her in contact with Bennét Blitz. Bennét had just broken up with a now-famous B-list movie actress and was looking for someone to fill the void. Enter Arden: five feet seven inches, 102 pounds, dressed to kill and chain-smoking Gauloises. Bennét took one look at her and fell in love, and when he asked her name, the sound of her voice made him certain: she was The Next Big Thing. He announced it to everyone. "Just listen to her!" he proclaimed, urging Arden to tell one of the many anecdotes from her crazy life so people could hear her voice.

Arden had been told before that her voice was unique, but she had never been told it was "fabulous." Some people had even told her she sounded like a cartoon character and accused her of inventing it. One reviewer had said that she spoke like a six-year-old with a cold and that her vocal register seemed permanently stuck at a C above middle C. Another reviewer had pointed out that she snarled when she spoke and ended her sentences on an upturned note, as if they were questions, which made everything she said seem like a judgment against itself.

Whatever people said about it, it was the voice Arden had, and Bennét was the person who found it amazing and inherently funny and urged her to turn her unusual adolescence into a performance-art piece so the whole of New York could get a chance to hear her (that was the point in the show when silver and purple streamers came down from the ceiling and the disco ball started spinning and Arden handed out daisies to the audience members and thanked them for coming).

And then she *became* someone—someone people lined up to see; someone who could get a table at the trendiest restaurant, even without a reservation; someone Jude Rosenthal wanted to fuck, wanted to date, wanted to sign. "My One and Only Arden" even made it back onto the charts for a few weeks, thanks to a contact Jude had at Z100.

Arden stubbed out her cigarette and lit another. What would become of her if no new idea ever arrived? Jude rarely came home before midnight anymore, and when he finally did come home, he was always reeking of pot and scotch and wanting to fuck her doggy-style while slurring obscenities and spanking her ass.

Frankly, Arden was shocked he'd been supportive this long. He'd been tremendous, though, truly. When the feng shui specialist and numerologist agreed that living on an odd floor could be the root of her creative drought, Jude had insisted they move right away. Within a month, they were in this bright, spacious loft in TriBeCa, living on the sixth floor, with several illustrious

Manhattanites as neighbors and one international rock star in the penthouse.

And at first, the move *had* seemed like the perfect antidote. Creativity flowed out of her, but not in the form of a new idea. Instead, she worked like a fiend to create the perfect environment in which to write her next masterpiece, and with such success, *Elle Decor* sent someone to take pictures.

But then one day there was nothing left to decorate, and Jude said it was definitely time for her to develop a new piece. But the summer was upon them and she continuously had to shuttle between TriBeCa and their summer rental in the Hamptons, a situation she found not at all conducive to the creative process.

Finally, Labor Day came and went and Tuesday, September 4, dawned upon them. Arden got up at eight o'clock, walked Sushi, dressed in her favorite pink Pucci dress, and went into her office. She lit some incense and said a few prayers she vaguely recalled from yoga, pulled out a fresh yellow legal pad and a pen, and then realized there was no way she could come up with even one word when the garish yellow of her legal pad clashed so hideously with the aubergine walls. She raced out of the apartment and tore through TriBeCa until she found a store selling white legal pads. Then she returned and tried to write again, but the white was worse. What an anomaly it was in contrast to the subtle, dark, English country house look she had gone for!

A new look was needed. English country house was all wrong for an office anyway. She couldn't even guess what she had been thinking when she had decided on the morose theme. Something light and airy would be better: white—the color of clouds, of snow—white crushed velvet—on the walls!—and a small white crushed-velvet tuft for Sushi to sit on in the corner.

She called a painter and went to the D&D Building in search of the perfect fabric. The new office would be complete by October. That thought alone was enough to lift Arden's flagging spirits. She and Jude flew to South Beach that weekend to celebrate the imminent return of her artistry. They got home Monday night, hungover but tan. After Jude had fallen asleep, Arden lay in bed imagining the journey she would make the next day to the most amazing furniture store near the World Trade Center. It had the perfect white desk for her office displayed in its window! She drifted off to sleep with this happy thought, and her sleep was relieved of the unremembered nightmares that had plagued her most of her life.

Tuesday, September 11, was as magnificent a morning as Arden could have desired. The sky was a brilliant, cloudless aqua, the sun reassuringly strong even at the early hour of eight. She dressed and walked Sushi, then returned to the apartment just as the first plane slammed into the north tower.

9/11. How much odder could you get?

One, three, five, and seven—these were odd numbers she could handle. Nine? Eleven? Arden had often wished she could have gone straight from eight to ten. Then maybe nothing would have happened.

She was nine when her parents took her up to the Berkshires on a family retreat weekend offered by their temple at Camp Schneider, where young families went to learn how to make a proper Jewish home. While Doris and Alan hunkered down with the rabbi and fifteen other couples to learn how to prepare and properly celebrate Shabbat and Havdalah, Arden went to a play group for children, led by the assistant rabbi. He was especially attentive to Arden, since she was the youngest child there and, by even an objective eye, the prettiest. Arden was pleased. She loved his attention, never having received any from her own father, who came home from his accounting job every night drained and disinterested in anything but the evening news and a glass of Metamucil.

By the end of the first day at Camp Schneider, Arden was already giddy with the power she felt she had over the assistant rabbi. She saw that only she could evoke a certain kind of smile on his sweet face, a face covered partially by a soft brown beard that made him look like one of the Muppets. And he did the nicest, most special secret things for her, too! Like picking her to lead the prayer over the challah before dinner and sneaking her extra cookies during dessert.

So she didn't think it was strange at all when he came into her room on the second night while the adults were watching *Exodus* on the big movie screen in the basement of the lodge and the rest of the kids were sleeping; didn't think it was strange when he asked her if she wanted to go with him to get a gift he had for her up in his room. She went willingly, even though his room was up on the third floor in a remote, spooky area of the lodge where the hallways were lined with cobwebs and the older kids said there were ghosts.

The gift was a milk shake from Friendly's. There it was, on the far side of the room, sitting on top of the bureau. Arden started for it, but the assistant rabbi caught her arm and told her she could have the shake but that first she should come and have a bedtime cuddle with him on his bed. He would tell her a bedtime story, the story of Jonah and the whale, and then the next day when he taught it to the other children, she would already know it and could be his helper in telling it.

At first when he cuddled her in close to him, she had felt protected, almost as if God himself had chosen her for some kind of personal intimacy. "Once upon a time, there was a man named Jonah," the assistant rabbi began, and then his finger was making a little circle around one of her nipples through her thin yellow nightgown. Around and around and around it went, occasionally stopping and changing direction. And then somehow his fingers were inside her underpants, and she stopped breathing, stopped feeling, had no recollection of anything but ". . . and Jonah lived happily ever after. The end." And then there was the shake, chocolate, and a warning that God had picked her to play an important role in the world and that he, the assistant rabbi, would personally see that she fulfilled her very special destiny, but she definitely shouldn't tell anyone what had happened between them, because God only chose people who could keep a secret. If she did tell, God would be angry and see to it that her life was cursed. And she didn't want that, did she?

She certainly didn't. And the assistant rabbi *had* been gentle with her and *had* given her a shake and *had* called on her several times when he taught the story of Jonah the next day, so she tried not to mind what had happened, even went up to his room again that afternoon before the buses were set to take everyone back to Great Neck.

Later, when the bus pulled into a rest stop along I-84, he gave her a bag of M&M's and told her God was proud of her; she had passed an important initiation; she would certainly be one of his special select angels on earth, as long as she kept her trap shut.

And so it went every Sunday after Hebrew School, either in the assistant rabbi's study or behind the heavy red velvet curtain that surrounded the ark in the sanctuary. Occasionally it was in his car, and once it even happened in her very own garage after he dropped her off one afternoon from Hebrew School. On it went, Arden dutifully allowing the assistant rabbi to molest her to his heart's content, even hurt her (which he did when he rammed his fingers up inside her or choked her as he shoved his big penis into her mouth), until one day, sometime shortly before her tenth birthday, he disappeared. She remembered the date because he gave her a Ballerina Barbie as an early birthday present, and that was the last time she saw him until her eleventh birthday, which, by coincidence, happened to fall on the weekend when she was sent along with the rest of her fifth-grade class back up to Camp Schneider for a Hebrew School joint retreat with a youth group from Woodmere.

"*Shabbat shalom*," he said to her as she got on the bus. At first, she didn't recognize him without his beard, but as she made her way down the aisle, she felt his stare on her back and knew. She studied the faces of the girls from Woodmere, wondering if any of them were spending afternoons with the assistant rabbi like she had.

If any were, they didn't that weekend.

She pretended to be asleep like the four other girls in her room, but his hands were big, and when he covered her mouth and lifted her out of bed, she didn't fight.

This time, he had ice cream for her and whipped cream and sprinkles, which he put on his penis and made her lick off. He kept putting on more and more sprinkles and more and more ice cream until she told him she was full, and then he said it was his turn to eat ice cream. He took the ice-cream scooper and dipped the handle into the ice cream and then ordered her to lie back. Then Arden felt a tear through her vagina, like a sharp rock slicing up her insides. She remembered nothing more about that night except what he said to her afterward: "Sometimes God gives his angels on earth strange dreams, but everyone knows that what happens in dreams isn't real, so you shouldn't tell anyone what just happened, since it was just a dream and people don't listen to girls who make things up." He said God would punish her, in fact, if she told what she had just dreamed, since he didn't tolerate angels on earth who told people stories that weren't real.

What had *ever* seemed real to Arden after that? Even when she witnessed the plane fly into the first tower and the ensuing inferno that sent people flying through the air close enough for her to see the color of their ties, even when she watched the towers actually collapse and day turned to night like something biblical—even *then* she didn't shed a tear. It was horrible, she *knew,* but she didn't *feel* anything, not deep down. (And the furniture store with the cool desk in the window stayed closed for a month afterward, which put quite a damper on the whole office-renovation plan.)

Naturally, Jude put the apartment on the market. The whole neighborhood had become nothing short of creepy once all the celebs fled, only to be replaced by an endless stream of fat, tacky, American flag–sporting tourists trudging down to get photos of Ground Zero. And the policemen! And the National Guard! How much more of a creative buzz–kill could you get?

Besides, no one else in the building was staying. The art gallery owner on the eighth floor, who always wore the most gloriously chic three-inch mules, even to walk her dog, and her husband, the most handsome young artist, whose papier-mâché rolls of toilet paper were fetching as much as fifteen thousand dollars apiece from certain important international buyers, had moved out a week after the attack and were now safely ensconced in an Upper East Side town house; and the gay fashion designer, who had recently been dubbed "The Most Exciting Undiscovered Talent in Fashion" by a trendsetting English magazine, and his actor/model boyfriend, who was soon to appear in a supporting role in a film starring Gwyneth Paltrow, had sold their fifth-floor one-bedroom apartment and had moved to L.A.; which meant that with the exception of the über-famous but recently rehabbed rock star who lived in the penthouse, there was really no one worth being in the elevator with left in the building.

And Arden knew: ordinariness rubbed off. It was like an insidious germ, and she had no intention of being exposed. It was a drag, though, having the apartment shown. It meant that there were days—today, for example—when she'd have to get up and be dressed and out before noon so she wouldn't be around when the prospective buyers showed up. Arden checked the time: 11:45. She only had fifteen minutes. What would she do today anyway? If only the neighborhood weren't so damn negative, she could at least get something creative done!

The intercom buzzed and the doorman announced the broker and client.

"They're *early*," Arden said. "They'll have to wait."

"My client doesn't really like to wait." (It was the broker on the line now.)

"But I'm still *here*," Arden pointed out.

"It's okay with my client."

"Oh, is it?" Arden smirked. "Well then, come right up."

Arden decided she shouldn't be forced to dress before she was ready, so she tightened the belt of her pink satin robe, lit another cigarette, unlocked the door, and sat herself back on the divan in the living room, where she knew she looked most picturesque.

The doorbell rang.

"Entrez," Arden sneered.

And then a miracle: in walked Arden's heroine, the world-famous performance artist Lydie K.

Into the vestibule and across to the middle of the living room Lydie floated, dressed in form-fitting black leather from head to toe, a magenta silk shirt beneath the jacket the only shock of color. When she reached the center of the living room, she stopped. "I hope you don't mind our barging in," she said, looking like a rare jungle orchid, poised, as she was, on top of her three-inch Sergio Rossis, "but I have a video shoot that was supposed to start at one, and for some reason those assholes just moved it to noon."

"Not at all." Arden smiled. "Cigarette?"

"No thanks. I quit."

Arden took one last drag of her own half-smoked cigarette and dropped it into a Diet Coke can on the floor. "I'm trying to quit, too," she said, standing up.

Her idol turned to the broker and said, "What are we waiting for?"

The broker took Lydie all around the apartment while Arden frantically made the bed in the master bedroom before Lydie and the broker got there.

"You've done a fabulous decorating job," Lydie said when she and the broker finally made their way to the now-immaculate bedroom.

"Not really," Arden said. "I just sort of threw it together."

"I don't know why you'd want to leave this place," Lydie said, "but it's perfect for what I'm looking for, so I'm glad it's on the market."

"Forgive me for asking," Arden squeaked, "and you don't have to answer—I mean, I don't mean to pry"—Arden could feel herself flush—"but, um, don't you live in the San Remo? In a duplex? I just, um, I remember seeing your apartment in—"

"Yeah, *Architectural Digest* did a spread last year."

"So why are you moving down here to a two-bedroom?"

"I'm just looking for a studio," Lydie said, studying the view of Ground Zero from the bedroom windows. "I'm working on a show about September eleventh and I want something near where it all happened. It's very inspirational, you know? This energy. These policemen. The tourists. The *air*."

"If you wear a blindfold and hold your nose," Arden said, trying to be funny but sounding bratty instead, even to herself.

Lydie did a pirouette and said, "I just want to throw open the windows and write! Create! Go, go, gooo!!!" She swept out of the bedroom and grabbed her purse off the floor near the front door. "Shall we?" she said to the broker.

"Thanks for letting us up early," the broker said to Arden, who had followed breathlessly. "We'll talk."

"Good luck," Arden said.

She could hear the sharp click of Lydie's spikes on the terrazzo floor in the vestibule, then the sound of the elevator arriving, opening, closing. . . .

Arden remained in the doorway, unable to move. Inside her

bony chest, her heartbeat accelerated. A thin film of sweat had formed at her hairline and her breath came short and fast. *"Lydie fucking K.,"* she whispered. Then she propelled herself across the hallway, into the kitchen, and over to the telephone.

It rang before she could start dialing. It was Jude.

"Oh thank *God*," she said, sighing loudly in relief. "You're not going to fucking believe what just happened! Lemme just get a cig."

"It's done," Jude said when she got back on the line. "Start packing. I accepted an offer on the apartment. As soon as you decide—"

"What?" Arden screamed. "No, we can't—who—you already heard from Lydie's broker?"

"What, are you psychic, babe?"

Arden lit her cigarette and sucked furiously. After a tense exhale, she said, "Well, you'll have to call back and tell her we've changed our minds. I finally have an idea. And I need to be in this apartment to execute it. And I don't want any more upheaval in my life right now. *Please.*"

"Arden," Jude said in that overly calm tone that made Arden want to vomit, "you're being—"

"I am *not* being unreasonable. Didn't you fucking hear me? I have an *idea.*"

"That's great news, doll face. What's the gist?"

Arden told him she didn't want to dilute it by overdiscussing things. She just wanted to start writing.

Jude asked her what he was supposed to do.

"Talk to her," Arden implored. "For God's sake, change her fucking mind."

She hung up, flung open the windows, and inhaled. Her nose wrinkled involuntarily. "Pew!" she said to Sushi, who was watching with interest. She slammed the window shut, scaring Sushi, who ran out of the room barking, and went straight to her office.

Out came the yellow legal pad. Out came the pen. At the top of the page she wrote in her tiny backward-slanting script:

THE DAY LYDIE K. CAME TO VISIT

I wasn't expecting anyone. She just came, like anybody else, with a broker, to see my apartment. Lydie K. Lydie fucking K., standing with a broker in the living room.

She paused. What next? What, exactly, did she intend to say? Shit, she'd *had* an idea. It had been there. She'd felt it. But now it was gone. "Fucking shit," she whispered. She picked up the phone and called Jude.

"He's on the other line," his secretary said. "Would you like to leave a message?"

Arden told his secretary to have Jude call her back the *second* he was off the other line, then slammed down the receiver and stood, hand still on the phone, feet rooted to the floor, waiting for Jude to call back. He didn't that moment, or the next. Outside, Arden could hear the trucks honking and groaning under their loads as they jostled up Hudson Street. "Move it!" she heard someone shout.

I live five blocks from Ground Zero, she added to her new piece.

Arden dropped the pen and picked up the phone again. Jude was still on the other line.

"What the *fuck!*" she screamed at the secretary, her voice climbing into the stratosphere by the time she reached the end of the sentence. Then she composed herself enough to say in a lowish-pitched, calmer voice, "Please have him call me when he's available."

He didn't call for an hour, during which time Arden smoked five more cigarettes and changed outfits, until finally she settled on a navy pleated miniskirt, which she paired with a tight burgundy wool sweater, navy-pink-and-white argyle kneesocks, and low-heeled black Mary Janes. She outlined her large brown eyes in dark liner and shadow, and braided her brown hair in plaits down the sides of her head. After some contemplation, she decided the outfit would work only with supershort bangs, so she got out her scissors and cut some, a decision she instantly regretted when she remembered that Lydie had once said in an interview that bangs were the equivalent of milk: fashion suicide.

Lydie's hair was shoulder-length, layered, and very blond.

Arden sat down on the closed toilet seat with Sushi in her arms and cried. When she was done crying, she washed her face and reapplied her makeup. Finally, Jude called back.

"Hey," he said, as if nothing much were up. It was completely infuriating.

"So?" Arden demanded.

"So, what?" Jude said. Then he shouted, "Tell him to hold!"

"Did you retract our apartment?"

"Working on it. Not sure we should. Lydie's a pretty—*Tell him I'll call back!*—Lydie's a pretty cool cat and she's willing to pay top dollar. Can you hold a minute, puss?"

There was nothing left to smoke of her cigarette and she ground the smoldering butt angrily into the envelope that the camp reunion "Save the Date" card had come in.

"I gotta take that call," Jude said when he came back on the line. "Honestly, I'd give some thought to where you'd like to move."

"Will you just fucking *talk* to Lydie and explain the situation? Or do you want me to do it?"

"I'm having a drink with her at six," Jude said. "Just chill out and start working on your new idea. I'll be home late. I forgot to tell you. I have a dinner. *Tell him I'll be right there!*" he shouted. Then, in that overly calm voice, he added, "*Ciao, bellissima.* Don't wait up."

Arden slammed down the phone and stomped into her office. Why should Jude have drinks with Lydie and not invite her to join them? She grabbed a pen, picked up her legal pad, and began to write ferociously:

> *She was smaller than she looks on TV and in the movies. She was smaller even than she looks onstage, which I suppose is part of what makes her such an amazing talent—such an amazing presence. She wanted to buy my—*

Arden paused, crossed out the word *my* and replaced it with *our.* She crossed that out, too, and settled on:

> *—***the** *apartment to use as a studio. She wanted to be down here near Ground Zero, to smell the smelly air, hear the groan of the trucks, see all the tourists and policemen and the National Guardsmen—*

Arden stopped writing again, revolted by the image of all those stupid-looking Rangers in their ugly brown uniforms and Smokey the Bear hats. The outfits reminded her of her camp uniform, and she hated anything that evoked that loathsome place.

Back to the legal pad.

Lydie is the one who made me realize, Write what you know.
Write who you are. Write your reality. Well, my reality is this
apartment. This apartment five blocks from Ground Zero,
where I can still see the smoke rising from the—

Arden stopped again. There was Lydie, eager to fling open the
windows, to marinate in the dust, the stink, the asbestos, the
sticky, irritating patriotism. Arden was at a loss. This just wasn't
her subject. (If she had to hear "God Bless America" one more
fucking time—)

She put down her pen and went to the window. Out on
Hudson Street, people were rushing this way and that, all on
their way somewhere.

"I should get a job," she said to Sushi. What would she do,
though, and why? She didn't need any money. Not married to
Jude. She supposed she could always go back to styling fashion
shoots, but she really had lost touch with that world, especially
after her second bout in rehab. What else was there? The night
scene had always interested her, but that would entail running
into Bennét, and he hadn't taken their breakup particularly well.

Why fight it? She lit up and sat down. She was destined to
be a performance-art diva. There clearly was nothing else for her
to do but stay calm and wait for inspiration.

Several weeks passed, during which time inspiration stayed at
bay. And then one evening, Jude came home from work and
asked Arden where she planned to go. Arden was lying on the divan, smoking and trying to come up with an idea.

"What the fuck are you talking about?" she said, exhaling toward the ceiling.

"Well," Jude said, pouring himself a scotch, "Lydie gets the apartment on the first of the month, which is in"—he took a sip of his drink, turned his back to her, and looked out the window—"which is in four days."

Jude was wearing the royal blue Calvin Klein shirt she had given him for his birthday and there was a large unattractive sweat stain between his shoulder blades. There were also sweat rings around his armpits. It wasn't hot in the apartment. Something was up.

"Didn't you— I thought—" Arden searched for the right question to ask. "I thought the deal was *off*. Isn't it— Wasn't it— Didn't you—"

"Nope," Jude said with eerie calm. "The deal is on. Very *much* on." He turned then and looked at her, a queer smile on his lupine face.

"Excuse me?" she said, the right side of her upper lip beginning an involuntary dance of rage.

"Why should I excuse you?" He was still smiling queerly. He flipped his hair and fixed his gaze on her in such a way that Arden had to get up and move away. She paced from one corner of the living room to the other and back again, her upper lip stuck now in a full-on snarl. She retrieved a cigarette from a pack hidden in a porcelain vase on top of the piano and smoked furiously for a few long moments.

"So what are we going to do?" she finally asked. "Where do *you* want to go? Why is everything always *my* decision?"

Arden noticed the smallest hint of guilt on Jude's face before he dove back into his drink. Finally, he said, "I'm not going any-where, babe."

There was a stare-off. Then Arden said, "What the fuck are you talking about?"

"What part of 'I'm not going anywhere' isn't clear to you?" Jude replied debonairly.

Arden eyed the vase on top of the piano, wondering whether she'd actually kill him if she smashed it over his head. If she screamed and cried and flung the vase against the wall, would he change his mind? She thought about yelling "You useless piece of shit!" or something like that, but in reality she only managed to say in a tiny, tight voice: "I'll have another idea soon, Jude. I wish you'd have greater respect for the artistic process."

"I have tremendous respect for the artistic process," Jude shot back. "If nothing else, my interaction with Lydie over the past few weeks has confirmed that."

It was the movement of his steely gray eyes, the quick flicker to the left on the word *interaction*, that told her she was in trouble.

"What on earth do you expect me to do?" she cried. "What the fuck am I supposed to fucking *do* in *four fucking days*?"

"Get out," Jude said.

Arden asked for clarification.

"What part of 'Get out' are you having difficulty with?"

Arden was speechless.

He tossed back the remainder of his drink, placed it on the kitchen counter, grabbed his coat, and left.

It would suck, Arden knew, going back to Great Neck, but she couldn't think of what else to do. She had never had many girlfriends. She found them too competitive and demanding, and they had always eyed her with suspicion, even when she had been a knobby-kneed eight-year-old with the same Snoopy on her bed as everyone else and the same collection of Barbie dolls and Wacky Packs and puffy movable stickers.

"I don't know why everyone wants to make my life miserable," she said to Sushi as she waited for one of her parents to pick up the telephone.

No one answered.

She hung up and called again, but again there was no answer.

She pressed redial four times in a row in case her parents were having dinner or sleeping, then finally left a message, letting them know that she was on her way.

"He'll have to pay me alimony," she said to Sushi as she swept her eyes across the apartment she had decorated with such vigor.

The suitcases were stored in the hall closet, above the coats and behind the hats and scarves. Arden got a stool and climbed up, wobbling slightly in her thin-heeled mules. Her luggage was way in the back, behind Jude's gorgeous Gucci set, given to him recently by a satisfied client. It was with enormous effort that she managed to pull down the floral-embroidered suitcase, the floral-embroidered dress carrier, and the floral-embroidered duffel bag (one of the many glorious gifts she had received for her Bat Mitzvah). Then she went to the bedroom and began, scarf by scarf, skirt by skirt, thong by thong, to pack.

She called her parents from Penn Station two hours later and got the machine again, which she thought bizarre since it was 8:30 on a Thursday night and they both usually went to bed by nine on weeknights. When the train arrived at the Great Neck station, she called once more. There was still no answer. She screamed into their answering machine for them to pick up, but they didn't, so she hung up, smoked a cigarette, and took a cab.

Doris and Alan were sympathetic but firm. They agreed to keep Sushi but refused to keep her. Doris called it "tough love," and Alan kept saying, "We're just doing what Dr. Roberts advised. We want you to get better. We're your parents. We love you."

Arden swore she was off drugs, but to no avail. Doris made her a sandwich of some leftover brisket and gave her a doggy bag of chocolate-covered graham crackers and some cantaloupe cubes.

"Where am I supposed to sleep tonight?" she pleaded when they walked her to the door. "This is nuts. Do you want me to sleep on a bench at the train station? It's freezing out."

"You're a big girl now," Alan said, not allowing any emotion to creep into his voice. "You've made it perfectly clear to us time and time again that you can take care of yourself. Now come on. Your mother and I need to go to bed. We both have to work in the morning."

Sushi, who had been snacking on brisket for half an hour and was now tucked under Doris's arm, gave a loud belch.

Doris wiped away a renegade tear that was sliding down her cheek and opened the front door to let her daughter out.

Jude allowed Arden to come up, which Arden thought was a good sign. She had changed on the train into the blue top with the butterflies on it that Jude had purchased for her in the Frankfurt air-port during their layover from Bora Bora. He had made her put it on right away and then fucked her in it in the shower stall of the first-class lounge while they waited for their connecting flight back to New York. She thought the memory might soften him a bit when he saw her wearing it, but it didn't. He blocked the doorway and told her she was trespassing.

"But I still *live* here," she said. "I have four more days."

Jude told her that it was, in fact, *his* apartment. The contract was in *his* name. *He* had paid for it. It was, therefore, *his*. When Arden reminded him that they were still married, he laughed and said, "You think we're actually married? That was some drunk fisherman, not an ordained rabbi."

"Fucker!" Arden screamed, yanking the aquamarine engage-ment ring off her finger and throwing it at him. Jude ducked and the ring hit Lydie, who had come to the door to speak to Arden personally.

"Shit!" Lydie cried, clutching her forehead. "I'm cut!"

Arden tried to push her way past Jude so she could tend to the injured star, but Jude wouldn't let her through. Then Arden noticed what Lydie was wearing: it was her very own bathrobe—the pink silk robe she had left behind the door in the bathroom.

"Cunt!" Arden yelled, slithering past Jude and grabbing at the robe.

Jude pushed her away roughly and slammed the front door in her face.

"I want my stuff!" Arden screamed, pounding on the door. "You can't keep what's mine!"

Arden was so angry, she was hyperventilating. She reached into the side pocket of her purse, where she kept her cigarettes, but came away with only a handful of loose change, a bobby pin, and an old gum wrapper.

"Motherfucker," she said under her breath. She dumped the contents of her purse onto the floor and found a squashed, nearly empty pack of Dunhills. She lit up one of the two slightly crushed cigarettes, and frantically tried to formulate a plan. Unfortunately, nothing came to mind. There was no way to be prepared for sudden homelessness. How was she, Arden Finkelstein, born and bred in Great Neck, Long Island, in a two-story house with a pool and barbecue in the backyard and a frilly canopy bed in her pink bedroom, supposed to deal with this absurd turn of events? It wasn't possible. It simply wasn't possible.

And yet, undeniably, once again, it was.

Just as she smashed out the last little bit of cigarette on the wall by the elevator, the front door of Arden's former apartment opened a crack and out came a garbage bag. In it was a stash of mail, the pink silk robe, three sweaters, a Calvin Klein floor-length formal that had come back from the dry cleaner's that evening, a set of hot rollers Arden had stolen from her mother when she was thirteen, and nine half-full packs of cigarettes culled from every hiding place Arden had ever created in the apartment, including a pack of Gauloises she had slipped behind the refrigerator. If Jude—or, worse, Lydie—had unearthed those, there really was no going back.

✳

It was nearly 3:00 A.M. and Arden's feet were killing her, stuffed, as they were, into pointy-toed patent-leather spikes, but she knew if she could keep dancing just a little bit longer, her perseverance would be rewarded.

"*Thirsty?*" she shouted, knowing she probably couldn't be heard over the throbbing music.

The man shrugged and wiped some sweat from his bushy eyebrows with the back of his thick arm.

"You want we should take a break?" he shouted back.

One Kamikaze shot later, they were in a taxi, heading uptown.

"Come, come," he said, gesturing toward the living room as she stood, terrified but resolute, in the entry gallery to the lavish apartment on the twenty-sixth floor of Trump Towers. He wriggled his sausage-like fingers in the air as if summoning magical spirits, and she took a few steps forward.

"Can I just get a glass of water?" she asked when he grabbed her around the waist.

He pointed her in the direction of the kitchen and told her to join him in the bedroom with a glass for him, too. She took her time, hoping he'd pass out before she got there, but he was waiting for her, sitting in a yellow silk upholstered chair in the corner of the room. On the floor, in a heap by the closet, were his clothes.

"Cigarette?" he offered, holding out a pack.

"Thanks," Arden said, unbuttoning her coat slowly as she took microscopic steps in his direction. When, at last, she reached him, he lowered the pack of cigarettes down to his crotch and smiled. His teeth were crooked and yellow.

"Why don't you smoke *this* instead?" he said, leaning back in the chair and closing his eyes.

✳

Arden slept for a few fitful hours. When she awoke after the requisite nightmare, she slid out of the bed and tiptoed around the apartment. There was three hundred dollars in his wallet. Arden took the money and returned to the lobby of the apartment in TriBeCa. The super had been in Vietnam and was as kind as he was insane, and agreed to let her keep her stuff in the building until she found another place to live. It wasn't ideal, but it was better than being out on the street with all her worldly belongings surrounding her in old shopping bags from Bergdorf's and Barneys.

She went to the storage room and freshened up. At the top of her suitcase was a Prada dress from the recent season. She chose it, plus a pair of black knee-high suede boots, and changed behind some boxes with "Kramer, 14th floor" written all over them. Lisa Kramer—formerly Bernstein—had gone to Arden's temple in Great Neck and had been a few years ahead of Arden at Willow Lake. Even so, Arden had never spoken to Lisa, not even when she ran into her in the lobby or the elevator. Lisa's husband was a banker, or something straight and business-y like that, and she was nothing but a housewife with two little kids who always had food on their cheeks. Arden wondered if she should knock on Lisa's door and ask for help. Jews were supposed to help one another, wasn't that right?

Deciding against it, Arden left the building.

The lobby of the SoHo Grand Hotel was quiet but not empty when Arden sauntered in at 8:30. She made her way to the second-floor lounge, grabbed the morning newspaper and some magazines that were lying around for guests, and got comfortable in a club chair next to a large potted palm. She pulled out a small journal she always kept with her in case she got an idea, then began sorting through the newspapers and magazines.

"Job Possibilities" she wrote at the top of a page in the notebook. After an hour, there was nothing written beneath the heading. She couldn't go back to the gallery world. She'd *been there, done that,* and it hadn't paid particularly well, not to mention the fact that she'd fucked anyone who mattered in that world already and most people knew Jude, which wouldn't help; Artist's Model would never cover rent; she had no experience as a waitress and she wasn't about to flip burgers; Personal Assistant would probably require a high school diploma; she had no experience as a masseuse and couldn't afford a course now; she couldn't type; she certainly couldn't be a paralegal since she didn't know what one was. In short, she had no idea what she was going to do to make money.

Glancing across the room, she saw a couple of businessmen leave two twenty-dollar bills on their breakfast table before getting up to leave. She made her way over to their table, pulled out her notebook, leaned down on the tabletop and wrote, "Tra la la la la" on it. Two minutes later, she was back on the street, forty dollars richer and full from the croissant they had left in the bread basket.

It was a beautiful day. SoHo was packed with tourists and shoppers and locals enjoying the unseasonably warm weather. She wandered aimlessly up West Broadway, stopping in a few stores along the way just to kill time, when, outside of Ralph Lauren, someone called her name. Her first instinct was to hide, but she didn't have time. Within seconds, Wendy Levin, an old bunk mate, was upon her.

"Arden? Is it *you*? Oh my God! Your hair—it's a little different. I wasn't sure— Look at you!"

"Look at *you*," Arden said, nodding her head at the infant lounging cozily in the baby carrier strapped across Wendy Levin's chest.

"This is Samuel," Wendy said, smiling proudly. "But we're calling him Sam. It was my husband's father's name."

Arden congratulated Wendy, and Wendy said, "The congratulations should only go to Sam here. Isn't that right, Sammy? Today we're four months old!"

"Are *we*?" Arden said. "Mazel tov."

"Tank you," Wendy said in a baby voice and then, in her own register, she explained that she never ran around shopping like this—she wasn't *that* kind of mom—she didn't even live here in the city, but she was in a terrible bind. Her nanny had quit the day before without any warning. She had come into the city to interview someone, who, it turned out, had no decent references, and now here she was with three other sons at home.

"Do you have any names for me?" Wendy begged. "I've always preferred word of mouth to an agency. I'm looking for a full-time live-in nanny. Preferably legal, but cash off the books is fine."

Arden shook her head. She glanced at her watch and looked up in despair. "I'd love to chat, but I have to get to—"

"Look, illegal is fine," Wendy said. "I mean, who cares, right? I'm offering five hundred and fifty dollars for five days, seven hundred for full-time live-in. Only child care, no cleaning—I mean, I expect her to help out with things like grocery shopping and all that, but I have a great housekeeper, so there wouldn't be any heavy cleaning. A driver's license would be a plus, since it's New Jersey. So? What do you think? Seriously. Anyone come to mind? This is an emergency."

It was amazing how easily Wendy had swallowed the story, Arden reflected as she unpacked the few things she had decided to bring with her to Short Hills. The bit about her degree in early childhood education from Oxford was especially inspired, Arden thought. And the horrible asshole who had run off with all her money was really not so far off. Wendy had been especially sympathetic when Arden described the boating accident on Long Island Sound that had claimed her parents' lives.

It was a further amazement to Arden to think that the once-formidable Wendy Levin was now nothing more than a well-toned, well-manicured, well-dressed suburban mom. Sure, there were all the tennis trophies around the house, but when Arden asked what they were from, she had learned that Wendy was simply the Orange Lawn Tennis Club ladies' champion. It was a far cry from the superjock camper everyone had thought would win the U.S. Open one day.

Wendy seemed happy enough, though, as she showed Arden around the house and property, both of which were nice, if a little generic. It was a house filled with boy things: basketballs and mitts, superheroes and dump trucks. Outside there was a pool and tennis court and a small putting green where she and Seth practiced their short game, whatever that was. The grounds were beautifully landscaped and, according to Wendy, looked gorgeous in the spring when everything began to bloom.

"It's not much at this time of year," Wendy had said apologetically, leading Arden through the kitchen to her new room, which was small but lovely in a Laura Ashley, matching chintz curtains and bedspread way. She couldn't complain. She had her own bathroom and a television set and a phone she could use to make local calls to set up play dates for the kids. It sure as hell beat the street.

She had dinner that night with Wendy and her handsome, dark, curly-haired, slightly nebbishy husband, and the three older boys: David, who was seven, Ben, who was five, and Eric, who had just turned three. Eric was fair like his mom, but the other two were carbon copies of their father. It was amazing how genes transferred. Arden didn't look anything like either of her parents. Maybe if she had, she reflected, she wouldn't have turned out so badly.

After the kids were in bed, Seth disappeared into his office and Arden and Wendy stayed up until ten sipping herbal tea in the cozy dark den, reminiscing about camp. Wendy was excited about the upcoming August Willow Lake reunion. Arden agreed it sounded like fun but told Wendy she had no plans to attend the event.

Neither she nor Wendy alluded to their own messy past or the night in the woods with Ali. There was an implicit understanding that either the events had never happened or that they had happened too long ago to matter now that they were both adults in a dire situation: Wendy needed a nanny and Arden needed an income and a place to stay. Who cared about the past? Arden was more than happy to let bygones be bygones. Hadn't she been trying to do that most of her life anyway?

There were only two tough parts to the whole nanny thing, and neither one was the diapers, which turned out to be no big deal. The smell of Ground Zero had been a lot worse, and you certainly couldn't wipe *that* away and throw it into a hermetically sealed Diaper Genie.

No, the problems were technical. One was all the laundry, especially the hand wash, which was murder on Arden's nails. The other was the "no smoking in the house" rule, which was a major challenge at night and had Arden shivering on the back patio at 2:00 A.M. on many occasions, which in itself wasn't much of a problem, except that it often meant dealing with Seth, who seemed to have insomnia at the same time she did. There was no question about his intentions. He had all but propositioned her straight-out. Normally, she wouldn't have had qualms, but she needed to keep her job, and she knew if Wendy caught them, she'd be back out on the street. Lately, she had taken to wearing a nicotine patch to bed and keeping Nicorette gum on hand. Anything not to jeopardize her position.

Sometimes Arden caught Wendy staring at her. Sometimes Arden caught Seth staring at her and Wendy staring at him. Most of the time, she averted her gaze or retreated to her room. She was still biding her time until she got an idea. Then she'd be on her way, and she didn't want any trouble in the meantime.

One evening, after the boys were in bed, Wendy called Arden into the kitchen.

"I'm sort of embarrassed about this," Wendy began, "but

Seth and I were invited to Dafna Shapiro's engagement party—you remember Dafna, right?"

"I would say so," Arden replied. "We were all in a little log cabin together for quite a few summers."

Wendy smiled awkwardly. "Anyway, she's having an impromptu party in Vail and—"

"I'm completely fine taking care of the boys all weekend," Arden said, relieved that the plan didn't involve her staying alone in the house with Seth. "You don't need to worry about *anything*. Just have fun. And give my love to anyone I might know from camp."

So off Wendy and Seth went. On Friday morning, Arden took the older boys to school and walked with Sam around the Short Hills mall until school was out. In the afternoon, she took David to ice hockey practice, Benjamin to tae kwon do, and Eric to gymnastics. In the evening, she did the Sabbath prayers with the kids just like Wendy and Seth did, gave them their chicken fingers and broccoli, let them watch *Toy Story* on DVD, and put them to bed.

Everything went smoothly on Saturday, too. David and Benjamin had basketball, Eric had a play date, and Sam stuck to his eating and nap schedule. Arden even had time to give herself a pedicure. When Wendy called to see how things were going, Arden was able to report honestly that everything was fine.

But early Sunday morning, things began to unravel. Sam woke up screaming at 3:00 A.M., right after Arden had fallen back asleep herself. He screamed until four o'clock, waking up the other boys, who ran around the house like hoodlums. At 6:30 she finally put them all in the car and drove to the emergency room.

Sam, it turned out, was suffering from an advanced case of

constipation. The doctor on call gave him an enema, after which he pooped, smiled, and fell instantly asleep. Arden drove to the International House of Pancakes and treated the older boys to chocolate-chip pancakes before driving them to Hebrew School, where, thank God, David and Ben were set to stay for lunch and afternoon games.

When Arden returned to the house with Sam and Eric, she was exhausted. The baby was still sleeping off his anal trauma, so she put him into his crib. Eric, too, was tired, even though he claimed not to be. She put him in front of a video and, by the time she returned with a sippy cup of milk for him, he was asleep.

Too tired to walk through the house to the back terrace, she opened the front door, sat down on the stoop, and lit up her first cigarette of the day. For a few delicious minutes, Arden smoked and stared out at the front lawn, her mind blank.

It wasn't until she was lighting up her second cigarette that she noticed the young guy shoveling the last of February's snow out of the neighbor's driveway, his jet black hair glistening in the noonday sun. Hers was auburn now and she missed her black hair suddenly. She had always been a sucker for black hair anyway, even if it did remind her, unpleasantly, of Jude.

Back and forth across the driveway he shoveled, until he reached the edge closest to the front of Wendy and Seth's house. Then he put down the shovel, removed a packet of cigarettes from one of the pockets of the light parka he was wearing, and leaped over the white picket fence that separated the two lawns.

"Got a light?" he asked. He had a hot accent, Spanish or Mexican. Something that sounded a little illegal.

"Sure," Arden said, offering him her own cigarette to light

off. They smoked together for a while in silence, Arden's mind moving over Sam's schedule and what time the boys had to be picked up.

"Would you like some hot chocolate, or a beer?" she asked, standing up.

She had seen enough cheesy late-night TV to know what came next. First Arden took him to the kitchen, went to the fridge, and took out the bottle of Cristal that had been chilling in the back since she had arrived at Wendy and Seth's house. She popped the cork, grabbed two champagne flutes, and nodded for him to follow her.

They made their way through the front hallway, up the staircase, and into the master bedroom. Clothes came off along the way. There was tossing and turning in the sheets. There was a move to the bathroom. There was oral sex on the marble countertop between the sinks.

Unfortunately, the cheesy late-night TV show played out true to plot when, twenty minutes into the steamy episode, Wendy and Seth burst into the house shouting, "Surprise! We're home!"

The Jacuzzi in the master bathroom was on full force so neither Arden nor the snow shoveler heard the shouts clearly, but they did both hear a door slam and stopped kissing.

"What the fuck?" the snow shoveler said in his adorable accent. Arden had turned off the water jet.

"Hel-lo!"

They both heard the greeting distinctly.

They scrambled out of the Jacuzzi and desperately began searching for their clothes in the twist of sheets and pillows, which were now mostly on the floor.

The snow shoveler was dressed and shoving his feet into his work boots when Seth entered the bedroom holding Arden's shirt, which he had picked up as he crossed the threshold to his room.

"Nice," Seth said, taking in the full nakedness of the nanny he had lusted after for three months.

The snow shoveler ran out of the room, bumping into Wendy, who was on her way in.

"What on earth . . . ?" Wendy said.

Seth just laughed.

"I'm so sorry things didn't work out with Rude."

"*Jude,*" said Arden, smirking slightly at what she knew was Bennét's intentional lapse in memory.

They were sitting side by side in a black leather banquette in the main bar at Esmé, a new club Bennét was managing. In the perpetual evening of the dark interior, Bennét looked cool as ever with his wisp of a soul patch, blue-tinted glasses, and a tan snakeskin Gucci suit. It was somewhat depressing, though, being inside a club at ten o'clock in the morning. No candles were lit, no scantily clad girls wriggled by, no kiss-kiss, no wave, no *call you soon* rang through the stale, stagnant, boozy-smelling air. And the silence! What was a club without a pulsing beat? It was this: this sticky black leather banquette where Bennét had agreed to meet Arden for a brief tête-à-tête before his day began.

Bennét wasn't as heartless as Arden had feared. He had a new girlfriend, which helped, sort of. It meant Arden couldn't win him back, as had been her goal, but at least he wasn't jealous anymore, so he wasn't out to ruin her. He offered her a job at Esmé right then and there and told her she could start that night. Then he checked his watch, said he had to get somewhere, and escorted her out.

Arden showed up for work that night in a form-fitting black Lycra minidress with chiffon ruffles on the hem, paired with high black suede boots. She asked for Bennét but was told by Duane, the assistant manager, that Bennét wouldn't be in that night. She asked where she would be working, because if it was at the door, she wanted to keep her coat on. Duane told her to check her coat and report to the ladies' lounge on the lower, lower ground level, where someone named Pearl would tell her what to do.

"You've got to be fucking kidding me," Arden said when Pearl told her the job included wiping vomit up off the floor when the girls missed the bowl.

Pearl, an overweight middle-aged woman from Trinidad, was the men's room attendant, and she told Arden she didn't kid about anything. Pearl suggested Arden put a few of her own fives in the tip bowl to encourage the girls to be generous. It seemed ludicrous to Arden that the fat lady was in the men's room instead of her. How many women would want to give the pretty, skinny, chic girl a big tip, if at all!

Jenna and Ilana did, but they also wanted her to join them in a threesome, which Arden wasn't into, even though Jenna and Ilana were both attractive if you were into body piercings and neon-colored hair. It was tempting. It would mean a bed to sleep in, Arden presumed, and a shower and clean towel, she hoped. But they mentioned something about nipple clamps and a vibrator with electric probes, and Arden felt, desperate as she was, that even *she* might be out of her league.

Days merged into weeks, which merged into some time frame Arden couldn't put her finger on. It had been freezing for a time, and Arden had spent most nights sleeping next to the heater on the floor of the bathroom. Upstairs, in the bathroom in the VIP lounge, Arden had discovered a shower, and she used it every morning before the cleaning crew arrived at nine o'clock.

Somewhere along the way, she had stopped getting her period, which was a relief, since she wasn't pregnant. That she was undernourished and underweight didn't matter to her at all. She usually spent her slim earnings on food only once a day, preferring to save the rest of her salary for the future. More often than not, she managed to get something free: a pretzel from a park vendor, some rotting fruit from one of the Korean markets, a bowl of soup from one of the nearby restaurants that catered to the club crowd and knew of her situation. If she spent her money on anything else, it was only for cigarettes, Diet Coke, and, every now and then, washing her clothes at the Laundromat. She also shopped occasionally for cheap but fashionable outfits, since she had long ago stopped going to the storage room in the building in TriBeCa, where her things were still waiting. The fear of encountering her former neighbors, not to mention Jude and Lydie, kept her at bay. There were even some days when she no longer remembered she had lived there at all.

She saved the bulk of her money in an envelope from Chase

Manhattan that she kept tucked into her underpants. Soon she'd have enough to rent a cheap apartment somewhere.

Eventually, it was warm out, and then, for a spell, unbearably hot. Arden learned survival tricks: department stores and subway cars were way too air-conditioned but a relief, and the grass in any of the city parks was just fine for sleeping as long as the police didn't make you leave. Sometimes she found a bed for the day by sleeping with someone from the club—a bartender, a patron, one of the bouncers—or she found a businessman in from out of town, a bored husband, a waiter whose English was bad. If she couldn't find a place to sleep, then she sleepwalked through her day, passing her time in stores, just looking and dreaming and trying not to fall over. Sometimes she slept on the job, dozing on the stool next to the row of sinks, her head leaning back against the towel dispenser.

One night, one of the bartenders, a lean young Colombian named Miguel, offered her coke, which she accepted gladly. Soon, it became a regular feature of her night. Miguel met her in the coatroom before the club opened, Arden sucked him off or let him fuck her against the wall, standing up, and then he gave her coke. Every now and then he gave her speed, too, which was great, or ecstasy, which was okay but made her do things she otherwise might not, like let a woman eat her out one night in a bathroom stall while Miguel watched. Crystal meth was cool, too, except that it made Miguel insatiable. When they did crystal meth, he needed Arden to get him off over and over, and sometimes he did nasty things, like fuck her in the ass, which hurt.

There were times, lately, when she'd had to give him some of her savings. One night, he suggested they try heroin. She said no, but she knew it would only be a matter of time.

Every now and then, during the day or in the early part of the night, before the club got crowded, Arden would take out her journal and try to write a few notes about things: the weather, what she was wearing, what other people were wearing, what kinds of people came into the lounge. Once, Lydie came in, and Arden asked, "Still with Jude?" Lydie looked at her as if she were a cockroach and said no, but Arden thought she was lying. She was wearing a big amethyst ring that looked exactly like the aquamarine engagement ring Jude had given her. Later, Arden wrote in her journal:

> *Saw Lydie tonight: white leather pants, black see-through T-shirt with rhinestone logo—DIVA—pink bra, black boots. We made eye contact in the mirror over the sink while she touched up her lipstick. Lip liner. Ew. She didn't put a tip in my basket, thank God.*

Other notes included:

> *Girls in tight pants should wear a G-string.*

> *Black chick with skinny legs looks great in white micromini and shaved head.*

> *Cloudy today and cold. Where am I?*

> *Should I throw myself into the tracks?*

Waste, waste, waste. Taste, taste, taste. Why, why, why? May as well have married a banker.

She often touched the Chase envelope, feeling it through her clothes, and thought about what she would do with the money she was saving. Soon she would rent something simple, maybe on the Lower East Side, where it was chic, or near the club, where she'd be sure to find something cheap above one of the meatpacking companies. Then she would start writing in earnest. Then she'd be on her way.

"What are you doing down here?" the tall, well-built, good-looking guy asked.

"What are *you* doing down here is more to the point," Arden answered.

He had a tattoo on his left tricep, and she asked what it represented. He flexed for her and she could see it was the Twin Towers draped in an American flag.

"I'm serious," he said again, oblivious to the looks he was getting from the ladies, who didn't want him in their lounge. "What the hell are you doing down here? You're a star. Look at you! You should be upstairs partying with me and my buddies."

He sounded like he was from somewhere deep in Jersey, Staten Island, or Queens. A few months back, Arden wouldn't have given him the time of day, but now he seemed like someone who really understood her; who saw her for what she was. "A star," he had said. A star buried in a bathroom.

"Come upstairs with me," he urged, taking her by the forearm. "Come on. Let's go."

She explained to him that she couldn't just get up and leave—she was working, she explained, feeling simultaneously terribly sorry for herself and also hopeful that a solution for her future had finally presented itself in the form of this tattooed, chiseled, patriotic hero.

He scribbled down an address on a paper towel with an eye liner that was in one of the baskets near the sink and told her to meet him when she got off work.

"Chad," he said, extending a large hand.

"Arden," she replied, her hand disappearing in his large, forceful grasp. "What are you, in the marines or something?" Arden asked.

"Or something," he said, smiling. He had a wonderful smile and very white straight teeth.

Arden was about to ask him what that "something" was, but just then a young girl rushed into the lounge and threw up in the sink. A second girl rushed in after her who looked at Arden and said, "Um, can you do something? Like get a wet cloth or, like, some Pepto or something?"

"Just hop on the E," Chad said to Arden. "It's easy. See you later." He winked at her, and she knew she'd be sleeping soundly in a bed in a matter of hours.

She had second thoughts when she reached her destination. The house was a dilapidated wreck on a desolate block in the middle of nowhere. But she was exhausted—the sky was already turning pink—and it sounded like the party was still going on—that is, if the music she could hear was coming from Chad's apartment. She rang the buzzer and the door clicked open.

It was a bachelor party for a guy named Richie. He was one of the ones she remembered most clearly: tall, like Chad, but lankier, not as pumped, with dark stubble on top of his shaved head and a scar that cut diagonally across his left cheek. He was the one who went first. Then came Chad, because, as he said to a cheering chorus, he had "found the little slut." After Chad came someone named something like T.J. or M.J. or J.J. The rest were a blur. They took turns holding her down, but she didn't struggle much anyway. She was way too weary; she wasn't even there. When they started in with beer bottles, she screamed, and then someone broke one over her head and she blacked out.

When she came to, they were gone. She put her clothes on and left the abandoned building. A few blocks away, she found a pay phone. When the police came, they went back to the building with her, took down her story, then dropped her off at St. Vincent's for an exam.

There was no way to tell right away if she had contracted AIDS or whether or not she had gotten pregnant. Her anus and the area around her vagina were torn, her wrists and ankles were chafed, her lower lip was split, and she needed twenty-four stitches in her head and forehead where the beer bottle had cut her. Other than that, she was fine.

A few hours after she was admitted, her parents showed up like a pair of suburban angels in their matching white sweatsuits and sneakers. While Alan handled the paperwork, Doris wrapped Arden in her arms and together they cried. Then Arden checked out of the hospital, got into her parents' blue Mercedes station wagon, clamped the seat belt shut, and fell asleep.

✳

Arden had harassed her mother for years to redecorate her child-hood bedroom, but as she lay in the pink canopy bed, cuddling with Sushi and looking across the room at her poster of John Travolta and Olivia Newton-John embracing in a big pink heart, she felt a level of comfort that had eluded her for years. Next to the poster was a large bulletin board, which hosted the memora-bilia of her lost childhood and squandered adolescence: a series of skating patches from her lessons at Parkwood Ice skating rink in Huntington; Great Neck Junior High's drama award, which she had won three years in a row—fifth grade, sixth grade, and seventh; a collage of Tom Cruise and Mel Gibson; tickets from a Madonna concert; a program from *The Nutcracker* signed by Patricia McBride; a small beige certificate with a willow tree drawn on it in Magic Marker and an inscription that said "For Excellence in Gymnastics, Arden Finkelstein, Willow Lake Camp, 1981."

In the lower right-hand corner of the bulletin board was a photo that had retained its vivid Kodak color even after twenty-four years. Across the bottom of the photo was the caption "Willow Lake Camp, Bunk 16B, 1978." There they all were, in a pyramid. On the bottom, on hands and knees, was their coun-selor, a brown-haired girl of about nineteen, whose name and salient attributes Arden no longer could recall. Next to her was Beth Rosenblatt, who might as well have been oinking, she so re-sembled Miss Piggy. And then there was Wendy Levin, looking, even on her hands and knees, like a water buffalo compared to the gazellelike Dafna Shapiro, who knelt next to her. On their backs balanced Laura Berman, who was snarling; Jessica Bloom, who was smiling as if for a magazine cover; and Pam Mandel-baum, who looked like an owl with her oval face, hooked nose, and round, darkly shadowed hazel eyes. Pam had dropped out after two summers, even though she was popular because she was so good at tennis.

Above them balanced a girl Arden thought was named Amy Baumgarden, who was squinting and who had lasted only three summers and was the worst girl in their age group at swimming but the best girl in their age group at jacks. And then there was Ali Cohen, who looked, even with a queer sort of half-smile, like a fish; an ugly fish; a bottom dweller; something vaguely related to dinosaurs.

Finally, like the cherry on top of a sundae, there she was, way up high, the smallest girl in her bunk that summer, sporting bangs and pigtails and grinning gloriously despite the fact that the moment after the photo was taken the pyramid toppled, sending Arden crashing down onto Pam, who crashed down onto Beth, who dislocated her shoulder and spent the rest of the summer with her arm in a sling.

Arden felt a pang of enormous nostalgia and sadness, not for the fates of the other girls, but for her own lost innocence so guilelessly displayed in the photo. She reached into the drawer of her night table and removed the letter her mother had handed her that morning. It was from Ali Cohen, inviting Arden to participate in a documentary.

Arden's first reaction had been to fold up the letter in disgust and stick it in her drawer, but the question in the letter had nagged at her all morning. Ali wanted to know what the defining moments of Arden's life had been.

Arden looked at the photo on the bulletin board once more and reached for the pack of cigarettes on her night table (her parents had finally relented and agreed to let her smoke in the house as long as she kept it to her own bedroom and nowhere else).

Ali Cohen . . . Ugly Ali Cohen . . .

She had ruined Ali Cohen's camp experience, she and Wendy together. Arden had been a bad camper; a bad egg, a bad girl. Was it genetic or circumstantial? she wondered now. Both her parents were good; boring and clueless, but decent nevertheless.

When had it begun, her badness? One memory came immediately to mind: her seventh birthday, when her mother let her skip school to see a show at Radio City Music Hall. "When I grow up, I'm going to be a Rockette," Arden had said to her mother between acts.

"Don't be silly," her mother had replied. "Jewish girls don't grow up to be Rockettes."

"I hate you," Arden had said, loudly enough for the large black woman in the red hat sitting next to them to turn to her mother and say, "Can't you control your child?"

In response, her mother had yanked Arden up the aisle, and home they went. Did that mean she was already a bad apple by seven? Arden didn't think so, although now that she was soul-searching, she did remember stealing a doll from Melissa Jackson's bedroom at Melissa's birthday party, while everyone else was eating cake on the floor in the living room. And she remembered taking a little gold bracelet from Rena Trowler's cubby at school when no one else was in the classroom and then throwing it into the garbage can in the cafeteria later. When had that been? First grade? How old are you in first grade? she wondered. Six?

Arden closed her eyes and thought back to camp. Had she been bad at camp? She certainly didn't look bad in the picture on the bulletin board. She looked like a normal, happy kid.

She *was* a normal, happy kid at camp, in the beginning anyway. Those first few summers had been a welcome respite from the horror taking place in Great Neck with the assistant rabbi. Those first few summers, camp had been something she looked forward to. She liked gymnastics and pottery and enjoyed singing in the musical her age group put on. She liked Friday-evening services, sitting on top of the hill overlooking the lake, singing the Sabbath Prayer song from *Fiddler on the Roof* while Tabitha, the music director, plunked away on an electric piano set up on the side of the hill.

A sigh filled Arden's soul as she remembered the beauty of those services, when nothing was asked of her but to sit with her fellow campers, an equal member of the community.

And she had had some friends, too, before Wendy plucked her up. Laura Berman, Dafna Shapiro, Beth Rosenblatt. In those early summers, they had all been friends. Wendy was someone they all admired back then, but not someone they feared.

She had just wanted Wendy to like her, Arden reflected, lighting a fresh cigarette and exhaling sadly. But who didn't? Everyone wanted to be liked by Wendy, starting that very first summer in 1978, when the Kodak was taken. Arden was eight that summer and Wendy was nine. Not recently nine, either. Wendy was a full calendar year older than the other girls because she had repeated second grade when she switched from public to private school. But she had decided to stay with her school age group rather than go ahead a group when she started camp. Because of this, Wendy had had an advantage over the other girls when it came to sports. She was a full head taller than most of them and much more coordinated.

But it was hard to hate her, even with her unfair advantage. It was hard because she was such a gifted athlete, and not just at the usuals, like soccer and tennis, but also at things like archery, waterskiing, diving, and lacrosse.

In addition to her athletic gifts, she was also blessed with a terrific singing voice. The combination of her height and talent made her a shoo-in for the male lead in their age group's play every year. With her short-cropped blond hair and taut, straight body, she could pass for a boy even without the help of a costume. That first summer, she was Baron von Trapp in *The Sound of Music;* the next summer, she was Daddy Warbucks in *Annie* and somehow managed to steal the show from Jessica Bloom, who had established herself as the number one contender for the female lead in their age group; the next summer, Wendy was Harold Hill in *The Music Man* opposite Jessica's Marion the Librarian. And so it went, summer after summer, until that sixth summer, when Arden got cast as Sandy in *Grease* opposite Wendy's Danny Zucco.

Yes, *Arden* was Sandy and Wendy was Danny, and everyone was shocked about the unfair casting (Jessica sobbed when the cast list went up), except for Arden, who wasn't shocked at all. She had always been theatrical, but her shyness had prevented her from doing a decent audition in her early camp years. But by then, she was no longer shy in front of the girls in her own age group or in front of Hillario, the flamboyant theater director, with whom she felt an odd kinship. Plus, she was familiar with all the songs from *Grease,* since her parents had taken her to see it on Broadway for her ninth birthday and she had memorized every word even *before* the film had come out, and she'd gone to see *that* an astronomical thirteen times.

And so began a fast and intense friendship. Not only did she and Wendy rehearse together every day but, as chance would have it, that summer they were also put on the same team for color war, which meant they did most of their activities together, too. Wendy, of course, was better than Arden at everything, but Arden wasn't a bad athlete, either—good enough, at any rate, to be one of the starting five players alongside Wendy for basketball; good enough to play right wing to Wendy's center forward in field hockey; good enough to be on the A team for softball, even if she did hit last and play catcher while Wendy pitched and hit fourth. And Wendy was encouraging to Arden, too, urging her to try sports like waterskiing and sailing and even kayaking, which Arden ended up enjoying, even though she thought she would feel claustrophobic in the thin, red, giant-sized kazoo.

Arden's rise in popularity due to her association with Wendy was instantaneous. Now counselors singled her out and joked with her, not to mention girls in upper age groups and even Jack Travanti, the waterskiing instructor all the girls had a crush on.

For a month and a half, things were bliss. *Grease* was a big hit and things with Wendy were harmonious. But as the summer wore on, Wendy began making suggestions for activities that required Arden to behave in ways that made her feel uneasy. Short-sheeting a bed was one thing; so was stealing someone's Pringle potato chips, fruit rolls, cans of tuna, or squirt cheese.

But as July gave way to August, Wendy's ideas became increasingly radical and mean and aimed at their bunk mate Ali Cohen, who was, for no real reason and a million unfair ones, the object of everyone's derision.

"Let's cut Ali's hair while she's sleeping," Wendy suggested, which meant she expected Arden to do it while she stood by laughing. "Let's throw Ali's purple sweater into the rafters!" "Let's throw Ali's teddy bear into the lake!" "Let's dip Ali's hand in warm water while she's sleeping and see if she wets the bed!" "Let's give Ali a swirly!"

And *she* was the one who ended up pushing Ali's head into the toilet bowl while Wendy flushed and flushed, cackling at Arden's side like a witch.

Arden rolled away from the bulletin board. She felt terribly sleepy, but sleep wouldn't come. For long minutes, Arden thought about Ali, recollection and realization moving over her like slow-spreading syrup. She hadn't wanted to hurt Ali, and yet she had to admit that she had *enjoyed* being mean to her; had *enjoyed* the power she felt inflicting misery, frustration, pain, embarrassment. And then, to share that thrill with Wendy!

But one night, while they were on a camping trip, Wendy suggested they stick a mascara wand up Ali's ass.

"Gross!" Arden had said, sure Wendy couldn't be serious. When they were all in the tent that night, Wendy showed Arden the pink tube of Maybelline she had stashed under her pillow. Still Arden didn't think Wendy was serious.

They all got into their sleeping bags. Wendy read aloud from a dirty magazine she had stolen from the bus driver. Then, one by one, they fell asleep, including Arden.

"Now," Wendy had whispered, giving Arden a shove.

Together, Arden, groggy and still half in a dream, and Wendy, full of enthusiasm and with a kind of demonic energy, gagged Ali with a bandanna, ordered her not to make a peep, and dragged her into the woods not far from the tent.

"*Pull down her pants,*" Wendy ordered. She had already wrestled Ali to the ground and was now sitting on the terrified girl's back while she pinned Ali's arms down at her sides.

"Do it," Wendy said. Without thinking, Arden followed orders.

But Ali clenched her ass tightly and the mascara wand wouldn't go in.

"Shove it in *hard*," Wendy ordered.

Arden tried again, but the mascara wand bent.

"Here," Wendy said, grabbing the wand. She spit onto her fingers, swabbed Ali's anus, and shoved the wand in hard.

Ali let out a moan and Arden, horrified, ran. She ran back to the tent and got into her sleeping bag, panting more from the awful situation than exhaustion. She had done something terrible; she had done something really wrong. Ali was crying out there, a mascara wand sticking out of her ass, and Wendy was sitting on her back, laughing. Arden knew she had to do something! She wriggled out of her sleeping bag and returned to the woods.

"Stop," she said to Wendy, who was still sitting on top of Ali. "Take it out. Take it out or I'm going to get a counselor."

"Don't be such a wuss," Wendy had said. She didn't move, so Arden ran to Ali, pulled the wand out, and pushed Wendy off. All three girls rolled around on the ground, and then they saw flashlights and heard a counselor shouting, "What's going on there?"

Wendy did the talking. She told the counselors they had all gotten up to pee. Whatever she had said to Ali in Arden's absence had made Ali keep her mouth shut.

Ali must have been in shock, Arden reflected, disgusted with herself.

After that night, Wendy wouldn't talk to Arden anymore or even look at her. Arden didn't know whether to be glad or relieved. Soon, Wendy was hanging out exclusively with Dafna, who slept in the bed next to Wendy's, and with Jessica, who had been cast as the lead in the end-of-summer all-camp musical opposite Wendy.

One morning, Arden found a dead frog on her pillow when she returned from breakfast. Another morning, all of her underwear was tied to the flag line and raised with the flag in the center of campus while the rest of the campers looked on, laughing. Arden knew it would only be a matter of time before Wendy stood by cackling while either Jessica or Dafna held her own head down in the toilet bowl. Luckily, there were only three more weeks of camp to get through.

Fresh off the plane, Arden had begged her parents not to send her back. No go. Her parents insisted she return the next summer. To Arden's unquantifiable relief, Wendy wasn't there the following summer. Rumor had it that she had been recruited to play soccer for the junior Olympic team and was already advancing through the junior tennis ranks, as well. Arden thought she might have a chance at starting over, but for some reason the ostracization of the previous summer stuck, even though she was cast as Adelaide in *Guys and Dolls*.

As soon as she was back in Great Neck, her campaign began. She begged her parents not to send her back for her final summer. She told them that she had no friends, she hated sports, she was picked on or ignored, she despised the lake. But her parents believed in Willow Lake's reputation as the finest Jewish summer institution on the East Coast for girls and reassured Arden her luck would change now that everyone had had a year to mature and forget about silly things.

And so, the summer Arden was fifteen, she returned to

Willow Lake. That was the summer she got kicked out for smoking behind the bunk during rest hour. What Aunt June didn't
know was that she had gotten the cigarette from one of the
handymen, a seventeen-year-old local boy named Paul, who gave
Arden the cigarette in return for a blow job, which Arden had
performed with admirable skill "for someone her age," he told her
afterward. "You're a regular dirty Jew," he had said, slapping her
hard on the butt. At the time, the comment had seemed like a
compliment, but now, as Arden lay in her bed, staring up at the
canopy overhead, she was overcome by a wave of self-loathing.

She jumped up, sending Sushi tumbling to the floor in a
small white ball of yelps, and raced down the hall to the bathroom. Splash after splash of cold water over her face did nothing
to relieve the feeling. She took a steaming shower and scrubbed
everywhere, even beneath her nails and inside her belly button.
Still, as she dried herself, taking care around her still-bruised
lips, she felt, in her heart of hearts, that she wasn't clean.

She went back to the bedroom and sat on the edge of her
bed. She studied her bedroom, searching for some sign, some
clue, *something* that could help erase this awful feeling that had
come over her.

Across the room, on the top shelf of her bookcase, her school
notebooks were still lined up in chronological order. She went to
the case and pulled down the last book in the group.

Past doodles, past math problems, past notes in French, past
homework assignments and dates for tests written in large block
letters, past lists of boys' names and a diagram of photosynthesis,
Arden found what she was looking for: a blank page.

She went back to her bed, notebook in hand, and got into a

comfortable position for writing. "My Defining Moment," she wrote
at the top of the page in her minuscule backward-tilting script.

> *I was nine years old when my parents thought it would be
> a good idea for us to go on a family retreat. It was one of those
> completely queer-ass, seventies-inspired, touchy-feely events
> where grown-ups learned how to bless wine and challah and
> felt their children were being uplifted because they were play-
> ing in nature and learning Hebrew folk songs.*

Arden put down her pen for a moment as the main room
of Camp Schneider invaded her memory. She saw the late-
afternoon sun streaming in through the stained-glass windows,
illuminating a giant spiderweb by a heating grate in the corner
of the room; she saw a pool of dust on the floor near the fireplace and the crown molding around the ceiling, its gold paint
peeling above the sliding doors that opened onto the dining
room.

> *It all began with a song the assistant rabbi taught us that
> first day. "Repeat after me," he said. "It is a tree of life to them
> that hold fast to it and all its supporters are [clap] happy."*
> *I was very musical and caught on quickly.*
> *"Good!" the assistant rabbi said, smiling straight at me. He
> asked me my name and I told him.*
> *"Excellent, Arden!" he said. "Now let me teach you the
> chorus. It's just one word, which you repeat over and over. It's
> a word I'm sure you guys know. Who can tell me what shalom
> means?"*

We all raised our hands, but the assistant rabbi called on me. "Arden!" he shouted. "Tell us what shalom means!"

I knew the other kids were jealous that I was getting so much attention, but it didn't stop me.

"Hello, good-bye, peace," I said proudly.

Arden put down her pen. "*Shalom,*" she said aloud, listening to the strange word. "*Shalom,*" she repeated, lowering her voice. The word sounded prettier when she whispered it. It sounded like a lullaby. "Hello, good-bye, *peace,*" Arden explained to Sushi, who looked up at her, confused. She rubbed the dog behind the ears and Sushi resettled herself in the cove of Arden's pelvis. "*Shalom,*" Arden whispered one more time, and, certain now of her new idea, the words began to flow.

Thou Shalt Honor Thy Father and Thy Mother

"Your mother and I are worried about you."

Ali nodded, his phrase barely audible over the din of the lunchtime diners. A piece of rice had fallen off Ali's fork and landed on the top of her hugely protruding belly. With another six weeks to go, she couldn't imagine how her body could expand one more inch.

"Your sisters are worried about you, too."

"I'm sure," Ali said, picking up the rice and rolling it under the rim of the white china plate before her.

"I think you should let—"

Here it comes, Ali thought, having waited through the entire meal for him to bring it up, but he was interrupted by an old family friend who was passing by the table.

"Steve! Ali!" The friend, a gentleman in his early seventies by the name of Abe Greenwald, grasped Ali's father's arm and they shook hands firmly, like two men of the world. "God bless you," Abe said to Ali, nodding at her stomach. "Any minute now, eh?"

"Any," Ali said, standing to give Abe a kiss. She had called him "Uncle Abe" well into her twenties.

"Sit, sit," he insisted. "If you stood up every time someone you know walks by at this place, you'd never be able to finish an olive even!"

Ali's father and Abe laughed and Abe said his good-byes. He was the fourth person to stop by their table during the course of their lunch to interrupt with a boisterous hello.

"Nice to see Abe walking again. You know he had a hip replacement a few months ago," Ali's father said as they watched Abe leave the unassuming Italian restaurant, a virtual hole-in-the-wall on upper Madison Avenue so integral to the social doings of the wealthy locals that most had house accounts and the waiters called them by name.

"Come on," her father resumed. "Why would you turn your back on this?" He gestured to the room. "Is it really so bad? Let me help you and Renny move up here, if for nothing else than so you can be nearer to your sisters and your mother."

"And you and Ruthie," Ali said, unable to keep the bitterness out of her voice.

"You know," Ali's father began.

He and Ruthie had recently abandoned Scarsdale and moved to an apartment on Seventy-ninth and Fifth so they could enjoy his retirement more.

"It's like this," he said, nodding his head slowly, which he did whenever he was gearing up to make a point. "You're the one daughter I've never felt the need to lecture. You've always made your own choices and I've always felt you've made the right decisions for yourself. But there's one piece of advice I feel the need to give you in my advanced age and this is it." He paused to wet his mouth with the last few sips in his water glass. Then he leveled his gaze at her, took a theatrical breath, and said, "People disappoint each other all the time, Alison. It's one of the unfortunate parts of growing up. It was never my desire to hurt you or your sisters or your mother. I love you all. But I couldn't live with the duplicity anymore, and Ruthie makes me happy in ways your mother didn't and couldn't."

"How can you say that?" Ali tried to keep her voice down, without much success. "Mom gave her life to raising us and taking care of you, and now you've left her for some subservient nitwit?"

"Ruthie isn't a nitwit," her father said. "She's very cultivated and caring and has two wonderful grown children of her own who are interested in meeting you if you have any interest in meeting them."

Ali smirked but didn't press the point. She understood her father even if she wouldn't give him the benefit of knowing that. Sharon Cohen had not been an easy woman to have as a wife; she hadn't been an easy woman to have as a mother. While it was true that she had been both doting and loving, Ali knew it was a fallacy to suggest that her mother had *given up her own life* in service to her family.

Sharon Cohen was a stunningly self-involved person and vain to the point of neurosis. Her appointments over the years with plastic surgeons, dermatologists, decorators, manicurists, colorists, personal shoppers, travel agents, tennis and golf pros, not to mention her weekly massage, had all but eclipsed everything but the most pressing family matters. Everything had to be *just so:* her face, her hair, her body, her clothes, the house, *their* clothes, the places they vacationed—it was no surprise that she had lined up a surgeon to take care of the small imperfections in her daughters' faces. She herself had had so much plastic surgery by the time she turned fifty, she was barely recognizable.

Ruthie looked old. She didn't even color her hair. Ali's sisters endlessly criticized their father for choosing to run off with a woman who was a visual downgrade from their mom, but it made sense to Ali, even though she wished it didn't.

"I understand your loyalty to your mother, and so does Ruthie," her father continued, as if he were inside her mind. "It's perfectly normal, but your mother is a grown-up and she's been doing pretty darn well on her own, if you ask me."

"Stop," Ali said. "Just stop. This is ludicrous. I don't see how you expect me to listen to any advice you have to give me regarding my personal life, since you've made such a train wreck of your own."

Ali's father signaled pleasantly to the waiter for the check and took a pretend sip from his empty water glass. "People disappoint each other," he said when there was nothing left to do. "That's all I'm trying to say. I know that's crappy for you to hear, but you only have one life, and I think you have to try to fulfill yourself, even if it means disappointing people you don't want to disappoint."

"Then you have to give me the freedom to disappoint *you,*" Ali said, the weight of the conversation much more difficult to bear than the weight of the baby inside her. "I know you wish I'd marry Renny and I know you and Mom and Robin and Andrea and Mara and Karen and, for all I know, *Ruthie,* all want me to move uptown. That's all I've heard for the last five months. But it's not the right place for me. I'm not an uptown girl."

"That's where I disagree," her father said. "And I know my opinion is only that, and that you don't need to accept it, but I think you're a lot more of an uptown girl than you think."

"Look at me, Dad." Ali ran a hand through her shoulder-length black hair, which was currently streaked with pink.

Her father shrugged. "That's just something you do to get a rise out of your mother. Me, I don't even notice anymore. For years, I thought you were gay, so I'm just happy you're going to give your mother and me another grandchild. But I'd feel better if you'd please live uptown. You'll always be you, wherever you live. You won't suddenly become some Stepford Wife if you move here. You'll just be closer to people who can support you. Closer to the best schools. Closer to Central Park. And I can tell you from very firsthand experience that kids are tough. They don't make life easier. Speaking of that, when are you and Renny getting married?"

"We have no plans to marry at all," Ali said. The baby was kicking her hard under her rib cage and she readjusted herself in her chair.

"Sit still," her father suddenly ordered. "I need you to listen to me." His features, usually so benign, hardened in his lined and infinitely caring face, and the cutting tone that he usually reserved for the courtroom entered his voice as he said, "Don't be ridiculous. Get yourself the same lawyer your sisters used to draft a prenup—I think they used Bernie Glatt—then ask your mother to make you a wedding. I'm sure she'll be thrilled to help out. It'll give her something to do. But for Christ sake, don't bring a bastard into this world."

"You know, Dad"—and now Ali matched her father, tone and

features pointed—"I find it interesting that Renny's parents have said nothing this whole time but congratulations, while I've heard only—"

"You've heard only joy and support from us," her father shot back.

An eavesdropper might have thought he was furious, but Ali knew he was merely frustrated.

"Your sisters adore you. We all adore you. We just don't want you to hurt your child. And I think you're hurting both it and Renny by refusing to get married. I don't even understand why. Against whom, may I ask, are you rebelling? If it's your mother and me, forget it. Neither of us cares. We're too old. If it's your sisters, you're wasting your time. Their self-involvement precludes them ever accepting you unless you're exactly like them, and you never will be, so get over it. Really, Al. You're too old to rebel. At this stage of the game, you should just live your life."

The noise in the restaurant had reached an earsplitting decibel and it felt like the baby had hooked a foot beneath one of her ribs. It was time to go anyway. She had a 2:00 P.M. appointment.

"I'm sorry to cut this conversation short," she said, trying to sound polite, "but I have to be somewhere else soon, so . . . if there's no more to this . . ."

Ali's father sighed and everything about him softened. They had never been able to fight, she and her father. They were too much alike.

"Renny's a nice guy. A great guy. You don't need a Suit. You need a kindred spirit. Let him be a father. Let him have a right to his own kid. Help him be a man." His eyes pleaded with her and she wanted to please him, but she knew her decisions had to be her own.

"If you don't think he's the right person for you," her father continued, "then you'll still have my support, and your mother's support and your sisters' support. If you need to move on and find someone who can give you a different kind of life, then do it. Do it for your kid, Ali. Do what you need to do, for God's sake. Life is short. Take it from your old man. And who even knows when these crazy terrorists are going to unleash a dirty bomb right in the center of Manhattan and do away with all of us. *Live,* Ali. *Live.*"

Ali wanted to speak; she tried to form the words *I'm trying,* but her throat had constricted. "Gotta go," she finally got out. She gave her father a peck on the cheek and squeezed his shoulder. It felt frail beneath the navy blazer. "Thanks for lunch," she said, managing to contain her tears until she reached the street.

"So what do you think?" the broker asked. She was rail-thin and walked with her hips jutting forward, like Nancy Reagan.

Ali had made up her mind about the apartment on the way up to it in the elevator. It had a smell, that elevator. It smelled like mothballs and Nivea and a little bit like the bologna sandwiches her mother used to send her to school with in first grade. In her current state, it made her fight hard not to gag.

The hallway leading to the apartment had that smell, too. The apartment itself wasn't as bad. The windows had been thrown open and an icy draft carried the smell of dirty slush through the cramped three-bedroom on Eighty-third between Second and First.

"I think the kitchen needs a little work, maybe some new appliances and some updated linoleum—"

"I'll think about it," Ali said.

"It's a hot market," the broker reminded her. She blew her nose and stuffed the Kleenex up her sleeve. "An apartment like this will go by the end of the week. And eight hundred thousand is a steal for a prewar building with a doorman."

Prewar? Maybe pre-Vietnam, but there was no way this hulk of bricks and terrazzo was any older than Ali. It just smelled older. "I'll be in touch." She smiled.

"What about the one on Seventy-sixth and First? And the one on Ninety-seventh? Remember how much you liked the living room?"

True, the living room had had a fireplace with a beautiful mantelpiece, but the kitchen in that apartment was from the Carter administration, and she had seen a dead mouse on a glue strip behind the toilet in the master bathroom. Ali checked her watch. Arden would be waiting. "I'll definitely let you know." Smile hopefully! Channel Dafna! she told herself. "And thank you so much for your time."

The subway stalled halfway between Grand Central and Times Square and she was twenty minutes late for her meeting with Arden.

"Are you okay?" Arden asked, jumping up to help Ali as she made her way into the editing suite.

"Fine, fine. Just got stuck on the subway."

"I was worried you were having the baby."

Ali reminded her that it would be another six weeks.

"So *what*?" Arden said. "You shouldn't be running around the way you do." Arden grabbed Ali's parka and bag and pulled a chair out for her to sit in. "You don't want to have it prematurely, and if you don't stop running around this much, you will." She practically forced Ali into the chair. "Have some water. And I bought you some Ovaltine, if you want me to mix you a shake."

Ali had asked Arden to be her assistant in November, after her moving confessional. The arrangement was working out perfectly. Arden had a great eye for editing and had learned the computer program Pro Tools quickly. And with the exception of the constant cigarette breaks, she was a hardworking and caring protégée, especially since the money Ali was paying was minimal. But Arden was still living at home and said she was just happy to be doing something productive with her time.

"I'll only drink a shake if you have one, too," Ali said. She'd been trying to add some meat to Arden's skeletal figure, so far to no avail.

"I found some hilarious footage of us," Arden announced. "Look." She turned on the screen. "You, me, and Beth at a swim meet. Check out my kneecaps—they're bigger than my legs."

"They still are," Ali said, studying the footage.

"And look at this." Arden stopped stirring Ovaltine and ran to the editing machine. "Look at this." She fast-forwarded and stopped at a lacrosse game.

"Jesus," Ali whispered as Wendy Levin clobbered her way across the pitch. "What a brute."

Arden gave Ali a quick, wary look and Ali stopped the footage.

"I don't blame you," Ali said.

"I'm just—" Arden paused, struggling with something she couldn't seem to articulate. Finally she said, "I'm just sorry, you know?"

"I'm sorry, too," Ali said, "for everything *you* went through. And for getting you kicked out of camp."

"I'm glad you did," Arden smiled. "I hated it."

They sat in silence for a while, Ali sipping her Ovaltine and Arden fast-forwarding through some more footage. Then Arden got up to get her own shake. When she returned, she said, "You know, when I was working as Wendy's nanny, I once logged on to her computer." She took a long sip, as if wondering whether or not to proceed.

"And?" Ali prompted.

"And when I clicked her AOL favorites list, the first thing that came up was some lesbo chat room. It was like totally gay, you know?"

On the screen before them, Wendy raced across the field, tackling her opponents and—score! She threw the ball out of her lacrosse stick with enough force to hurt someone. And there was Miss Carol, cheering on the sidelines.

"I think it's a mistake to jump to conclusions about people," Ali said.

"But don't you think it might be interesting for the documentary to show that one of the J.A.P.s is actually a L.A.P.? I mean, even from a commercial standpoint, it's pretty sexy. Everyone loves a lesbian who dresses well."

"If Wendy doesn't want to do an interview, there's not much we can do," Ali said, thinking about the footage she had but was still uncertain as to how to use. She had thought many a night of sending it anonymously to Wendy's husband, but something always stopped her, some nagging moral safety belt that kept her from careening over the edge of ethical reason.

Wendy must be suffering, Ali reasoned, and that much was

good enough. It was only the thought that maybe she *wasn't* suffering, but instead enjoying occasional dalliances with both sexes, that made Ali uneasy. It wouldn't be fair if Wendy were getting laid left, right, and center and enjoying it all, *plus* her cushy little life in Short Hills, where she reigned as her country club's tennis queen. That *would* be unfair.

But if she were tortured? This always made Ali smile. If she were unhappily married, with four little kids in Short Hills, and secretly a sad lesbian with no way of fulfilling herself except through clandestine arrangements like trysts in tents at camp reunions—well, that would be good. Very good. Retribution enough.

Of course, retribution might be better if Ali included the scandalous footage in the documentary. It would be even better if she could get Wendy to indict herself somehow.

"Do you have Wendy's cell phone number?" she asked.

"I *so* fucking still do." Arden beamed.

"Let's see if she picks up. Call her from your cell phone. She'll never pick up if she knows the call's coming from me, and she might not answer if she doesn't recognize the office number."

Arden dialed on her own cell phone.

Wendy picked up on the second ring.

An Outing at Willow Lake

✳

"I don't have time for a French," Wendy said. "I have to make it home by noon. Just do two coats of Like Linen and let's call it a day."

"As you wish," Natalia said. Natalia had been doing Wendy's nails for almost eight years now. Her Polish accent was heavy, but her English was good enough, and she was one of Wendy's most trusted confidantes.

"You must use stronger moisturizer," Natalia cautioned, massaging the callus on the inside of Wendy's palm; it was at the base of her thumb, where she gripped her racket too hard sometimes.

"Just skip the massage today," Wendy said. "I'm seriously in a rush. I'm having Arden for lunch."

"Arden?" Natalia looked up. "I thought she was fired by you, no?"

"No," Wendy said. "Well, *yes,* but I really had no choice. I *had* to fire her. But I didn't *want* to fire her. I always liked Arden." Wendy omitted the fact that she wanted to have sex with Arden, but there were some things you couldn't say to your manicurist, no matter how tight the bond.

"Should we try oval today?" Natalia asked. "I think will look better and is more fashionable now than square."

Wendy nodded her assent. As Natalia filed, Wendy thought about the moment she first realized how badly she wanted Arden Finkelstein as a lover. It hadn't been during Arden's months as Wendy's nanny—although Wendy now had to admit she had probably been lusting for her back then without articulating it to herself. But Arden had been the kids' *nanny,* and Wendy did have some parameters of decency when it came to her private lust. Besides, it had been well before her official outing. (God, how she hated that word! It sounded so *gay.* Honestly, it grossed her out.)

"You don't like shape?" Natalia asked.

"I do," Wendy said. "It's fine."

It was after the pizza cookout on the first night of the reunion, after the encounter in the bunk with Dafna.

"Cut the cuticles, or just push back?" Natalia asked.

"Just push them today," Wendy said, recalling the way Dafna had looked as she slipped off her miniskirt. They were all in the bunk, changing for Friday-evening services. Afterward, they were all going to go down to the beach for singing and a bonfire with s'mores.

"Did you see Ronnie Lipton?" Dafna had asked while she changed. "Her tits are out of control. I wonder where she bought them."

Dafna was wearing a fuchsia thong, the same color as the watermelon they had all consumed with such merriment during the cookout. Dafna had no cellulite and a perfectly flat stomach.

"Do you think there are more boob jobs or nose jobs here?" Beth had asked.

"Noses," Wendy had said, wriggling into her jeans self-consciously. She had felt like a giant. The rest of her former bunk mates looked like they had been starving themselves since their Bat Mitzvahs.

"I'm just dying to know how many people our age have tried Botox," Dafna said. She'd pushed down her thong, and Wendy had had to work hard not to gasp. Dafna was bare. Completely bare. Wendy had felt herself almost start to tremble. Plenty of women in the locker room at Can Do Fitness Club, where Wendy went for her workouts, had Brazilians, but they still had a little landing strip of pubic hair. Wendy had never seen a completely nude wax job in person, only on the models in *Playboy* and on the porn she watched sometimes—well, every day actually, as soon as she got back from tennis.

"I'm just gonna call the kids," Wendy had said, raising her cell phone. "See you all down there."

Wendy had scrambled out of the bunk. Still, she hadn't missed the sight of Dafna's perfect breasts as she took off her tank top.

She began to run. Once the fantasies started, Wendy was helpless to stop them. That's what her life had become: an endless submission to her sexual fantasies. She had found the spot in the pine cove behind the bunks without a problem and tumbled to the ground. Under the branches, over the pine needles and withering cones, at last she had felt safe.

She stuck her hand inside her jeans and began to rub.

Bonnie had come first—Bonnie, her son David's phys ed

teacher at Hartshorn, with her wavy black hair cascading over muscular shoulders, her thick, strong thighs poured into gym shorts. Bonnie had once flicked a mosquito off Wendy's cheek with a surprisingly soft touch. Bonnie had once asked Wendy in for a special teacher/parent conference to discuss David's athletic gifts. Wendy had once even called Bonnie at home, but when another woman answered, Wendy had hung up fast.

Next came the children's physician, Dr. Margaret, tan and tall, with limbs like a man's beneath the skirts or dresses she always wore. Wendy had often imagined that Dr. Margaret got it on with her nurse, Anne, a tiny blond waif in her early twenties who spoke in whispers and soothed all the children after Dr. Margaret plunged a needle into their arm.

And then, the surprise: Arden. At first, it was Arden as a twelve-year-old camper, all brown eyes and long lashes and pink lips, sitting on the steps of the Willow Lake theater in her white camp midi and a pair of navy blue shorts. But the image quickly changed and Wendy saw Arden as she had looked taking care of the boys in jeans and a T-shirt, her slightly concave chest heaving under the weight of Sammy in her arms. Then she saw Arden smoking on the terrace in her pink silk bathrobe, or doing the laundry in that oversized light-blue oxford she often wore with nothing underneath. Wendy began to imagine making love to Arden on the laundry machine and—

"Ridge filler?" Natalia asked. "You have a split."

"Yes, please," Wendy said. "Whatever will fix the problem."

As if *anything* could fix the problem!

Carol's ultimatum was impossible to meet. It would be like death to cut herself off from that pleasure. She had waited so long for it! It was only possible to consider if she could replace Carol with Arden. But to live without a woman, *any* woman—the thought made Wendy shudder.

"You don't like?" Natalia asked anxiously.

"They look perfect," Wendy said, hardly noticing.

"Why you shake your head, then?"

"Just thinking," Wendy said. "Trying to decide what to serve for lunch."

She couldn't go back to life before the reunion. She had been online half the day in chat rooms and driving herself mad with all-girl porn and magazines. She had even had trouble concentrating on tennis. Once Carol came into her life, everything had become perfectly balanced. Every Wednesday night, Wendy drove into the city on the pretext that she was having a girls' night with Dafna and Beth. Then she would spend a few rapturous hours with Carol at her apartment, on Seventy-fourth between Park and Lex.

The arrangement suited Wendy perfectly, but not Carol, who had given Wendy until April 1st to make a choice. The rush seemed unreasonable to Wendy. After all, they had been involved only since the end of August. Six months of bliss seemed a scant amount of time upon which to base such a major decision. But Carol had lost a close friend when the Twin Towers fell and felt life was potentially too short to waste even a moment.

"You don't realize what we have," Carol said, "because this is your first experience, but I'm telling you, this is what most people wait a lifetime for."

"You pay now," Natalia said, "before polish, and I walk you to your car wet."

Wendy produced the forty dollars a manicure at Salon La

Mode cost with tip, then laid out her hands for polish. Carol preferred it when Wendy wore color, but today Wendy felt like she should present a less vixenish look, especially if she was going to make any sort of overture toward Arden. She hated herself for even thinking about cheating on Carol. It was enough that she'd been cheating on Seth all this time. But Arden—the thought of those lips and those long, skinny legs and those tiny little breasts and those eyes; those eyes that expressed so much pain—

"All set," Natalia said. "I don't know where your mind is today, but I wish you luck with lunch. What did you decide to serve?"

"Tuna salad," Wendy said, deciding on the spot, since it was the easiest thing to make. "Thanks." She kissed Natalia on both cheeks. "See you next week."

She made it home with barely enough time to change. Luckily, she was prepared. She had obsessed over what to wear since receiving Arden's call two days earlier and had finally decided on white flannel pants and a simple cashmere top with her Gucci loafers. It was a great look for her, Wendy knew, and the sweater (TSE) felt luscious to the touch, which she hoped Arden might discover.

Arden Finkelstein pulled up in front of Wendy and Seth's house on Minnisink Road twenty minutes late. By that time, Wendy was in the throes of an anxiety attack so severe, she had already taken a Valium to calm herself. Consequently, she had had trouble mashing the tuna fish and mayonnaise and had dropped half of it on the floor. Sometimes Valium did that to her, made her a little uncoordinated and groggy. Now she gulped down a Diet Coke, wiped up as much of the tuna off the floor as she could with the single square of paper towel she had torn from the roll, cursed herself for giving the maid the day off today, and ran to the door to greet her guest.

"Hello!" she said too brightly. Arden looked delicious in a long, clingy gray cable-knit dress only she could pull off with that maddeningly skinny body of hers. On her feet she wore furry snow boots which Wendy told her to leave by the front door. She was wearing pink socks with red and white hearts on them which Wendy found excruciatingly adorable. "Was there traffic on Route Forty-six?" She could feel her pulse racing. "Sometimes it gets a little backed up by the Mobil station. It's better if you make the right and go the back way, but I didn't know how to describe it to you." Wendy knew she was blathering, but she couldn't control herself. Right now, the Diet Coke and her nerves were winning the battle over the Valium.

"It was no problem getting here," Arden said. "Sorry I'm a little late."

"Sometimes with the snow, it's better to take the main road. I always feel a little safer, although I don't know why. It can get so slushy. And sometimes kids go sledding in the street, and I'm always so afraid of an accident." As Wendy chattered on, she ushered Arden into the kitchen, where she lit a Diptyque tubéreuse-scented candle to remove the smell of tuna. It also gave the room a romantic glow she knew Arden would notice since Arden had always been so aesthetically sensitive. "Please," Wendy said, pulling out a chair. She instantly regretted it, realizing she should have led Arden to the sofa in the den, where it was dark and cozy. There was nothing sexy about sitting at the kitchen table. "What can I offer you?" Wendy said, finding her manners through the miasma of her mind.

"Um, just some water would be great."

Her voice! It sent chills of desire through Wendy's body.

"Coming right up." Wendy smiled.

Of course Arden wanted Wendy, too, Wendy was sure. Why else would she have called? They had unfinished business, she and Arden. It was so clear, it didn't need to be discussed.

"So I came here for a reason," Arden said.

Wendy took a sharp breath and cocked her head. "Well, you don't need to come right out with it! Let's ease into things, enjoy a little wine. I have white—is that okay?"

"Oh, just water," Arden protested, but Wendy ignored her and poured two glasses of chardonnay.

"Let's go into the den," Wendy said, leading the way, in hopes that Arden would follow, which she did. "Why didn't you come to the reunion?" she said *en route* to the couch. "How have you been? I've been worried sick about you."

"I've been fine," Arden said, lingering in the doorway.

"Sit! Sit!" Wendy patted the paisley cushion beside her. "Tell me what you've been up to. Have you found another position? You know, you can use me as a reference. I'll give you a good one. Seth is the one who insisted you go, not me." Wendy felt better immediately. At least she had gotten *that* off her chest.

"Actually, I've been working in the film industry," Arden said. "Just learning some basics. It's a lot of fun."

"Film," Wendy said, nothing registering in her mind but the way Arden smelled, which was slightly tart, like a green apple.

"Have you done your interview yet with Ali?" Arden asked.

"Ali?" Wendy felt jarred just hearing her name. "Ali Cohen? Don't tell me you did one?"

"I did."

God! Those eyes!

"It was great."

What a beauty!

"Very therapeutic."

"Really?" Wendy managed, Arden's words finally registering. She was surprised. She had always taken Arden for a rebel—someone who would have laughed at Ali's annoying letter.

"So what was your *defining moment*?" Wendy asked playfully. "I hope to God you told Ali it was when she ratted on you and got you kicked out of camp. That would have given her something to think about." Wendy tossed back some wine and licked her lips. She could hardly wait to use them. Carol's lips were thin and chapped. Arden's were full and shimmering. What lip gloss was it that gave them that glaze?

"I think Ali's had plenty to think about," Arden said gravely.

Aware of the reprimand and grasping the subtext immediately, Wendy said, "Well, she seems to have come out of everything fine and dandy. Not that it excuses what we did—"

"What *you* did," Arden said. "Really, it was you. I was there, that's for sure. But I already made my peace with Ali about that during the interview."

"So, was that your defining moment?" Wendy smiled seductively, wishing Arden's skin wasn't covered so completely by her dress.

"No, my defining moment was being molested by the assistant rabbi at my temple when I was nine years old. That was the real biggie."

"Goodness," Wendy said. She sat up straighter and tried to focus on what she had just heard through the distancing filter of the Valium. "Goodness," she said again as the words and their ramifications sank in. *Those eyes so full of pain!* "How tragic," Wendy said. "Arden, I didn't know."

"It's okay," Arden said. "No one knew. I didn't tell anyone."

"But I was your best friend!" Wendy felt terrible.

"For a few weeks."

Wendy felt worse. She put her white wine down on the table next to Arden's untouched glass and reached for Arden's hands. "I'm so sorry," she said, meaning it with all her heart.

"Me, too," Arden said, pulling her hands away.

Making a pass at Arden no longer seemed like the right thing to do. In fact, Wendy didn't know what to say or do at all.

Arden took care of the moment, asking Wendy once more why she was ignoring Ali's letters.

"I don't think she'll understand my defining moments," Wendy answered truthfully.

Arden asked Wendy why she was so certain Ali wouldn't understand.

What was up with Arden? Wendy wondered. She was so irritatingly *earnest*—not at all the Arden Wendy had been expecting.

"She might understand," Arden was saying. "She's a lot more accepting than you think. At the very least, you should have the decency to return her letters and calls."

"No," Wendy said, unable to comprehend Arden's insistence in pursuing the point. "Come *on*. I deeply doubt some smug purple-haired, pierced-nose *poseur* is going to get a thing I have to say, especially when she's already biased against me. You know, I went to that reunion with the sole purpose of apologizing to her, but she was so smug and hateful, I couldn't bring myself to do it."

Arden asked Wendy what she thought Ali's pose was.

"Look, there's no *way* she's going to understand me!" Wendy said with a sudden force that took her by surprise. "You want to know my defining moments? Marrying Seth when I was twenty-four; the birth of each of our sons; winning tennis matches at Orange Lawn; cheering on the sidelines at David's and Ben's soccer games; taking Eric to swim class; watching Sam try to crawl; managing all of our lives, running the house, organizing sitters and vacations and summer camp and after-school activities. Every moment I'm *alive* is a defining moment! What kind of asinine question is she asking? What is she looking for? She's trying to fry us. Don't you get that? She wants to catch us at something. She wants to embarrass us. It's so obvious!"

"*Whoa.* Chill *out*," Arden said, reaching for the wine. "I didn't mean to make you nutty. I just think it's bad form not to come clean like the rest of us. It's a really interesting project. It might behoove you to participate."

Arden took a long sip of wine and an alarm bell began to ring in Wendy's mind. Were Arden and Ali lovers? Ali certainly had looked like a big dyke at the reunion with that awful hair. "Did Ali send you?" Wendy asked. "Is that why you schlepped out here today? Did Ali actually *send* you?"

"She didn't *send* me," Arden said. "I sent myself because I wanted to set the record straight with you, too. Look, I'm sorry I fucked up as your nanny. It was totally uncool to screw the snow guy in your bed and drink your Cristal and soak in your hot tub, but I do want to say that I took really good care of your kids and you should know that. You should also know that your husband gave me the creeps and I think you should keep an eye on him. But that's your business and not mine. For all I know, you *both* have wandering eyes."

Arden paused and looked at her hard, and Wendy stood, hoping to end the get-together.

"I'm also really sorry that things happened when we were campers that should never have happened," Arden continued. "I regret my behavior, I really, really do, and I'm sorry I let you coerce me into such deplorable actions."

"I think you should go," Wendy said, simultaneously feeling betrayed and trying, unsuccessfully, to stifle heartbreak.

Arden made her way to the front door.

Wendy followed, desperate to salvage the situation.

It was Arden who made the first allusion. Once her boots were on, she looked up from the floor and said, "I wasn't going to say this, but I think someone should and I think that someone is going to have to be *me,* because there's probably no one else brave enough or close enough to you to know this or tell you, but I think you should know that—that I *know* about you."

There was a deep silence in the house. Then Wendy offered Arden a hand up and the two women stood within touching distance.

"What is it you think you know?" Wendy asked, her heart beating wildly.

"I *know* about you. That's all. I know about your little collection of magazines in your underwear drawer and I know about your favorite Web sites and all that. That's all I'm saying. I'm not judging it. I'm not exposing it. I'm just letting you know that I know, and I wish you all the best." Arden turned to go, but Wendy stopped her.

"Can you just tell me one thing?" Wendy tried to control her tone, but she could hear herself almost begging. "Are you in the same boat?"

"The same *boat?*" Arden eyed her queerly. "What kind of boat? You mean the lesbo boat?" Arden's lip snarled and her eyes scrunched up, as if she had just passed a raw sewage plant. "You're on your own there, babe," she said jauntily. "Sorry. No boats at this dock. I'm not even into sex with anyone at the moment. I'm just trying to clean myself up."

"Well, you're doing a good job," Wendy said, clinging with all her might to decorum as she felt reality slide away. "I congratulate you. I'm sure it's been hard."

"Just do the right thing," Arden said. "That's what they always tell us in rehab. Just do the right thing."

After Arden left, Wendy went back to the kitchen table and sat in the chair Arden had abandoned earlier. She dropped her head and let the hot tears burn down her cheeks, fill her nose, land on the table. After a fuzzy amount of time either passed or stood still, she checked her watch. It was 1:35. What day was it? Wednesday? She looked at the *New York Times*. Yes, it was Wednesday. Carol would still be on her lunch break.

"*I can't,*" Wendy sobbed into the phone as soon as Carol answered. "*I can't do it. I can't leave this and I can't leave you. I don't know what to do.*"

"Hey," Carol said soothingly. "Hey. Calm down. Let's calm down. What happened, love? What's happened?"

"I just can't leave this," Wendy said. "I can't. I need my house and my country clubs and my family. I need it. And I need you, too, and you can't make me choose! *You can't!* I'll just end up *dead!*"

Wendy dropped the phone and sank to the floor. She could hear Carol's voice calling her, but she couldn't respond. There was nothing for her but sorrow. Eventually, she stopped weeping enough to get back on the line.

"Carol?" she sniffed. "Are you still there?"

"I'm still here," Carol said gently. "I want you to take a nap. Can you do that for me? Can you nap until the boys get home?"

Wendy said she would.

"Are we still going to do Palm Beach this weekend so we can talk this through in person?"

Wendy said they should. Then she hung up the phone, blew out the candle, climbed the stairs, went to the master bedroom, hung up her lovely pants and lovely sweater, got into her lovely La Perla nightgown, took another lovely Valium, climbed into her lovely lavender upholstered bed, where she was greeted by lovely four-hundred-count Pratesi sheets, and fell into a lovely drug-induced sleep.

Naturally, Wendy had jumped to her son's defense when David was beaten up by some nine-year-old boys at Hartshorn who were jealous that he had been chosen for the Milburn soccer traveling A team instead of them.

"Ignore those losers," Wendy had advised as she dabbed hydrogen peroxide on his cuts. "They're just jealous of you. Kids your age shouldn't go around hurting each other." Wendy had gone so far as to call the school principal and the head of the Phys Ed Department. When it happened a second time, she called the bullies' parents.

"What kind of kids are you raising," she had chastised, "that they think it's appropriate to brutalize a fellow classmate, especially someone younger?"

Tortured by memories of her own behavior as a child, that night Wendy hadn't slept well. What kind of parents had *she* had?

What kind of kid had *she* been that she had thought it was okay to brutalize *her* classmates?

Her parents had been wonderful, her life at home unfettered. She and her two brothers had been raised in a beautiful suburb of Philadelphia, where their father had a thriving corporate law practice and their mother worked as a docent at the Barnes Foundation. True, she had been a tough kid. Her brothers had beaten each other up, like all brothers do, and Wendy had been beaten up herself and had had to learn to fight back, like all younger sisters of tough older brothers. But she had always been a leader among her classmates and popular at camp and Hebrew School. She had always excelled.

So she had also always been a little brutal to certain girls. At camp, it had been Ali; at school, it had been Betsy Comer, then Amanda Goldberg. But it had seemed okay. She had never gotten in trouble for it. It had seemed like something that had been her right, something that came with the territory when you were taller and stronger than everyone else.

Once she went to the University of Michigan, it all fell by the wayside. She got wrapped up in the tennis team and joined a Jewish sorority and did all the things her friends did: went on dates, made out with cute Jewish boys, even lost her virginity sophomore year to Mark Abromowitz, a senior who played number two men's singles. She hadn't enjoyed it, but most of the girls she knew hadn't enjoyed their first experience with sex, either. Then again, most girls she knew didn't have crushes on other women, which, at that point in her college career, she had to admit she did.

There hadn't been any lesbians in her high school class—none she had known about anyway. At U of M, lesbians roamed the campus freely, holding hands, dancing together and kissing at parties. Being a lesbian was cool in Ann Arbor. But not in her circle. She had thought once or twice about joining a women's organization, but she never did. She couldn't. She wouldn't. She didn't want to be gay. Being gay meant being outside the mainstream; not shaving your legs and armpits (ick!); piercing your nipples (ickier!); going to rallies and being political (boring). Lesbians wore thick-soled flats, not Gucci spikes. Lesbians were weird, not "nice Jewish girls." Lesbians were always marching around holding hands under banners and shouting slogans and letting their armpits go wild. She refused. She simply refused. She would never give in to her deepest urges. Never.

After college, she played professional tennis for a year. It was awful. She traveled to Tokyo, Sydney, Prague, and Milan with nothing but her bag of rackets and tennis dresses to keep her company. She was isolated. She gained weight. She lost most of her matches. One night after a tournament, she let another girl on the tour kiss her, a Russian girl named Sylvie. Sylvie was tall and lanky and had short-cropped blond hair and a mouth like a horse. They had both been lying naked on their towels in the sauna at the tennis club. Wendy's eyes had been closed, and the next thing she knew, Sylvie was kissing her. Wendy had enjoyed it and kissed Sylvie back, but when Sylvie began fondling Wendy's breasts, she had gotten terrified and pushed Sylvie away.

"You're happy, no?" Sylvie had said, smiling her horsey smile.

Wendy ran out of the sauna, threw on her clothes, grabbed her racket bag, and fled.

The next day, she had to face Sylvie in a match. Wendy was up a game in the first set, but was forced to withdraw when she injured her left knee diving for a low volley. As soon as she got back to New York, she went to the Hospital for Special Surgery, which was where she met Seth. He fixed her knee, asked her out, and the two were married three months after her twenty-fourth birthday.

Seth was eleven years older than she was and knew what he wanted. And Wendy? Well, Wendy wanted whatever Seth wanted.

They moved to Short Hills and had children. Each birth seemed a confirmation to Wendy of her heterosexuality. She changed diapers and breast-fed and went to mommy-and-me classes and joined a tennis club and went out to dinner with Seth and their friends—other couples who were just like them. She felt normal. And normal was what she wanted to be. She wanted to be just like her neighbors; her friends; her brothers and their wives, with kids and dogs and cookouts on the Fourth of July and big Seders and happy Thanksgivings and family tennis tournaments.

That she fantasized regularly about that night in the sauna with Sylvie seemed harmless enough. She was a married woman. Her parents were proud of her. When she went home to Philly for Rosh Hashanah and Yom Kippur, her kids played with their older cousins while Seth joked around with her brothers and smoked cigars with them in her parents' den, and everything was as it should be.

That's all Wendy wanted: everything as it should be, even though nothing ever was.

✳

"Your hair looks nice," Seth said. "Have it blown?"

"Um," Wendy said, irritated with herself for having given up her morning tennis game to get her hair done, when Arden had neither noticed nor cared. At least everything on the home front was under control. Sam was already down and the other three boys were watching a video with their baby-sitter, Bianca. Seizing the rare moment of tranquillity, Wendy studied her closet, trying to decide what to wear. It was an "A" night at the club, meaning tie and jacket for the men, cocktail dresses for their wives. She settled on one of her more feminine outfits, a Valentino crushed velvet dress in red with an equally plunging neck and back. She usually favored her Gucci or St. John suits for the club, but tonight her body ached and her skin felt raw. She couldn't bear the idea of anything tight.

She put on a thong and a pair of black leather boots with silver spike heels, Sergio Rossi's latest, and went into the bathroom to do her makeup before putting on the dress so as not to drop any powder on it. Seth was at his sink, flossing his teeth. She hated the sound the floss made as it dug hidden particles of food and plaque out of his teeth. She regarded her face in the mirror and tried to black him out. She looked tired and her eyes were a little red. She put in some drops and closed her eyes to allow the drops to do their work, which was when Seth put his hands around her waist and began to kiss her neck.

She kept her eyes closed. It would be easier that way. She could imagine Seth was someone else. He was kissing her shoulder now and his hands were working their way up to her breasts. His touch repulsed her and his kisses made her cringe. Where was her imagination? Why couldn't she find an image? A person? Where was Bonnie? Where was Arden? Where was Carol? But no one came to Wendy's tired mind.

"Mmmmm," she moaned, knowing she should. The more encouragement she gave, the hornier Seth would get and the sooner the ordeal would be over.

Seth pushed her to her knees and dropped his pants. "Take me in your mouth," he ordered, and, her eyes still closed, Wendy did what she was told.

David needed new cleats and shin guards for soccer. (She reached up and stroked Seth's balls. That usually sped things up.) And she needed to find the lost cartridge for his Game Boy. Benjamin had probably put it in the hamper, his favorite new hiding place.

"That's so good," Seth was saying. "I love what you're doing, baby. Let me give you some loving, too." He pulled himself out of her mouth and led her to the bed. "Those boots are too much. You look like a naughty member of the Gestapo. Turn around. I want to see that great ass of yours."

She climbed onto the bed on all fours and let him do his business. While he pumped away, she noticed that one of the buttons on the upholstered headboard was coming loose. She made a note to talk to her decorator about it. She hadn't spoken to Lugene in ages. She wondered if he was even in New York, since he split his time between New York and L.A. now, with occasional trips to Milan.

She was getting dry and it was beginning to hurt. It was time to end things. "I wish my arms were longer so I could slide my finger into your ass," she said in a seductive voice.

Bingo. Game over. She returned to the bathroom and began to apply concealer.

Wendy had found Dafna and Beth within minutes of arriving at the reunion. From the check-in desk on the terrace of the main house, she had located them by Aunt June's garden, to the left of the infirmary. When Wendy came upon them, they all squealed in delight like long-separated loved ones, even though they had seen one another a scant three weeks earlier at the Parrish Art Museum in Southampton, where Wendy and Seth rented a house every summer. Dafna and Beth had come up to Maine together from the city. They compared travel notes with her, then suggested they all have a seat on the Adirondack chairs, which was when Ali—strange Ali, unrecognizable Ali—entered the picture.

Right away, Wendy knew she was in some kind of trouble. There wasn't anything specific that Ali actually did. It was just the way she spoke—with a kind of breathtaking authority—that had made Wendy feel small, even though, had they been standing side by side, she would have towered over Ali by several inches. And then there was the "defining moment" bullshit at the beach party. Wendy had listened hard, trying to discern a subtext to Ali's words. She didn't trust the person who claimed to be Ali.

"I'd be happy to share my own defining moment," Ali had said cheerfully. Even in the dark on the beach, where Wendy stood with the others, she had felt Ali's gaze resting on her.

"I'll be right back," she had said, knowing there was no law that claimed she had to participate. "I see someone I want to catch up with."

Wendy had walked away purposefully and searched the crowd of women on the beach and around the bonfire to see if there was anyone she recognized.

"Wendy Levin," she heard, "I've been searching all over for you."

Wendy had turned in the direction of her name and her eyes found the face of Miss Carol, her former bunk counselor and onetime lacrosse mentor. With a rush of relief, she threw herself into Miss Carol's arms.

"I thought I saw you at the cookout," Miss Carol had said, holding Wendy at arm's length. "*Look* at you. You look terrific."

"Not really," Wendy demurred, mesmerized by the warmth in Miss Carol's lovely blue eyes. "Look at *you*," she had managed in return, taking in the rest of Miss Carol, who, by the light of the moon, looked as blond, fit, and preppy as she had all those years earlier.

"You look like you've eaten nothing but Wheaties and whole milk since I saw you last!" Wendy had said.

"Grape-Nuts," Miss Carol had countered. "And whole-grain toast. That's it."

They both laughed and Wendy had almost instantly forgotten about Ali and her ridiculous "defining moment" interrogation.

"I hear you're the mother of four now," Miss Carol had said, leading Wendy down the beach, away from the group of singers and up toward the grassy knoll where the Sunfishes and Flying Juniors were stored for the night.

Wendy asked where she'd gotten her gossip, and Miss Carol replied, "Ali Cohen."

Wendy tensed and, as if sensing it, Miss Carol asked Wendy if she'd like to sit down.

"I'm the one who got her to do the documentary," Miss Carol explained proudly as Wendy lowered herself onto the beach. "When I saw her film last year at the Palm Beach Film Festival— have you seen it? *Children on the Roadside*?"

Wendy hadn't.

"It's an incredible piece about the children of migrant workers in the Hamptons, and I told Faye and Ron that they had to hire Ali to do something about Willow Lake."

It was oddly exciting to hear Miss Carol discuss her life outside of Willow Lake. As a camper, such a life had seemed impossible for a counselor. Wendy asked Miss Carol if she lived in Palm Beach.

"New York. Upper East Side," Miss Carol said. "But I grew up in Palm Beach and I go down every year for the film festival. My mother's on the board."

Was Miss Carol one of them? That, too, seemed impossible. Well, she wasn't entirely one of them. She wasn't Jewish. No Jew could possibly be that preppy.

"You're not a member of the tribe?" Wendy asked skeptically.

"Honorary," Miss Carol answered. "But at this point, I feel like I'm at least ready for my Bat Mitzvah money."

Off to the right, Wendy could see Ali, who was still talking with the other girls. She asked Miss Carol if she knew Ali wanted to interview them.

"I hope you're going to do it," Miss Carol said. "I'd be especially curious to hear what you've been up to since you wowed us all as a camper."

Wendy shrugged and rolled her eyes, hoping Miss Carol would find another subject so she wouldn't have to detail her failure to achieve any of her early potential.

"I assume you're still as athletic as ever," Miss Carol said.

Wendy was careful not to reveal too much hubris as she shared her most recent victory: the Orange Lawn Tennis Club's ladies' A-team singles championship, which she'd clinched the day before for the eighth year running.

"That's awesome!" Miss Carol said, giving Wendy's arm a squeeze. "Why the sad face?"

How could Wendy explain that it wasn't a sad face but a face working hard to conceal attraction? She couldn't. Instead, she explained that people were sick of seeing her win. Other than the officials at the club, no one even offered more than perfunctory congratulations, including her husband.

"The price of fame," Miss Carol said. "It's lonely at the top."

Wendy said she wouldn't really know about that; it was one thing to win your club tournament, but it wasn't like she'd taken home the Wimbledon Cup every year.

"The girls who do the tour make a lot of sacrifices," Miss Carol said, putting her hand on Wendy's back. "And very few of them, if any, have four sons and a happy marriage."

"Well," Wendy managed, looking up at the night sky. Miss Carol's hand felt good; it felt natural, unthreatening, and she let it stay there as they caught up on the intervening years. The moon made a white stripe across the water and Wendy remembered how, as a camper, she had wished she could run across the path and go straight up to the sky. She shared the thought with Miss Carol, which was when the hand began to move—up a little, down a little . . .

Wendy turned and looked into Miss Carol's eyes, and what she found there was a look that could only be described as lust.

"I have to call Seth," Wendy said, practically jumping up. "Find out how the kids are doing."

"O-kay. Nice catching up!" Miss Carol called out as Wendy ran away from the beach.

She ran and ran, up the hill and across the campus, until she reached the cold, dark bunk where she threw herself into her sleeping bag fully clothed. Wendy heard the sound of rustling in the ceiling. She remembered how once, as a camper, a bat had gotten into her bunk. She turned on her flashlight and shined it all around the ceiling but saw nothing.

Why had she come back to Willow Lake? she wondered as tears filled her eyes. It was a mistake, a stupid, demoralizing mistake. It would have been better to stay home with Seth and the boys. Tear after tear rolled down Wendy's cheeks to join the bath of shame in which she was soaked. Miss Carol's hand had felt so good! Her *nearness* had felt so good! Wendy reached into her jeans so her hand could catch up with her already-wandering mind. It was Miss Carol she thought of as she rubbed away her misery: Miss Carol doing all kinds of things to her a nice Jewish girl should never even think of—

Wendy let out a cry in the dark that echoed, ominously, in the rafters. There was nothing for her to do but lie on her back and stare helplessly up into the dark.

Every time the car curved around the circular entrance to Mountain Ridge Country Club, Wendy breathed a sigh of relief. Although she professed to Carol to despise her and Seth's frequent get-togethers there, in fact she usually enjoyed them. There was something so permanent and reassuring about the massive stone and brick structure, built in 1929 by Clifford Wendehack, whoever he was (Wendy only knew his last name because of the plaque on the front of the building). "Poor Clifford," everyone always said when they made their toasts. "If he only knew!"—meaning, if only he knew the club was entirely Jewish now, he might not be so pleased.

Seth turned the car over to the valet and took Wendy's arm as they entered the building. The dinner tonight was being held in the grand ballroom, where all "A" dinners were held, as opposed to the "B" meals (jackets but no ties for men, pants—except for jeans—for ladies), which were held in either the dining room or the clubhouse; and then there were Wendy's favorites, the "C" barbecues in summer (only shirts and shoes required), which were family affairs and were held on the terrace or, in the event of rain, in the sunroom.

Tonight, they were meeting the Farbers and the Gottliebs in the library first for drinks. Like Seth, Ed Farber was a surgeon at the Hospital for Special Surgery. His wife, Julie, was an excellent golfer, and the four of them often played together in the summer. The Farbers had introduced them to the Gottliebs, which was lucky, since they lived only a few blocks away in Short Hills and had kids the same age as David, Ben, and Eric. Barry Gottlieb ran some kind of hedge fund (Wendy never could quite grasp exactly what he did, but she knew he was worth a bundle) and his wife, Michelle, played tennis at Orange Lawn. They spent a lot of time together as families, so it was nice, for a change, to socialize just as adults.

Both the Gottliebs and the Farbers were already in the mahogany-paneled library, a room the decorators of Mountain Ridge could have lifted right out of Cliveden, given all the wood paneling and green leather seamed with brass studs. There was even a tapestry of a unicorn over the fireplace, which tonight was picturesquely ablaze.

Hellos with hugs and kisses ensued, along with a full appreciation of the ladies' outfits, and within minutes Seth was sitting by the bar drinking scotch and nibbling almonds with Barry and

Ed, and Wendy was ensconced with Michelle and Julie on the leather sofa in the corner of the room, where they had the best view of the other sofa in the library, which was presently holding the notorious Shira Miloff. The girls were aghast. Shira was sitting practically on the lap *not* of her husband, who was at the bar with the other men, but on the lap of her best friend's husband, Micah Friedman.

"Where's Lynn?" Wendy asked, wondering why Micah had been left in the precarious position at all.

"She's in the bathroom," Julie whispered. "I swear to God! You can't even go pee, for fear Shira will fuck with your man."

"What a slut," Michelle said.

"What a fashion victim," Julie added. "I don't care if she *was* featured in *New York* magazine because of her obnoxious obscssion with Azzedine Alaia. Who even *admits* that kind of thing?" Julie shook her head in disgust. "She's a complete anorexic embarrassment to this club and she looks like a kid playing dress-up in that Prada. Jewish girls really shouldn't wear Prada at all. It only looks good on the Italians."

Julie herself probably only weighed ninety-six pounds, wet, and was wearing a dress Wendy was pretty sure she had seen in the Prada department at Neiman's, but she kept her mouth shut.

"I heard she gets herself off having phone sex with all her friends' husbands," Michelle said.

Julie demanded a source.

"It's common knowledge," Michelle replied.

"It is," Wendy confirmed.

Lynn returned from the powder room and Shira wobbled up from Micah's lap in her four-inch Jimmy Choos, waving innocently but fooling no one.

"Poor Lynn," Michelle said. "Someone should warn her."

"I don't think so," Julie rebutted. "I don't think it's good practice to meddle in people's marital affairs."

"Agreed," Wendy said.

"You have a point," Michelle conceded.

There was a silence. Everyone in Short Hills was talking about Julie's husband, but no one knew how to bring the topic up with Julie. It was rumored that he'd been discovered in a pair of women's underpants. Apparently, he had a whole secret stash discovered by Julie's maid, who quit on the spot, since she was a staunch Catholic and didn't condone monkey business of any kind. It was just a rumor, but still.

Wendy tried a change of topic. "Are you guys going to Morgan Ringelstein's Bat Mitzvah next Saturday?" But it was too late. Julie's eyes were filling with tears, and Michelle initiated an exodus to the powder room.

"What am I supposed to do?" Julie wailed. "Everyone thinks I'm married to some freak, but it isn't like that. Ed's a normal guy. God, if this gets out around the hospital . . ."

Michelle suggested counseling and Julie said she had already found an expert.

"So there you go!" Michelle said. "It'll all be fine."

"I know," Julie said, wiping under her eyes. When she had gained full composure, she turned to Wendy and said, "How about you? How are things with you and Seth?"

"Fine," Wendy replied. "Why?"

There was a brief pause, and then Julie said, "Only because you were complaining about Seth's insomnia after yoga last week and I wondered if it was affecting your sex life."

"Not really," Wendy offered.

"I wish Barry would get goddamned insomnia or something so that he'd stop wanting to fuck me so much," Michelle blurted out. "He's become a fucking Viagra junkie and it's killing me. It takes him for-*ever*. I mean, let's face it. It's just hard to get through sometimes, isn't it?"

Wendy laughed in solidarity with her friends and they all touched up their makeup and returned to their men.

The pitch sailed toward her slow, straight, and slightly outside.

A chorus of voices was cheering, "*Go,* Wendy, *go! Do* your *best! Can't* you see that you're better than the rest! *Go, Wendy!*"

Wendy smiled triumphantly even before the bat made contact with the ball, sending it way out past the farthest fielder and into the middle of the hockey pitch. She rounded the bases, just like she had so many times when she'd been a camper, her adrenaline surging, glory undeniable.

"Chickee wee! Chickee woo! [Clap, clap.] Wendy!" her grown-up teammates cheered, offering high fives as she returned to the bench. Then chimes rang out over the PA system, announcing the start of the milk-and-cookie line, and her team erupted once again in a series of chants and cheers as Wendy was hoisted up into the air. Her team had won, 4–1, and Wendy had scored two of the runs off homers and batted the other two runners in.

Wendy's coming, better watch out.
Wendy's coming, give a loud shout.
From the east to the west

From the north to the south
Wendy's on the war path
So . . . look out!

Wendy couldn't believe anyone still remembered the cheer, but on it went as the women carried her to the steps of the main house. As they put Wendy down, the first person she saw was Miss Carol, who was standing on the top step of the terrace.

"That last one was a hell of a swing," Miss Carol said. "I thought it would end up in Nova Scotia."

"My God!" Wendy exclaimed, surveying her former mentor in daylight. "Has everyone been in a time capsule except me?" Miss Carol was wearing the same kind of plaid skirt and Izod shirt she had worn when she had taught Wendy to master a lacrosse stick so many years ago, and her hair this morning was back in its familiar French braid. She looked beautiful and solid, reassuring and classic.

"I trust the hubby and kids were fine," Miss Carol said as they waited together on the milk-and-cookie line.

Wendy told her the kids had been asleep when she called.

"You must have followed their lead," Miss Carol said playfully. "I didn't see you later around the fire. We had beer. It seemed very sacrilegious and fun."

Wendy didn't know what to say. She felt inexplicably nervous, as if Miss Carol had access to her fantasies. They reached the table and Miss Carol took a cookie. Wendy hesitated. She had noticed several other women pass by the cookies with a rueful laugh and a shake of the head.

"Oh, go ahead," Miss Carol said.

Wendy laughed and helped herself to a large chocolate-chip.

She was reaching for a cup of milk when Miss Carol asked her if she'd like to sit for a minute.

Wendy took a breath and looked into Miss Carol's face. The look she saw in those blue eyes and the tone she heard in Miss Carol's voice were both normal enough, but in each Wendy detected, or perhaps simply hoped for, a hidden agenda. Wendy opted to ignore her instincts and the fantasies they elicited. "I have a date," she explained, "with Ali and the gang."

"Busy, busy," Miss Carol said. "See you later, then." She waved to Wendy and went off to join a different group. Wendy felt a pang of jealousy, but she had made the commitment to Ali to participate in her documentary, and after everything that had happened, she felt the least she could do was stay true to her word. Still, she regretted that she couldn't join Miss Carol. She certainly wasn't looking forward to the interview with Ali. She hadn't figured out a good strategy yet. Should she apologize on-camera? Should she pull Ali aside between takes and apologize privately? Should she just go on pretending the events had taken place so long ago that they no longer mattered?

When she reached the Adirondack chairs, nothing more than a gossip session was in progress. "Andrea Weiner?" Dafna was saying when Wendy sat down with her Dixie cup of milk. "Fat and living in Greenwich with two kids."

"Leah Winkle," Ali said.

"Social worker in San Francisco," Dafna answered. "Twins. Husband in tech."

"Ellen Tarnakoff?"

Dafna was unruffled. "Moved to London. Divorced. Works for the BBC."

Dafna had the skinny on everyone in their age group, even

Chloe Weinstein, who had stayed for one summer. "Mom. Park Avenue. Older husband. On the board of the Cooper-Hewitt."

As Wendy took her seat, Ali looked over at her with such unmasked hatred, it made Wendy shudder and she spilled some of the milk. *The irony!* Here Wendy had spent so much time focusing on the appropriateness of her desire to apologize, it had never occurred to her that Ali might not want to hear an apology anymore. What was more, Wendy no longer felt like apologizing; not to this Ali anyway. This Ali had turned out fine; this Ali was someone to avoid.

"Tell me more about your wedding plans," Ali said to Beth as Wendy crushed the Dixie cup in her fist. "How about your dress?"

"Vera Wang."

"It's gorgeous!" Dafna gushed. "I helped her pick it. Tight bodice. Organza."

"It's satin now," Beth said, as if the dress had been diagnosed with cancer.

Wendy stopped listening then. How could she possibly concentrate? "I'm *sorry!*" she wanted to shout. "I'm *sorry, okay?!* Can we just establish that so I can enjoy this weekend? I was young; I was an idiot. I'm *sorry.*"

That's what she would say, she decided. She waited for Beth to finish her description of the *chuppah* so she could deliver her brief monologue, but chimes rang out over the PA system, Ali put the camera away, and the women dispersed to their final activities before lunch.

*

Wendy stood, paralyzed, before the sumptuous Mountain Ridge buffet. After as much consideration as she could manage, she wandered back to the table with nothing but a handful of carrot and jicama sticks, a few glistening supersize pale green olives, small servings both of the cucumber salad and the endive, walnut, pear, and blue cheese salad, and a small triangle of pumpernickel bread on which was perched a perfect orange slab of smoked salmon topped with dill.

She passed on the pigs-in-the-blanket and spanakopita, even though they were usually her favorites. She passed on the raw bar, fresh and plump as the shrimp looked, festive as the oysters seemed, succulent as she imagined the crab and lobster claws were. She had passed on the cheese platter and the antipasto and the chopped chicken liver, and the whitefish salad, pickled herring, and chub. She had passed on the mini egg rolls and pizzas and on those wonderful cheese puffs Mountain Ridge always did. (What was in there, some fancy cheese, or was it Velveeta that made them so tasty?) She didn't even help herself to the yellowtail or salmon sushi or to any of the California rolls or inside-out spicy tuna rolls, although she was sure one of the other women would bring some back for the table.

There was no need to examine the second buffet table. Judging from the chefs in their tall white hats and the red heat lamps, there was prime rib, beef Wellington, or rack of lamb tonight (possibly all three), and there was always salmon and swordfish, chicken, and one or two pasta dishes, as well as risotto and at least four different kinds of vegetables. It was all just too much for her bloated brain to get around tonight.

What had Julie meant by asking how things were going with Seth?

She nodded at Barbara Nusbaum as she passed by Barbara's table. Barbara smiled back, even though Wendy knew Barbara probably hoped she would trip and break her arm. Barbara had lost to Wendy in the tennis finals for the last three years in a row. They saw each other every Tuesday and Thursday morning at tennis clinic and often joined each other as a doubles team; still, there was no great excess of friendship between them, despite Wendy's best efforts to dispel the tension.

Why did she think of this club as her home anyway? It was like swimming in flashy jewelry with a bunch of barracudas!

Wendy took her seat and eyed the plates of the other women. Michelle had taken three of the open-faced smoked salmon sandwiches and a few squares of cheese. Julie's plate contained two pieces of yellowtail, two California rolls, and a single lonely shrimp. Across the table, the men seemed to be preparing for a coming famine, their plates piled high with everything but carbohydrates, since they were all doing the Atkins Diet. Wendy had tried explaining to Seth earlier that scotch was not on the Atkins program and by drinking it he was undoing the diet, but he didn't seem to get it. Since starting the diet, he had already gained four pounds.

"I don't think they should have someone unintelligible. That's all I'm saying. It's a time for language acquisition, and I think a heavy accent makes it hard on them."

Wendy knew right away that Michelle was kvetching about the new teacher at B'nai Jeshurun. Michelle's daughter, Madison, and Wendy's son, Eric, were in the same nursery school class there. Julie's younger son, Zach, was too young, but she was concerned already about next year.

Julie asked Wendy what she thought about Ms. Pakula.

"Eric likes her," Wendy said.

Michelle began to list a series of facts discrediting Ms. Pakula's credentials.

It wasn't that Wendy lacked interest in the conversation, but she felt almost overcome with fatigue. She looked around the dining room and made eye contact with a waiter, who came right over and vowed to bring her a Diet Coke within seconds. Seth noticed when the waiter returned with it and he gave her a look (Ed had splurged on a fabulous bottle of wine), but she raised her hand and closed her eyes, letting him know it was a quick remedy and not something that would ruin their good time.

Michelle and Julie were trying to figure out whether Nina Rosenman's necklace was from Bulgari or Harry Winston.

"Nina's husband buys her major jewels every time she lets him have anal," Michelle said.

Julie's jaw dropped and she insisted on knowing Michelle's source.

"It's common knowledge," Michelle said.

Julie looked at Wendy and Wendy said, "It is," even though she'd never heard the rumor.

There really was something soothing about the giant crystal chandeliers and the muted golden glow they cast upon the room. During the summer, when it stayed light out late, Wendy never noticed the chandeliers. Her gaze always rested on the endless green vista of the golf course, which was visible from every spot in the grand ballroom, and on the sky as it melted from blue to pink and then to fuchsia lavender when the sun made its way below the horizon. Tonight, however, the feeling of comfort in the room was intensified by the fact that there was nothing to be seen out the green velvet–dressed windows but the reflection of the diners enjoying themselves within.

"Anyone want more?" Seth was already up, empty plate in hand.

The group declined, but Seth kissed Wendy on the forehead as he passed her seat and whispered that he'd bring her back some whitefish salad.

Under normal circumstances, she would have been pleased. But she wanted an excuse to get away from the table, so she got up after a moment to stop Seth from bringing it back.

Only a few moments had elapsed between their departures. Still, she couldn't find him. He wasn't at the appetizer table. Wendy looked over at the second table, but there was no sign of him there, either. She finally located him by the desserts, standing beside Shira. He was looking down at her and they were sharing a laugh about something. She tossed back her long brown hair and wriggled her nose at him. Wendy didn't move. Something primal in her recognized their body language. She did a quick about-face and returned to the table.

"You okay?" Michelle asked.

"Fine," Wendy said, and really she was. Her mind was working quickly now, moving over a series of possibilities. If Seth was cheating on her, it would be better for their marriage. She wouldn't have to feel so guilty about her own situation and she could even avoid sex with him more frequently. She wasn't thrilled that Shira seemed to be his lover (Lord only knew what diseases she might carry, given her reputation), and Shira was someone who flaunted her conquests as casually as she flaunted her nonexistent breasts with their perpetually erect nipples through her ridiculous sheer tops, which meant that at some point (and perhaps already), Wendy realized, people would be feeling sorry for her.

Would that be so bad? If anything ever leaked out about her

own affair (*please God, please God, let no one ever know her affair was with a woman!*), people would understand. They would say she had been pushed to do it, or, better yet, consider it proper retribution.

Seth returned to the table with another slice of beef topped with blue cheese. There was no sign of any whitefish salad. He winked at her across the table and launched immediately into a conversation with Barry and Ed.

Wendy turned toward her friends, who were going on about Shira.

"I'd cut her off without a nickel, if I were him," Julie was saying.

"I'd write her a *check* to get lost," Michelle said. "She's a complete psycho."

Wendy began to wonder if they knew about Seth and Shira; if perhaps they were tearing Shira apart in Wendy's defense. She joined the attack, adding little comments here and there, but her ears strained to pick up what the men were talking about, in hopes that she might discover a shred of fact to fortify her suspicion.

"Ron Dayne is dead wood," Seth was saying. "They gotta give Tiki Barber more carries. The guy's on fire."

"Kerry Collins is having a good season, too," Ed added.

"They're my *boys!*" Barry exclaimed, as if he knew the players personally.

Julie was shaking Wendy's arm. "Your phone. It's ringing."

Wendy apologized. The club had a policy prohibiting cell phones, but she had forgotten to turn hers off tonight. By the time she yanked it from her purse, the ringing had ceased. Hoping it might have been Carol, she excused herself from the table, left the dining room, and actually went all the way out to the parking lot, where her phone would get the best reception.

She checked Recent Calls and her own home number came up. Bianca! Wendy's heart began to pound as soon as she pressed the dial key.

Eric had a 104-degree fever. He wouldn't stop crying.

"Hold him straight up," Wendy said, thinking it was probably an ear infection, which apparently always felt worse when the child was horizontal. "Give him some Tylenol. Use the dropper in his medicine cabinet. I think it's two dropperfuls for a child his age. Just make sure it's the Tylenol for toddlers, not Sam's infant Tylenol. I'm on my way."

Wendy raced back to the table and told Seth the news. She offered to go home by herself, but Seth didn't let her finish the sentence. "Are you nuts? It's *Eric*. Of course I'm going home with you. He's my son, too."

Seth took Wendy by the hand and together they left the table amid a flurry of best wishes from the Farbers and Gottliebs.

Miss Carol stood at the edge of the dock, the white-blond hair on her arms highlighted by the late-morning sun. "Mind if I come along for the ride?"

"Fine with me," Wendy said, jumping off the dock and into the lake. The water was cold but refreshing and she giggled a little, happy to be in Willow Lake after so long an absence. She bobbed in the water while the boat circled around her, wondering if she'd remember what to do.

"Hit it!" she shouted, giving Miss Carol and Water Ski Jack the thumbs-up sign. She got up on one ski immediately, as if eighteen years hadn't lapsed between that moment and her last on a water ski. She cut left across the wake, leaning low toward the water so she made an arc of spray around herself. Joy filled her as drops of water hit her face and she cut across the wake in the other direction.

It was funny that Seth and the boys had never seen her water-ski. Of course they had all seen her downhill ski. They had spent their winter vacations for years skiing in Vail with the Farbers. Everyone knew Wendy could get down even the steepest black diamond, but there was nothing that could compete with her prowess on a water ski. If only her family could see her!

But they didn't see her. Even if they were here they wouldn't see her. No one saw her. She wasn't even certain she saw herself.

"Looking good!" Water Ski Jack shouted as she glided to a graceful finish right at the dock.

Wendy clasped her hands over her head, the Willow Lake gesture for "A-OK."

"Looking *very* good," Miss Carol added, jumping out of the boat and onto the dock. She offered Wendy her hand and pulled Wendy out of the water with a single strong yank.

Chimes had already rung. It was time for lunch. Wendy threw a pair of shorts over her suit and joined Miss Carol for the walk up the hill.

Dafna, Beth, and Jessica had saved Wendy a space at the lunch table they were sharing with the other girls from their age group. Several were full-time mothers, like she was, and she felt at home with these women, even regretted that she hadn't been friends with them back when they had been campers together.

At a nearby table, Ali was filming a familiar scenario. Each girl at the table, one by one, put a finger to the side of her nose and the last to remain unaware was singled out. "Pig!" everyone at the table screamed, and then the serenade began: "Every party has a pooper, that's why we invited you! Party *poo*per! Super-*duper*!"

Wendy looked over toward the "Pig" table and caught Miss Carol's eye across the dining hall. Miss Carol winked. Wendy winked back and asked the girls at her table if anyone knew Miss Carol's last name.

"She's *Miss Carol*," Dafna said. "How could she be anything else?"

"But she's really only a few years older than we are," Wendy pointed out. "Isn't it funny that we've always called her 'Miss'?"

The rest of the girls dismissed the question, but Wendy got up and went over to Miss Carol's table. As a camper, it had been prohibited to "table-hop," and Wendy experienced the quick tinge of pleasure that accompanies a forbidden act as she planted herself on the green bench to Miss Carol's left.

"Payne," Miss Carol answered. "But you can call me plain old Carol at this point, unless you want me to call you *Miss* Wendy."

"That's *Mrs. Abrahms*," Wendy said, laughing at how absurd it sounded here in the dining hall of her youth.

"You up for a lacrosse toss during free swim, *Mrs. Abrahms*, or has my rival, Ms. Cohen, already booked you?"

They made plans to meet at the lacrosse shack and Wendy returned to her table. She had, in fact, scheduled the dreaded "defining moment" interview with Ali for free swim, but Wendy reminded herself that schedules at camp were no longer binding and gave herself permission to skip the irritating interview.

Carol was waiting on the bench in front of the lacrosse shack, two lacrosse sticks in hand. "Shall we?" she said to her old protégée.

They tossed a ball back and forth for a while, but Wendy was worried that Ali might see her from the Adirondack chairs where they were supposed to have met. Ali hadn't been at the lunch table when Wendy returned to it and she had failed to find Ali all afternoon. She had asked Dafna and Beth to tell Ali she couldn't make it if they ran into her, but who knew whether or not that had happened.

Wendy leaned her stick against the side of the shack, apologized for her lack of enthusiasm, and asked Carol if they could take a walk instead.

"Have you seen the new pioneer shed?" Carol asked.

Wendy hadn't, so off they went. Wendy followed Carol past the tennis and basketball courts, across the soccer field, and into the woods near the stables. Eventually, they came to a small wooden cabin surrounded by six small green tents. The site of the tents brought on the memory of the night she had so violated Ali at the campsite, and for a moment Wendy disappeared into an abyss of regret and shame.

"Would you like some water? There's a tap inside the shed," Carol said.

Wendy shook her head, unable to speak. *It was unthinkable!* And yet she had done it.

"You okay?" Carol asked. She put her hand on Wendy's shoulder.

"Not really," Wendy whispered.

"What is it?" Carol asked, her voice filled with tenderness. "Can you tell me what's wrong?" She tried to take Wendy into her arms, but Wendy pushed her away.

"I don't know how to take it back!" Wendy cried, desperate for a salve for the burden of her guilt. "I don't know what I'm supposed to do!"

"Are you sure I can't help you?" Carol asked. She stroked Wendy's hair.

Wendy stood still, too frightened to speak; too frightened to move; almost too frightened to breathe.

"I think I *can* help you," Carol said. "But I can go if you'd prefer to be alone. I just think I know what you need. What you *want*."

Wendy remained motionless and watched as if it weren't her hand Carol lifted to her lips. *"Oh,"* she gasped involuntarily when Carol kissed the inside of her palm. "Oh," she murmured again as Carol's mouth came toward her own.

The kiss felt amazing. Carol's lips were deliciously soft, her tongue probing but not intrusive. They kissed for a long time and Wendy never once tried to pull away, even when Carol's hands reached up to cup one of her breasts.

"Come with me," Carol said, taking Wendy by the arm. "We can go inside one of the tents."

Wendy tried to resist, reminding Carol that she had an interview with Ali.

"Just come with me," Carol said gently but firmly, as if she were trying to encourage a new camper to pick up a lacrosse stick. "I haven't felt this kind of chemistry in years. You don't need to be afraid, Wendy. It's only pleasure. You deserve it, and you don't have to tell anyone. *I* certainly won't. I'm attracted to you and you're attracted to me, and we're adults now, so we can do as we choose."

"But I have to go apologize," Wendy said, as eager to follow Carol as she was to run back to camp. "Ali's waiting, and I owe her one."

"You can apologize later," Carol said. "I'm sure whatever it is can wait."

Uncertain, Wendy took Carol's outstretched hand.

It felt right in her own. It felt like the first right fit in Wendy's life.

They barely spoke in the car on the way back from Mountain Ridge, but it wasn't awkward. They listened to the radio. As they pulled into their driveway, Wendy said, "I hope he's okay."

"He'll be fine," Seth said, but he ran ahead of her into the house.

By the time Wendy got upstairs, Seth had Eric on his lap and was asking him questions. "Does your throat hurt?" A nod. "Does your tummy hurt?" Another nod. "Does your ear hurt?"

Eric shook his head vehemently, then clutched his right earlobe and started crying again.

"Should I call Dr. Margaret?" Wendy asked, down on her knees at Seth's side. She was rubbing Eric's back, which was drenched in sweat.

Seth nodded and Wendy went to her room while Seth stayed with Eric. The two older boys were up now and they climbed into Wendy's bed, listening, wide-eyed and silent, while she talked with the doctor.

Dr. Margaret said it was most likely an inner-ear infection

but that since Eric had said his stomach hurt, too, which wasn't that common a symptom with ears, they could take him to the emergency room if they were worried.

Wendy told the boys to stay in her bed, then ran back down the hall to get Eric. It probably was just an ear infection, but she knew it would be horribly painful until he was on an antibiotic and it had kicked in, and morning was a long time to wait to get antibiotics.

"Let's go to the emergency room," she said, poking her head into Eric's dark room.

"Shhhh," she heard. "Shhhhh."

She tiptoed into the room and ran into Seth, who was tiptoeing out. "Asleep," Seth whispered. "He went out in my arms. I propped him up against a pillow. He doesn't feel as hot. The Tylenol's working. I think we should take him to Dr. Margaret first thing in the morning unless he wakes up again."

When Seth was in doctor mode, there was nothing more reassuring. Everything he said sounded like the only possible option.

In the dark, Wendy tried to find Seth's eyes. It was too dark. All she could do was cling to his chest.

"Hey," Seth said, "he's going to be fine."

"I know," she murmured, the tears beginning to fall. "I know. I just—I just love you so much."

"I love you, too," Seth said, holding her tighter.

They made their way hand in hand to their bedroom. David and Ben were asleep in their bed. Seth picked up David, who smiled groggily at his father before falling back asleep in Seth's arms. Wendy got Ben, who didn't wake up at all until she had tucked him in and was almost out of his room.

"Don't leave," came a tiny voice in the dark.

"I'm not leaving," Wendy said. "I'm just going back to my room. I'll be close by."

"If you leave me, I'll be lonely, Mom. *Stay*," Ben begged. "Stay in my bed."

Part of Wendy wanted to cuddle with her son. He never spoke like this anymore, obsessed as he was with his older brother.

"Mommy has her own bed," Wendy said. "I'm going to be right down the hall, though, okay? If you need to get me, you can. Daddy and I are just down the hall."

Ben asked if Eric was going to be okay.

"He's going to be fine," Wendy assured him. She started out of the room again, but Ben stopped her once more.

"I love you," he said. "I love you as high as the Empire State Building and to the moon and back."

It was the game they used to play when he was Eric's age! Wendy melted.

"I love you to the bottom of the ocean and back up to the top of Mount Everest," Ben said.

"I love you that much, too," Wendy said. "I love you from Cairo to California and from the North Pole to the South Pole."

"Is that farther than from the bottom of the ocean and back?"

"About the same," Wendy said. She went to his bed and kissed his forehead. "Good night," she whispered. "Sweet dreams."

Silence now in the hallway. Suddenly aware of a ravenous hunger, she went downstairs to the kitchen and opened the fridge.

Juice, milk, some leftover chicken fingers. She ate the chicken fingers but was still hungry. She scanned the shelves until her eyes landed on the tuna salad she had made to eat with

Arden. She grabbed the bowl and ate the tuna directly from it with her fingers. When she was finished, she washed her hands, went upstairs, slid out of her clothes, put on her favorite old T-shirt, and got into bed. Seth was already there, the light on his side off.

"Honey?" she whispered.

Seth made a faint sound.

"Good night," Wendy said. She searched for his hand but couldn't find it. Content to touch her toes to his calf, she whispered another good night.

"Hmmm," Seth said. "Ummm, hmm," like he was struggling to respond even though his mind had already been claimed by a dream.

To Everything
There Is a Season

*

Ali was lying on the floor with her knees up to her ears when Renny slid in behind her and whispered, "Don't push too hard, hon, or we'll have the baby right here."

Under different circumstances, Ali might have been irritated by his tardiness, but Renny was working on a film and Ali celebrated his lateness rather than punish it. "At least I'd have a breathing coach who knows what he's doing," Ali said.

Renny put his hands on her big belly and kissed her forehead. "What did the doctor say about this weekend?"

"He said I'm fine to travel as long as I take it easy."

"Did Dafna give you the list of everything she wants covered?"

Ali nodded, then exhaled slowly to the count of seven. They were getting dirty looks from the Lamaze teacher.

"Are we the only video crew?" Renny asked. "She didn't hire anyone else, like someone who actually knows what they're doing?"

Ali shook her head, then did the series of short exhalations.

The teacher told them they could return to their seats, and Renny helped Ali off the floor.

After class, they grabbed a cab home.

"I think we should go with the house in Carroll Gardens," Ali said as the cab sped past Sixty-second Street.

"If it's what you want," Renny said. He was holding her hand, but he didn't give it the little squeeze he usually did when he was enthusiastic about something.

"The place I saw today uptown smelled like old people," Ali said, trying to make him laugh. "And a little bit like bologna."

The blocks slipped away and Renny's hand slipped away, too. He didn't care anymore. He'd given up, she knew. His indifference hurt. She needed his certainty. It was the quality she loved about him most. She reached out and found his hand on the seat and tightened her grip as they made their way home in silence.

That night as she lay in bed, Ali thought about the report. Arden's visit to Wendy had been both exhilarating and sobering. Clearly, the woman was miserable. There was really no need for Ali to use the footage she had. And yet she couldn't destroy it. It felt like something she might need; something she might want to send to Wendy so Wendy could examine the truth about her life. . . .

What was the truth about her *own* life?

As if he could sense her inner-turmoil, Renny turned over on his side, away from her, and wrapped himself more tightly in the sheets. It pained her. They used to sleep with their legs intertwined.

This was the truth: Renny was not the person she was supposed to marry. He wasn't rich, he wasn't Jewish, he wasn't Ivy League—although Ali thought he was as smart as any of her classmates had been at Brown. The Upper East Side meant sellout to her. The Upper East Side meant the address in the return portion of an envelope for him. Renny didn't care whether they moved to the Upper East Side, the Lower East Side, or Morningside Heights for that matter.

This was the truth: her refusal to marry Renny *was* a rejection of who he was, plain and simple. But it wasn't even based on her own criterion for rejection. It was based on the sum total of bullshit opinions held by people she claimed to despise for the narrowness of their views! Ali shuddered at her hypocrisy.

Outside their bedroom window, an argument began to rise in Spanish. Ali didn't understand a word, but she found herself siding with the guy. The girl was too shrill. She sounded guilty and sulky. The girl began to cry and the guy stopped yelling.

She'd miss this, she realized, the sounds of her neighbors. It assuaged her loneliness. It made her feel part of the bigger picture.

In his sleep, Renny turned toward her and wrapped a long, heavy arm across her belly. She picked up his hand, kissed it, and placed it on the sheet next to her. By the light from the clock radio, Ali watched as his eyelids fluttered and the eyeballs beneath them rolled like marbles under dough.

She loved Renny more than anyone she'd ever loved and more than anyone she could ever imagine loving. He was warm and supportive, handsome and strong, considerate and hardworking—in short, all those things she liked and respected in a person. She couldn't imagine ever losing him.

"People disappoint each other," her father had said. The words felt like a blessing to her troubled mind. *People disappoint each other. People disappoint each other.* She repeated the phrase over and over, holding Renny's hand, until it became the lullaby that finally eased her to sleep.

Stormy Weather

✳

When Jessica Bloom began her bike ride, it had seemed like the perfect day for a wedding: the sky was blue, the weather balmy, and the humidity, although noticeable, was nothing out of the norm. In the last ten minutes, however, the sky had darkened, the temperature had dropped, and a few rolls of thunder told Jessica she better turn back. Nevertheless, she pushed forward until the end of "To Life," from *Fiddler on the Roof*. She was always inspired by it and could no sooner halt her forward momentum in the middle of it than halt during the final fabulous moments before an orgasm.

The song finished just as the first hard drops began to fall. She turned around and pedaled harder than ever, helped by the frantic pace of the instrumental version of "Can-Can," but the music was no match for the storm, even with the driving quarter notes, and she was quickly drenched and panting as she did her best to navigate her way through a bombardment of flying palm fronds. Without the music, she might have been terrified, but the accompaniment made it seem like she was on the set of a movie, and she had no problem summoning the right amount of *chutzpah* tinged with fear, just in case the camera in her mind came in for a close-up.

Her aunt's condo on Worth Avenue, where she was staying, was still a healthy ways away. In the much nearer distance, the magnificent Breakers Hotel towered above the tossing palms. In a few hours, she would be dancing in the ballroom there at Dafna Shapiro's wedding. She couldn't wait. She'd had to miss many of her friends' weddings as a result of a career that kept her on the road much of the time. But Dafna's wedding happily coincided with Jessica's performance at the Royal Poinciana Playhouse as Sarah Brown in a highly acclaimed bus-and-truck tour of *Guys and Dolls,* and tonight Jessica's understudy, Brooke, was going to go on for her, and Alec, who played Sky Masterson, was going to call in sick so that she'd have a date. And not just any date. The most handsome man on the planet was going to escort her through the night—dance with her, pull out her seat before she sat down, help her down the stairs and into the taxi when it was time to go home. And all of this in front of an audience made up of her camp friends and her mother! It would be perfect.

Jessica looked longingly at the double towers of the Breakers, symbols of old money, old values, and Gentile refinement. Her mother and stepfather, friends of the groom's parents, would be arriving there in a few hours. Jessica wished it were sooner, so she could have a legitimate reason to pull up on her bike right now and hang out in the lobby. But she couldn't see herself standing in the plush digs, dripping water and shivering until the rain let up. Without even her Platinum card on her to prove she could belong there if she so chose, Jessica felt completely at a loss. All she had was her rented bike, her Walkman, and a tape of musical-theater tunes. Her best bet, she decided as "Can-Can" turned into "I Hope I Get It" from *A Chorus Line*, was to bike over to the Palm Beach Bungalows, where the rest of the cast was staying.

By the time she got there, she looked like she'd been out for a swim in her workout clothes.

"Can you ring up to Alec for me?" she asked the ancient, obese concierge.

"Alex?" he yelled back.

"Al-EC," Jessica said slowly and loudly. They went through this exercise every time she came by, and she was getting tired of it.

The concierge rang up to Alec's room then announced that Alec was out.

"Can I just go up?" Jessica asked, trying to sound charming through chattering teeth.

"Sorry," the concierge said, shaking his head. "Can't let you wander the halls. Security. Those are the rules."

Jessica knew about rules. In the Fifth Avenue duplex where she had grown up, no shoes were allowed past the front door, no jeans at the dining room table, no cursing or raised voices in front of the staff, no TV until homework was done, no staying out past twelve o'clock on Friday or Saturday night unless accompanied by an adult, and on they went. She decided to change tactics.

"Did you actually see Alec leave this morning? I wouldn't be surprised if he's just asleep up there."

"Even so," the concierge said. He sucked his teeth.

Jessica knew Alec was up there and so did the concierge, but there was nothing she could think to do to bend the rules. She couldn't see him accepting a couple of bucks in a handshake the way the guys in the garage used to take tips from her father. She didn't have any money with her anyway and doubted her musical tape would make for good barter. The box of doughnuts she had binged on that morning would have gotten her a lot further, she suspected.

Jessica checked her watch. She had a little more than an hour before she had to get to the theater for the matinee. It was enough time for a quickie.

"Can you try his room one more time?" she asked sweetly. "Sometimes he doesn't answer the phone."

It hadn't occurred to Jessica to have sex with Alec that morning when she left the condo on her post-binge bike ride, but now that the thought was in her head, she couldn't let it go. She needed Alec to fuck her. It wouldn't make him love her; that, she knew. She had already given up that hope long ago. But it didn't hurt to pretend. It was sick, she knew. But by now, it's what she was used to.

It hadn't always been that way. She had once had high hopes. And if Alec ever straightened himself out, they'd make an excellent couple. Even the director had commented on their chemistry after the first read-through way back in August. Of course it wasn't hard to be attracted to Alec, with his movie-star good looks. Together, he and Jessica made quite the pair. She had the blond hair to match his and the same sparkly blue eyes, and then there was her charming button nose and a classic hourglass figure that called to mind the screen goddesses of the fifties—the perfect complement to his Rock Hudson physique. She'd been over the moon when she realized Alec was interested in her, too, and for a few magical months she stayed there. But, as it always seems to, the plot thickened. He insisted on keeping their relationship a secret. There were rumors of other women. There were bizarre lapses of memory. There were inexplicable absences.

It had taken months to finally form the connection between the sweet smell that oozed from his pores and the scotch he drank every night after the show. How was she supposed to have recognized the smell of Glenlivet? Alcoholics were people who roamed the streets and asked for money, not devastatingly handsome thirty-two-year-old actors. What did she, a Jewish girl raised on Shabbas wine, know from scotch?

She made adjustments. They had sex in the late morning or early afternoon, after he had been to the gym and steam room and sweated out most of the poison. They did it between shows on matinee days or before going to the theater in the late afternoon because he could still get it up before he hit the bar at night. There was no way she could compete with Glen, though. Glen was Alec's first love. And after Glen, it was bitters. It was bitters in the morning and Glen in the evening, and in between there was Preparation H under his eyes to take down the puffiness and endless cups of black coffee and visits to the steam room. Ultimately, Jessica was someone Alec dreamt up during the day, which, when you got down to it, was really just a giant haze for him.

But what a lovely haze! For Jessica anyway. Alec was a generous lover—attentive, daring, sensual. His cock was as beautifully formed as the rest of him, and when it worked, it worked like a champ.

"How's the show going?" the concierge shouted at Jessica.

"Oh, you know," she answered pleasantly, omitting the fact that she was sick to death of doing the same show every night and twice a day on Wednesdays and weekends; omitting the fact that the cast was made up of the most dysfunctional, competitive, nasty performers this side of the equator; omitting the fact that she spent most of her days binging and puking; omitting the fact that on certain days she felt like the last ten years of her life had been a waste.

"Your friend Alec gave me a little concert the other night," the concierge said, smiling broadly. Jessica could see how many teeth he was missing, which were quite a few.

"I'm sure he did," Jessica said, smiling back but shivering dramatically, in the hopes that the old man would take pity on her and let her past the reception desk so she could go up to Alec's room.

She shouted, "Alec always lets me in, even if he's out. I have a key."

"Sorry, toots," the old man shouted back. "I'd love to help, but rules is rules."

Jessica looked around the lobby. The rose-colored paint was peeling from the walls as if they had come down with a case of psoriasis, and three of the five lightbulbs in the tarnished chandelier were burned out. An enormous water bug darted across the floor and disappeared behind the concierge desk. She was revolted, but outside the rain was still coming down in sheets and she desperately wanted a shower, a fuck, or both.

"Look, I'm sure Alec's up there," she said, wishing she could drop her father's name to some effect; but there was no way this concierge would know who Jerry Bloom had been.

"Well, if it isn't Jessica Bloom!" Nancy called out, coming to Jessica's rescue as she emerged from the stairwell. She was dressed like the character of Adelaide, whom she played in the show, in four-inch hot-pink mules, a pair of leopard-print leggings, and a tight aqua sweater with a plunging V-neck. Even with her arms full of folded laundry, you could still see plenty of cleavage. "What in *God's* name happened to *you?*" she asked in her signature husky alto.

"Got caught in the rain," Jessica replied, wringing out her shirt so it made a small puddle on the floor.

"Well, for heaven's *sake!*" Nancy shouted. "You come upstairs with me right this minute and let me wrap you up in my pink terry-cloth robe which is still warm from the dryer!"

She made it sound like it was going to be a roaring good time, and Jessica smiled at the concierge as she waltzed past him to the elevators.

"Ask me how do I feel, ask me now that we're cozy and cling-ing," Jessica sang, filling Nancy's tiny, dark room with her shimmering soprano.

"Well, aren't *you* happy!" Nancy called out from the kitchen, where she had gone to get Jessica a cup of tea. "Get laid today already, or are you just happy to see me?"

"Happy to be *warm,*" Jessica replied, snuggling deeper into Nancy's robe, which was, indeed, still warm from the dryer.

It was odd, this role reversal. Usually, it was Jessica who mothered Nancy. Jessica had lost count of the number of times she had discovered Nancy crying in the dressing room a half hour before showtime, swearing never to see Herb again. Herb and Nancy had played opposite each other as Nathan Detroit and Adelaide in nine different productions of *Guys and Dolls* beginning in '89 and had been sleeping together since opening night of the first production. Herb lived in New York with his wife and their four teenaged kids when he wasn't on tour, but mostly he was on tour, with Nancy, who was single and clearly past forty-five, although she told people she was thirty-six.

Jessica knew Nancy's reasons for not being able to perform as well as she knew her own lines for the show: Nancy's back had gone out from fucking Herb in some bizarre position; her bladder infection was back from too much sex; her hemorrhoids were on fire from Herb's fucking her in the ass. Her mascara would run in muddy streams down her face as she told Jessica she *couldn't make it,* that *she was going to go back on the bottle*, and Jessica would hold her until Nancy became calm enough to wipe the makeup off her face and start over so she'd look pretty by curtain time.

"There now," Nancy said, emerging from the cramped kitchen with a teacup in hand. She made her way across the living room, stepping over ginger ale cans and dirty plates and almost tripping over a saucepan filled with cigarette butts before placing the steaming mug into Jessica's hands.

"So let's get some good gossip in before we have to go to the fucking theater," Nancy said, lowering herself down next to Jessica on the sofa.

Jessica glanced at her watch, wondering how long she'd have to stay in Nancy's room for it not to be considered rude to leave. She needed to get some relief for her anxiety before the matinee, and she knew no amount of witty repartee with Nancy would eliminate it the way a roll in the hay would with Alec.

"Stormy weather, eh?" Jessica said.

"Oh come *on!*" Nancy howled. "I don't give a shit about the weather! Tell me one coupling you've heard of recently that will give me the giggles. I need *something* to keep me interested in going to that goddamned piss hole of a theater this afternoon."

"Okay," Jessica agreed, deciding there was no harm in playing along. "Tony Carangi and Denise DuPret."

"Tony and Denise?" Nancy threw her head back and let out a guffaw. "Lemme get this right. You mean Tony who plays the drums and my Hot Box Girl, Denise?"

Jessica nodded, hoping she could borrow some dry clothes and room-hop now that she'd provided the information Nancy wanted.

"Now that's a fucking weird one." Nancy settled more deeply into the couch. "Denise is a foot taller than him! I mean, you and Alec I could understand."

Jessica asked her what she meant.

"Oh *please,*" Nancy said, rolling her eyes. "I lived in the next room over from him in D.C., and was across the hall from you in Philly. What do you think, I'm blind, deaf, and dumb?"

"Could you hear us?" Jessica asked, mortified but oddly proud, too.

Nancy said she hadn't heard anything but that she knew Jessica wasn't visiting him for the conversation.

"He happens to be a very good conversationalist," Jessica said, feeling the need to defend her lover.

Nancy asked Jessica what proof there was of Denise and Tony, but a loud rhythmic thump started hammering into the wall behind the sofa. Low grunts and higher moans of "Oh oh oh!" could be heard clearly, then the distinct sound of skin slapping skin.

"Jeremy," Nancy said. "He's at it morning, noon, and night, God bless him."

Jeremy was the dance captain, a gorgeous muscular twenty-five-year-old with a demonic suggestion to his features and a well-known penchant for picking up men on street corners.

"I barely notice anymore," Nancy said. "It's become like white noise to me."

Jessica asked who was in there with him, but an urgent series of knocks on the door precluded an answer.

"You don't get much of a break here, do you?" Jessica said as the knocks continued.

Nancy raised a brow but remained seated.

"Aren't you going to answer?" Jessica asked. The knocks on the door were becoming violent.

"Certainly not," Nancy said.

Jessica asked if she should go, but Nancy issued an even more emphatic negative. "You stay right where you are and finish your tea," she ordered. "I can't answer that fat fuck's every beck and call."

"I know you're in there!" Herb yelled. "You can't keep me out!"

"Oh no?" Nancy yelled back from the couch. "Watch me!"

"I should go," Jessica said, getting up. Between the pounding on the door and the banging on the walls, she felt as if she were in a construction zone.

Nancy shot Jessica a look of resolve and said, "Stay right where you are. We were having a perfectly nice conversation. Herb can't interfere every time he has a fight with his tired, old bag, pathetic excuse for a wife, and expect me to drop everything and play nurse."

"Open the door!" Herb yelled.

"Go into the bathroom," Nancy said, cocking her head at Jessica.

Jessica obeyed while Nancy unlocked her door and let the beast in.

"What kind of games do you think you're playing?" Jessica heard Herb say. "You can't keep me out."

"What makes you think I want to see you right now?" Nancy countered. "I have a visitor."

"You were entertaining the Queen of England, I suppose?"

Then Jessica figured he must have seen her teacup, because she heard something crash, followed by, "You slut! Whaddya offer? A blow job and a cup of tea as a lunchtime special? This your version of happy hour? Where is he?"

Then Nancy was screaming and Herb was yelling, but Jessica couldn't make out what they were saying, because they were yelling over each other. Then the door slammed and Nancy was calling out for help, which Jessica took as her cue to reenter.

Nancy was crumpled on the floor by the window. "I'm bleeding," she sobbed. "Get me some Neosporin from the bathroom. I cut my foot."

"Should I call the police?" Jessica asked, running back to the bathroom. There was no Neosporin, only soap, which Jessica rubbed on the end of a wet washcloth.

"No. No police," Nancy said when Jessica returned with the washcloth. She wasn't crying anymore. She was sitting on the chair near the window, smoking a cigarette. "Watch the cup," she croaked. "Don't cut your feet. I hope I don't get rabies." Nancy took another drag of her cigarette and exhaled toward the window. "I kicked that fucker so hard, I think he lost some teeth."

Jessica stopped dabbing for a moment and took a closer look at Nancy's foot. Were those *teeth* marks below her toes?

"He tried to hit me," Nancy said, stone-faced. Within a second, though, the waterworks were back. "What if I kicked out his teeth?" she wailed. "How will he go on? What if I hurt him? Oh God oh God oh God . . . what have I done?"

"You could call the police," Jessica suggested.

"Baby, go into my room and bring me one of the orange pills on the night table."

Jessica asked what they were for.

Nancy averted her gaze as she answered, "My nerves."

"Come on," Jessica said. "You don't need one of them."

"Yes, I do!" Nancy shouted. "That asshole's given me a bladder infection from fucking me so hard, and hemorrhoids from ramming his porky fingers so far up my ass. I wish I had herpes so I could give them to him!"

"Okay, Nancy," Jessica said in the voice she usually reserved for her mother's worst breakdowns, "just calm yourself, okay? Herb is gone and I'm here with you and everything's going to be okay, okay? You're going to have two great shows today, one with me and one with Brooke." Jessica rocked Nancy in her arms and stroked her hair until Nancy finally stopped shaking. "It's twelve-forty-five," she whispered into Nancy's hair. Nancy's roots were white. "We have forty-five minutes before we have to get to the theater. I'm going to bike back to the condo so I can get my dress for the wedding tonight. Can you meet me at the theater in forty-five minutes, or do you want to go back to the condo with me? We could call you a cab if you want and I could get my bike later."

Nancy wiped her eyes and mumbled something unintelligible.

"I do have to go home, though," Jessica said with a little more authority as she tried to disengage from the still-clinging Nancy. "You should move into my aunt's place with me for a while!" she added. "There's plenty of room, and I'm pretty sure the sofa in the living room is a pullout."

"No," Nancy said, letting go of Jessica and wiping her cheeks with the back of her veiny hand. "Thanks for the invite, but I don't sleep well in a new place." She looked up at Jessica with glazed eyes and added, "But I'll think about it. How 'bout that? Maybe we could be roommates for a while."

"Let's pack a suitcase now," Jessica said, instantly regretting the words that continued to tumble out of her mouth. "You can take it to the theater and then grab a taxi over to the condo after the show tonight. Why not?"

"Poor Herb," Nancy whispered.

Jessica's mind began to race. Forty-five minutes was enough time for a quickie. That's what she needed: a quick fix, one fast roll on the sofa, something for herself, for heaven's sake; something she could think about during Dafna's wedding that would bring a smile to her face and help her forget the hopeless dysfunction of her own ridiculous personal life.

A slim stream of sunlight penetrated the room through a frayed corner of Nancy's drawn shade. Jessica crossed the room and pulled aside the blind. It was still overcast, but the rain had stopped and the sun was trying to shine through.

"I better get home," Jessica said. "The rain's let up."

"Can I at least loan you some dry clothes?" Nancy offered, already rummaging through her clean pile.

Jessica left Nancy's room with a bright pink pareo wrapped around her waist and a yellow T-shirt that said SHIT HAPPENS across the front. She laughed at the sight she imagined she must have been as she stumbled down the hallway, her eyes squinting against the shock of the lime green carpet and the bright floral wallpaper after the twilight of Nancy's room.

The elevator was slow to come. Jessica was about to begin listening to her tape when a door slammed at the far end of the hallway in the direction of Nancy's room.

"Ciao ciao!" she heard Jeremy call out in his distinct, effeminate voice.

"Shhhh," someone else replied, and Jessica found herself smiling in anticipation as Jeremy's mystery lay made his way down the hallway. Would she have news for the cast today! It would be the perfect reason to barge into Alec's room uninvited. She would be the bearer of good gossip, and who wasn't welcome with that!

The elevator arrived before the mystery figure rounded the bend. Jessica was dying of curiosity but also dying to get laid. She got on the elevator and pressed the button for the sixth floor.

"Can you hold the door?" a familiar voice called out just as the doors began to slide shut, and a moment later Alec came striding onto the elevator.

Jessica had always enjoyed a good hora, but her dress was strapless and her shoes were high, and the combination seemed too precarious for participation. She certainly wasn't missed. Most of the guests had flocked to the dance floor and were clapping and stomping joyfully as they did the famous grapevine.

Dr. Seth Abrahms, the husband of Jessica's former bunk mate Wendy Levin, had also stayed behind at the table. He had been sitting across from Jessica for a good portion of the night, but now he stood up and moved to Alec's abandoned seat on Jessica's right.

"It's quite a success, this wedding, wouldn't you say?" Behind his wire-rim glasses, Seth's hazel eyes twinkled mischievously.

"It certainly is a showstopper," Jessica said. Hundreds of lanterns were hanging from the ceiling, and in the centers of each table grapes cascaded over the edges of huge tureens, which were surrounded by low vases of peonies and white votive candles. "It reminds me of the set for the party scene in *My Fair Lady* I did at the Goodspeed." Jessica sighed

"So you're the actress," Seth said.

Jessica nodded.

"That's sexy."

"Is it?" Jessica said hopefully.

"A woman who works?" Now it was Seth who nodded. "I think that's *incredibly* sexy."

"And you?" Jessica asked. "What do you do?"

"Orthopedic surgeon," Seth said, his eyes narrowing like a wolf's.

"I'd say that's sexier," Jessica ventured.

Seth laughed and said, "How do you see that?"

"Working with your hands all day?" Jessica giggled. "Checking patients out in those flimsy paper gowns . . ."

"It has its moments," Seth said, "but not every patient looks like you."

There was no way to mistake the lust in his tone. Seth was an attractive man: tall, dark, fit, and handsome in a Jewish orthopedist way. He had long white fingers with black tufts of hair on the knuckles, but they were fingers that looked very capable.

"Too bad you're on the road so much," Seth said. "Otherwise, I'd make sure we saw more of you."

On the dance floor, Dafna and Dan had been lifted above the crowd in their chairs and were whooping in glee as they bobbed above their guests. Jessica threw her head back, aware that it made her hair fall flatteringly around her bare shoulders. Then she said, "I get back to the city enough."

"Well, you'll have to let us know when you're coming to town. We're in Short Hills, but it's nothing to go in to the city." Seth's eyes narrowed again as he added, "I'm in all the time."

Jessica didn't know what to say. She was having fantasies of Seth crawling under the table and going down on her. In the movie in her mind, plot twists like that were perfectly plausible.

He asked her how serious she was with Alec.

"Not at all," Jessica said, shaking her head in disgust as she watched Alec join the other men in lifting Dafna's parents in their chairs. A cheer rang out as Dafna and her father "danced" together by holding on to the same white napkin. "Alec is a fag," Jessica said. "An alcoholic fag at that. But do me a favor? Don't tell your wife, or my mom, for that matter. I think they'd both be heartbroken, and life's just too short."

"You think?" Seth said, tilting his head slightly to the right and looking at her slyly. "I think of it as long. Long and wonderful and full of moments when you can do things you only dream about."

Seth's eyes wandered down to her lips, and Jessica knew if they were alone, he'd be kissing her. There was no sign of Wendy anywhere in the ballroom.

"You don't smoke, do you?" Jessica asked.

"I'd love a smoke," Seth replied. He opened his jacket to reveal a pack of Dunhills in his inside breast pocket.

"Don't you dare tell anyone I smoke sometimes," Jessica said as he pulled out her chair.

"I don't tell anyone anything they shouldn't know," Seth said so close to her ear, his lips brushed her skin.

They made their way through the crowded ballroom and out into the hallway.

"Follow me," Seth said, striking off down the dark, somber passage that lead toward a set of sliding doors—and out they went.

The night air felt refreshing after the air-conditioned ballroom. The terrace overlooked the ocean, and a gibbous moon illuminated the waves just enough to make her and Seth's clandestine smoke seem condoned by Mother Nature.

"Does Wendy know?" Jessica asked as Seth lit her cigarette.

"Know what?" Seth paused and looked at her hard. "That sometimes I smoke?" He paused again. "No. She wouldn't be happy about it, and I firmly believe that what someone doesn't know can't hurt them."

They were standing in view of the door. Without a word, Seth took her by the elbow and led her across the terrace and down some steps to the beach. When they got there, however, they came upon another couple already in a hot embrace.

Seth began to pull her farther down the beach, but he stopped when he saw what Jessica was already gaping at. There was no way not to see. The moon was too bright. She tried to block Seth's view, to steer him away, but it was too late. One of the people in the embrace was his wife. The other was Miss Carol.

Jessica froze. She knew what was about to occur in the

movie in her mind: Seth would say, "Wendy? Is that you?" and Wendy would look up, caught and panicked. Seth would storm off while Wendy chased after him, saying, "Wait! I can explain! It's not what it looks like!"

But that's not what happened next at all. Seth led Jessica silently back up the stairs and then, when they were safely hidden behind a palm on the upper terrace, he said, "Well, I guess I'm not the only one in the family with extracurricular interests."

Jessica was still stunned. Then, realizing the parallel, she said, "I found out Alec's been sleeping with a man just this afternoon. Must be something in the air."

Jessica took a final drag of her cigarette, wondering if Seth was hurt and not showing it, or if this was something that occurred regularly; if perhaps her own unbelievable situation was more common than she thought.

"Shall we?" Seth said after they had each ground their stubs into the stone terrace.

"Shall we *what*?" Jessica said, a hint of mischief in her voice.

It was clear from the way Seth strode toward the double glass doors that the game was over.

They were almost back at the ballroom when they ran into Arden, who looked frantic.

"Have you seen Renny?" Her voice was high enough to shatter lightbulbs. "Ali's water just broke!"

"There's no one out there who's a better listener, who's more supportive, who knows how to make everything seem fun, who can make a better dinner reservation."

There was a smattering of laughs and applause and Dan

continued to toast his stunning bride, who virtually floated next to him in a Vera Wang confection of chiffon, satin, lace, and beading.

"Dafna's exceptionally kind, exceptionally loyal, exceptionally beautiful, and, let's face it, exceptionally sexy." More laughter. A few whistles. "I think she'll make an exceptional mother one day." Hoots and applause. When things quieted down, Dan turned to face his bride and said straight into her eyes, "I love you, Mrs. Dan *Rosen,* and I look forward to loving you till death do us part."

The band burst into "Love Is a Many Splendored Thing," the audience cheered and sighed and wiped away tears, and Dan kissed his Dafna to the flash of bulbs and the rolling of the video camera, which was now being manned solely by Arden.

Across from where Jessica stood at the edge of the dance floor, Wendy and Seth were standing side by side. Wendy was crying and Seth handed her his hankie. A few people down from them, Beth slouched in her bridesmaid's dress, the tears sliding down her round cheeks faster than she could wipe them away with the one free hand she had. In the other hand, she clutched the bouquet she had caught. The flowers, lily of the valley, had already wilted. They struck Jessica as a pitiful consolation present for someone whose own engagement had ended in abortion.

Jessica cried, too, overwhelmed with a sudden bout of self-pity. Forget about the shock of discovering Alec's secret life; forget about the shock of discovering *Wendy's* secret life. Those were mere trifles when compared to the larger hurt so clearly summed up by the spectacle taking place in the center of the dance floor.

This could be my wedding, Jessica thought jealously. Jessica had dated Dan Rosen once, years ago, when he still had all his hair. They were set up on a blind date brokered by Steve Lazarus, Jessica's stepfather, who was one of the senior managing directors at the investment bank where Dan worked. It wasn't exactly a *blind* date. Jessica and Dan had more or less grown up together. Dan's father, like Jessica's, was a second-generation Jewish real estate tycoon and the two had worked together on many a deal, not to mention played uncountable rounds of golf together. He and his heavily jeweled wife had dined many times at the Blooms' various residences during Jessica's youth. And Dan himself had always figured in the shadows of Jessica's social consciousness in places like Georgica Beach in East Hampton, or in the pew behind hers at Midtown Temple, or at the box across from theirs at the U.S. Open. But he had always been "one of the icky older boys" and she had ignored him, even though he was—according to her mother, who had heard it from Steve—brilliant, nice, funny, and *Jewish* (a point her mother had stressed, since she had vigorously disapproved of the Catholic actor/bartender Jessica had been dating at the time of the setup, who wore a turquoise cross around his neck).

Luckily for Dafna, Dan hadn't been "the one" for Jessica. She'd been bored from the moment she sat down to the moment she told Dan she'd love dessert but she had an early audition the next day so had better be going. She'd gotten the job, an out-of-town gig, and two days later she was on her way to Denver, the phone calls from Dan left unreturned on her answering machine in New York. Once she was back in town, she avoided Dan's eye when they saw each other at High Holiday services, a small price to pay, she felt, for the freedom from his company.

Did Dafna actually love him, Jessica wondered, or did she

just want to get married? Dan certainly was the kind of guy every parent hopes their daughter will bring home: well educated, well mannered, wealthy, well dressed. He had an excellent job and a house in the Hamptons and an amazing collection of contemporary art in his five-thousand-square-foot SoHo bachelor pad. He and Dafna probably had a nice circle of friends who went to dinner together and to the theater and the movies.

Jessica knew she would never have a relationship like that as long as she continued to do musical theater. She could really only date other actors or musicians, since bankers and lawyers and people with "real" jobs and "real" lives wanted to be with women who were free for weekends away and eight or nine o'clock dinners with friends at chic restaurants. But that wasn't her life.

Musical theater was her life. It was all she had ever done and all she ever imagined doing. *It* had chosen *her,* not the other way around. Her earliest memories were of putting on shows in her parents' enormous living room for their frequent illustrious guests. Her mother, who herself had a lovely but slight soprano and often entertained her guests with some of the Italian songs she recalled from her days studying opera, had told Jessica all her life that she was Broadway material. For Jessica's high school graduation, she got a charm bracelet from her mother that contained a miniature gold Oscar, Tony, and Emmy.

"You deserve all of these," Jessica's mother, Lainey, had said when she put it on her daughter's wrist. And really Jessica did.

When her father died unexpectedly at fifty-nine of a heart attack, she was only fifteen, away at camp for her final summer. Jessica had been shocked to learn of her father's sudden death and had grieved, naturally, but when given the choice to leave camp early or stay until the end, she had opted to stay. It wasn't that she hadn't loved her father. But she loved him the way some people love the president: as a remote, powerful person who's working hard to bring prosperity and peace to his constituents.

When she did return home, she wasn't surprised that her mother didn't come to meet the chartered plane that had flown Jessica from Maine directly to the East Hampton airport. Her dramatic imagination was already well formed and she imagined her mother swathed in black and crying on the four-poster bed in the giant master bedroom on the second floor.

Jessica was surprised, however, not to find her mother anywhere in the house once she arrived at the Bloom family manse on Further Lane. It was Consuela, the cook, who found her employer unconscious on the floor of one of the bathrooms on the third floor, surrounded by empty vials of Vicodin and Valium. She was still breathing and the chauffeur got her to the Southampton emergency room fast enough to save her life.

Jessica had always assumed the suicide attempt had been a result of her mother's devastated heart. It wasn't until years later, when Jessica was twenty-five and trying to get the upper hand in her battle with bulimia, that she finally learned the real reason for the suicide attempt. Jessica's therapist had insisted that she confront her mother for details about the event and thus Jessica found out that her father had cheated on her mother with Consuela's niece, Rosita, a lovely twenty-two-year-old Dominican girl who sometimes helped serve at the Blooms' large parties. Lainey had discovered the truth the morning Jessica was coming home from camp, when Rosita showed up asking for child support. There was no way to deny it: the baby boy in Rosita's arms bore an uncanny resemblance to Lainey's late husband. And if there had been any lingering doubt in Lainey's mind as to the claim of the baby's paternity, it was eliminated when Rosita proceeded to describe to Lainey the shape of her husband's penis, an easily identifiable body part, since it was shaped like a banana and curved to the left. There was nothing left for Lainey to do but call a lawyer, which was the last thing she did before swallowing the pills.

After Lainey recovered from the suicide attempt, she became a very different kind of mother. Jessica had been used to a mother who had given her tremendous freedom and privacy. But now Lainey became suspicious and was neurotic about the truth. "Tell me," she'd insist. "Do you like this outfit on me? *Don't lie.*" "So *tell me.* What did you do today at Sarah's house? The *truth.*" "I want the truth. Do you smoke?" "The truth, Jessica. Have you touched a penis?" "Have you given anyone a blow job?" "Don't lie to your mother, Jessica. I want to know if you're having sex." "Do you love me? Don't lie. I want the truth, even if it'll hurt. I can take it."

What choice did Jessica have? Naturally, she became an expert liar. And what was acting, after all, but expert lying? Acting was the perfect career for her; came as easily as breathing. And then there was her voice, the voice she'd tried to destroy every way imaginable: smoking, puking, staying up too late, screaming over loud music, never doing a single one of the vocal exercises her expensive voice teacher had assigned. But there it was, strong and clear as always. She'd had the lead in every play since kindergarten.

Musical theater was what she did. When she was a senior at Vassar, an agent came up to see her as Sally Bowles and signed her on the spot, and then Jessica graduated and went to New York and started being sent on auditions right away. One job led to another and now here she was, almost twelve years later, doing the same thing: going where she was sent, doing what she did best, enjoying her moments onstage and getting through the moments when she was offstage, drifting from lover to lover as the shows and their locations changed.

Jessica dreamed of getting cast in a straight theatrical production and fantasized that the actors in those casts were smarter and classier, with fewer addictions and fewer homosexual tendencies. In her imaginary scenario, TV would be even better, with film being the ultimate. Everyone on a film set would be funny, friendly, talented, sexy, thoughtful, noncompetitive, supportive, and inclusive. There wouldn't be a list of all the twelve-step meetings in the neighborhood every time they went to a new location. People would drink a glass of wine, a few beers, or maybe a martini or two after a day of shooting and that would be it. They wouldn't sneak off to snort coke in parking lots and bathrooms; no one would worry about AIDS or herpes or catching someone else's genital warts. They'd eat dinner at 7:30 or 8:00 every night instead of snacking at 6:30 before call time and then pigging out at 11:00, after the curtain went down, only to puke it all up by 11:15.

But Jessica was enough of a pragmatist to acknowledge that that was probably not ever going to be her reality. There was plenty of time to think every day about the status of her life. She only had to be at the theater Tuesday through Sunday nights from her 7:30 call until the curtain came down at 11:00, and on Wednesdays and the weekends she did matinees. Other than that she was free—free to exercise, sightsee, read, shop, binge, puke, cry, and ask herself what the hell she was doing with her life.

The answer was always the same. What she was doing was this tour; this bus-and-truck tour produced by a third-rate touring company that played dinner theaters and glorified school auditoriums and which had reached its peak of glamour at the Royal Poinciana Playhouse here in Palm Beach. Before the tour, she had been doing a workshop for a new musical that probably would never be produced, and after this tour she'd probably continue doing more of the same. She was thirty-three years old and had landed only five TV and film auditions in her entire career. What a musical theater veteran had once told her was true: once you're known in the business as a musical-theater actor, it's nearly impossible to break out of the genre.

Jessica knew L.A. was the answer. Fuck her voice. She could sing in the shower. Fame was in L.A., and fame was what she needed. Fame would lead to money, which she didn't need but which would put her into contact with people with whom she belonged, with whom she felt comfortable, with whom she'd fit in. Laura Berman lived in L.A.. Jessica had read her name just the other day in the *Guide to L.A. Super Agents*. They'd had a good time together at the reunion. She'd give Laura a call. Dafna would know her number.

"Laura Berman?" Dafna exclaimed when she and Dan stopped by Jessica's table on their way around the room. "Of course I have her number. I ran into her sister at a dinner party in Greenwich literally four days ago. But you can just call William Morris."

"Have you tasted your own cake?" Wendy asked. "It's fantastic."

"So glad you like it!" Dafna shouted. "Gotta make it around

the room before all the old biddies go home!" And she and Dan were off in a froth of tulle and tuxedo.

Jessica was swallowing her first bite when Alec took the seat to her right. She ignored him.

"What's with you?" Alec whispered.

"How do you guys like the grapes?" Beth asked. "They were my idea. I was going to use grapes in the centerpieces at my own wedding, but Dafna liked the idea so much, she asked if she could copy it. Can you imagine? Dafna copying something from *me*?"

Jessica smiled in Beth's direction and lifted a second forkful of cake to her mouth. She swallowed without registering any taste and returned the fork mechanically to her mouth. For the next few minutes, she chewed and swallowed, chewed and swallowed, her mind crowded with revolting images. The same gorgeous cock she had been sucking for seven months had not only been in another woman's pussy (she was sure of that from his own admissions) but potentially in another man's *ass*. Just thank God they'd always used condoms.

"Are you going to eat that?" she asked Alec. Before he could answer, she drew his plate over.

The band started playing "Oh What a Night," and Wendy turned to Seth. "Oh, honey!" she shouted. "It's our song!" There was such desperation and sadness in her tone, Jessica had to avert her eyes from Wendy's face.

Seth told Wendy he was too tired to dance, so Jessica turned to Alec and told him to hit the dance floor again.

"I've been on the dance floor all friggin' night," Alec whispered. "Can I just sit here next to you for a minute and enjoy how pretty you look?"

"No, you can*not*," Jessica said, popping another piece of cake into her mouth.

"Lighten up," Alec said, taking a sip of the scotch that materialized as if from the centerpiece.

"Come on," Wendy said to her husband. "It's our song. Let's dance."

Jessica ate the last forkful of cake on Alec's plate, wiped her mouth, turned to Alec, and said, "If you're upset about the way I've treated you this evening, why don't you go cry on *Jeremy's* shoulder?"

"Ah," Alec said, a pleasant smile gracing his face, as if she had just told him she'd overheard him singing something lovely.

"Wendy!" Alec said as Jessica reached for the platter of *petits fours* and chocolate truffles. "Would you be so kind as to honor me with a dance?"

"Are you sure?" Wendy asked, looking toward Jessica for approval.

"Go 'head," Jessica said. "*Please.* I can't stand up for another second in these heels."

Jessica wiped away the mascara smudges from beneath her eyes and touched up her makeup so there was no visible sign of her purge except a light case of bloodshot eyes and a red mark over her right knuckle which came from her hand scraping against her upper teeth as she rammed her index and middle fingers down her throat.

When she returned to the ballroom, she discovered that most people had already left. Alec was still sitting at their table, alone, sipping his scotch. He told Jessica that everyone else from their table had gone to the Seafood Bar for more drinks but that he had waited for her because he didn't know if she wanted to stay.

Jessica was drained but oddly not tired. She found her mother and stepfather and kissed them good night. Then she walked Alec to the entryway of the grand hotel, asked for a cab, put him inside, and said good night.

Alec rolled down the window and summoned Jessica over.

"I'm sorry," he said. "I really am."

Alec's eyes were even redder than hers and he was slurring his words, but she could tell he knew what he was saying. "I wish I weren't who I am," he added.

"Me, too," Jessica said, taking a step back.

There was a group of wedding guests drinking at the Seafood Bar and Beth was hanging all over the arm of the photographer while he continued to shoot the guests. Good for Beth, Jessica thought. Why not? Not everyone needs an investment banker or a lawyer.

Jessica left the bar and searched in the many rooms that dotted the large footprint of the ground floor, but Seth wasn't in any of them. It was an insane thought, she knew, that he might be feeling the same yearning compulsion to be with her that she felt to be with him, but in the movie in Jessica's mind, a meeting between them would make a nice third-act plot twist. She checked each of the terraces and around the pool and even out by the beach. Finally, she had to concede the camera wasn't rolling; didn't even exist. Seth was upstairs in his room, sleeping in the same bed with, or perhaps on the sofa across the room from, Wendy, his dutiful, delightful dyke of a wife.

Defeated, Jessica returned to the main lobby. Only one clerk was on duty and she went over to him. He was young, possibly not yet twenty, and Jessica was sure he'd comply with her request. She smiled at him and leaned in so he couldn't miss her cleavage as she asked for her mother's room number.

The clerk smiled back at her, his blue eyes conveying a desire to please, but he told her he couldn't give out the room number, could only ring up to the room, if that's what she'd like.

Jessica thanked him but declined. She'd had enough of *that* game for one day.

The plush sofa in the center of the lobby offered her, at least temporarily, the comfort she so desired. Her feet ached and a blister had formed on the side of her right big toe. She flipped off her Manolos, tucked her feet beneath one of the lovely soft crimson pillows, and took a deep breath, basking in the opulence of the surroundings. Her admiration, however, soon turned to despair. It was hers, but it wasn't hers. She could be here, but she couldn't. It was hard to synthesize into a single emotion that was comprehensible.

Jessica looked around the lobby. There was no food anywhere, no bowls of nuts or dishes of chips. She eyed the young blue-eyed clerk and thought about asking him to slip out onto one of the secluded terraces with her. In the end, she simply picked up her shoes and left.

Jessica's aunt was in New York for the spring, so it had made perfect sense for Jessica to stay at the condo. For the most part, Jessica was grateful. She could shop to her heart's delight on Worth Avenue, binge and puke in private, lounge around the lovely private pool, read on her own bougainvillea-trellised balcony, and she didn't have to worry about roaches in the kitchen and bathrooms, unlike the rest of the cast, who were over at the Palm Beach Bungalows.

Although all of these features were undeniable luxuries, her lips nevertheless curled down in displeasure every time she opened the front door. The decor alone was enough to put her in a state if she let it. The wall-to-wall carpeting was mauve, the wallpaper was beige and had streaks of silver running through it, and a breakfront containing Hummels and other porcelain figurines took up most of the living room. It was difficult, in fact, to believe that her aunt was even related to her mother, who was known far and wide for her exquisite taste.

Jessica went straight into the bedroom, avoiding the kitchen, where temptation lurked, and flicked off her shoes. The bedroom wasn't much better, what with the mauve, beige, and metallic silver motif carrying through. True, it was better than the hotel. Still, she was alone and lonely and there was no way she could consider this apartment *home*.

Soon it would be time to go to the theater and perform. Dafna, Dan, Wendy, Seth, and her mother and stepfather would all be out in the audience. It would be fun. She was good in the show, even though Nancy, as Adelaide, always got the most applause. Adelaide had all the funniest lines. But Jessica had the voice, and she knew her friends would all be impressed and overlook the fact that she was at the Royal Poinciana Playhouse on Poinciana Way in Palm Beach, instead of at the Richard Rodgers Theater on Forty-sixth and Broadway in Manhattan.

Jessica removed her American Airlines frequent-flier card from her wallet, sat down on the edge of the bed, and picked up the telephone. Her understudy, Brooke, would be thrilled. Surely the producers would let her finish the run. There was only one more month left: four more cities, none of them all that important.

A flight was leaving for the coast the following night at 8:00 P.M. She could go straight from the matinee. She even had enough miles to upgrade to business class.

The grapes on the *chuppah* and tables were a nice touch, Jessica reflected as she began to pack her bags. Fertility, sweetness, "To life, To life!" and all that. Good for Beth for coming up with it. Something beautiful had come out of her strife. Three cheers for Beth, Jessica thought, reminded of the way the girls used to cheer for one another at camp.

Chickee wee! Chickee woo! (Clap, clap.) Beth!

Chickee wee! Chickee woo! (Clap, clap.) Dafna!

Chickee wee! Chickee woo! (Clap, clap.) Me! Jessica thought as she put Scotch tape over the opening of her shampoo. That's right, she thought, putting the shampoo into her suitcase. They'll see. They'll see. They'll all cheer for my wonderful life one day, too.

Joy

✳

In retrospect, the wedding couldn't have been more perfect. Surrounded by immediate family only, Ali and Renny said their "I do's" at the Palm Beach Municipal Hall, with lunch following at an Italian restaurant Ali's mother had found off Worth Avenue that closed off the back section for them. The milk had begun to engorge Ali's breasts after six days of difficult pumping (Joy's mouth was too small to latch onto Ali's breast, so she'd been pumping and feeding Joy on a bottle), but she felt lovely anyway in a loose floral sundress she had picked up in the Breakers gift shop. The entire ceremony lasted less than five minutes and was conducted by a judge, who wished them all well without mentioning God once (although everyone heard Fiona and Pete both murmur something about "the Father, the Son, and the Holy Ghost" and Ali's entire clan shouted *"Mazel tov!"* when Renny kissed his bride).

It had taken a lot longer to get the actual marriage license. The line at the Palm Beach city hall had moved slowly and the process had taken more than an hour and a half, robbing them of precious time at the hospital, where Joy was struggling to put on the requisite pound and a half before she could be released from the pediatric ICU. It was hard to believe such a tiny thing was a whole person, but at four pounds two ounces Joy Cohen McCann was just that: alive, well, and breathing on her own.

Renny was the one who had suggested the name Joy. They had never finalized their name selections, even though Ali's sisters had told her to preorder two different versions of thank-you notes, one with a boy's name, the other with a girl's. They had narrowed their choices down to a few—Claire, Ella, Serena, if it was a girl; Zachary, Jason, Aiden, if it was a boy—but Joy seemed perfect. Joy was the only thing Ali felt.

Soon they'd all go back to New York. Renny's family was leaving that night, Ali's dad was going in the morning, and the rest of the Cohen clan would be departing on various flights. Only Robin and her mom planned to stay until Joy was ready to go home. Then they would accompany Renny, Ali, and Joy back to Teterboro on the private plane, which, at last, seemed like a very relevant item to have in one's closet, so to speak.

Laura Does a Mitzvah

∗

"I want them to see Tanya *tomorrow*," Laura said into her phone, making a note in her Palm Pilot with her other hand to remember to pick up her dry cleaning on her way home from the office. "And send the producers flowers from me, too."

Laura's assistant, Marni, told her that Tanya was in New York shooting *Letterman*.

"Fuck," Laura said, as much to the needle in her arm as to the news. She adjusted herself so the IV rested in a slightly more comfortable position. She couldn't write in her Palm when the needle was in. It was the same every time: she tried, but it always hurt. "Just tell her she has to get her ass back to L.A. by noon. Stick her on the first plane out. Explain that it's the role of a lifetime. It *is*. I read the script. This could be an Oscar if she plays her cards right."

A brutal wave of nausea rolled over her and she told her assistant she had a call coming through on the other line. She put the phone down fast and closed her eyes. She hated the way it moved in so quickly, with only the vaguest hint of a warning: a change in the taste of her saliva, a sudden all-over clamminess, a weird muscle spasm that began in her cheeks and drew her mouth into an involuntary grimace. She tried to will the feeling away, but it increased, until she was forced to hold the Baggie up to her mouth.

Nothing came up.

As suddenly as it had come, the nausea receded, but then she was boiling, prickles of heat stabbing her all over her body. She wished she had chosen her new teal Gucci dress instead of this fitted black Donna Karan pantsuit. Her leather boots felt like cement shackles, and the weather was warm enough for sandals. What a fool she was! If she had worn the dress, she also could have worn her new cream kitten-heel Manolos! But her office was so damned over-air-conditioned and the hospital was usually an icebox, too, or else became one when she finished the treatment and the waves of heat disappeared, leaving her with shivering gooseflesh.

It would be over soon enough. Then she could go back to the office for the afternoon and bury herself in work. She'd have to get Tanya in for the producers tomorrow. She'd get this role for Tanya if it was the last thing she did!

Beneath her auburn pageboy-style wig, sweat trickled down Laura's scalp. She wanted to scratch her head, but her phone was ringing again and she had to answer; would answer unless she was actually vomiting, and even when *that* had occasionally happened, she'd wiped her mouth, said hello, puked some more, and gotten back on the line.

Jessica Bloom was in town, Marni informed her, and wanted to know if Laura was free for lunch.

"Jessica *who*?" Laura asked.

"She says she went to Willow Lake with you. She was in your bunk."

After flicking through a mental Rolodex of the girls she had mostly hated, Laura landed on a blond-haired girl who was always singing.

"She wants to know if you're free for lunch and I noticed you don't have a lunch scheduled for today."

The thought of food was enough to drag the edges of Laura's mouth south again. Why was Jessica bothering her? What on earth did she owe Jessica Bloom?

"Jessica Bloom?" she said to Marni. "You've got to be kidding. I can hardly remember which of the annoying bitches she was!"

Which wasn't at all true. She remembered all the girls in her bunk clearly. She'd just seen most of them at the Willow Lake reunion, one week before she had discovered the lump.

Laura readjusted her position in the chair and closed her eyes. Jessica Bloom, Wendy Levin, Dafna Shapiro, Beth Rosenblatt, Ali Cohen—Ali had looked great. What a transformation. Only Arden hadn't gone back, which was a shame. Laura had been looking forward to seeing Arden. She'd always had such quirky style.

Arden was good at gymnastics, Laura recalled, suddenly remembering a morning when she and Arden had helped each other do back walk-overs on the low beam, which was set up on the grass outside the gymnastics barn. Arden had a funny voice—a high-pitched nasal voice that sounded comical all the time. Arden tanned well. Arden wasn't homesick at camp. Arden was unfettered. Arden was liked.

Laura remembered more now: Arden, with the sun making her crystal ponytail holder gleam, telling Laura she could do the back walk-over on the beam if she stopped worrying about falling. "You can do it," she had said in that funny voice of hers. "You *can* and you *will*." And then Laura had realized she could. She could and did, again and again, one back walk-over, then another, then another.

Laura could remember everything now about that morning: the way the light had filtered so gently through the oak trees; the way the regular noises of camp had seemed to disappear while she and Arden spotted each other and laughed and urged each other on. She could see herself then, too skinny in a sky blue leotard but already feeling fat, especially next to Arden, who had a perfect gymnast's body.

Laura felt sad. What a waste of energy, to have been that upset about herself at ten! She had had ribs she could walk her fingers up, like a ladder, but she remembered clearly thinking that she was disgustingly fat. Laura studied the spot in her arm where the needle slipped into her vein. If only she had known what was in store, she would have worked harder to enjoy her childhood.

Arden had enjoyed her childhood. In Laura's memory, Arden was always smiling. They had been friendly, she and Arden. And Jessica, too, Laura had to admit. She had been a little bit friendly with Jessica, too. Still, they had never stayed in touch. It wasn't like she and Jessica had a history together.

So why was Jessica bothering her? Laura could guess. Jessica wanted Laura to become her agent. Story of Laura's life. *Everyone* wanted Laura to be their agent. Well, it wasn't going to happen. Laura had her hands full with her current clients. And it wasn't like she was the best company on earth right now. She hadn't told anyone she was sick, not even Marni, and the subterfuge was exhausting.

But why *should* anyone know? It was enough that her older sister and brother knew. Brooke was driving her crazy with her constant phone calls from Greenwich. Easy for her to care. No tumor for Brooke. No panicked moment in the shower for Brooke. No *"What the hell is that?"* for Brooke. No "Shit, oh shit, oh shit" for Brooke.

Whoopee for Brooke. Always easy for Brooke. Team captain at camp. Senior class president at Beverly Hills High. Editor in chief of the *Yale Daily News*. Cute Wall Street boyfriend. Beautiful wedding. Beautiful kids. Beautiful dog—a golden retriever named Brandy. *Blech.*

And Steven? Okay, so he cared enough to send e-mails. He was a *ski instructor,* for God's sake. And not even year-round! He was a ski instructor in Aspen in the winter and God only knew *what* in the summer. Mountain bike tour leader? Was that what he had told her? She couldn't keep it straight, he was such a flake. And he was smart, too. And handsome. People had always said how much he and Laura resembled each other and their mother.

Laura understood why he had checked out. It made sense. Enough had been enough. They had both gotten away, Brooke to the East Coast, Steven to the Midwest. It was better this way. They had all stopped being a family a long time ago, which was part of the reason Laura found it so infuriating that Brooke had told their father about the cancer.

"If I can be there for you in anyway," he had said, "please let me know."

Why should she give him the pleasure of being there for her now? He hadn't been there when she had wanted him there as a teenager. He had simply moved out one day to live with one of the aerobics instructors from the gym he belonged to in Brentwood. Did he pay for Brooke to go to Yale? Did he pay for Steven to go to Cornell? Did he pay for her to go to Harvard? And that would be, no. What an asshole. He had made their mother do it. And she did, wonderful, capable woman that she was. For fifteen years, she was the number one broker for high-end properties in L.A. For fifteen years, she had schlepped from palace to palace and brokered deals worth millions.

And then she died, two weeks short of her forty-seventh birthday, when her car crashed head-on into some fool going too fast around the lethal curves of Laurel Canyon.

Nice try, Dad, Laura thought, trying to reenter the scene with his two blond-haired twin brats from wife number three (a makeup artist named Trix, whom he'd picked up while she was stretching by the Santa Monica pier after a run; a makeup artist with a pierced nipple and blond hair down to her waist and a vocabulary that encompassed about twelve different expressions, ranging in complexity from "Cool" to "Oh my God!" to, on the extreme end, *"Awesome,"* which she reserved for only the most dramatic moments in a conversation).

Who the fuck did that idiot think she was, giving Laura a photo album of pictures she had taken of her father with the twins. "To look at during chemo," Trix had said. "To take your mind off things and help you focus on life."

"Oh, thanks," Laura had said, wondering how her father could stand it.

"Please let us know if we can help," Trix had said so earnestly. *"Please,* Laura. I *mean* it. You're welcome to *move in* with us."

Trix had a miniature Italian greyhound that shook all the time.

"I'd love to move in," Laura had said with matching sweetness, "as long as you promise to put your dog down first."

"I'm just trying to be nice," Trix had said, her lip quivering. "I wish you wouldn't take your bitterness out on me."

"Why not?" Laura had said.

At least they weren't bothering her anymore.

Laura suddenly realized that she had never gotten back to Marni. She checked the line. Marni was still there. "Sorry," she said. "I ran into someone I had to talk to. Can't you tell Jessica I'm out of town?"

Marni admitted that she'd already told Jessica that Laura would be back in the office in the afternoon. Marni apologized profusely and Laura softened. Then the curiosity that had made her so good at her job kicked in and she began to wonder: what if she *did* have lunch with Jessica? Maybe it would be interesting. Maybe Jessica was on the verge of some kind of fame Laura should know about. She was a little old for stardom, but one never knew in this business.

"Can you get me a table at the Ivy?"

Marni said it wouldn't be a problem just as Laura's doctor entered the room with a bright smile on his face.

"Would you consider television?" Laura asked.

"Television would be great," Jessica said. "Gosh. Television would be a dream. I mean, I'd love to be a movie star—who wouldn't, right? I just can't do musical theater anymore."

As Jessica spoke, she moved a tomato from one side of her salad plate to the other. Laura had to force herself not to look.

"It's too grueling, too limiting," Jessica was saying. "And I'll never get married if I spend all my time with gay men, right?"

Laura knew she should laugh along with Jessica, but she was nauseous again, and the sight of the tomato Jessica was tormenting made Laura feel perilously close to throwing up at the table—not a risk she could take in a dining room that currently contained an Oscar winner lunching with her manager in the far right corner, a studio head in another corner, and several other tables of important players between them.

"So, what about you?" Jessica was asking. "Dating anyone? I don't see a ring on your finger, so I'm going to assume you're not married."

"Nope and nope," Laura said, gripping the edge of the table.

"I've heard it's murder meeting men out here, but I figured if I could get myself on a show or two, maybe into an acting class, I'd start getting into the flow of things. And I'm sure you have a whole long list of your rejects I'd be more than happy to date."

Jessica was trying so hard and Laura wanted to be polite, but she could feel the corners of her mouth dipping down again. "Excuse me," she managed, seconds before the first heave hit.

She barely made it to the bathroom stall before the bowl of lentil soup she had managed to get down her throat came right back up. Waves of chills, followed by waves of sweat, rolled over her body, leaving her too weak to stand. She slumped to the floor and rested her head against the wall. Tears were forming in her eyes, but she didn't dare shed them, in case her makeup decided to start its own smear campaign of her face.

For long moments, Laura worked to control her rebellious body. She breathed deeply, trying to visualize strength, trying to visualize good health, trying to visualize the gift department of Fred Segal. Nothing was helping. She was too weak to get up.

Was this the end? Was she going to die in the bathroom at the Ivy? If she had known she was going to die today, she would have worn her cream-colored Prada dress with the lace along the neckline and at the hem. How sweet she would look—like a meek little angel. The thought made her happy and she tried to convert the feeling into strength, but nothing happened when she sent the message to her body to rise. If she didn't return to the table soon, Jessica would wonder what was happening.

"Get *up*," Laura whispered to herself. This time, her body obeyed.

She was still wiping a puke stain off the pristine white collar of her blouse when Jessica came into the bathroom.

"You know," Jessica said, moving in closer toward Laura and speaking in a tone that reminded Laura of the way actresses speak on tampon commercials, "*I've* struggled with bulimia for most of my life, so if you want to talk, I probably know what you're going through."

Laura stopped rubbing the stain and studied Jessica, wondering how to respond to the bizarre but reasonable assumption. Jessica fished in her purse for a moment, then pulled out a pack of Certs. She offered one to Laura.

"I'm not bulimic," Laura said, taking the mint. She fished through her own bag and pulled out her favorite lipstick, Chanel's Power Play.

"I've been working hard for a few years now on acknowledging that I have a real disease," Jessica continued. "My therapist is convinced that's part of the cure. I'm also trying this drug called Norpramin. It's used to treat Alzheimer's, but my psychopharma-cologist has had a lot of success using it on clients with eating disorders."

Jessica had finished applying her lipstick and now returned it to her purse. She put a little powder on her cheeks and nose, then turned away from the mirror. "Shall we?" she said, nodding her head toward the door.

Once back at the table, Jessica resumed preaching. "It's nothing to be ashamed of if you *are* bulimic. Millions of women in this country suffer from it. It's a vicious disease."

"I don't have bulimia," Laura said in a quiet, even tone. "I have cancer. It's quite a different disease. Unfortunately, it some-times makes me puke."

Jessica made a dramatic gesture of shock.

"It's not public news," Laura continued. "I've never missed a day of work. So if you don't mind keeping quiet about it, I'd be grateful."

Jessica relaxed her face and dropped her hands from her cheeks, but her eyes remained wide. "Laura, I had no idea. I— Why didn't you— I'm so *sorry*," she stammered.

"Whatever," Laura said with a shrug.

"May I ask what kind—what your— How can you still work?"

Their waitress approached the table, saving Laura from an answer.

"Would you like anything else? Coffee? Dessert?"

"Just the check," Laura said. It was close to two. She had to get back to the office. She wanted to make sure her assistant had reached Tanya.

"Thank you *so, so* much," Jessica said when Laura handed the waitress her credit card. "I'd be more than happy to pay myself. I'm the one who asked you to lunch, and I had no idea how sick—"

Laura shot Jessica a stern look, which shut her up.

"Let me be clear," Laura said, waving and smiling as an executive from Paramount passed their table. "My health is not public information. That means I don't want the word coming out of your mouth in relation to me. I don't want you calling Dafna, or Wendy, or any of the other Willow Lake girls you're still in touch with. I don't want you sending me flowers or e-mails or asking my assistant how I'm feeling. It means you don't know. Got it?"

Jessica barely nodded, then whispered, "I'm so flattered you chose to share it with me."

"Don't be," Laura said. "I just didn't want you to think I puke for sport."

Jessica's face took on a hurt expression, and Laura realized how callous she sounded in light of Jessica's own revelation. She apologized.

"It's okay," Jessica said, clearly wounded. Then she added with a smile, "Hey, I wish I weren't bulimic, you know? But what can I do? I just get up every morning and try. That's what I'm doing here right now. Just trying to move myself forward, get to the next place."

Laura had to admit Jessica's optimism was admirable. Nevertheless, as Jessica followed Laura out of the restaurant and waited by her side while the valet went to get the cars, there was nothing Laura could think of that she, personally, could do to help move her former bunk mate forward.

All Laura really wanted to do was to tell Jessica to get lost, but she never did anything rude in public. Hollywood was too small a town and her career was too important to her. If Oscars were given for Best Performances in the Workplace, Laura surely would win one for her role as the brilliant, icy agent who never loses her cool. When she had first started in the business, she had been less careful. She had cried to her boss once when a boyfriend cheated on her and had yelled once at an intern in front of a roomful of colleagues. But she had watched and learned, and now she was one of the best agents in the business.

"Well, good luck," Laura said to Jessica as the valet pulled up in front of them with Laura's midnight blue Mercedes. She had bought the car for herself not long ago as a thirty-third birthday present and still felt a thrill every time she saw it. Before she got in, she turned to Jessica and said as evenly and unemotionally as she could, "I wish I could help you somehow, but I just can't right now. I'm sorry."

"It's okay," Jessica said.

She looked disappointed but not shattered.

"I appreciate your honesty." Jessica smiled and her words seemed sincere. Then she said, "You know, I'm not doing anything tonight. I'm staying all by myself at the Peninsula. We could hang out together at the bar if you're up to it. Or, if you're too tired, I could drop by with a video, or we could catch up some more on our lives."

"I have a date tonight," Laura said, kissing Jessica good-bye. "Thanks anyway."

On the way back to the office, the nausea returned and Laura had to pull over to puke. She only narrowly missed hitting the car in the lane next to hers and could hear the driver cursing her as he went by. Nothing came up, but she couldn't shake the feeling of wretchedness. The sweating was back, too. Soon, she knew, there'd be chills.

Three to six months. The words swirled around in her head, meaning everything and nothing. She had thought she had dealt with all the shock a person could handle. Hearing you have cancer at thirty-two is about as big a shock as you can get. And no matter how she had tried to prepare over the last few months for the possibility of the doctor's words, she simply didn't have a personality that allowed for such negativity.

But there was no way to avoid the negative with a prognosis like that. The cancer had spread. It was in the lining of her heart now and in her bones. The doctor hadn't said "six months to a year," or "six months, then we'll see where things are." He'd said "three to six months, unless there's a miracle." And then he said he was sorry and left the room.

But *she* hadn't left the room. She'd had to stay and finish her treatment. She'd had to taste his words in her mouth, chew his "sorry," vomit it into the toilet over lunch with Jessica, and now here she was, driving down Sunset Boulevard, rushing to get back to the office so she could make Tanya more famous than she already was and then meet with a new young girl people were calling the next Jennifer Aniston.

She made it back to the office, but not until she had pulled over two more times. Marni had been unable to reach Tanya directly but had left several messages and reserved a ticket for her on an American Airlines flight that would get her into L.A. in time for a meeting with the producers. And her three o'clock was no Jennifer Aniston; she wasn't even Jessica Bloom.

✳

When Laura got home, it was already dark. She had made two stops along the way, one to pick up her dry cleaning and the other to pick up some Häagen-Dazs mint ice cream and a bag of taro chips. She flicked on the switch by the front door and the apartment flooded with soft, pleasing light. What an oasis her home was at night! The white sofas and carpet seemed suspended in air and the lights from the Hollywood Hills in the distance twinkled outside her floor-to-ceiling windows like tiny fairies. The cleaning lady had been there that morning, so the apartment still had the delicious fragrance of lemon-scented cleaner. Laura breathed deeply, smiled, was overcome by nausea, and put down her things.

Sitting at the kitchen table, she checked the "To Do" list in her Palm Pilot: all her errands were complete. Next, she checked future appointments: a facial was scheduled for Thursday, but that was it. She made a note to cancel the facial, then decided to give the appointment to Marni. She had waited eight months for the treat with one of L.A.'s top facialists. Why not let someone else enjoy it?

She sorted through her mail. There was another letter about the Willow Lake documentary from Ali. This time she had included an e-mail address for personal updates, in case Laura didn't have time to participate in person.

Willow Lake hadn't been so bad a place. If she had been less tortured, she would have really loved it.

"Woulda, coulda, shoulda," she said aloud, quoting her favorite *New Yorker* cartoon, which showed a man lying on a couch in his therapist's office. "Woulda, coulda, shoulda," says the shrink. "Next!"

She had thought it would be more delicious than it was, eating ice cream in the bathtub. She put the bowl aside and opted instead for a liquid dinner of chardonnay. After her bath, she studied herself naked in the full-length mirror on the outside closet door in her all-white bedroom. She looked like a freak. She looked like the Bride of Frankenstein. The scar from the mastectomy was purple, garish, totally unchic. She averted her gaze, looking at her arms instead. There were her veins, a reassuring blue road map to her living self. The longer Laura stared, the longer she was able to see only the scary track marks from the chemo. They were ugly, and she was grateful for the reminder, so she could stick to the task at hand.

It always came down to this, didn't it? What was a girl to wear? Laura studied the contents of her closet, which were arranged by color, season, and length.

The cream-colored Prada she had envisioned in the bathroom at the Ivy seemed way too girlish now, too frivolous for the occasion, but her more severe outfits (the black Jil Sander suit, today's Donna Karan, last week's Helmut Lang, the Armani she had bought in Milan when she went to visit Tanya on the set of her second big film) all seemed too austere, too dramatic, too self-conscious.

What kind of statement did she want to make? Something dressy seemed inappropriate, but lingerie of any kind seemed somehow clichéd.

She went through her entire closet item by item. Each outfit elicited a different memory, and she let herself linger in each one. The last time she had had sex, she had begun the evening in her emerald green Tocca slip dress and her amazing Michel Perry emerald spike mules. When she tried it on now, she looked like a kid playing dress-up, but the afternoon she had worn it to her friend Jamie's wedding, she had looked fantastic. She knew she had, and so had Steve Tremblaux, the actor next to whom she had been seated and in whose bed she had awakened the following morning. He had called to ask her out afterward, which was nice but unnecessary. Laura didn't date actors. They were usually too messy and always wanted her to do too much.

The celadon top from that thrift shop on Melrose had always been a favorite. The last time she had worn it was the day she took a young client named Annabel Hutchins to lunch to celebrate her booking a starring role in a pilot. Annabel was going to be a star. Everyone in Hollywood was talking about her. And Laura had discovered her, signed her, negotiated her very first job as a young secretary who has an affair with her boss in a canceled but critically well-received series.

The white see-through Donna Karan! Laura laughed, remembering how shocked Tanya had been when Laura had met her for dinner in it. Of course she had worn a slip beneath it, but Tanya had asked Laura if she was wearing any underwear and Laura had admitted that it just wasn't possible in an outfit like that.

The navy Chloé pantsuit with the Bakelite buttons was pretty spectacular. How many celebratory lunches had she had in that outfit? Too many to recall now. But it wasn't right for tonight, so she put it back in the closet.

By 11:00 P.M., she had gone through almost everything, even jewelry, and was completely exhausted. She finally settled on a beautiful lavender silk nightgown and robe ensemble her mother had given her for Hanukkah a few months before she died. It felt soothing against Laura's skin now and she remembered for a moment how wonderful it had been as a child to hug her mother first thing in the morning, when her mother was in the kitchen in a silk robe.

There was one robe in particular that she had loved. It was the palest blue nylon with a three-quarter-length sleeve edged in pale green satin, and there was extra fabric in the skirt, so when her mother spun around in it, the robe flew out around her like a 1950s ball gown. God, how Laura had loved that robe!

The more Laura remembered that robe and how it had felt when she once snuck into her mother's closet and tried it on while her mother was out, the deeper the pain became around her throat. She sat down on the floor in the middle of her room and hugged her knees and rocked herself as she sobbed. While she rocked and sobbed, she suddenly remembered the words Jessica had said at lunch: "I just get up every morning and try. That's what I'm doing here right now. Just trying to move myself forward, get to the next place."

Jessica was a good person. She had offered to be with Laura tonight. She had offered to be a friend. There would be nothing in it for Jessica—Laura had made that clear—and yet Jessica had made the effort anyway. It had been a long, long time since anyone had wanted to be Laura's friend without wanting something in return for it.

Laura wiped her eyes and cheeks and got up. The e-mail she composed to Marni went as follows:

I won't be coming in today.

Please send a new actress named Jessica Bloom in to meet the producers, instead of Tanya. Jessica is staying at the Peninsula. Call her first thing.

Also, please take my facial Thursday at Ole Henrikson at 2:00 p.m. If you can't use it, please cancel.

Laura sent the e-mail, then opened to a fresh document. She wrote quickly, without thought, just noting the salient things that had marked her life post–Willow Lake, which, when she got down to it, weren't many. She had graduated with honors from Harvard, gone straight into the agenting business, worked her way up to the senior position in which she found herself now, and along the way had dated eight different men, two for significant periods of time (Keith, a fellow talent agent at William Morris, for three years; Lawrence, a screenwriter, for two). There was no one in her life at the moment, thank God. She wrote that she had lived the life she had wanted to and that she was proud of the work she had done. She added that if she could say anything to young campers, it would be for them to try to enjoy their youth. Without rereading her letter, she pressed Send, signed off, and went to the kitchen.

The refrigerator was nearly empty, but she disposed of two lemons, an onion, a clove of garlic, a nearly empty jar of "no sugar added" strawberry jam, an unopened jar of country Dijon mustard, and a small carton of ruby red grapefruit juice. Then she filled a large glass with water and returned to her bedroom.

She was in pain now, her body throbbing. She opened the

vial of Vicodin, a fresh prescription she had had refilled today at the hospital, and poured the pills out onto her bed. They were hard to swallow one by one, but she managed to get all thirty of them down.

It was a few minutes after midnight. Laura lay down on top of her bed and turned on the television. Tanya was being interviewed by David Letterman, who was laughing at something Tanya had said. Tanya looked elegant—elegant and classy. When Laura had first discovered Tanya, she couldn't dress at all. She had come straight to Hollywood from a Florida trailer park wearing a spandex halter top, itsy-bitsy cheek-showing denim cutoffs, Candies, and an anklet. Now she was wearing a black sleeveless cocktail dress with a plunging neckline and a long silver necklace that had Gucci written all over it. Laura took the credit. She had gotten Tanya the best stylist in Hollywood.

"What did you do when you found out you'd gotten the role of Sweetie?" David asked her.

"Oh God," Tanya said, smiling her winning smile ear to ear. "That's easy. I called my fabulous agent, Laura Berman, and we just shrieked together on the phone for like ten minutes." Then Tanya turned directly to the camera and said, "If you're watching this, Laura, I want to thank you. You're the best, babe."

Laura smiled back at Tanya, feeling pleased. She was very sleepy—sleepy and happy. Happiness that began in her feet, spread up her legs, moved through her pelvis, her abdomen, down her arms, up her spine, across her shoulders. She felt like she was floating above the bed, floating up to the ceiling, floating out into the night, into the twinkling lights in the Hollywood Hills.

From somewhere far away she could hear the telephone ringing and her sister's voice saying, "Laura? You there? Helloooo?" Then Arden came in through the window in her sky blue leotard, a reassuring smile on her face.

"You can do it," she said clearly to Laura. "You *can* and you *will*."

Shalom

"I love it!" Robin said. "We watched it last night."

Ali thanked her sister and asked what her nieces and nephews thought of the old footage of her mom and aunts.

"Nikki didn't recognize any of us," Robin said. "Let's not forget, it was before we did our noses. But Rachel recognized Karen because of the mole."

Robin wasn't the first person Ali had heard from. Many of the Willow Lakers who had received the documentary had written letters, sent e-mails, or found out her number and called. Ron and Faye had sent it as a gift to everyone who had attended the centennial reunion and now included it in the information packet they sent to prospective campers and their parents, a nice perk, but certainly no necessity, since the waiting list was long for a spot at Willow Lake, which, after a century, remained the premier Reform Jewish summer institution in America for girls.

Robin asked if Ali had heard from Mara or Karen, who had watched the video with Robin, or if Andrea, who'd been unable to make it last night, had made any comments yet.

"It's only eight-fifteen," Ali said, still exhausted from her night with Joy.

"I've usually spoken with everyone by eight," Robin said, "including Mom."

"Well, no, then," Ali said. "No one else has phoned in yet, and I don't have any idea if Andrea has even seen it." That it had taken her sisters over a month to get around to viewing it wasn't even a big deal. Ali was used to their ignoring her work—not that she wasn't grateful for Robin's call. It was thoughtful and sweet. Still, Ali had another matter on her mind this morning. She wished Robin a good day and got off the phone.

Joy had been up since 5:00 A.M., when Renny went into her room to kiss her good-bye before leaving for his shoot. Now Joy was asleep, finally, in her Snap-and-Go car seat, which was currently resting on the floor of the kitchen. Ali finished reading the *New York Times,* lingering over an article in the real estate section about the rise in prices for apartments on the Lower East Side.

At 8:45, she put aside the paper and took Joy into the nursery. Relieved that Joy remained asleep, Ali put the car seat on the floor, then put the diaper bag on the changing table and began stuffing it with all the things Joy might need during their outing: two outfits in case she spit up, an extra pacifier (where on earth did those things disappear to?), four diapers, two burp cloths, Balmex, a rattle, a plush toy, wipes, extra circular pads to put in her bra in case her nipples leaked through the pads that were in there already, her cell phone, and, even though Arden had printed out directions, just to be on the safe side, a map of New Jersey.

Oh, and one last thing—the one thing that couldn't be forgotten: the videotape, which she wrapped in a diaper cloth and stuck in the outside compartment, where she usually kept a stash of Wash 'n Dri towelettes.

Joy slept on, the little angel, while Ali snapped the seat into the car. It was their first outing together alone in the car, and Ali felt a grave sense of responsibility as she pulled out of the spot in front of their new apartment on Stanton Street, a location she loved, even more so because she learned after she and Renny closed on it that her paternal grandmother had grown up on the very same block.

It was easier to get to New Jersey from where she lived than it was to get to the Upper East Side: just a straight shot across Delancey, a quick jog over to Broome, then—whoosh!—right into the Holland Tunnel and there she was. It was such a beautiful day, even the industrial wasteland beyond the Pulaski Skyway couldn't ruin it. Once she hit I-78, the ride even got pretty. Everything was in blossom, and the weather was warm enough for an open window. When her mission was complete, Ali thought she might even find some nice park around Short Hills to stroll in with Joy before she made her way back home.

The house was exactly where Arden had said it would be. The only thing that had proved inaccurate so far was Arden's description of it. It was nicer than Arden had described it. Arden had made it sound like a generic mansion, but Ali thought it had much more character than that. All the windows in the front of the white-shingled neoclassic traditional contained flower boxes overflowing with red geraniums and ivy, and the brick walkway leading to the front door was lined with all kinds of pretty flowers, the names of which Ali didn't know. There was a large tree in the front yard, too, an oak or elm—Ali hadn't paid enough attention during pioneering sessions at camp to know—but it was one of those big old permanent-looking trees, and it had a tire swing hanging from one of the branches. Near the tree, an abandoned red bicycle sat waiting on the ground for an occupant. A few feet from it lay a yellow Wiffle bat. It was all very Norman Rockwell—very heartwarming, very nice.

There weren't any cars parked in the driveway. Joy was awake now, so Ali picked her up and went to the front door. She rang the doorbell and waited, but there was no answer. She thought about leaving the videotape on the front stoop but decided against it. It was only for Wendy. She couldn't take the risk of someone else finding it. The whole point was for Wendy to understand the choice Ali had made: the choice to spare her; the choice to be a mensch.

Ali rang the doorbell again, but no one came, so she went around the back of the house, where she found the door leading from the terrace into the kitchen ajar. She could hear the sound of vacuuming within.

"Hello?" she yelled, taking a few tentative steps into the kitchen.

The vacuuming stopped and a uniformed housekeeper arrived from an archway leading into another part of the house.

"Yes?" the housekeeper said. "May I help you? Mrs. Abrahms no here. She play tennis today, then go with boys to activities. She back around three."

Ali introduced herself as an old friend, then asked if she might sit for a moment to feed Joy, who had begun to fuss. The housekeeper nodded and offered Ali something to drink, which Ali declined. "I won't be long," Ali said. "I'll be fine. I don't mean to disturb you. I'll just leave Wendy a note, if that's okay."

"As you wish," the housekeeper said, returning to her work.

It was amazing how much you could get away with when you had a baby in your arms! Ali slipped out onto the terrace, sat down on a green wicker rocking chair that overlooked the swimming pool, and began to feed Joy. The grounds were gorgeous. Lucky Wendy, Ali thought. Then she took it back, remembering everything she had heard from Arden and Jessica. "*Poor* Wendy," Ali said to Joy. "Poor, poor Wendy."

As if she understood, Joy gurgled and spit up.

"That's okay," Ali said, wiping up the mess and reattaching Joy's mouth to her nipple.

As Joy continued to feed, Ali basked in contentment. She thought back to the conversation she had had last night with Renny and knew she had answered correctly when he had asked whether or not she was happy about the decision not to finish the documentary about her former bunk mates. There really was no point. Between Laura's death and Wendy's refusal to participate, she was missing too many essential participants. Besides, Beth was pursuing a book deal for herself based on her wedding manual, so at least some attention was being paid culturally to the life and times of the Jewish American Princess. Jessica was on her way to sitcom stardom, having landed the lead role in a show on NBC after just narrowly missing getting cast in the movie Laura had set her up on, so she didn't need any negative exposure right now. And Ali didn't want to give her any negative exposure anyway. After interviewing Jessica, she felt as close to her as she did to Dafna and Arden, both of whom Ali now considered dear friends.

It wasn't hard to put the second documentary to rest at all. She didn't feel much like working these days. She was too busy with Joy—too busy feeding her, bathing her, kissing her, squeezing her little arms and legs, marveling at her tiny fingers with their perfect rectangular nail beds, luxuriating in the softness of the light brown peach fuzz on top of her head, basking in the warm, velvety, baby-lotiony smell and feel of her body.

She didn't plan to stay away from work forever. In fact, she had already begun collaborating with Arden on a script about a young girl who gets molested by a rabbi on a family retreat weekend. They even had a producer lined up, and he had agreed not only to let Ali direct but to let Renny shoot it.

Ali had worried that Arden might want to star in it, but Arden couldn't have been happier with the arrangement to cast someone else. Although she'd enjoyed her stint as Ali's assistant, she spent most of her free time now, when she wasn't working on the screenplay, studying for the LSAT, which she planned to take in May. She had decided that law school was her true calling. (Actually, it had been Renny's idea, but Ali never let on she knew that.) Arden's plan was to become a prosecutor specializing in cases of molestation. If she had any success, she'd be able to feel like she'd put her theatrical skills to good use, rather than using them in hopes of landing free entrée to a nightclub.

Ali smiled as Joy suckled, thinking about how wonderfully Arden's life was turning around; and she, Ali Cohen-McCann, had been an integral part of that.

When Ali finished burping Joy, she returned to the house. The maid was eating her lunch now in a small room off the kitchen. The door to the room was open and Ali could hear the woman talking back to a TV set. Ali took the moments alone to survey the kitchen. Was there any spot to leave the video? The sill over the sink? The counter next to the phone? Neither place seemed suitable.

Ali tiptoed through the archway and found herself in a large formal entryway. Several doors opened onto it, one leading to what looked to be a den, another to a dining room. Across the room, doors led, respectively, to a formal living room and to yet another hallway.

In the center of the foyer, a staircase beckoned. Up Ali went, the documentarian in her noting every detail: the plush chocolate brown carpeting on the staircase, the Magic Marker on the wall in the hallway, the decor of each of the children's rooms (navy, red plaid, green plaid, light blue). There were toys everywhere: soldiers, trains, baseball mitts, trucks, tanks, dinosaurs. Ali kissed Joy's head, thankful that her only child was a girl.

The master bedroom was at the end of the hallway.

"Hello?" she said as she entered.

No one was there. All was peaceful in the beautiful bedroom. To the right of the bed was a sitting area facing a large bay window that offered views of the landscaped grounds below.

"Isn't it pretty?" Ali said to Joy as they went to the window. "See the birdie?"

They watched a bird fly from one branch of a cherry tree to the other. When it flew away, Ali abandoned the window and entered the dressing room. For a moment, she hesitated. Then she went to the drawer almost as if under a spell.

And there it all was, just like Arden had reported, beneath the underwear and bras, beneath the socks and the knee-highs: magazines and a few videotapes—*College Girls, Tits on Chicks, Teen Lesbian Sluts*. Ali closed the drawer quickly and looked around. No one was up there.

She could just slip her video in with the others. Eventually, Wendy was bound to find it. And what a shock that would be! She had even written a little note on the label: "Dear Wendy, It was so nice to see you enjoying yourself at the reunion! Love, Ali."

Ali reopened the drawer, then closed it without depositing the video. Someone was calling for her. "Miss!" she heard. "Miss! You must move your car! Is blocking the garbage truck!"

Ali raced out of Wendy's room, down the hallway and the stairs, through the foyer, into the kitchen, and out the back door. A large green garbage truck was waiting at the entrance to the driveway, where Ali's car was indeed blocking its way.

"So sorry!" she yelled to the guys. Once she was in her car, she decided to go. She could always come back later, maybe after lunch. She moved out of the way and the truck proceeded up the driveway to the custom-made white-shingled hutch where Wendy and Seth's garbage lived. As one of the garbagemen began hoisting the garbage bags into the truck, Ali realized she shouldn't go without checking Joy's diaper first.

"Are you wet?" she asked as she jumped out of the car to check. "Yup," she said, pleased with herself for remembering. She put on a clean diaper and raced over to the truck.

"May I?" she asked, holding up the diaper.

"Go 'head," one of the guys said, smiling knowingly.

Ali tossed the diaper into the truck and turned to go, but as the compacter began to grind, she had a second thought. She reached into the diaper bag and tossed the videotape into the truck as well, where, within seconds, the small black rectangle was crushed into nonexistence. Satisfied, she got back into her car and told Joy it was time to find a nice place to enjoy the rest of the day.

About the Author

Isabel Rose is a summa cum laude graduate of Yale and received an M.F.A. in fiction from Bennington College. She has written several screenplays, and she cowrote the 2003 release *Anything but Love,* in which she also starred. Rose also entertains regularly on the New York City night club circuit with her nine-piece band. She is currently making her debut CD and is working on her second novel. For more information, go to www.IsabelRose.com.